Hyzy, Julie A.
   Artistic license

2/01

Artistic License

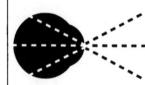

This Large Print Book carries the
Seal of Approval of N.A.V.H.

Artistic License

Julie A. Hyzy

Thorndike Press • Waterville, Maine

Published in 2004 by arrangement with
Tekno Books and Ed Gorman.

Thorndike Press® Large Print Women's Fiction.

The tree indicium is a trademark of Thorndike Press.

The text of this Large Print edition is unabridged.
Other aspects of the book may vary from the original edition.

Set in 16 pt. Plantin by Minnie B. Raven.

Printed in the United States on permanent paper.

Library of Congress Cataloging-in-Publication Data

Hyzy, Julie A.
    Artistic license / Julie A. Hyzy.
        p. cm.
    ISBN 0-7862-6549-3 (lg. print : hc : alk. paper)
    1. Women artists — Fiction.   2. Pregnant women —
Fiction.   3. Separated people — Fiction.   4. Art thefts —
Fiction.   5. Large type books.   I. Title.
PS3608.Y98A88 2004b
    813′.6—dc22   2004046026

With much love, this novel is dedicated:
To my family,
Curt, Robyn, Sara, Biz, Paul,
and little Brian.
And to good friends,
For their heartfelt encouragement.

As the Founder/CEO of NAVH, the only national health agency solely devoted to those who, although not totally blind, have an eye disease which could lead to serious visual impairment, I am pleased to recognize Thorndike Press* as one of the leading publishers in the large print field.

Founded in 1954 in San Francisco to prepare large print textbooks for partially seeing children, NAVH became the pioneer and standard setting agency in the preparation of large type.

Today, those publishers who meet our standards carry the prestigious "Seal of Approval" indicating high quality large print. We are delighted that Thorndike Press is one of the publishers whose titles meet these standards. We are also pleased to recognize the significant contribution Thorndike Press is making in this important and growing field.

Lorraine H. Marchi, L.H.D.
Founder/CEO
NAVH

* Thorndike Press encompasses the following imprints: Thorndike, Wheeler, Walker and Large Print Press.

Acknowledgments

This novel is the fulfillment of a dream for me. And so many have helped me, in so many ways, to achieve this dream. With a full heart, I know I'm the luckiest girl in the world to know such wonderful people as these:

My family, of course. Without their support, without their belief in me, none of this would be possible. Thank you, Curt. And Robyn, Sara, and Biz — remember, girls: always follow your dreams! Thanks to my brother, Paul, for his boundless enthusiasm, and to Grandma and Auntie Claudia for their constant support, and to my always-great Garbarczyk and LaPlace families.

Thanks to Dean Wesley Smith, who very generously gives of his time and his vast knowledge on the AOL writing message board. I count Dean and his wife, Kristine Kathryn Rusch, not only as some of the best writers and teachers out there, but also as good friends. Their Oregon Coast Professional Fiction Writers' Workshop taught me much, and gave me the opportunity to work with an incredible group of extremely talented people, who are also a rock of support. Good Rolls!

Through the magic of AOL, two groups of writers from around the country come together weekly to chat and learn. Thanks much to the Queue and the WAMers for reading my stories and always offering valuable critiques.

Closer to home, many thanks to everyone in our Novel Writers' group — who welcomed me even when I only wrote short stories. Special thanks to John Welsh — Carpe Dictum! And to Earl Merkel, novelist and friend, who's always willing to help.

And to very dear friends, Rene and Mike, and Karen and Dennis, who patiently listened to me babble about my dreams — thanks for putting up with me! And to Deirdre, who pushed.

Thanks also to some very special people: J. Michael Major whose constant, cheerful, "You can do it!" makes me smile; and my editor, Debbie Brod, who read my manuscript and decided it might have promise. Thank you.

I must mention Ray Bradbury, whose stories continue to inspire me, and who answered my overdue fan letter last year with a phone call that will "live forever" in my memory.

And finally, heartfelt thanks to my great friend and writing partner, Michael A. Black. Without him, *Artistic License* would still just be a dream. He convinced me to write this first novel and he read every word of it (countless times) as it transformed from a jumble of ideas into a finished manuscript. He'll complain that I give him too much credit, but the truth is, if it weren't for Mike, this novel wouldn't be here now.

Thanks, everyone. Love you all.

Chapter One

Annie held the white stick in her shaking hand and stared. There was no mistaking the tiny pink plus sign.

She couldn't be.

Taking a ragged breath, she squeezed her eyes shut and whispered, "Please," hoping to change the result by sheer force of will.

But when she looked, the plus sign was still there. Unwilling to meet her own eyes in the bathroom mirror she sat down, hard, on the tub's curled edge. How was it that a small piece of plastic could so profoundly affect so many lives? Even now, she was sure that somewhere, another woman sat just as she was sitting, seeing a blank spot instead of a plus sign. Disappointed, and perhaps not for the first time.

The bathroom walls closed in on her, their pale pastel tiles growing brighter through the tears that worked their way hotly to her eyes. With another deep breath, she realized how tenuous her hold on calm really was.

Resting her elbow on the sink's

countertop, she massaged her temples. Buying the home test had been hard. Taking it even worse. The night before, she'd driven to a grocery store ten miles away just to avoid running into people she knew, feeling like a shame-faced teenager who'd let her boyfriend do the nasty and whose period was late because of hysterical fear.

But instead of an adolescent, thrown by hormonal urges into a dizzy moment of awkward intimacy, she was a married woman who'd slept with her soon-to-be-ex-husband in a moment of weakness.

What was I thinking?

Two months ago, she'd felt invincible. Two months ago the world was open to her and she'd been ready to embrace it for the first time in years. But two months ago she'd tried to let Gary down easy. In the final page of the unpleasant book of her marriage, she'd sought a compassionate ending.

It had been pity sex. And now she was pregnant.

With her breath coming in noisy, uneven pulls, Annie picked up the pieces of the test kit and placed them back in the box, trying to fit each item back in the plastic tray neatly, as packaged. She pushed the emptied and rinsed collection cup back into its niche, only to have it pop back out to dance across the countertop. Grabbing it, she jammed again, still unable to get it to fit. A hiss of frustration shot from her lips as she scooped all the pieces with both hands, and slammed them into the wastebasket. Crumpling the flimsy page of directions, she suddenly remembered a paragraph about errors in readings.

The nearly see-through paper was misshapen and creased, covered on both sides with minuscule black print offering everything from directions for use in four languages, to reminders about practicing safe sex. Annie smoothed it out, breathing slowly. She grasped the paper in her left hand, tried to read, then brought her right hand up to help steady the sheet, her eyes scanning the page, searching for words like "false" and "positive." When she found them, she raced through the paragraph, making the words blur, both before her eyes and in her mind. Taking another steadying breath, she started again.

The wording was precise. False positives were virtually unheard of.

The breath she'd been holding fell out of her in a sob. She tried to suck it back in before she lost control, but fear and desperation bubbled up to the surface. Her body trembled once in an attempt to maintain control, but her next gulp of air heaved forward in a moan.

Her mind, wired to always try to solve problems, to remain detached enough to see a challenge through to its logical solution, was overwhelmed to the point where she could do nothing but let herself feel the anguish. *My God,* she thought. *How could this have happened?*

And, all too well, she knew how it had.

Three days after their fifth wedding anniversary, Gary had received the divorce papers. He'd shown up at her door, holding them in his hand.

"Gary," she said, surprised to see him.

He ran his free hand through his chestnut brown hair, pulling it up and out of his face for a moment, though whether that movement indicated nervousness, or the need for a haircut, Annie couldn't be sure. His eyes, the color of dark chocolate, wavered a moment before he spoke, as if he was deciding what to say. He thrust the neatly bound sheaf of papers out toward her. "What is this?"

She held herself against the door, the heavy wooden one she'd found at the Kane

County Flea market. It was fine-grained golden oak, and had beveled glass set into an oval shape in the center, which sent rainbow prisms of light into the house on sunny days. Browsing the stalls at the market, she'd seen it leaning against a white panel truck, and tried to negotiate the seller down, knowing all the while that the excitement in her eyes kept the wiry old man from lowering his price. As they'd loaded it into the back of their van, Annie, barely containing her glee, had repeated over and over, "This will make the house ours." Gary had simply shrugged.

Now Annie gave him a look, one that she hoped conveyed the message, "you don't really expect an explanation, do you?" and he raised his eyebrows in question.

With a sigh, she opened the door a little wider and he stepped inside.

Gary stood in the center of the small hallway, looking around. "Lot of changes since I was here last." He moved into the living room, and Annie wondered if he was as unsure of himself as he seemed. He gave her a hesitant grin and walked across the room, stopping at a painting above the couch. "You've gone back to your water-colors, I see."

Annie bit her lip. The fact that he noticed surprised her. He certainly hadn't noticed much about her in the years that they'd been married. "Yeah, I'm experimenting with oils and acrylics, too," she said, then cleared her throat. "Was there something you wanted?"

Gary kept his back to her as he examined the picture. "This looks like that place we went for our first anniversary. The backyard of that bed and breakfast in Galena."

"You remember that?"

He turned, and his brown eyes sparkled. "I remember how much you loved that garden. And how I complained about you using up three rolls of film trying to capture it in different lights."

Annie smiled, "I was a little obsessed, I guess."

"And all I could think of was how beautiful you looked as you agonized over every shot, and I wanted to *be* those flowers, to have your attention like that."

"Gary . . ." her voice held a warning.

"Yeah, sorry." He rolled his tongue over his front teeth, and sighed. "About these papers . . ."

"You knew they were coming."

"I did. But it hit me harder than I expected."

Annie shook her head and picked up her purse. "We've been separated a while. The only thing left was the paperwork."

"This is just . . . amazing. Looks like you got your inspiration back." Gary reached to run his finger along the picture's silver frame, then turned to her. "Is that because I'm out of your life?" He chewed his lip and set his jaw, as if the answer was of no consequence, but Annie had known him long enough to recognize the tiny glint of pain in his eyes.

She took a breath before she spoke. "I was about to head out . . ."

"Where you goin'? Donagan's?"

"Yeah."

"Mind if I come along? Haven't eaten yet, either."

Why hadn't she been stronger?

In the kitchen, Annie flipped through her calendar. Seeking to find some order to calm her thinking, she counted forward by weeks. Her due date would be February eleventh. *Due date*.

Memories of that fateful day, of Gary's lopsided grin and its effect on her, floated through her mind.

The same charm that had pulled her in all those years ago had worked its magic again. And yet, something had been different. Gary had been more persistent than usual. More self-deprecating. And, whether manufactured or not, it was an attractive change. And while Annie had been able to remain cognizant of the fact that there was a divorce ahead of them, she'd felt herself slip into old comforts during dinner at Donagan's.

"Ahhnna! Gahry!" the hostess said as they walked in, rolling her r's and elongating their names. Annie had never learned what country Elena had come from, but it was likely Eastern European. "It is too long that I see you!" She moved forward, kissing them both on the cheek.

Annie smiled politely, understanding that Elena believed they'd gotten back together. She was about to say something, but couldn't quite come up with the words to explain that being here together didn't mean being together. Gary returned Elena's embrace and shot a beaming grin over to Annie, as he asked, "Is our table open?"

It was, of course. At seven-thirty on a weeknight, Donagan's was relatively empty. They kept up with Elena's brisk step, following her path along the well-worn carpet, her tight black polyester skirt bouncing side to side with every shift of her hips, as she wound her way past empty pre-set tables.

Truth be told, the restaurant had seen better days, and was dwarfed both in size and class by the franchised eateries that had cropped up all over this little Chicago neighborhood. With wobbly chairs, and fat teardrop-shaped candleholders swathed in red fishnet on each table, Donagan's maintained a level of shabby charm. She and Gary had started coming here for dinner when they were first married. The menu was basic, the food homemade, and the helpings big enough for leftovers the next day.

Elena came over with oversized red leather binders with tassels hanging off the side. She turned to Annie and asked, "Glass of the Riesling?" with a look of pride for remembering.

"That would be wonderful."

"Mr. Gahry?"

Gary ordered a Manhattan and closed the menu as Elena left. He smiled at Annie and she wondered how the finality of the divorce would affect him. She'd been careful to avoid interactions, but had anticipated Gary's need to talk it through. Tonight's conversation was inevitable. Annie was just surprised it had come up so soon. Nonetheless, it was their chance, she hoped, to say good-bye.

They sat in silence until Elena reappeared with their drinks. She took their dinner orders, winked at them, and left.

Gary watched her leave. "Well," he said.

Annie took a sip of wine, then another. She put the glass back down with a nervous laugh. "Yes," she said. "Well."

"Annie," he said, moving the red-sheathed candle to reach across the table for her hands. There was a tiny hole in the white tablecloth between them. "I'm not going to fight you. I know how you feel about some of the choices I've made. There's nothing I can do to change that." He winked. "Not yet, at least."

He gave both of her hands a little squeeze, as he continued. "What would you say if I told you I'm going to win you back? One way or another. That I'll be the husband you want me to be?"

She pulled her hands away, and when she noticed the concern in Gary's eyes that her movement caused, she tried to make it seem nonchalant and so she picked up her wine glass, and played with it. The wine glistened before her eyes, and she took a sip, a long one, feeling the delightful smoothness as it eased down her throat, warm and tingly.

She sighed. "Gary, we had some good years. But you've promised me that before. We have very different outlooks on life. That isn't going to change."

"*I* can change."

"You won't."

"But divorce, Annie? We can't let that happen. I *will* change."

"Gary," she said, her hands folded on the table, her gaze unwavering, "it's better this way."

"We'll see," he said.

She watched him as they talked, and tried not to be pulled into those dark eyes that sparkled when he looked at her. It was something that she suspected he was capable of turning on and off. Right now the charm was in high gear. It had been at least six months since she'd seen him, and despite her misgivings, she couldn't help feeling flattered by his attentions.

When Elena dropped off a second glass of wine at the table, Annie held up her hand. "What are you trying to do to me? Another glass and you'll have to carry me out."

Gary grinned and gently pushed the glass toward Annie by the base. "One more. We're having a nice time, aren't we?"

They were. Dinner arrived and they talked as they ate. Gary was attentive, listening, and asking all the right questions. He'd been surprised to find out that she'd quit her job at the architectural firm, and sat back in his chair as she explained.

"It's time, Gary. I've been waiting for the right time to strike out on my own. All my life I've wanted to create. To do 'art.' But the time isn't going to present itself to me on a silver platter. I have to grab it. And that's what I'm doing. I'm cutting ties and I'm going for it."

He was shaking his head in a way that conveyed amazement. "What's happened to you?" He held up his hands and sat forward, "Don't get me wrong; I think this is great. But you always wanted to have everything just *so* before you tried it on your own. You wanted security. What changed?"

Annie's brain was working perfectly, but her mouth was finding it difficult to form words. "Maybe," she said finally, after taking another sip of her Riesling, "I need *in*security to push me. If I don't have a safety net, then I can't let myself fall, can I?"

And before the glass of wine was finished, she'd told him her plan. She would work on her artwork, her paintings, her passion, by day. Eventually, she hoped to find a gallery to represent her. In the meantime though, for income, she'd paint walls.

"Paint walls?"

She hurried to explain, "Not like a house painter . . . I mean I'll do murals and faux finishes and things like that. Artistic stuff. And I figure that if I market my talents to corporations and businesses, I'll use non-business hours to work, like at night, leaving my days free for the real art I want to do."

"You plan to sleep at all?"

She giggled. "I'll manage."

"Murals, huh? Like what?"

"Whatever they ask for. I already did one back at the house."

"You did? Where?"

"In our room."

Gary lifted an eyebrow.

Annie bit her lip, "Er . . . my room."

They'd walked home, as they always had. Gary took her hand as they left the restaurant and winked when Annie looked at him. "You've had a couple of glasses of wine tonight, sweetie. Don't want to see you fall and smash that pretty little nose of yours."

And she'd let him hold her. Feeling comfort in the warmth, she felt the stirrings of femininity. It had been a long time. For the past several months, all her time had been taken up with setting up her business, getting paperwork together, insurance matters settled, and advertisements done. She hadn't thought about meeting anyone, hadn't considered the possibility.

At her door, or their door — her mind felt muddled — she let Gary pull out his key. He reached over and touched her cheek. "I've missed you so much," he said in a soft voice.

A part of her mind remained logical and detached, but it was getting harder and harder to pay attention to reason. The wine in her system had worn down her resistance. Companionship, conversation, having a person to share her dreams with — she'd forgotten how seductive those things could be. Her knees and elbows were feeling liquidy, and an agreeable warmth had started from her toes and was in the process of working its way upward.

She knew better. She should have kept quiet.

But she said, "I miss you, too."

The sparkle in his eyes turned into something more as he moved almost imperceptibly forward. His face was so close that she could feel his breath pleasantly warm on her cheek. For a moment that lasted no more than a second, but felt much longer, they stood there, eyes locked, inches apart, until Gary tugged her closer and their lips touched, softly.

And when he asked to see the mural in their room, Annie told herself that until they split things up, the house was half his anyway — that he had every right to see it. Ignoring the alarm bells that whispered beneath the heavy blanket of wine, she invited him inside.

June fourth. Seven weeks, three days ago. And how much had changed since then.

With the calendar date facing up at her, Annie sat in her kitchen, elbows propping her chin, staring at nothing. Memory fragments flipped through her brain like a poorly edited movie. She ought to call her sister Karla.

She ought to splash cold water on her face and get started.

She knew what she ought to do, but she also knew she had no energy for any of it.

With a sigh, she closed her eyes. Then jumped as the phone rang.

Instinctively, she moved to answer it,

stopping herself with her hand poised over the receiver as it rang a second time. She looked at the clock. Nine in the morning meant that it was probably a telemarketer and she didn't feel like dealing with that at the moment. The answering machine could pick it up.

Sitting down again, she heard her own chipper voice on the tape and waited while the machine clicked and beeped.

"Annie?"

It was Gary. Thank God she hadn't picked up.

"Umm. I . . . I need some help here."

You and me both, she thought.

"Could you meet me tomorrow? In the morning? At . . . uh . . . the, hang on . . ." Annie heard him talking with someone in the background, and from the muffled words, she assumed Gary's hand was over the mouthpiece. When he came back, his words rushed out. "Yeah, sorry. I'll be at the court building. The one at Twenty-sixth and California, courtroom 324. You'll be able to find it, won't you? And bring some money. Cash. As much as you can, okay?" He mumbled a few more details as Annie scrambled up, reaching for the phone. "Nine o'clock tomorrow. Uh . . . Bye."

Annie lifted the receiver just as Gary hung up.

She waited, as if expecting it to ring again, while she tried to sort through the hundred questions that were flying through her mind. She replayed the message, twice.

With a numbness borne of confusion, Annie sat down. The window across from her framed a small part of the bright, cloudless July sky. A beautiful day. Picture-perfect. Her mind registered that tidbit the same detached way it recognized her own hands, folded like a schoolgirl's, resting on the gleaming oak table top, poised in anticipation.

Chapter Two

Sam Morgan sat on the pink-striped seat of the white wrought iron chair and stared at the long blank wall across from him. He glanced at his watch. Ten-thirty. Annie Callaghan was due here any minute and he still didn't have any ideas for the mural he'd hired her to paint.

Okay, that wasn't true. He'd had several dozen thoughts, but none of them grabbed him. None of them fit with his visions for this place. He craned his neck to glance around. What had once been a large free-standing sports bar in the center of the Chicago suburb of Tinley Park was now Millie's Ice Cream Parlour and Restaurant. The old owners, caught in a sting operation for selling liquor to minors, had had their license revoked and they'd gone under. A little clean-up, a little change in décor, and now the place sparkled.

Warm honey-colored oak gave the restaurant an air of yesteryear. The massive former bar took up one wall along the far side. Now it served as the soda fountain, with a brass footrest running the length and Tiffany-style lights hanging above. Two teenage boys behind the counter, dressed in white long-sleeve shirts with striped vests and bow ties, pulled sundae glasses from the rack over their heads and spun them with cocky flair. Ragtime piano syncopations provided the background music, giving the impression of having just stepped back in time to the Victorian era.

In the past three months since he'd opened Millie's, the place had really gained a following. July's hot weather kept people scurrying in for air-conditioning and frosty treats. Sam hoped to keep it open eight months each year — which wouldn't be bad for a Chicagoland location. The first three Millie's, in Georgia and Florida, stayed open year-round. With any luck, he'd be able to start selling franchises soon.

Grabbing the chair by its seat, he repositioned himself to be able to see the front door of his shop. The restaurant opened every morning at eleven in the summer months, and he'd planned to discuss plans with Annie for a little bit before the lunchtime crowd hit. He was still surprised at himself for hiring her. Although she hadn't said it in so many words, he'd gotten the distinct impression that he was her first client.

Her portfolio, though filled with pictures, featured different views of only four rooms: a living room, a bathroom, and two bedrooms. One of the bedrooms had been painted to resemble an African jungle, with Victoria Falls and Mount Kilimanjaro in the distance.

"Wow," he'd said, pointing to the photographs. "I'll bet that room would be hard to sleep in at night. Make you feel like there'd be wild animals coming to get you."

"It's not so bad," she'd said. "I find it kind of soothing."

Sam had nodded, realizing these were pictures of her own home and, despite the business savvy she exuded, this Annie Callaghan was just starting out. She'd stood next to him as he flipped through her book, her blue eyes bright with anticipation every time he looked over to her. And that's what did it for him. While good business sense told him that he should hire a "name" to do the work he wanted, he sensed that Annie had spunk. And he was a sucker for enthusiasm.

He looked at the wall again. Ten feet tall and about twenty feet wide, it was going to be a massive project. He wondered about that.

And Annie Callaghan hadn't been wearing a wedding ring. He wondered about that, too.

He heard a tap on the glass door behind him, and turned. Annie waved without smiling. Sam gestured her in.

"Sorry I'm late," she said.

"Don't worry, I was just sitting here thinking," he said. "Trying to figure out what'll work. Any ideas?"

Annie bit her lip and smiled a little.

"Actually," she said, "I'd given it a lot of thought over the week and I came up with some preliminary sketches. . . ." She dug through her large black portfolio and riffled through some papers, her arm up to her elbow inside it. She pulled out a few sheets, frowned, then put them back. "I know they're here. I put them in yesterday."

Sam watched her search, then search again. She blew her bangs from her forehead, concentrating on her work. Her hair was reddish-brown, with gold highlights, just a bit shorter than shoulder length and it kept flipping into her downturned face. She tucked it behind her ear for the fourth time in the space of a minute and he could see her teeth clench in frustration.

"Hey," he said, wanting to put her at ease. "Why don't you just tell me your ideas for now? We can look over the sketches later."

Her eyes flashed with embarrassment as she looked up at him. "Great way to start out, isn't it?"

Something was different about her today. Gone was the cheerful confidence and contagious exuberance. Sam ran a finger over his bottom lip and shook his head, "Not a problem. What have you got?" They hadn't signed a contract, though he'd verbally given her the job last week. He wondered if that had been too rash a move on his part. But years ago, he'd felt as though he'd needed a hand when he was starting out. This was his chance to help someone else.

He watched her nod her head to herself, almost as if she was counting to ten before continuing. "I'm sorry." She flashed a smile at him, one that was wry and sad at the same time, but for the first time since she walked in, he noticed a glimmer of hope in her eyes. "It's been a rough day."

Sam reached his hand out toward her, but didn't quite touch. "You okay?"

"I'll be fine. I just rushed over without

checking everything first. I never do that. I'm always so conscientious. I mean . . ." Annie's hands danced in front of her, gesturing, ". . . people *complain* about how conscientious I am. This is so unlike me." Then, as if she was suddenly aware of talking too much, she stopped abruptly, smiled a businesslike smile, and walked over to the big blank wall to begin.

Fifteen minutes later, as Annie described her third option for the wall, the one that she admitted was her personal favorite, Sam found himself being caught up in the idea. Whatever had been bothering her earlier had taken a back seat to the natural zeal that bubbled up. He wondered what the problem had been, then forgot to worry as Annie made him see, with her words, the whimsical fairy tale mural she'd envisioned.

"What I mean is, look around," she continued. He did. "This is a place where parents are going to want to bring their kids and the kids are going to beg to come. You've got the ambiance going with the antiques and furnishings." She trailed her hand along the back of a dark oak bench. The booths, which had been here when the place was still a bar, had lined the walls. Sam had them relocated to the center of the shop and then invested in small, square, wrought iron tables to line the perimeter of the place. These could be pushed together or pulled apart, depending on the size of the party being seated. The booths in the center were great for couples on dates, who preferred the high-backed privacy of the solid wood seats. The entire area had been painted in pinks and greens, and the windows in front expanded to allow lots of light.

The blank wall was directly across from the windows and would be the focal point as customers walked in. Annie stood in front of it, gesturing.

"Okay. Little girls."

Sam raised a questioning eyebrow and she continued.

"The way I figure it, little girls are the ones who'll be most interested in the wall, but that doesn't mean we aren't going to include elements that'll pull the boys in too. So, here . . ." she waved her hand on the far right end of the wall, ". . . would be a castle. Not just any castle, but one with all sorts of little surprises, with windows, at different heights, where the kids could look and pretend they're seeing inside. And maybe we could have a knight taking a bath, or a dog stealing some food. Fun things."

She walked to her left and Sam wondered at what point she'd forgotten he was there. She seemed lost in the magic of her own creation and even though he listened to the description, he found himself more interested in the transformation that had come over her. With great gusto she gestured and pointed, laughing a bit at herself as she spoke, and apologizing for running off at the mouth. Yet she continued.

"The best part, or, well, my favorite part, of this mural would be the hidden pictures." She turned toward him, smiling as she spoke. Her eyes sparkled and it seemed as though her speech was having a hard time keeping up with her brain, her words were coming so fast. "I thought that we could make it almost like a puzzle. Maybe when you have the menus reprinted you could put in a legend of what they need to look for. Simple things, like paintbrushes and buckets and brooms. But we could also hide other things, trickier ones, that'll keep the older kids guessing as well."

Sam, caught up in the idea, took a moment before he responded. "That sounds like a lot of work, and I know we talked about price . . ."

"I'd love to do it, and I'm not asking for more," Annie interrupted. "It would be great for my portfolio and it would make it even more fun for me."

"How long do you think this will take?"

"Probably . . ." Annie said, her voice high with excitement. Then, as if she'd just remembered something unpleasant, her shoulders dropped and she looked away. When she spoke again her voice was quieter, more controlled. "I'm not sure. I would think maybe a month, but it might be a bit longer, depending on the hours I can put in."

Sam wondered at the change in her. "You'd want to work during the hours we're closed, wouldn't you?"

"Mostly, yes," Annie said. "But I can adjust to whatever times are convenient for you. And, I could start right now."

"Well then, Ms. Callaghan," he said, gesturing, "my wall is yours."

Annie went out to her car to get her supplies. *No time like the present,* she thought. *It'll get my mind off of my troubles.* For a little while, she'd been almost able to pretend life hadn't thrown her the curveball it had. She could almost forget.

On the passenger seat of her blue Ford Escort were the sketches she'd looked so hard for inside. *Damn, that'd been humili-*

ating. Her first client and she'd made every possible mistake. She'd seen the doubt in his eyes for just a moment, and it had almost been enough to make her grab her things and leave. Hoisting her backpack to her shoulder, she grasped her tackle box of supplies and took a breath, glad she'd had the fortitude to stay.

She wasn't quite sure how she'd managed to land Millie's Ice Cream Parlour as a client, especially when she'd slipped and practically admitted that all the pictures she had were of her own home. Some business-woman. Still, this Sam Morgan seemed like he'd be a nice person to work for. For a big guy, he had a quiet manner of speaking. At her five-foot-four, everyone looked tall, but she figured he topped six feet. In his late thirties, he didn't look like a man who'd made his fortune selling ice cream, not that Annie thought there was a stereotype for that; Sam looked more rugged. Tougher.

Both times she'd seen him, however, he'd been wearing a long-sleeve white shirt and black pants with matching black vest, dressing up the outfit with a red, white, and blue garter around each upper arm. It took a pretty masculine man to carry that off with the panache that Sam did.

Rattled at first by the solemn way he'd

watched her, she'd started second-guessing herself, wondering if he disapproved of her ideas. But once she'd started to explain, to get into the dreams behind her designs, he'd smiled, energizing her.

Maybe it was his great teeth. Maybe his self-conscious glance — as if feeling guilty for finding pleasure in the plan. But whatever it was, his character-rich face transformed from serious and handsome, to smiling and downright gorgeous. And the more she'd explained, the more interested he seemed to become.

Balancing her supplies as she opened the front doors, she thought about the little bit he'd told her. This was the fourth Millie's he'd opened, though the three others were in Georgia and Florida. Assuming things went well here, she wondered if she might earn a chance to work on the other locations, too.

When she settled her drawing supplies on the floor near the wall, she saw him make his way from behind the bar to the kitchen area. Grabbing the sketchbook, she called, "Mr. Morgan."

He turned. A smile twitched at his lips. "Even the little kids who come in here don't call me that," he said, "so let's go with Sam."

"Okay . . . Sam," she said, feeling a little odd saying his name for the first time, "and . . . Annie's fine."

He nodded.

"Here, while I get started. I found those sketches after all. They were in the car."

Sam paged through, spending a couple of minutes on the first two before flipping to the third one. "Wow," he said. "You described this perfectly. This is exactly how I saw it." He looked up at the wall, then back to her with a grin. "This is excellent."

Annie let go of the breath she'd been holding. As he moved off to oversee the food preparation, she stood in front of the blank wall and stared. She touched the wall, laid her palms against it and said, "You are going to do great things for me, you understand?" And with that, she began to draw.

Two hours later the castle was roughed in and Annie took a bathroom break. When she returned, Sam was standing in front of the drawing, with a milkshake in his hand. "You like chocolate, I hope?"

Annie was startled. She'd forgotten to eat and, now reminded, her empty stomach started to feel funny. "Thank you," she said, as she took the shake from him. For the first time she noticed Sam's eyes. They were an unusual shade of blue, a color that reminded Annie of a favorite crayon she had when she was little. Azure blue. "This is wonderful. It's so thick."

"Hand-dipped," he said, "and the ice cream's homemade."

She pulled a big spoonful up to her mouth and Sam gestured for her to sit in one of the booths. "You'll be more comfortable."

It was as if the chocolate shake was the last remaining food on earth, Annie thought. She couldn't stop herself. She was starving. Sam sat across from her, watching her. She could tell from the look on his face that he was amused.

"Been a while since you had one of those?"

Annie smiled, a little embarrassed. "This is just so good."

"I could have the guys make you a burger or something."

Annie licked some of the cold chocolate from the end of the long spoon, "No, this is perfect. Hits the spot." She glanced up at him, "Thanks."

"Well, while you're working here, just let us know when you want anything. Food and drink on the house, okay?"

"Sounds great."

"How's it going? It looks like you're really moving along."

"I'd like to get as much as I can roughed in. I'm finding that working here has improved my day." She looked away for a moment. "A lot."

"I'm glad," Sam said. "You're welcome to stay as late as you'd like. I have to warn you though, it's going to get crowded in here, soon."

Annie nodded. "I figured. But as long as I'm just drawing and I don't have to worry about paint and kids and all, I should be okay."

"Well," he said, "let me know if you need anything."

Standing up, Annie realized that she needed to go to the bathroom again. Geez, after one milkshake? So this is what pregnant is like, she thought as she pushed open the door to the ladies' room. At least I don't have morning sickness. She grimaced. Yet.

After washing her hands, Annie looked at herself in the bathroom mirror. The fluorescent overhead lights didn't do much for her coloring, but she looked into her eyes and thought that maybe, just maybe, there was a touch of resilience there after all.

Had it only been this morning that she'd almost fallen apart in her bathroom? She shook the excess water from her fingers and reached for a hand towel, still watching herself. She would get through this. She had to. She had a client now.

In the short amount of time that Annie spent in the washroom, the restaurant had begun to fill up. It wasn't crowded, yet, but two soccer teams and three moms with kids in tow were settling into the booths and tables. A white-bloused, black-skirted teenage waitress greeted them as they sat, introducing herself to each of the groups with a little tilt of her head and cheerful "hi." Her nametag read: Milissa, and Annie watched as she helped the moms get the babies into the wooden high chairs, and pass out crayons and coloring book menus to toddlers. Smiling, unruffled, unrushed, she talked to each of the little ones as though they were her best friends.

Annie wondered if she'd ever feel that kind of ease around small children. Her hand absently grazed her abdomen. She'd think about that later. Right now, back to work.

So deep in the project, Annie didn't notice the time.

"You've gotten pretty far," Sam said, startling her.

The windows had gone dark and there were few customers left, stragglers, sitting in the high-backed booths, laughing quietly.

Annie stepped back to get a better look at the overall picture. "Yeah," she said, pleased with herself; trying to sound casual, "it's starting to shape up a little. I think I might even be able to start painting a couple of areas tomorrow."

"Before the drawing's finished?"

"Now that I've found the plan," she said with a wry look, gesturing to the sketch on the floor by her feet, "I know where it's going. And I think it's more exciting for the customers to watch me paint than to do all this pencil work."

"Lots of kids bothering you today, I noticed."

"Didn't bother me at all," Annie said. "And they seemed to be comfortable asking questions." She shrugged. "I kind of enjoyed that part."

They were silent for a moment. Annie looked at her watch and started to gather her things.

"Early tomorrow?" Sam asked.

Annie started to answer, but then remembered Gary's message about court in the morning. "No. It'll be late. I'm not really sure what time. Is that okay?"

"Any time is fine."

Surprised to find a parking spot in front of her house, Annie pulled in and shut off the Escort. She'd have to get Gary to clear his stuff out of the garage one of these days so she could start parking there again. Gary. Her heart dropped when she thought of him. Court tomorrow.

She rested her head back for a moment and shut her eyes. The exhaustion was overwhelming, although she hadn't noticed it till she'd sat down. Now all she wanted to do was go to bed and hope to wake up to find out that today had all been a bad dream.

To be honest though, there were parts she'd liked. Working had felt good. She had been able to push all the unpleasantness out of her head while she drew. It was as if while she worked, she was not only creating art, but also creating a little bubble of happiness — a place where she couldn't get hurt.

Her steps made taps on the sidewalk as she made her way to the house. Seven wooden steps led from the irregular, moss-framed sidewalk to the whitewashed planking of the cottage's front porch. In the city of Chicago, famous for its sturdy bungalows, the cottage could be considered a poor cousin. After their mother died and Karla moved to Boston, Annie had bought out her sister's share. It was small, but it had lots of charm.

When Annie and Gary first married, they viewed the home as an opportunity to own real estate and watch the investment grow. They knew that when babies came they'd have to move to something bigger. But that was five years ago when he had eyes only for her, and babies seemed like the natural course of things.

Annie sighed as she fitted the key into the lock. An expensive addition to the antique door, she'd ordered this retro-designed deadbolt from a catalog that specialized in period hardware. When Gary moved out, she considered changing the lock, but hadn't gotten around to it, yet.

Annie kicked off her shoes inside the front door and slid them out of the way with her stockinged foot. The living room was dark, with just the cool glow from the streetlights in lines across the sidewall from their shadows through the blinds. She walked across the room, her silhouette breaking into the neat patterns of light and she reached down to turn on a lamp. The warmth of the yellow room chased away the shadows and she dropped her drawing supplies on the coffee table by the couch.

Time to call Karla. Annie had been both anticipating and dreading this phone call all day. In the kitchen now, she flicked on the overhead light that always reminded her of an upside-down cake on the ceiling, and reached for the phone. It was nine o'clock in Chicago, which meant it would be ten in Boston.

Annie took a deep breath. The important thing was to sound strong. She had to tell Karla, but she didn't want to worry her. Especially since Karla was pregnant herself, due in four weeks with child number three. Pursing her lips, she blew out the breath, and dialed.

The phone rang, then rang again. Annie swallowed, finding it difficult to do so. This was going to be tough. And what if Chip answered? She wasn't in the mood for their usual cheerful banter. She took a deep breath.

As the third series of rings started, Karla picked up. "Hello?"

Annie opened her mouth, but no words came out. She held the phone and tried to fight the wave of emotion that overpowered her. But her sister's voice, and the comfort and safety it represented, was too much. "Kar . . ." she began, then stopped as she sucked in a breath.

"Annie?" Karla's voice held alarm, "What's wrong?"

Her eyes squeezed shut, Annie cried silently into the phone, forming words in her mind, unable to get them out. She made quiet noises that she knew had to be frightening to hear. Karla's words of encouragement, quiet and nonjudgmental, whispered through the phone line. Despite the fact that Karla couldn't know what was wrong, Annie knew she could count on her sister for support.

"It's okay, honey. It's okay. Whatever it is. It'll be okay."

After a little while, Annie quieted, and she felt her breathing become more regular, punctuated here and there with little hiccups.

The sisters were wordless for several minutes.

"Tell me about it," Karla said.

It came out in fits and starts, as Annie tried to explain, and rationalize and justify, knowing all the while that the attempts were for her own benefit. In trying to make this ridiculous situation sound sensible, she was trying to bring clarity to her own thinking.

Finally, when Annie found herself repeating things, Karla asked, "First things first. Did you make a doctor's appointment yet?"

Annie hadn't thought of that. "No. I just found out today."

"Listen, I want you to call your OBGYN and do that first thing tomorrow. Okay? Whatever else is going on, you need to take care of yourself. Especially now. You still go to Dr. Appleton?"

"Yeah." Annie wrapped the curlicued phone cord around her finger, unwound it, and wrapped it again.

"Good. I like him. And I think he'll be understanding."

"But . . ."

"I know. Now about Gary . . ."

As they talked, Annie could feel the tension slipping away like waves on a beach as the tide moves out. Less and less and smaller and smaller until she felt her entire body quiet like the sea when it's as still as glass.

"You sound tired," Karla said.

"I am. It's been an exhausting day."

"Get used to it. Fatigue is part of the

package. At least till the baby's born — then you move into bone-tired!" Karla laughed for a moment, then stopped abruptly. "I mean — I'm sure everything's been really rough. You need a good night's sleep."

Annie started to say something, but Karla interrupted. "Hey, how's Uncle Lou? Have you seen him lately?"

"Oh my God!" Annie stood up and looked at the clock. It was late. Too late. "I was supposed to stop by there today. He knew about my first day on the mural job and wanted to hear all about it. Geez."

"Annie, don't worry. You know him; he probably got wrapped up in some *National Geographic* article and forgot all about it. How's he handling retirement, anyway?"

"Hates it. Can't stand the fact that he isn't following every big news story anymore. Spends half his day rewording the feature stories in the *Tribune*. Then he hands them to me with this chicken scrawl all over it and says, 'Isn't this much better?' "

Karla laughed. "*Is* his better?"

"I have no idea. I can't read it with all the cross-outs and arrows. It's a mess. But I tell him it is, and assure him that the newspaper just isn't as good anymore without his contemplations on page three."

"I miss him. Even if we can't ever get him to stop talking about newspapers. Does he still go into the whole process of how newspapers used to get printed?"

"Every time he finds a new audience," Annie sighed, smiling, "but I think he's getting desperate and he started in on me again the other day about the magazine sections. I swear I can recite the steps to four-color press in my sleep."

"Well, give him a kiss for me," Karla said.

"I'll do that. Hey, Karla?"

"Yeah?"

"Thanks."

"That's what big sisters are for."

Annie hung up the phone. She stood there with her hand on the receiver for a couple of extra seconds, before turning toward her bedroom to decide on the right kind of clothes to wear for bailing your soon-to-be-ex-husband out of jail.

Chapter Three

Two lines of people waited to walk through metal detectors. Annie stood immediately inside the doors of the Twenty-sixth and California courthouse, trying to get her bearings. Those coming in after her elbowed their way past, mindlessly brushing her out of the way. Annie looked around before choosing the right-hand line, grasping her purse just a little tighter to her side when a teenager dressed all in black came up behind her. He was wiry and unkempt, wearing a collar-type necklace boasting little silver triangles that you'd expect to see on a dog named Spike. Every couple of seconds his arms gave a jerky wiggle, and his chin lifted. His eyebrows, nose, and ears were pierced and he played with a stud on his tongue, running it around his teeth, making little clacking noises.

Annie looked around the entryway, trying to take it in at once, feeling out of place among all these other people who seemed to move along as though they did it every day. What bothered her most about the boy behind her, and he couldn't be more than seventeen, was the look in his brown eyes. Vacant, dull. As though any hint of life had been snuffed out over his short years.

One of the officers just beyond the metal detector yelled something. Annie was surprised to see him motioning to her.

"What?" she asked.

He pointed. "Females over there."

Despite light coming in from the glass wall across from them and from the skylights above, the whole area felt dreary and dark. Even the guards standing watch by the detectors, crisply dressed and armed, seemed drained of life as they waved the lines forward, said "Next," and nodded. Annie made her way around a temporary wall — no wonder she'd missed this — and took her place behind the last woman standing there.

Like cogs on an assembly line, each person stepped up, each piece needing to be checked, but each piece no more important than the one before, and certainly not worth breaking into a reverie over. The guards' eyes were dead, nearly unseeing, giving those who walked by a cursory glance and then returning to the deep stare that hid personality and thought from the outside world.

The alarm went off as Annie walked through. The bright red light above the plastic doorway blinked while chimes rang.

She turned to the nearest guard. "Why did that happen?"

"Step back, please." The black deputy gestured her backwards. She didn't meet Annie's eyes, but seemed to focus on the ground as she spoke without inflection. Her navy blue shirt was adorned with Cook County patches. Both her shirt and her matching pants were too small for her stocky build. She had what Annie had heard referred to as a coffee-table butt, protruding so far out the back that it almost formed a ledge behind her. Surrounding it were the tools of her trade, which did nothing to enhance her shape. She looked strong, yet seemed passive. Annie stepped back as indicated, and the woman waited till she'd cleared the barrier, then wiggled the fingers of her right hand when it was time for Annie to try again.

"I'm so sorry," Annie said as the alarm bells rang once more. "What am I doing wrong?"

"Step to the side, ma'am," the woman said, flicking her hand. A white woman with dyed red hair, dressed identically to the other guard, waved Annie over. She carried a large metal-detecting baton and Annie felt like a criminal holding her arms out to the side as it was waved slow motion all around her body. She glanced over to the line of people waiting to walk through. With her out of the way, the line was moving again. How embarrassing. And yet, not one of them even looked at her. Their eyes were focused ahead, as they took tiny forward steps, to take their turn.

After two passes with the wand, the guard sighed. "Sorry, but I have to do a search."

The deputy's hands patted down her sides, and even while Annie gritted her teeth as she endured it, she could tell that the woman wasn't paying strict attention. The search was cursory at best. Fortunately, it was also quick.

"Okay," she said, looking for her next subject.

"What set off the alarm?" Annie asked.

"Dunno," she shrugged. "Happens sometimes."

Annie followed the groups of people moving down the wide corridor to her right, hoping they were headed the same direction she was. Hoping she didn't look as lost as she felt. Bond hearings were straight ahead, according to the sign. So she kept walking, looking for the right room.

A portly female bailiff, wearing a crisp, white long-sleeve shirt and black pants, her blonde hair pulled up in a bun, stood guard outside courtroom 324, preventing entry. Annie looked at her watch: eight twenty-five. She'd gotten here earlier than she'd expected.

Wooden benches lining the marble walls of the old building were occupied by a diverse group of people: white, black, Hispanic, Asian, some in suits, some in T-shirts, others in ethnic garb. Annie moved farther down the hall to a huge window covered with an art-deco iron lattice. She wondered if it was to prevent anyone from jumping out in an escape attempt.

She was amazed at how many small children were present, some in no more than a diaper and an undershirt, some in heavily ruffled dresses and patent leather shoes. She wondered if they were destined to come here often over their childhood years, even though most of them were too young to understand what was going on. And if over time they could become desensitized, so comfortable in this environment that it became their way of life.

A man stood to the right of the window,

looking out over the boulevard below. Pale and short, maybe five-six, he had an odd, disturbing look about him, as though his face wasn't put together quite correctly. His thick glasses, dark hair, and deep-set eyes gave extra prominence to an already sizeable nose and though he was clean-shaven, his face was dirty. Annie smiled politely as he glanced up at her. She figured him to be in his early forties. He nodded an over-eager greeting and said, "Hi," with a little catch of excitement in his voice. A striped tie, badly skewed to one side, revealed a wrinkled white shirt, and the suit he wore was blue and shiny, as though he'd ironed it. She wished she hadn't decided to wait here, but the crowded corridor didn't offer many other options.

Annie moved to the far left of the window and curved her fingers around the metal latticework, to watch the cars below. The man to her right was staring at her; she could feel his eyes move up and down her body. Damn that Gary for putting her in this situation. But there was safety in numbers and she could be relatively assured that he wasn't carrying a weapon. Although the fact that the guards downstairs had let her through without determining what had set off the alarm was disturbing.

She watched a red car veer left onto one of the side streets below. Back when she was little, she'd taken swimming lessons at the Boys' and Girls' Club somewhere down there. Spaulding Street? She couldn't remember.

"Hey . . . you Annie Randall?" the guy next to her asked.

Startled, Annie looked over. How did he know her? She'd taken back her maiden name, Callaghan, some time ago. He waited, his eyes alert, something in them amiss. His voice still had that eager tone to it and she felt herself cringe. "Uh . . ." she said, wondering if she should answer.

He seemed to take that as an invitation and moved toward her, hand extended. "You gotta be. Gary told me to keep an eye out. You're some looker. Lucky guy." He smiled. If it was possible for the man to get less attractive, his smiling did it.

Annie, unsure, shook his hand.

"I'm Pete," he said, "frienda' Gary's."

"You're *not* his attorney?" Annie said, hoping her repugnance didn't show.

As if that was a compliment, Pete let out what could only be described as a guffaw and shoved his glasses higher up on his nose. "Naw," he said, with that little catch to his laugh, "I'm his roommate. I'm lettin' him stay with me for a while, till he gets everything all fixed up with you."

Fixed up with me? Annie bit her lip, not trusting herself to speak. She looked at her watch.

Pete spoke up again. "They ain't gonna let us in till quarter to nine. Trust me." He nodded at her, his eyes widening as if to emphasize the point. Then he winked. "I been here a coupla times myself."

Annie pulled her lips tight as he moved closer and put his arm up against the metal grid, settling in, it seemed, for a chat. "Um," she finally said, shifting and looking down the hall. She felt the need to get away. "I . . ."

Pete gestured, his mouth open, a smirk tugging at one corner in a knowing way, "I know what you're lookin' for. Down the hall and to your left a ways," he said, winking again. "Can't miss it. Next to the water fountain."

"Thank you."

At ten to nine she emerged from the ladies' room and found the courtroom open, the same bailiff now standing with her back propping an open door. The small room was filled almost to capacity and she pretended not to notice Pete waving her over, indicating that he'd saved her a seat. Despite the fact that the room had been empty moments ago, a wave of body odor and warmth hit her as she jammed her way inside. The air-conditioning available apparently wasn't strong enough to combat the mass of humanity gathered here. The bright sun poured in from floor-to-ceiling windows to her right, and she could see little dust motes dancing above the people's heads. She sidled in to the right, and moved till she was almost in the farthest back corner of the room, giving her a panoramic view of the families and lawyers here to lend their support to the innocent-till-proven-guilty crowd.

The spectator section was separated from the actual courtroom by a wall of angled glass, giving the place a stage-like feel. Annie wondered if the people inside couldn't see the audience, or if they'd just become used to performing in front of a crowd. They moved about as though no one watched, coming to the center door only to call the occasional witness.

When Gary was brought before the judge nearly an hour later, led from a side room by another bailiff, Annie stood up straight. She'd been leaning against the relative cool of the marble wall, yawning in the room's close heat, fighting a losing battle with fatigue. For a moment she almost didn't recognize him. What she recognized was his shirt. It was the Hawaiian shirt they'd bought on their honeymoon, still bright-colored — polyester being one of those few things that never fade — with a pattern of large red parrots and green and yellow leaves. She was amazed that he'd choose such a thing to wear to court, then realized that he'd probably been arrested in it and hadn't had the opportunity to change.

Gary looked exhausted. His eyes scanned the room, looking for her, she thought. Maybe he couldn't see through the glass. Pete gave a self-important, low-key wave, but Gary obviously didn't notice; he kept searching until he was forced to face the judge, who cleared his throat and read the charges.

Judge Abernathy was a black man of about fifty, with salt and pepper hair and rimless half-glasses that he wore near the end of his nose. He spoke slowly and clearly, stopping every few sentences to be sure Gary understood the accusations.

"So, Mr. Randall," he said, leaning on his elbows and focusing on Gary, "you have been assigned a Public Defender. I ask you, do you accept the services of the Public Defender for purposes of this bond hearing?"

Gary appeared momentarily confused, but answered, "Yes, your honor."

"You are charged with burglary; how do you plead?"

A slim, brown-haired man in a gray suit sitting next to Gary at one of the front tables shuffled some papers, then held up a finger in a gesture for the judge to wait. Gary's lawyer, Annie decided. Judge Abernathy cocked an eyebrow and tilted his head. The lawyer shuffled more papers before he stood, answering, "Not guilty, your honor."

After some debate and discussion between the Public Defender and the State's Attorney about Gary's current state of unemployment, his lack of a criminal record, and his marital status, to which Gary had replied "married," bond was set. Annie didn't know if she'd be expected to say or do anything during the court proceedings, so she waited, her eyes widening as she heard the bail amount.

She hadn't noticed that Pete had made his way over until he spoke to her. "Don't worry," he whispered in her ear. She tilted her head away from him. "You only have to come up with ten percent of that." Nodding, she inched away, but he hadn't finished. His eyes were alert again. "You got that much on you?"

He was so close she could smell his breath. Stale, as if he hadn't brushed his teeth this morning. She pushed herself tighter into the corner, but had to ask, "So what do I do now?"

Gary, being led out of the courtroom, cast another wild look toward the spectators.

"Follow me," Pete said. Annie figured she had no choice.

Her head spun trying to follow the procedure for bond payment. The petite red-haired woman in charge of Gary's bail sat behind bullet-proof glass and didn't look up unless she was repeating a question or asking for an ID. Annie supposed that when you did this every day for eight hours at a time, you'd get pretty efficient, but she was still surprised at how quickly they were done. She'd handed over the cash, signed a few things, heard a couple of thumps as paperwork was stamped "PAID," and was out the door with Gary, Pete, and a large white receipt in under ten minutes.

★ ★ ★

It had taken her till nearly four o'clock to get back to her mural at Millie's. By then the afternoon crowd had diminished, and the pre-dinner lull had begun. Annie pulled open the brass-handled door, catching the quiet strains of the ragtime music as she entered. She stopped for just a moment to quell her mind, to shake off the unpleasant business of court this morning and to center herself on the job she'd been hired to do. The aroma of fresh coffee wafted toward her and she smiled. This was only the third time she'd come into Millie's, but she found that she could depend on the sights, smells, and sounds to cheer her up. Just by walking in the door.

Sam was behind the counter, scooping ice cream. He looked up as Annie passed, greeting her with a lift of his chin. Surprised that he didn't smile, she wondered if he was annoyed with her for starting so late in the day, but when she looked back, he was immersed in conversation with the fountain boys.

Within twenty minutes, she had herself set up.

"Hungry?" Sam asked, coming up to stand behind her.

Annie, sitting on the floor, glanced up at him, her brush poised, ready to touch the wall for the first time with paint.

"This must be how you look to all the little kids," she said, her face tilted upward. "But no, I grabbed something to eat on the way, thanks."

"How do I look?"

"Really, really, tall."

Sam grinned, "I just want to give you fair warning. It's Friday night. Date night. The place is going to be jumping pretty soon and it won't slow down till nearly closing time."

"Would you rather I wait to start painting another day?" she asked, pulling her paintbrush back.

"It's up to you. I just thought you ought to know."

Annie looked at all the paints she'd just mixed. Each of the small glass jars had a screw-on lid, so the colors could be pre-served, but she was anxious to get started, to throw herself into the project and forget about Gary and Pete and whatever non-sense they were involved in.

"You know," she said, turning back to him, "I'm just going to work on this one section. It's the very beginning and I want to get the colors just right because it'll set the tone of the whole wall. Maybe after I get that done, I'll work on more of the sketching again."

"Like I said, it's your call. It can get pretty rambunctious in here on the weekends."

"Thanks for the heads-up."

Annie grimaced as Sam left. She'd hoped to get an earlier start on the day, to get at least this foreground area done before the crowds came in. If it hadn't been for the blasted business at court, she could have had this section done by now. It was like she was spinning her wheels all day. Even making the doctor's appointment had been difficult, although she'd been happy to find out that they could take her next Friday. But the fact that she had to make an obstetrical appointment in the first place is what angered her most of all.

She'd chosen to keep the pregnancy secret from Gary, at least for now. Maybe forever, she thought, wryly. And this Pete was a loose cannon. How did he figure into the picture?

Leaving the courthouse in the morning, Annie had expected an apology, some sense of embarrassment, even a humble explanation for the burglary charges. But as they walked across the street to the parking garage, Gary and Pete seemed to have an agenda of their own. She felt like a mother duck, with the two errant ducklings in line behind her.

Gary quickened his step to keep pace with her, studying the bond receipt in his hands. He'd wanted to keep it, promising to pay her back as soon as he could, but Annie grabbed it back from him when he'd finished reading. Pete stayed a few feet behind. "Thanks a bunch, Annie," Gary said, "I mean it. I didn't know who else to call."

Annie didn't slow down.

He continued, "Pete, here, doesn't have that kind of money, otherwise I wouldn't have bothered you."

She stopped and looked at him. "It's not like I can afford this either, you know," she said, her voice sounding more panicked than she expected.

"You'll get it back," he said.

"But not till you have your court date. And if you miss that, I'm out even more money. Money I can't afford."

Gary shook his head. "I wouldn't do something as stupid as miss my court date," he said.

"Yeah well, I didn't think you'd try something stupid like burglary either."

Pete stood a respectable distance away,

his eyes switching between them, tongue in the corner of his open mouth. She knew he was watching with eagerness to see what would happen next.

"I said 'not guilty,' remember?" Gary's eyes, wide in amazement, stared at her, but she doubted their sincerity.

"You say a lot of things that aren't true."

Pete snorted. They both looked at him. "She gotcha there, bud."

"Keep your mouth shut," Gary said.

With a shrug Pete looked away, but the smirk stayed on his face.

The small group resumed walking and when she was still about thirty feet from her car, Annie realized why they were following her. "You don't have a car here, do you?" she asked Pete.

Hands in his pockets, he shook his head. "Gary said we could catch a ride with you."

Annie looked at her watch. It was almost noon. She looked away and then back at them. "Fine. Where do you live?"

Gary gave directions, leading Annie to the far southwest suburb of Oak Forest.

After they exited the expressway and drove down a bit, Annie spotted a Wendy's. "Hang on," she said as she pulled into the drive-thru. "I'm starving."

"Wendy's?" Pete said from the back seat in a disparaging voice. "There's a McDonald's down a little further, why don't we go there?"

Annie half-turned as she eased next to the speaker. "Because I like Wendy's. Is that okay with you?"

Pete made a face and grumbled. "McDonald's got that game goin' again. Thought maybe we might win somethin'."

Annie turned to them, "Do you want anything?"

At the pickup window, Annie, amazed at her level of hunger, paid for the orders, then eased into a parking spot to open her cheeseburger. She took three bites in rapid succession.

"What's the hurry?" Gary asked, unwrapping his chicken sandwich.

"Mmm?" Annie swallowed, and took a drink of her iced tea. "Just can't wait to get rid of you two."

Gary took a bite and chewed slowly, watching her. "You know," he said, "you look different from the last time I saw you. Is everything okay?"

Pete piped in, "McDonald's got better fries."

Annie shot him a withering look, then turned back to Gary. "Yeah, everything's just great." He would miss the sarcasm, she was sure. "Why?"

"I'm sorry I didn't call you," he said, putting his hand on her knee.

She stopped chewing and stared at him until he took his hand back.

He kept talking, his voice low, "You know, that was a very special night for me."

You don't know the half of it, she thought. He had a strange look on his face, a mixture of "give me sympathy" and eagerness. As though he was ready to ask yet another favor. For the briefest of moments, she was tempted to let loose, to tell him about the pregnancy, to make him feel the helplessness, the fear, the anxiety that she'd been feeling.

"Yeah," Pete said, his mouth full of ketchup-laden fries, "Gary tole me all about it. He couldn' believe you put out that night."

Annie's mouth opened, but no sound came out. With one motion, she shoved the rest of her lunch back in the paper bag and smashed it into Gary's chest. "Get the hell out of my car."

There.

Annie shoved her bangs out of her eyes

with the back of her hand and stepped closer to the booths, careful not to block the path of the waitresses. Not too bad for a start. It had taken the entire evening, but the castle itself now had a first coat of paint, and although there was much to add later in terms of embellishment, a lot of the planned flourishes were roughed in. The level of detail was what made her most excited. She knew this section was key — she would need to get this part just right, and surprisingly, she'd done it on her first pass. There was something to be said for attacking a job with excitement, she thought. She'd channeled every ounce of emotion she'd been internalizing into creativity. The wall looked splendid. Just splendid.

She blinked her eyes and yawned. Time for a break.

The restaurant would close in fifteen minutes and the place was just about empty. It would be so nice to work tomorrow morning while it was quiet. The kids coming and going had slowed her down, although they all seemed interested in what she was doing. She looked at her watch. Yep. If she wanted to get an early start, she'd have to give it up tonight. Even the excitement of the project wasn't enough to keep her eyes open.

Two boys came by and asked if they could paint, too. Annie smiled and told them no but that maybe once the picture was finished, they'd want to come back and find the hidden pictures. The boys, about four and six years old, made faces at her, and complained about never getting to do anything fun. She was about to ask them where their mother was when a large man came from the booth section, and reached both boys in three strides. Placing enormous hands on each of them, he tilted their heads upward till they met his eyes. "Your mother wants you back at the table."

The whining stopped instantly and although the boys grimaced, they allowed themselves to be led back. The big man glanced at Annie before he turned. His short, almost crew-cut hair was dark, but the tips had been highlighted blond. Annie wasn't great at guessing heights and weights, but this guy was even bigger than Sam; she bet he topped two-eighty. He wore khaki pants and a dark shirt with a dark gray jacket, despite the humid weather. Judging from the bead of sweat that formed on his upper lip, Annie didn't think he'd chosen it for warmth. He nodded, "Sorry, miss."

"Not a problem," she said, feeling like there was more going on than she realized. Turning back to her supplies, she began sorting and packing.

Sam walked up. "Calling it quits for tonight?"

"Yeah, I think I've about had it. How does it look?"

He stepped back a few feet. "I think it's great. Where did this come from?" he asked, pointing to a small section near the bottom of the wall.

"Oh, that's the legend," she said.

"I don't remember seeing it in the original sketches," he said.

"It wasn't. I just got the idea tonight. A little artistic license. It's what I'm best at."

"It looks like it tells a story, with pictures."

"It does. I got carried away. Took some extra time, but it gave me some more ideas, too."

Sam nodded in a way that made Annie believe he was pleased. "Same time tomorrow?"

"I thought I'd come in early. Like eight? Is that okay?"

"I'll be here," Sam said. "Take it easy, though. Get some sleep."

"I'm just going to clean up, and then I'll head out."

In the ladies' room, Annie waited for the water to warm up in the sink before thrusting her hands beneath the stream. She had to keep pressing the hot water plunger to keep the water flowing, scrubbing the paint off her fingers till it stopped, then pushing it again, until she finally felt as though her hands were clean enough. The walls of the bathroom, reflected in the mirror before her, had been painted a dark shade of beige to complement the teal-colored stalls. While the restaurant exuded a minty cheer, the bathroom was dull and lifeless. The ragtime music being piped in didn't fit at all. Annie nodded her head, looking from side to side. Maybe once the mural was done, she'd be able to talk Sam into letting her perk this room up, too. *And then,* she thought, *my portfolio will have . . .*

Like a punch in the stomach, she remembered the pregnancy. Even if she'd be capable of working for the entire term, she'd have to consider what life would be like once the baby was born. The kind of money she could expect to make would have been enough to keep her going, what with the savings she'd put aside. But it wouldn't be enough to cover baby expenses, or to hire a sitter. And she certainly couldn't count on Gary for financial support.

Thank heaven she'd taken out a health insurance policy when she left the architectural firm. Otherwise right now, her grim situation would be even worse. She could try to go back, of course; the company had been sorry to see her go. But despite the anti-discrimination laws on the books, they'd be foolish to take her back now, with a maternity leave looming in just a few months.

She'd been screwed. In more ways than one.

She'd been so concerned about this job, and so distracted by Gary's shenanigans that she hadn't taken the time to fully contemplate the enormity of her situation. One night of recklessness was going to ruin it for her. It wasn't fair.

High-pitched whining punctuated by yells and screams started, and grew louder outside the bathroom door. Moments later two children scrambled in, followed by their mother, looking less harried than she should, Annie thought, with the way the children were behaving. They were the same two boys who'd asked her if they could paint and whose father, or uncle, or something had taken control. They were shoving each other, and arguing, but because they were both shouting at the same time, Annie couldn't understand what they were saying. All she could make out was that their mother had apparently insisted that they come wash their hands.

She was dark-haired, early thirties, wearing a bright aqua sleeveless silk blouse, the buttons undone low enough to show the lace of her bra. The sag of her upper arms wobbled as she drew her arms up and out of the way as the boys tried to grab at her. Her movement caused a wave of perfume to assail Annie's nose. She was wearing that rose-smelling scent that had gained in popularity lately, but always reminded Annie of a funeral.

"Drew! Kevin! Stop it!" she said, her tone more vehement than Annie had expected, her voice low and raspy. "Don't touch me with those filthy hands."

Her slacks, white and tight-fitting, were secured by a skinny brown leather belt that would have looked much better on a slimmer woman. Olive-complexioned, she had enormous brown eyes, and acknowledged Annie's presence in a distracted way.

Both boys were now jockeying for position at the open sink.

"Let your brother wash first," she said through clenched teeth, tugging at the fabric of the older boy's shirt with just the pads of her fingers, keeping her long acrylic nails out of harm's way.

Annie moved to the side, to allow the older boy access to the sink, but he'd discovered a new distraction and was pressing his messy hands together, then pulling them apart to hear a sucking sound. He held them up to show the little brown and white lines that formed along the bones of his hands.

"Look, Mom!"

The mother held up her own hands in a gesture that said "get away" and locked eyes with Annie. She shrugged. "Boys," she said. "Can't control 'em." She looked up to the mirror and began rearranging her hair, using her perfect nails to pick at tiny wisps. With a surreptitious glance, Annie decided that she had palm trees painted on each nail. Tiny yellow palm trees on teal-colored nails. She matched the stalls nicely.

The younger boy turned around and held up his hands, evidently expecting his mother's approval. Rivers of blue, green and red snaked down his arms and Annie realized, with horror, that the boys' hands weren't covered with ice cream, but with paint.

Giving a little cry, she raced out the door, whispering to herself. *They just played with the paintbrushes,* she said. *The mural is fine. The mural is fine.*

"Annie." Sam stood, blocking her view of the wall.

She looked up at him, and knew.

"Let me see it."

Preparing herself to see minor scribbles, telling herself that whatever they'd done was easily rectified, she looked ahead and walked around Sam to the mural. Or what was left of it.

She stopped short, her mind refusing to accept what her eyes were seeing.

Her first thought was a rational one, *but I wasn't gone long enough for it to be this bad.* As if she could somehow lessen the damage by virtue of logic.

The castle was ruined. The legend obliterated. They'd uncovered her paints and used her paintbrushes and their hands to cover as much of the wall as possible. Had they simply tried to color in the penciled-in area, Annie knew she could have managed around that. There'd be no recourse now, but to start over. They'd smeared orange and green and purple over the section of castle Annie had been so proud to have completed today. The part that she'd improvised, the legend. The one with no sketch to refer to. It was gone.

Her mind registered that their favorite color must be orange. Thick blotches of it obliterated enough of the day's work as to render it unsalvageable.

"Annie," Sam said again.

She brought her fingers almost prayer-like up to her pursed lips and drew a deep breath through her nose. Sam moved closer, but she couldn't look at him.

"Please," she said. She blinked her eyes slowly, then swallowed. "Don't say anything. If you're nice to me right now, I'll fall apart."

The large man who had corralled the boys earlier stepped up, and looked as if he was about to say something when the two boys and their mother emerged from the washroom. He turned to her.

"Mrs. DeChristopher, I think I found out what they did with the paint."

The woman had both boys by their wrists, pulling them.

"Oh my God," she said. "I had no idea."

Annie wanted to scream. *Had no idea?* How could two small children accomplish this much destruction without their mother having any idea? What could she possibly have been doing that kept her from watching her children? Admiring her nails, maybe. Annie felt a tremble work through her body. She forced herself to maintain control, staring at the wall and trying to breathe.

Sam, called away by the kitchen workers, flashed Annie a look that told him how sorry he was for her, and left.

"Miss," the woman said, "I am so sorry for what these two little *darlings* did to your nice picture." She yanked them both forward, "Say you're sorry."

The two boys giggled.

"Drew!" she said. "Say it."

"I'm sorry." More giggling.

The woman was speaking again, but Annie was doing everything she could to keep from making eye contact. She knew, she just knew, that if the saying "if looks could kill" was true right now, this woman was going to be dead on the floor in a minute.

"Timothy here will write you a check. Tim?"

The big man moved forward, pulling a checkbook from an inside pocket. "How much?" he asked.

Scuffling at her feet, the two boys were

again making a nuisance of themselves, so the mother ordered them to sit down back at their table. With a grin they left the group of adults and Annie could only wonder at what mischief they had planned next. All she wanted was for them to leave.

"Miss?" Timothy was talking to her again. "Mrs. DeChristopher wants to make good on this. You just tell me how much to make the check out for and I'll take care of it."

Annie found her voice. "It's okay," she said, quickly. "Don't worry about it." She knew that her tone was conveying just the opposite, but she didn't want their money, she wanted her painting back the way it had been. There was no dollar amount that was going to make her feel good about this, so all she wanted was for them to leave her alone. "Just forget about it. It's fine."

Mrs. DeChristopher laid her well-manicured hand on Annie's arm and it was all Annie could do not to slap it away. "Honey, I can afford it. Let me make this right."

Honey? Annie thought. The woman was barely older than she was, although something about her eyes led Annie to believe that she'd had a tougher go of it. Calm was beginning to take hold. Annie breathed out slowly and spoke with amazing reserve. "No. Thank you anyway. I'll just look at it as a challenge." She smiled wanly and moved off, thinking it was the end of the discussion.

Mrs. DeChristopher wasn't finished. "Listen. You do good work. I seen what a nice picture this was before the kids messed with it. If you won't let me give you money for fixing it, then let me have some of your business cards. I know lotsa people who'd like this kinda thing painted in their houses."

Annie started to shake her head when it occurred to her that she'd be cutting off her nose to spite her face by refusing to hand out business cards. Wasn't the whole idea to expand her business? Of course, this wasn't the method she'd had in mind, but . . . She sighed deeply and managed a cool smile. "I'll get some. Thank you."

When Mrs. DeChristopher, her two children, and the man they called Timothy finally left, Sam locked the front door and came over to the wall, where Annie sat on the floor, her chin in her hands.

He started to sit next to her and said, "Is there anything I can do?"

What control Annie had maintained till then was lost. She fought the hot stinging tears and the solid lump in her throat but couldn't settle herself. Her face dropped into her hands and her shoulders shook as she tried to keep herself quiet. Aware of Sam next to her, she felt acute embarrassment yet couldn't manage enough strength to keep him from seeing her like this.

"Come on," she heard him say from somewhere on her right. Two hands took her by the shoulders, and because she'd never anticipated a situation like this, because she had no idea how to behave, she allowed herself to be led into Sam's office.

"Have a seat," Sam said, pulling the door closed behind them until it gave a little click.

There was more going on than a ruined mural; he would bet on it.

Annie sat in one of the two vinyl office chairs, and he took the other to wait for her to talk. Taking deep breaths, she seemed to be working hard to settle herself, but the veins in the hands she held over her face stood out, belying her tension.

"It's okay," he said, unable to think of anything more profound.

She had her head down, more, it seemed, to prevent him from seeing her cry than from dramatic display. Her small shoulders shook in eloquent silence, her crossed ankles were pulled far back under the seat. Her whole body was turned in on itself, as though she wanted to make herself small and crawl away to hide, to turn invisible. And for some reason, Sam knew he needed to prevent that. And not just because he was afraid of having a defaced wall on his hands with no artist to finish it. As her shudders slackened, Sam leaned forward, "Can I get you anything?"

Annie shook her head, her reddish brown hair barely registering the movement. Still looking down, she rubbed her forehead and massaged her eyes. "No, thank you," she said in a hoarse whisper, then cleared her throat. "I'm sorry. I shouldn't have let it get to me."

"Hey," he said, repeating himself, feeling lame, "it's okay."

She looked up then, her face flushed, her eyes red. Some mascara had run, black-smudged under her eyes. With a wry expression, she shook her head, "I bet I look really great right now, don't I?"

Sam smiled at that, thinking that she did, despite the tears. He chanced a bit of humor. "Never better."

She took it well, giving a short laugh.

He realized, as Annie looked around the tiny room, that she hadn't been in his office before. They'd managed to conduct all their business out in the main part of the restaurant. What was she thinking, he wondered, about piles of paperwork everywhere, in bins on the floor, and on top of his filing cabinet. Her eyes, he noticed, flicked over the mess, settling instead on the picture on the credenza behind his desk.

He hoped she wouldn't ask about it. Not today, at least.

In a minute, Annie turned her gaze back to Sam. He noticed her eyes had gotten bluer and brighter from crying and her breathing had resumed a more regular rhythm. She wiped at her nose and he got up to grab the box of tissues he kept on the cabinet, offering it to her. He didn't want to pry, but knew there had to be some way to let her know that he was willing to listen. This woman who'd popped into his life, who'd come across as so strong and resilient, was, all of a sudden, totally vulnerable. Or maybe he was imagining things. But something welled up inside him. A need to protect her, to make things right again. And yet, who was she really? He knew so little about her. She may not want someone butting into her life.

Taking the tissue box and settling it on her lap, Annie smiled at him. The sadness in it caused a tightness in his heart.

"I'm sorry," she began, "I'm behaving unprofessionally and I'm overreacting. I know it." Her eyes drifted toward the ceiling, unfocused, and he sensed she was fighting tears again. "There's a lot going on in my life right now," she said, starting slowly, then rushing her words as she looked at him again, "and I know that's no excuse. Everyone has problems. Mine are no worse than anyone else's."

He noticed her twisting a tissue in her hands together as she continued. "So, there's no reason for me to fall apart like this." She looked at her hands again, and he watched, interested, as she took a deep breath. Her face relaxed, and her composure returned, "It won't happen again."

"Annie?"

Her eyes flicked up to meet his. Wary, he thought. "Yes?"

"What else?"

She bit her lip for a long moment and the look on her face made him want to say something but he didn't quite know what. She seemed to be asking him with her eyes if he could be trusted. He tried to appear strong and understanding, all the while wondering what he was letting himself in for. When she put the tissue box on his desk and turned to him, he knew she was past crying.

Squaring her shoulders, she lifted her chin and started to talk.

Chapter Four

Annie hoisted her backpack from the passenger seat to her shoulder, and slammed the Escort's door shut. She kept most of her supplies for the mural in Sam's office, so she didn't have to lug them back and forth every day. He'd suggested she start doing that the same night she'd broken down and told him her sordid life story. Her backpack tonight was light, with only a couple of new paint tubes and a new drop cloth stuffed into it.

She took a moment to stare up at the moon, looking hazy through the dark clouds of the early August sky. Nearly eleven o'clock; she berated herself again for oversleeping. After dinner, she'd settled in for what should have been a short nap. Who ever invented the snooze alarm? She'd hit it so many times that it had given up and a half hour ago she'd awakened with a start, realizing she'd missed her nine o'clock goal by a long shot. Tomorrow, hopefully, the doctor would have some suggestions for how to combat the constant fatigue. Good thing she wasn't expected here at specific hours. And good thing Sam had given her a key.

It had been a hell of a week, she thought as she made her way toward the restaurant's front door. She could hear the high-pitched hum of the cheerful neon sign, bright red block letters spelling out the word "Millie's," the words "Old Fashioned Ice Cream Parlour and Restaurant" in white, in the kind of script you'd expect to see on the side of an old-fashioned coach.

She wiped her forehead with the back of her left hand, and grimaced at the thought of what the humidity was doing to her hair tonight. All day the temperatures had hovered in the mid-nineties and though she had air-conditioning at home, the compressor in her little Escort had gone out and she didn't have the funds to have it repaired yet. Grabbing the neckline of her gray T-shirt, she tried to use it as a fan, sending down what little air she could to cool herself, and she looked forward to painting in the chill of the closed restaurant.

Just as she was about to step up to the sidewalk at the front of the restaurant, Sam was at the door, holding it open for the last remaining patrons to exit. The four adults, laughing and talking, called good-night to him, as he waved and thanked them. Spotting Annie, he smiled and held the door open a little bit longer.

"Allow me," he said.

She stepped around him, "Thank you," she said, and then, "kind of late for customers, isn't it?"

Sam shrugged, "It happens. Most of the crew has gone home, everything's clean. Just Milissa and Jeff finishing up now." As they walked into the main dining room, she glanced over toward the kitchen where the two teenagers were cleaning the fixtures. Annie wrinkled her nose as the brisk scent of bleach wafted their way. Laughing and talking as they worked, the young people appeared oblivious to the rest of the world.

"Little romance blooming there?" Annie asked.

Sam clutched at his heart, "Ah . . . to be young again."

As she headed toward Sam's office, she took another look. Milissa's large brown eyes sparkled, focused on Jeff as she wiped the countertop. They seemed to be discussing a marching band competition, but neither appeared to be as interested in the discussion as they were with keeping each other's attention. They probably wouldn't remember details of the conversation later, Annie thought. And it probably won't matter if they don't.

Sam headed to the back to shut off the outside lights as she pulled out her supplies from his office and made her way toward her wall. At first she'd referred to it as "the wall," then "Sam's wall." Now it was "her wall." Shaping up nicely, she thought, despite some earlier setbacks.

Over the past week, she'd whitewashed the fingerpaints and started sketching again. The new castle was bigger, with more windows, and Annie had included a small dungeon area, seen through a lower-level window, where two boys were locked behind bars. She'd resisted the urge to have orange paint dripping from their hands, afraid it would look too much like blood. Drew and Kevin. That's what that Mrs. DeChristopher had called them. Or maybe she'd name them Gary and Pete.

Background trees were her focus today, and she climbed her stepladder to finish roughing in the branches. Leaves would come later, when she painted. Her right hand moved above the roof of the castle, her hip leaning against the top of the ladder, and she allowed herself to be immersed in the process of creation. Keeping an eye on perspective, she drew large, supportive branches and then went in to fill with smaller, more delicate ones. Most would be obscured once the leaves were in, but she liked to know that they were there.

Kind of like the backing she felt she had in both Karla and Uncle Lou, she thought. They weren't always seen, but she knew they were there and she could feel their unyielding support.

"Should you be up on a ladder?" Sam asked, breaking into her reverie.

Annie looked down, pencil in hand, taking a moment to focus. "I'm fine," she said, waving her hand in a dismissive gesture. She'd gotten pretty far in the past hour and was pleased. She looked back toward Sam. "Can I bother you for something to drink?"

"Sure." Sam looked skeptical. "But I don't want you to fall, or hurt yourself."

She flashed him a smile as he turned away. Ever since she told him about her pregnancy last week, and about Gary's incarceration, she'd felt, in a way, as if a load had been lifted from her shoulders. Almost as though Sam was a newly sprouted branch on her tree of support. An unexpected one.

Not having to keep secrets made it easier. A lot easier.

She remembered that evening back in Sam's office. She remembered taking a deep breath before she began, and in those couple of seconds, when she'd looked at him, felt as if she was seeing him for the first time. While they'd certainly had plenty of time for interaction while she worked and painted, he was, after all, Sam the employer. Sitting in the chair across from her, with his elbows on his knees and his whole body leaning forward, he was different. She noticed his eyes again. Their vivid azure blue contrasted to his lightly sunburned face and sandy colored hair, and they seemed to be reaching out to her, urging her to talk.

Taking a leap of faith, she had decided to trust him.

When she told him she was pregnant, he'd blinked and said, "I didn't think you were married."

She'd been about to explain, but he interrupted almost immediately, his eyes alarmed and apologetic, "That's not what I meant. Of course, you don't have to be married." Looking like he didn't know what to say next, he shifted in his chair as though it had just become excessively uncomfortable.

He pressed his fingers into his eye sockets as he spoke again, "Well, you know what they say happens when you assume. I just made the proverbial ass out of myself, didn't I?"

His embarrassed grin made Annie feel more at ease. "Sam," she said, as she leaned forward to touch his arm, "it's okay. Actually, I am married. That's the real problem."

While talking, she observed him, looking to see if she was shocking him in any way, knowing that the story sounded distasteful when put into words. But he kept a careful, bland expression on his face, and Annie wondered if that came from practice or great concentration. He'd managed to stay expressionless except for that moment where she said she was married. At that, she'd seen something flicker past his eyes. Something akin to regret. As though he'd been ready to hear almost anything, but her being married had surprised him. She wondered why he would have been disappointed. And for the briefest instant, considered what life would be like if she'd met Sam all those years ago, instead of Gary.

Now, up on the ladder, Annie erased a couple of lines, squinted, then drew again. The picture on Sam's credenza behind his desk came to mind. Sam, a petite blond woman, and a young boy of maybe twelve, standing together, smiling. Even though the picture was focused on the three people in the foreground, Annie could see, behind them, impressive antebellum pillars on the large white home and she'd been reminded of Tara from *Gone With the Wind.* His wife and son, she supposed.

Wow, she was thirsty. She climbed down the ladder, and noticed a glass of iced tea that had appeared as if by magic, on a nearby table. Sam must have come and gone without her noticing. He knew she liked her iced tea really cold, so the fact that there were only a couple of very small ice cubes floating at the top told her that it had been waiting for her for some time. Sitting, she squeezed the lemon into the glass and lifted the straw to her lips. Part of the beauty of working on this mural was how it captured her imagination so fully. She found that she lost herself in it more often than not. Gazing, now, from her booth about ten feet away, she was amazed at how far she'd gotten tonight.

"Ready to call it quits?" Sam asked, emerging from his office.

"I didn't realize you were still here."

He looked at his watch, "It's going on two o'clock."

"Time flies."

Sam sat down across from her. His eyes were a little bloodshot — but he was smiling. "And you're having fun?"

She sighed. "Yeah, I am." Her legs, strained from standing for so long, were starting to relax and the fatigue she'd begun to expect started creeping into them. She stretched them out into the aisle and slowly rolled her head. "But I should knock off soon, I suppose."

"What time's your appointment to-morrow?"

"Not till the afternoon. I've got time."

"Annie, go home. You're pregnant. You need rest."

"Is that your professional opinion, Doctor?"

Sam still smiled at her, but it was a sadder smile than she would have expected. "Have you told your . . . husband, yet?"

Keeping her eyes on the straw as she swirled her amber colored tea, she shook her head. "Not yet."

"Can I give you a little friendly advice?"

Annie looked up. His eyes were serious. She nodded.

"The sooner the better. He needs to know."

"I was going to wait till the divorce was final."

"Divorces," he said, as he looked up at the ceiling, then back down at her, "divorces are funny things. They take a long time and they can be nasty. If you keep the pregnancy from him, especially after you've seen the doctor, and you withhold it, well, it could be unpleasant."

"Like legally?"

"No, but . . ." he seemed to search for the right words. "Sometimes you can't undo things. And you look back and wish you'd handled it differently. Telling him is the right thing to do and you don't ever want to regret not doing the right thing." He shrugged. "You never know."

Annie looked at him. He sounded like the voice of experience.

"Trust me," he said.

Annie berated herself for not visiting Uncle Lou earlier in the week. She held her navy blue umbrella over her head and shut her eyes as the wind shifted, shooting a fine cold spray of water into her face. He was probably asleep, but this was the only chance she had now for a couple of days.

She knew the doorbell didn't work. It had been out of order now for about four years. He'd been meaning to get to it. The chance of his hearing her knock over the wind and the thunder was slim. She knocked a second time, harder, and with more of a beat, thinking that it would stand out from the outside noise.

When he answered, clearly wide awake, she was surprised. It was only noon. Usually he slept till at least two in the afternoon, then stayed up all night watching old reruns and reading magazines.

"It's been stolen again," he said, opening the door to let Annie in.

Uncle Lou's rather unruffled tone and the fact that he was always reporting recent newsworthy events rather than talking about his own life, kept her from reacting too strongly. She searched her brain for some memory of something he might have mentioned being stolen a first time.

"Here," he said, leading her to the dining room table. Except for the reddish wooden ball-and-claw legs under the table, a person coming into the room would never know that there was a shiny mahogany table under all his clutter. Covered from end to end with newspapers, magazines, and assorted detritus, it resembled the beginnings of a Girl Scout paper drive.

Uncle Lou shoved an article into Annie's hands, which she didn't bother to read, knowing he'd recite the information to her in a minute anyway. The fact that he had his half-moon glasses on told her that he was serious about his subject matter; probably had been reading all about it up to the moment she'd walked in. She knew better than to try to change the subject, but really didn't mind the diversion. Right now he was digging through an extra high pile at the far end of the table, the sweat beading over the top of his very round, very freckled, bald head. He was a short man, but what he lacked in stature, he made up for in verbosity.

"Just when it was due to be exhibited at the Art Institute, it's gone again." He was still shuffling, "What does that say about the city of Chicago?"

Uncle Lou looked up, his bright hazel eyes fixed on Annie, but she could tell he wasn't really seeing her as he continued.

"That we can't protect some of the world's treasures? These . . . that one in particular, read that."

"I thought you said it was illegal to reproduce copyrighted articles," she said, holding up the paper.

"Yeah, well, I make these for my own personal use, so I can cut them up and rearrange them so they read better. None of them leave the house. So, don't take that with you." He started shuffling through the papers. "Let me find the original for you." The tall pile he'd been digging through was now separated into three smaller piles, one of which he'd placed on top of yet another pile on the dining room chair next to him. Without looking, he grabbed at the uppermost papers as they slid sideways, catching them before they hit the floor. Annie knew that the seats of these ornately carved chairs were covered with maroon and cream striped fabric . . . the set had been her grandmother's. But she couldn't remember the last time the chairs were clear enough for the cushions to be seen.

"It's okay," she said, starting to read.

"Did I ever tell you about the time . . ."

"Your buddy got suspended for making illegal copies?" she finished. "Yeah."

He nodded, but didn't look up, muttering to himself, "I know it's here somewhere." He shuffled around toward the triple window on the long wall. Drapes that had been there when he moved in years ago were still there, the hem in shreds from the incessant scratching of Mr. Brown, his orange tiger cat. The top of the linen fabric hung limp in places where the upper edge had missed its hooks. Over the years the color had gone from bright cream to a dull beige. A fervent smoker until he'd retired, Uncle Lou's house still had a thin sheen of brown over everything. He'd had the whole interior of the house paneled with a fake woodgrain about fifteen years ago when he realized that his habit was discoloring the walls, saying that it saved him from having to repaint.

The second and third bedrooms of the house were packed with filing cabinets, boxes labeled with obscure codes, books, and magazines dating back to the nineteen-forties. More piles sat beneath the windows, towering three-fold over the cardboard boxes on which they rested.

Here in the dining room, which he used as his office, two paintings hung on the wall opposite the windows above the table's matching, and equally concealed, mahogany buffet. Annie had painted both of them, one of the Tribune Tower and the other of the Wrigley building, where Uncle Lou had held his first job. Watercolors, they were framed under glass, and last year, when Annie had taken it upon herself to help Uncle Lou clean up a little, she'd wiped them down. Years of neglect had caused a build-up of stickiness and it had taken several passes with the cleanser for the pictures to be bright again.

Clearing his throat with a wet, noisy snort, he stopped and turned to Annie, giving her his full attention for the first time. "I'll find it later," he said, then nodded toward the paper in her hands. "What do you think?"

"It's hard to read," she said tilting the paper different directions, "I can't make out the byline. Is this something you wrote?"

"No, no." He moved around the table and stood next to her. Wearing his brown leather house slippers instead of shoes made him seem even shorter to Annie. "You see this drawing?"

Squinting, and thinking that it looked liked black and white squirming potatoes, she waited.

"This one, by some German artist from the early fifteen hundreds? You've probably heard of him." Uncle Lou leaned over Annie's arm, his chubby fingers pointing to different paragraphs as he spoke, blocking most of the article as he did so. "I'm sure you learned about him during one of your art classes." He took the article from Annie's hands, "Yeah, here."

He began to paraphrase as he read, "Albrecht Durer, you know who I'm talking about." Uncle Lou's eyes flicked up and back down before Annie could respond. "Here's a picture he drew, maybe you'd see some significance in it. Looks like a bunch of unattractive naked women." He looked up, warming to his first tangent. "Now I know I'm not an art critic, but they say that this drawing here, what is it? About eight and a half by eleven? The size of this piece of paper? They say it's worth over ten million dollars. Hmph."

"I've heard of him," she said. "Isn't this the drawing that had been stolen from some German castle during World War II?"

"The same one. And all the hoopla not too long ago about it having been recovered. Remember that?"

Annie nodded.

"Well, it was supposed to come to the Art Institute next month for an exclusive showing, not that I would have gone." He paused to clear his throat again, and wiped the sweat that had formed on his upper lip. As he got more excited about the subject, his perspiration level rose and he was starting to look uncomfortable. "But now it's been stolen again."

Annie took the paper back from his hand. "You're kidding. When?"

"Yesterday or the day before. It was in the paper this morning." He resumed foraging through the piles on the table. "I know that's hard to read, and the original is here somewhere. But I want to know what's so special about this drawing. I mean, in your opinion."

"It's in today's paper?" she asked, trying hard to mask the incredulity in her voice. More than the loss of the drawing, Annie was floored that the newspaper article could have gotten so lost so quickly. It was mind-boggling, even given the disorder of the house. She leaned forward and patted him on the arm. "I'll pick up a copy later."

"Will you? Pick me up an extra one too, okay?"

"Sure."

"Hey did Gary ever get ahold of you?"

"Gary." Annie said the name with distaste. "He called you?"

"He stopped by a couple of nights ago. Meant to tell you when you phoned the other day."

Annie lifted Mr. Brown, the cat, from the oversized leather easy chair in the adjacent living room. She sat down, the stuffing giving a long, slow, whoosh, as she did so. This was her favorite place to sit. It was also the only place to sit, other than in the kitchen, and that was sometimes iffy. "What did he want?"

"He didn't say, just that he'd been looking for you and he was wondering how come you weren't ever home at night any more. Had some papers with him. And a friend."

"Pete."

"You know him? Well, I'll tell you, I didn't think much of that guy. Kept pulling at Gary the whole time they were here, telling him they needed to hurry."

"Did you tell them where I was working?"

"Nah, didn't think it was any of their business."

Annie leaned her head back and stared at the ceiling where a spider had made a home in the corner. She blew out a breath of frustration before she stood up. "I gotta go," she said.

"It's not the company, it's the hour, eh?"

She leaned down to kiss him, "Yeah, exactly. And, just to be safe, don't ever let Gary or Pete in here, okay?"

"Sure. And don't forget that copy of today's *Tribune*, okay?"

"I won't."

Chapter Five

Baby.
  Parents.
  Working Mother.
  Annie looked at the choice of magazines in the waiting room and shook her head. Nothing felt right. If she was going to be having a baby, she ought to be at least a little happy about it. She put down the *Sports Illustrated* that she'd taken to read. Probably a nod to the poor husbands who sat here, patiently waiting for their wives to be called. She'd paged through the entire magazine, so distracted that she hadn't realized it was the swimsuit issue until she put it down on the table next to her. A dark-haired woman, looking well past due, sat on the other side of the corner table. She glanced down at the magazine, then away. Annie could only wonder what the woman was thinking.
  With a sigh, she got up, just to feel like she was moving. She'd been scheduled for two o'clock, but the receptionist had told her that one of the doctors on duty had

been called in to the hospital on an emergency, leaving only one other to take all the appointments. She wanted to go home and take a bath. Her hair had gone completely straight from the rain, and limp strands kept falling into her eyes.

It was almost three now, but it seemed as though she and the other woman were the last two for the day. She hoped she'd get Dr. Appleton. She'd seen him for the past few years and found him to be quick and efficient. Not to mention that he was small-boned for a man. Precisely what one wanted in a gynecologist.

The other woman got called in. Annie watched, trying not to appear obvious, as the woman pushed herself up from her seat, leaning heavily on the chair's arms. She waddled to the office door, holding her left hand behind her back for support. She smiled at the nurse with a weary cheerfulness, and Annie wondered if the woman's face was always that bloated or if it had been caused by the pregnancy. Wearing a white summery shirt with big red polka dots, and wide red cotton shorts, she looked immense. *Am I going to look like that, too?*

Across the room, which was decorated in a soothing blend of sea colors, Annie noticed a collage of pictures. Making her way over to it, she saw that it wasn't a collage after all, but a bulletin board full of haphazardly pinned up photographs of some of the babies that these doctors had delivered over the years. Some were posed Christmas portraits, some were candid shots of toddlers with food smeared over their faces. Children ranged in age from newborn to college-aged, wearing everything from just a diaper to fraternity sweatshirts.

Would she ever put a picture up here?

"Annie Callaghan?"

She turned to see a smiling nurse, file folder in hand, dressed in blue pastel pants and coordinating shirt, holding the door to the examining rooms open with her butt. "Come on back, and we'll get you started."

The examination room was tiny, but pristine. A peach-colored paper robe and a white sheet had been set out on the table. Handing it to Annie, the nurse said, "It opens to the front." She went to the door. "I'll be right back."

"Thanks," Annie answered. But she couldn't help shivering. It was chilly in here.

After giving her plenty of time to change, the nurse returned. "My name's Noreen," she said, wrapping the blood pressure cuff over Annie's arm. In her late thirties, she was slim and dark-haired, with large eyes and a sincere smile. "When was your last period?"

"May tenth."

"Well then," she said a few moments later as she removed the cuff. "One-ten over seventy-two, excellent. You conceived . . ." she picked up what looked like a green paperweight with a dial on top and began to turn the indicators.

"I conceived on June fourth."

Noreen laughed. "Pretty sure about that, are you? This thing says May twenty-fourth, and it's usually pretty accurate."

"June fourth. Trust me." She hugged herself with her arms and shivered.

Noreen's brow furrowed a bit. "Here, put this sheet over you to keep warm. The doctor will give you a due date, but it looks like late January, early February to me. She'll be here in a moment."

"She?" Looks like it wasn't going to be Dr. Appleton after all.

"Dr. Guerzon. You'll like her." Noreen winked as she walked out the door, "She's very petite."

A petite dynamo, she should have said. Opening the door to the examining room wide as she entered, holding the neat little manila folder that held Annie's medical history, Dr. Guerzon glanced up, booming, "Hello Annie," in a light accent. About fifty years old, she was short and slim, with dark hair and Filipino features. She closed the folder and sat on the low-wheeled stool near the bed. Tilting her head in a friendly way, she said, "And how are you today?"

"All right, I guess."

"You took a test at home?"

Annie nodded.

"Morning sickness?"

"No. Not yet."

"You would have had it by now," she said, smiling. "You're very lucky."

Lucky? Annie thought.

Dr. Guerzon asked what seemed like an endless round of questions before and during the actual exam. Finished, she pulled her latex gloves off her hands and pronounced, "You're pregnant."

Annie's last chance for a reprieve was gone. She rubbed her eyebrows with both hands, keeping her composure. She'd held out the very slim hope that the home test had been wrong and the doctor would laugh and she'd be sent on her way, feeling a fool. But at least not a pregnant one.

Dr. Guerzon offered her arm to help

Annie sit up. Her eyes seemed to flash downward at Annie's left hand as she did so. "You're not happy?"

Annie shook her head, feeling the doctor's gaze take her in. Bright brown eyes, looking warmly alert, waited. Annie felt a bubble of emotion rise up and she fought it. She was through crying about this. It was time to deal with it.

"I'm getting divorced," she said.

Dr. Guerzon canted her head. "And the baby's father is . . . ?"

Annie's words rushed out, "No . . . no. It isn't like that." Her hands came up in alarm. "My husband *is* the father, but he . . . but I . . ." Annie took a deep breath, "I made a mistake. A very stupid mistake."

Looking at the folder in her hands, Dr. Guerzon played with one of her large pearl earrings. "You can terminate the pregnancy if you wish. It is still early."

There was utter silence in the room for several long seconds.

Dr. Guerzon stood up, her eyes on the manila folder as she tapped it against the palm of her left hand, "I'll send Noreen back with the name of someone who is very professional." She looked up. "I wish you good luck, whatever you choose."

Annie slid from the examining table and

dressed quickly, trying to ignore the goose bumps on her arms. Her teeth chattered and she realized the room wasn't cold enough to warrant that. Just as she was about to slide on her shoes, Noreen knocked discreetly at the door and came in.

"Hi," she said with a smile that didn't reach her eyes. She held out a prescription paper on which Dr. Guerzon had written a name, address, and phone number. "This is the information you wanted."

Annie took the proffered paper, noticed the wedding ring on Noreen's left hand. She wasn't much older than herself. "Do you have kids?" she asked.

Noreen smiled, almost reluctantly, as she nodded, "Yeah, three girls." Something in her eyes softened for a moment. "They're everything to me."

Outside, in her car, Annie waited till her vision cleared before shifting into drive. It seemed as though her eyes welled up at everything now. Hormones ravaged her body. There are choices in life, she told herself. Difficult ones. And we live with the consequences of our choices every day.

Traffic down Ninety-fifth Street crawled, as always. Annie leaned her elbow out the side window and rested her head as she contemplated her life. A white mini-van next to her beeped, the woman driving asking through pantomime if she could please cut in front. Annie waved her forward, then waited as she crept into the lane.

Lifting her foot from the brake, Annie's glance swept over the back of the white van in front of her. A diamond-shaped "Baby on Board" sign wiggled from its suction cup perch in the back window. Annie gave a humorless chuckle. "It's a sign!" she said aloud, rolling her eyes heavenward. "I get it; I'm pregnant."

As the van pulled further forward, Annie caught sight of the bumper sticker pasted brightly below the plates. She bit her lip as she read it.

She's not a choice. She's a person.

Annie hit "rewind" on her answering machine to listen to the message again.

"Hello, Annie Callaghan? This is Gina DeChristopher. We met coupla nights ago at Millie's Ice Cream Parlour. You remember?"

Annie frowned; how could she forget?

"Well, anyway, my boys have been pestering me to have their rooms painted in something real cool, like that castle thing you were doing, but maybe dinosaurs. Could you do somethin' like that? Give me a call."

Having found some scrap paper and a pen while the message replayed, Annie found herself copying down the phone number that Gina DeChristopher provided. Not that she would want to work with those two boys underfoot. But still.

She padded around her kitchen, seeking food, and thinking about the night of orange paint.

Empty refrigerator. Annie knew she'd have to go grocery shopping soon, particularly because she was hungry so often, and in unpredictable spurts. She would be fine, content, not even thinking about food. Then, without warning she'd need to eat something immediately. Often she found herself grabbing cookies, stuffing three or four into her mouth within the space of a minute. With the intense hunger satiated, she'd then be able to forage for something healthier.

Only once, late at night, too tired to move, had she ignored the hunger cravings, and had paid dearly, her head hung over the bathroom bowl until all she came up with was empty heaves. She wasn't about to make that mistake again.

Pulling out a sleeve of Oreos and a mug of milk to dunk them in, Annie sat at the kitchen table and looked out the window. The little white prescription paper with the scribbled note on it sat on her left. She resisted looking at it, instead concentrating on the neighbor's tree that she could see over her garage in the back, the storm clouds beginning to recede behind it.

She dunked the first cookie, the one that always tasted best, up to nearly her fingertips, and swished it around. Soggy things usually didn't turn her on, but milk-drenched Oreos were in a class by themselves. And she felt soggy today. The cookie melted in her mouth, and she savored the unique flavor and texture combination with a sigh.

This was the house she grew up in. That was the tree she saw everyday since she was old enough to remember. It had to be over fifty years old. And it would probably be here fifty years from now. She'd never found out what kind of tree it was, maple maybe; it hadn't mattered. What had mattered was that she and Karla had picnics in its shade, and had played with the little pale green whirlybirds that fluttered down every year. And had grudgingly raked the crispy leaves that landed in their yard, then jumped into piles they created.

Her parents had provided a wonderful childhood.

And now here she sat, with two phone numbers in front of her. She could call one, or both, or neither. But they were her decisions.

And Gary should be told.

She looked down into the dunking mug. All the cookies were gone and little brown crumbs had floated to the top. She never could make herself drink the leftover milk. And despite the fact that it was a waste, her mother had never forced her. "We all have our little quirks," Annie remembered her saying, "and when you know something is right for you, you hold onto it. It's what makes you who you are."

She looked up again at the neighbor's tree.

She looked at the two papers.

With a sigh, Annie moved toward the phone, and as she passed the wastebasket, she crumpled up one of the papers and tossed it in. She knew what was right for her.

The phone rang four times before a machine picked up.

"Hello," she said at the tone, "This is Annie Callaghan . . ."

Chapter Six

"Can we go somewhere . . . else?" Annie's eyes swept the apartment. "We need to talk."

"Sure," Gary said, with a shrug. His wrinkled brown T-shirt hung slack over ripped khaki shorts. He held his hands up against his chest as he surveyed himself. "Probably need to change clothes, huh?"

"Yeah. Probably."

"Hey, Annie." Pete's voice came from an enormous white leather recliner across the room. Slouched so low his stockinged feet dangled over the edge of the footrest, he was barely visible. Looking like he hadn't showered in days, he leaned forward from his cushioned comfort in interest. He was shirtless, and when he smiled at her, his mouth hung open, sloppy and wet like a dog's.

Annie resisted the urge to step back outside to wait, glancing at her watch. She shook her head. What a change from the solitude she'd enjoyed just hours ago.

That morning had dawned in golden-cloud splendor. Annie had watched the sun rise from the steps of her back porch, a hot mug of coffee warming her hands. She'd enjoyed the early hour chill, as the sky shifted in a slow-motion ballet, from gray to pink to yellow. Wearing the oversized blue sweatshirt from her sister, her arms pulled tightly into her sides, she'd felt immense comfort and a tingling of hope.

It was Saturday. She and Sam had agreed that weekend crowds were too difficult to manage around, so now every Friday, Saturday, and Sunday were free. It made perfect sense, and yet Annie found herself wishing she could be there every day. She'd sighed at the smell of the green grass, fresh with sparkling dew. Two empty days lay ahead of her. The big decisions were behind her.

But Annie had known there was one more thing she still needed to do.

And so, once the coffee mug had been drained and the sky transformed to its dazzling blue, she'd made the call and arranged to meet with Gary.

Her first thought, as she'd pulled up to the four level apartment complex, was that it might have lived a prior life as a flea-bag motel. Three long identical brick buildings ran perpendicular to the road, with dark green metal staircases at each end that looked recently painted. Parked in the littered lot, over weeds that had pushed through the cracked macadam, were large, expensive cars and SUVs. Each one shiny and clean, they stood in stark contrast to the beaten and tired appearance of the apartment building complex. Her little Escort was dwarfed and outclassed.

Annie had gingerly made her way up the stairs to Gary and Pete's apartment, avoiding dark puddles and broken beer bottles. Each of the apartments had a metal front door and, next to it, a set of sliding glass doors that served double duty as picture window. Not one looked inviting. All were hazy with grime and covered from the inside. Some with taped-up newspaper to protect the residents' privacy, a little room left open for light. Some with ripped and faded curtains. As Annie made her way to apartment 451, she realized that Uncle Lou's house probably looked just as bad from the outside, so she was in no position to judge.

She hoped to get this over with quickly. She'd planned to have their talk in the apartment if they could, for expediency's sake. Within seconds of arriving, however, she couldn't wait to leave.

"Why dontcha sit down?" Pete asked.

A pastel bed sheet had been thrown over the sofa, barely covering the many rips and tears in the upholstery. Assorted odd-color stains on the sheet kept Annie from getting too close. "I'm fine," she said, thinking that the room needed airing out. Despite the fact that it was a clear, sunny day, the front drapes were pulled shut and the room was dark. An air-conditioner hummed from a side window, but the combined smells of sweat and feet as they wafted warmly through the room were too much for the small unit and Annie felt something lurch upward in her throat.

She inched closer to the flow of cool air, taking in its metallic breeze. She'd be all right. *Just hurry,* she thought.

Gary poked his head out of a room near the back, "You want to go for lunch?"

"Sure," she said, thinking that if she stayed in this room much longer she'd never eat again.

"It'll have to be your treat, I'm a little short this week."

"Whatever."

From his relaxed perch in the huge chair, Pete spoke up. "There's a great place down the block, all Cajun food. Cheap too."

"Great, thanks," Annie said, looking around.

The chair Pete sat in was pristine, the white, spotless leather looking out of place in the dingy room. Holding a remote control aloft, he poked at it repeatedly, glancing down at it, then up, then down again between pokes. Annie listened to the buzz and half-spoken words that blasted from the big-screen television as he changed channels and adjusted the sound for the dozenth time since she'd walked in.

Now he muted the volume and sat looking at her, his large eyes blinking from behind his thick dark-rimmed glasses. What he probably meant as a smile came across as a leer.

Annie shifted her weight, "Nice chair," she said.

"You like it?" Pete said, that eagerness in his voice again. "Watch this, it's one of those massaging chairs."

With that, he pulled out a second remote, hit a few buttons, and noiselessly, the recliner started to pulsate. Even though he wasn't a heavy guy, Pete's flabby, hairless stomach echoed and amplified the chair's movements, the fat on his abdomen looking like frantic Jell-O. The demonstration went on for a few minutes while Pete explained all the different options in a voice that vibrated as he spoke. He started to stand up, grinning at her, "Hey babe, wanna go for a ride?"

Annie backed up, "No. No thank you."

"Suit yourself." He grinned again and laid his head back, sighing. "This is the life, Annie." She flinched when he said her name. His big eyes shifted her direction, looking frog-like beneath the Coke-bottle lenses. "You should get one of these."

"I probably couldn't afford it," she said, knowing her sarcasm would be lost yet again.

"Sure you could. If *I* got it for you." He pulled his head up again and winked. "This one kinda fell off a truck."

Gary walked back in the room, buttoning the front of his shirt. "All set."

Annie drove to a franchised restaurant that had just opened a few weeks earlier and they followed the hostess to a table near the back. It still smelled new, as if the lacquer on the light pine walls hadn't yet dried. Annie frowned at the preponderance of orange in the décor. It reminded her of the overeager little artists and their painting spree.

"Since when do you like hot wings?" Gary asked, after they ordered. "You never liked anything spicy."

Annie motioned indifference. "Just have a taste for them I guess."

"I'm sure glad you're picking up the tab today. You're never gonna be able to eat everything you ordered."

"Yeah, I probably will. That's actually what I want to talk to you about."

The waitress, a twenty-something blonde waif wearing an eyebrow ring and heavy black eyeliner, came back to drop off their drinks, having introduced herself earlier as "Candi, with an i." Leaning downward, she transferred Gary's Coke to the table from her unsteady tray, mistakenly setting it down in front of Annie. She pushed it forward too fast, causing some of the brown pop to slosh over the side. "Sorry," she said, not moving to clean it up. "I'll get you a few more napkins to take care of that . . . okay?"

Annie slid the Coke across the table. "I had the iced tea."

"Oh, yeah, sorry," Candi said, placing the second drink in front of her.

"Can I have lemon, please?" Annie asked.

"Yeah, sure." Annie wiped at the spill with her napkin, placing it, crumpled, at the end of the table to be picked up.

Gary's eyes followed Candi as she moved

away from the table. "Nice place here."

"You haven't changed much," she said.

"Hey, can't I appreciate the scenery a little? After all, you're the one who wants the divorce, right?"

"As a matter of fact, I do."

When Candi appeared with the buffalo wings, Annie asked, "Can I have that lemon, please? And more napkins?"

Candi let the platter hit the table with a thunk, flashed a smile of apology, and grabbed two empty plates from the table behind her. "Here you go. Will there be anything else for now?"

"The lemon? Napkins?"

Candi snapped her fingers. "Oh, yeah."

Before Annie could broach the subject at hand, Gary started talking about Pete, trying to make it sound, it seemed, as if the two roommates were having the time of their lives. She considered asking him about how he came to be arrested, but as he blathered she realized that she'd never get a straight answer. Truth was, she really didn't want to hear the song and dance he'd invariably come up with. She'd listened to his fabrications too many times to allow herself to be dragged in again, now. Her goal this morning had been to spend as little time with Gary as possible; she needed to get this over with so that when lunch was done, they could each go their separate ways. At least that was the plan.

Deciding, as he rambled, that Candi was not about to show up anytime soon, Annie got up and took four napkins from beneath silverware at a nearby unoccupied table. She resigned herself to just deal with lemon-less iced tea.

He waited till she sat down again. "You haven't really been listening, have you?"

"No," she said with a smile, "I haven't."

Gary flung his hands out, annoyed. "Then what's up?"

She took a deep breath. "Remember that night we went to dinner?"

Half of Annie's barbeque back ribs sat on the plate next to her, cleaned completely of meat. She could have finished the entire slab, but decided she'd take it easy and save the leftovers for lunch the next day.

Gary's patty melt sat untouched. He'd been attentive as Annie talked between bites, she sometimes gesturing with a half-eaten rib. She'd apologized for talking with her mouth full a couple of times, then had just decided to give up worrying about it as she plunged on.

"Gary?"

His eyes registered that she'd spoken. "Close your mouth."

He sat back in the oversized booth, pulling his lips together in a thin line. Annie was happy to have such tall seat backs give them privacy. Gary gazed upward, his face reacting to his unspoken thoughts. Curiosity made her wonder what he was thinking. But she discovered, to her immense surprise and relief, that she really didn't care what he thought. She was here to handle this — not to seek guidance.

When his eyes finally met hers again, they'd changed from the shocked, fearful look they'd worn a few minutes earlier. "I'm gonna get off that burglary charge, you know."

Annie wiped her mouth, then tore open the little wet nap packet to clean her hands from barbeque sauce. "Okay . . . ?"

"When I do, there won't be a problem getting a new job."

Annie could only hope her face expressed the skepticism she felt.

"No, really," he said quickly. "There's a guy I can call. All I gotta do is get acquitted. No big deal."

"That's great, Gary," she said without enthusiasm. "I hope it works out for you."

"Now you sound like, final, when you

said that. I should have some say-so in this too, you know."

"Why is that? I'm not asking you for anything."

"Listen," he said, leaning forward, his elbows on the table, his head pulled in low, "this baby's gonna grow up in a two-parent household. And have it better than I did, okay?"

"This baby will turn out better than you did, all right," Annie said, her voice rising. She took a breath to calm herself, to lower her voice. "But the divorce is still on track. That isn't going to change."

"Come on, Annie, think about it. Remember the night we . . . Well, remember dinner that night? I said that there was going to be some way I was going to get you back? Well, this is it. See? We probably shouldna gone to bed together that night . . ."

"Shhhh. Geez Gary, can you say that any louder?"

"Okay," he stage-whispered, "what I'm saying is, most people getting divorced don't go and have sex together, so like, the fact that we did, and you got pregnant out of it, says something."

"What exactly do you think it says?"

"That we're supposed to be together,

what else?" His face tightened up at the words; he looked away for a moment and she thought she saw his eyes well up.

"Don't shake your head like that," Gary said, continuing. He sat back again, his back making a whump sound as he did. "I'm not giving up this time. You'll see. Maybe this ain't the right time, but you'll understand soon."

"Understand what?"

He moved forward, hands outstretched. "That I can provide for you. I can provide for our baby. How much money can you really make designing walls, Annie? And how long is it gonna take till you get picked up by a gallery for one of your paintings? I mean, you're good, hon, but face reality."

He was feeding into the very doubts that had kept Annie tossing in her bed the night before. Why was it that everything seemed bleaker, even small problems over-whelming, at night? Rubbing her eyebrows, she remembered the morning's sunrise and the boundless feeling of possibility that had engulfed her. Life lay ahead, still beau-tiful, still exciting, even with all the bumps she knew she'd encounter along the way. Sitting there, with the emerging rays making their early appearance, she'd known that everything would work out. No, better than that. She knew she'd *make* everything work out. And Gary wasn't going to change that.

He must have seen the resolve on her face. "Okay, so maybe this isn't the time or the place to discuss this. And maybe you have to do this painting thing for a while before you come to your senses."

Come to my senses? She almost laughed as she stood up. If he only knew. She finally had. "You ready to go?"

He grabbed the doggy bag that held his entire sandwich. "So, where's this next job you got lined up? At some rich chick's house?"

"Yeah. Come on. I'll even drive you home."

"Pete's apartment? That ain't home."

"Well, buddy, it's all you got."

Chapter Seven

Annie pulled up in front of the DeChristophers' house and wished she knew how to whistle. In her mind she could hear the long, slow, appreciative sound she'd make if she could. Although being able to hear it above the din would be another matter, since the Escort was making wretched noises, puffing out dark bursts of smoke as she sat there idling. It wouldn't do to have Mrs. DeChristopher look out that immense picture window and see her sitting in her little blue car gawking and sweating. She pulled forward to park along the curb, having to ease down the block a bit to avoid parking next to a fire hydrant. The perfectly manicured and verdant lawns made her feel all the more conspicuous driving the pollution machine she called her car.

Grabbing her lightweight portfolio, she walked up a neighbor's driveway in order to keep from stepping on the grass. The homes had to be at least fifty feet apart from one another, with the DeChristophers' centered in a cul-de-sac, its wide three-car garage bordered with shrubs and trees arranged with artful precision, sporting a portable basketball hoop that could be adjusted for height. Red brick, the home was three stories tall, and judging from the side view, had a walk-out basement. Four levels in one house. With only two kids. Annie wondered if she'd ever be so well off.

"You coulda parked on the driveway," Mrs. DeChristopher said as she answered the door.

Momentarily startled by the woman's appearance, Annie answered, "Uh . . . that's okay." She didn't want to mention that her car sometimes leaked oil.

Turquoise sandals with three-inch heels made Mrs. DeChristopher taller than Annie remembered. She looked older too, standing in the bright sunlight. The little lines by her eyes probably wouldn't have been so noticeable if she hadn't caked so much designed-to-look-natural makeup on her face. Her sleeveless midriff matched the shoes with uncanny precision, but left a pouch of stomach showing over low-slung black shorts. The outfit would look iffy on a teenager and Mrs. DeChristopher was well beyond that.

"My husband's home today, ain't that great? Now he can meet you, too, and we can get all this taken care of in one day."

Annie wasn't quite sure what Mrs. DeChristopher meant, but she was so taken by the interior of the home that she wasn't paying strict attention. To her right, the living room gleamed. It was at least twice the size of Annie's. Sunlight reflected from the high-gloss cherrywood furniture and sparkled when it hit the gold and crystal table lamps. Both it and the dining room beyond were done like the kind she'd seen in interior decorating magazines. From the lush carpet to the coffered ceilings, they achieved cozy beauty. The living room furniture looked soft and welcoming, the dining room ready for a party, but one where jeans would be just as welcome as evening gowns.

The deep, wide foyer led back to the kitchen and as they walked that way, Mrs. DeChristopher's turquoise heels made sharp clacking noises against the marble tile floor. Annie snuck a look up the curved central stairway, marveling at the beauty of the white balusters and how they coordinated with the pale striped wallpaper. She wondered if Mrs. DeChristopher had decorated this herself, or if she'd had help.

They passed an open den on the left on their way to the kitchen, where a man sat, only the top of his head visible over the back of the computer monitor. Mrs. DeChristopher leaned into the room, both hands on the door jamb, her left leg lifting into the air a little. "That painter girl is here, honey," she said in a sing-song voice. She whispered to Annie, "This is the downstairs den. He uses this room for meeting clients and stuff, but when he's working he usually uses the upstairs den."

Annie saw his eyes as they snapped up in answer to his wife's call. Even without seeing the rest of his face, she could tell he was angry at the interruption. Shifting his glance, the eyes swept over Annie, and she got the decided feeling that he disapproved of her appearance. She'd worn navy blue dress slacks, and a cream-colored sleeveless cotton blouse. All those years working downtown had provided her with a decent business wardrobe and she wondered what about her could possibly have won such immediate dissatisfaction.

Apparently taking his silence as encouragement, Mrs. DeChristopher touched Annie's arm, leading her into the den. "Do you wanna talk in here . . . ?"

He cut her off. "You know when I'm in here, I'm busy."

Mrs. DeChristopher pulled Annie back

out of the room, rolling her eyes. When they reached the kitchen she said, "He gets in such a mood sometimes. Do you want some coffee or somethin'?"

"No thank you."

"Naw, really, you wanna Coke? Or you know, we got drinks too. Even though it's kinda early, I'd join you in a beer."

Annie put her portfolio down on the table and rested her hands on top of it. "You know, a glass of water would be great."

"Water, sheesh. That how you stay so thin?" She grabbed a glass from her shining cherrywood cabinets and moved to the fridge. Annie wouldn't have realized it was a refrigerator if Mrs. DeChristopher hadn't opened it to grab a can of diet pop for herself, and gotten ice water for Annie from the dispenser built into the door. The refrigerator had been outfitted to blend in perfectly with the rest of the cabinetry.

"He'll be out in a coupla minutes, I think," she said, sitting down and gesturing for Annie to do so as well. Annie sat facing into the kitchen, her back to yet another immense space, the family room. It too, had been decorated sumptuously, with big overstuffed floral couches, ornate tables, and knick-knacks and family photographs arranged so artfully that it seemed as though they'd been purchased with a particular positioning in mind. Maybe they had. And everything was so clean. How much time did it take her to dust all that stuff?

Mrs. DeChristopher stared at her nails. The palm trees were gone, replaced by moons and stars on a background of navy. Then it dawned on Annie that this woman wouldn't be the type to do her own dusting. The only question was whether the maid was live-in or come-and-go.

Mr. DeChristopher walked in just as Annie took a sip of her water.

"I'm Richard DeChristopher," he said with a slow nod of his head. "You must be the artist my wife has been telling me about."

His voice was raspy, polite. He was a tall man, slim, with brown wavy hair touched with gray and dark eyes that weren't brown, but maybe a very deep blue. Annie couldn't tell for sure. Looking as though he'd had a bad complexion as a youngster, with sunken cheeks that played up his bone structure, he reminded Annie of the actor, Christopher Walken, whom Gary once referred to as "our generation's bad guy." Age-wise, it was close. She'd put him in his late forties, early fifties.

The man moved with precision, as though calculating each gesture, and yet he seemed quite at ease as he did so, smiling as he took one of the open chairs at the table. He glanced at Mrs. DeChristopher briefly before speaking again. "My wife informed me of the small incident that occurred at your place of business," he said, folding his hands together and resting his forearms on the edge of the table. He did this slowly, drawing out the movement, as he directed his gaze to Annie.

Annie wanted to say that Millie's wasn't her place of business, she just freelanced there, but he hadn't finished, and he didn't seem like the kind of guy who'd appreciate an interruption.

"Let me assure you, Ms. Callaghan, that our sons have been dealt with regarding this matter." He gave another graceful nod. The smile was gone and the eyes were serious. For a fleeting moment, she felt sorry for little Kevin and Drew.

Annie cleared her throat, "I've brought my portfolio," she began, drawing her hands over the fake leather cover of the photo album, "if you'd like to see . . ."

"Ms. Callaghan," he said, in a way that was both condescending and friendly at the same time, "I have every confidence in my wife's ability to judge excellence." With controlled care, he leaned back, raising both hands nearly to shoulder level, gesturing to indicate the beauty of the home's interior. "Does she or does she not have impeccable taste? I suppose I'm just fortunate that she saw something of value in me." He smiled then, almost self-deprecatingly, but Annie thought it forced.

Mrs. DeChristopher smiled at the compliment, and Annie noticed for the first time that her teeth were stained, as from cigarettes. But the house smelled clean. Too much coffee, maybe.

After Mr. DeChristopher's gentle, measured tones, his wife's voice broke the silence with a shrillness Annie hadn't noticed before.

"How 'bout we go upstairs and I show you the room?"

"Great," Annie said, happy to be doing something.

Mr. DeChristopher stood, giving yet another slow nod as they left the kitchen. Turning first to his wife, he said, "I will leave you two women to decide what you will for my humble abode. If you need my assistance, I will be in the den." Then directly to Annie, "It was delightful to meet you."

As they walked up the stairs, Annie remarked again at how beautiful the home was and at how it reminded her of pictures she'd seen in magazines.

Mrs. DeChristopher turned, holding onto the high-polished handrail as she did. "Call me Gina, okay? Every time I hear 'Mrs. DeChristopher,' I think about my mother-in-law. Trust me, you wouldn't want to be confused with her neither." She glanced at the den door, which was now closed, and continued, in a whisper, "And my husband don't know, but I had a decorator lady in here to give me just a little help. She took all cash, so I never had to tell him. He thinks I'm some kinda decoratin' genius and I ain't gonna be the one to tell him otherwise." Wrinkling her nose, she pulled up her shoulders in a silent giggle and started back up the stairs.

There were four rooms stretching around an expansive landing at the top, another turn, and then an additional set of stairs leading them higher in the home. The fourth level that Annie had spotted from outside. She'd assumed it was an attic, but upon entering, found that it was a large room, nearly apartment-sized, with

several dormers jutting out in three directions. Despite the profusion of toys that
occupied the shelves along one wall, the
room was white-walled and immaculate.

"Well," Gina said, winded from the walk
up, "this is it."

"Wow."

"Yeah, it's kinda nice. The boys use this
as a playroom. I had it cleaned 'cuz you
was coming today, but usually it's a pigsty.
I figure if maybe you paint something they
like, maybe they'd try to keep it clean once
in a while. Hey," she shrugged, flipping her
hands out in a way that let Annie know
that she didn't really care one way or another. "You never know."

Annie pulled out her measuring tape and
started to write down the room's dimen-
sions. "You said dinosaurs, right? I'll come
up with some sketches for you to approve.
Then you can decide if it's what you
want."

"Whatever pictures you come up with is
fine. And don't sweat it. The job is yours."

"But I haven't given you a price yet."

"I don't mean to say nothin' honey, but
does it look like we're hurtin'? Whatever
you think'll be fair is okay by me."

Annie's head was swimming, digesting
that last bit of information when Gina

moved to the far end of the room and cracked open a window. She reached between her breasts to pull out a single cigarette. "You don't mind?" she asked.

This was her house, Annie thought. "No, go ahead."

"I don't have no more, 'cuz I have to sneak 'em and I can't fit more than one at a time in here." She gestured and giggled. "They get kinda smashed if I try. So, I'm sorry I can't offer you one."

"That's okay. I don't smoke."

Annie watched surreptitiously as Gina fished further, pulling out a book of matches. She lit the cigarette and took a long drag, blowing the smoke out the window. Annie saw her shoulders drop and her eyes close in obvious pleasure.

"Dickie don't like me smokin'," she said, eyes open now, taking a second pull.

"In the house?"

"He don't like me smokin' at all. But he don't let no one smoke in the house. Gets him really mad."

Pursing her lips to direct the smoke outward, Gina spoke again, breaking into Annie's thoughts.

"You got any kids?"

"Er . . . no." There was no reason to tell her about the pregnancy.

"It ain't no walk in the park, let me tell you." She touched at her hair, as though to straighten out any wayward pieces.

Annie kept measuring.

"You married?"

Annie hesitated, then shrugged. "I'm getting divorced."

"I'm sorry to hear it. He cheat on you?"

Why was she peppering her with so many questions? Annie glanced over at Gina, prepared to politely, but firmly, tell her that it was a subject that she didn't want to talk about, but the look in the woman's eyes was one of friendly curiosity. Like Annie was her girlfriend. She wouldn't have thought it possible for a woman like Gina to look guileless, but she did.

Annie sighed, "Yeah, I'm pretty sure. But that's not the real reason. He's just . . . I don't know. Used to have dreams. But didn't really want to work for them, I guess." She tried to come across light-hearted, but the arrest still irked her. "Turned into this low-life . . ."

"Sometimes they do that. Happens a lot."

Annie pointed to the south wall. "This one too?"

Gina nodded, "All of 'em. Let's crowd

the room with pictures so that maybe I can lose the two of them in here." When she laughed, it took years off her face and Annie wondered just how old she was.

"This is a big project, you know."

"Yeah, I figured. Hey, you got a lawyer?"

Annie, scribbling down numbers, gave Gina a look of utter frustration. "That's another thing. I had one. But I'd leave a message and it would take two weeks and five more phone calls before he'd return the call. I'm going to have to find a new one soon."

"You know . . ." Gina said, tapping one starred, navy fingernail against her teeth. "Maybe we could work out somethin'. My husband's a lawyer, handles lotsa stuff, divorces too. Maybe he could do that for you and you could paint the walls for us? Whaddya think of that?"

She finished her cigarette, taking it down all the way to the filter before she was through. Flicking it out the window with her right hand, she pulled a breath spray from a pocket with her left, in a smooth, practiced motion.

Annie opened her mouth, but no words came out. She thought about the intimidating man downstairs. Mr. DeChristopher as her lawyer? "I don't know . . ."

But Gina was excited now. She shot two blasts of Binaca into her open mouth. "Come on down," she said. "I'll ask him."

Before she could say another word, Gina was out the door. Annie felt as though things were moving too quickly, but Gina had made it down the stairs to tap at the door of the den just as Annie cleared the last step. She watched the woman poke her head in, leaving her back end hanging outside the heavy oak door. Leaning back out to the hall, she wiggled her fingers, gesturing Annie forward.

". . . needs a lawyer . . ." Annie heard her say through the opening. "Yeah, just a divorce. No . . . maybe you could? Yeah . . . what's that word you always use? Por Bueno?" She giggled, then looked out toward Annie. "Pro bono . . . I always forget that."

Annie put a restraining hand on Gina's arm, but she waved it away. Feeling ridiculous standing in the hall, as though waiting for some great beneficence to be bestowed on her, Annie moved toward the kitchen to collect her purse and portfolio.

"I'll give you a call tomorrow with a price, okay?" she said, making her way to the front door.

Gina caught her on her way out, her high

heels pattering again as she scurried over. "Nah. If you're free, just start tomorrow, like maybe ten o'clock? It'll all work out. Dickie says he'll think about handlin' your stuff for you. Ain't that great?"

"Who're the people in the picture with you?"

Sam looked up from the paperwork on his desk when Annie spoke. He'd had the ragtime music silenced in his office so that unless he concentrated on the music wafting in through the open door, he wouldn't be able to discern the song playing. Helped him concentrate. Her question broke the stillness of the room.

Standing in the doorway, Annie looked tired. He worried about her, thought that she pushed herself too hard, and had suggested more than once that she take the project slower. He wasn't in any rush to have it done. To be honest, he wasn't in any rush to have her gone.

She'd been here since nine o'clock and he knew she wouldn't stay late tonight since she had a new project starting in the morning. It was almost ten-thirty and she'd brought her supplies back to the office and was starting to pack it in for the day. He'd been surprised at how much she'd accomplished this past week. At the rate she was going, she'd be finished by the end of the month. Probably sooner.

Last week the wall had been a collection of scattered ideas and themes. Colors here, pencil sketches there. Tonight, for the first time, the painting had come together as a whole, the promise of what was yet to come, taking shape.

"Which picture?" he asked, realizing how foolish he sounded, there being only one picture in the room.

She gestured with her chin, "That one."

Sam placed his hands on his desk and half-swiveled his chair to look at the photograph behind him. It gave him a couple of extra seconds to pull his thoughts together. The gold-toned frame weighed heavy in his hand, heavier than he remembered.

"This was taken about five years ago. See, I had more hair." Holding the picture up, he attempted levity.

Annie moved closer to look at it. She smiled at him. "You haven't changed a bit."

"Actually, I have. Since this picture was taken," he said, gesturing to the chair in front of his desk. "Have a seat. That is, if you want to hear the story." He caught the attentive blue stare in Annie's eyes. "It's not a happy one," he said.

Chapter Eight

Gina DeChristopher opened the door, a black cordless phone pressed to her ear. She greeted Annie, mouthing a silent "Hi!" and with an exaggerated raise of her eyebrows. Looking out onto the driveway, she furrowed her brow and pantomimed driving a car, with a questioning look on her face. Annie pointed down the block, to the same spot she'd parked in before. She wasn't about to park on the driveway. Gina shook her head and wagged a finger.

Motioning expansively for her to come in, she said, "Yeah," into the phone several times in rapid succession. Still using amplified movements, she nodded to Annie, and rolled her eyes, pointing to the phone.

"I got one, Dory. Hell, I probably have a couple. I'll bring it with me. I'll see you in about a half hour. The boys are looking forward to it. Yeah." Gina moved her head back and forth in a manner that suggested amused impatience, while she and Annie stood facing each other in the foyer. "Okay, yeah. Bye."

Hitting the "off" button on the phone, Gina gave a dramatic sigh, then shouted up the stairs, "Kevin! Drew! You wanna go to playgroup you better get your little butts down here on the double!" Tugging her bright pink T-shirt so that it almost met the top of her white shorts, she shook her head.

"You're going out? I'm sorry, I guess I misunderstood," Annie said, shifting her tackle box of supplies from one hand to the other. "I thought I was going to start today."

"Yeah, sure. But I was thinkin' that it might not be a bad idea to have the two little guys out of your hair while you worked, you know?" Gina yelled up the stairs again before moving into the kitchen. "Here," she said, opening a drawer to the built-in desk along the wall, "you can have this."

Annie took the key. "Are you sure?"

Gina slammed the drawer shut with her hip. "Yeah, but do me a favor, okay? Just always ring the bell a coupla times or somethin' before you use it. I talked Dickie into making all the locks have the same key, 'cuz I just hate the noise they make when they jingle in my purse, so that one opens both locks on the front door. He don't like me giving out keys to people, but I know you're the trustworthy type. So, he don't have to know."

Annie, relieved to know that the kids wouldn't be around while she was painting, thanked her. "Is your husband home?" she asked, hoping he wasn't.

"Nah. He's downtown, I think. Sometimes he comes home for a while. If he does, don't worry. He won't mind you being here." She gestured for Annie to follow her back by the front door. Opening a panel, she pointed to the touchpad within. "If the burglar alarm is on, this here green button will be lit. You gotta press the numbers 4-3-3-8-3-1 and then 'enter' within sixty seconds of when you open the front door, otherwise it sets off. Can you remember that?"

"Sure." Annie repeated the number to herself.

"If you forget, I have them written on a piece of paper in that drawer where I got the key from. But you only got sixty seconds, so don't be too slow. The cops'll come. We've had that happen. And it's real embarrassing.

"Reset it when you come in, too, just press the numbers again, then this 'set' button. That way he'll think I let you in and he won't worry. As long as you don't tell him I gave you the key, okay?"

"Not a problem. I brought my lunch and some bottled water; is it okay if I keep it in your fridge?"

"Oh, hon," Gina said, dismay evident in her voice, "you just tell me what you like and I'll stock up for ya. You don't need to be bringin' your own food." She turned toward the stairs, catching herself on the fourth step. "Oh by the way, Dickie says no problem on the divorce thing. He's gonna handle it. Says that it's really no big deal for him."

"Really, Gina." Annie started to protest.

"Quit shakin' your head. We ain't takin' no for an answer anyway, so you just do what you do, and let him do what he does, okay?"

Why is it, Annie thought after Gina left, *that every time I think I get control of my life, someone steps in and tries to take it over for me?*

Annie sat on the floor in the center of the playroom and pulled out the preliminary sketches she'd come up with late yesterday. Her mind couldn't concentrate on the dinosaurs. Having Richard De-Christopher as a lawyer had its appeal. But this wasn't the way normal people went about finding legal representation. It felt odd. And yet, the idea of not having to incur attorney fees was tempting. So was the idea of having such a daunting advocate. She recalled feeling uncomfortable just being in the same room with him, and that had been when he was being friendly. Gary'd take one look at this guy and give up the fight. In a heartbeat.

Annie smiled.

A door slam on the first floor brought Annie out of her concentration. Stepping back, she assessed her progress, glanced at her watch, and did a so-so movement with her head. It was only after noon. Gina said she'd be out till four, at least.

While she'd originally planned to consult the boys about what they wanted on their walls, Gina thought it better to surprise them. As a result, all the toys had been placed in the basement and the boys weren't allowed up here until the project was finished. Gina had promised to try and keep them out of Annie's way as much as possible, while she was working. Otherwise the room stayed locked.

Scratching her forehead, Annie thought about her next move. Hunger pains shot through her stomach — quick and insistent. It was time for lunch.

Richard DeChristopher's voice boomed from the second floor den as Annie made her way down the stairs. Happy to not have to pass the open door, she made her way down, grabbed her lunch, and scurried back up the stairs, hoping to avoid him on the way up, too. Listening to her uneven breaths as she rounded the final stairwell, she shook her head. This was going to be her lawyer? A man so intimidating that she raced past his door, heart beating like a trip-hammer?

Back in the playroom, Annie realized that she had nowhere to sit. In her eagerness to provide Annie with easy access to all the walls, Gina had arranged to have all the furniture in the room removed. The stairs would have to do. Sitting on the second step from the top, directly outside the room's door, Annie pulled her lunch out of her bag. As she curled her hand around the roast beef sandwich, she realized what a loud noise paper bags make when they crinkle when the rest of the house is silent.

Mr. DeChristopher's voice droned low-tone assents. She could hear his irritation grow as the repeated word, "Yes," moved from an absent mutter to an imperative hiss. Taking a bite of the sandwich, she wiped mayonnaise from the corner of her mouth and tried to picture who was incurring his wrath at the other end of the phone line.

Immediately, Pete's face came to mind and Annie had to cover her mouth from allowing a giggle to escape. Unlikely. Mr. DeChristopher didn't strike her as the type to deal with such a low-life. Still, she knew it had to be a guy. DeChristopher apparently liked to come across as gentlemanly and deferential in front of women, but she sensed that his view of the fair sex was just that. Look nice and stay outta my way.

"When can you get it here?" His voice held a sharpness that carried all the way up the stairs and she could picture his face as he spoke. Annie bet that the person on the other end was Timothy, the guy who'd accompanied Gina to the ice cream parlour. And that he'd just "acquired" some piece of evidence key to a trial DeChristopher was handling. No, she thought, better yet . . . DeChristopher had something on someone else and was going to blackmail him, and the thing, whatever it was, had gotten into Timothy's possession in some nefarious way.

Snaking her hand back into the bag, Annie reached for her stash of Oreos. Almost felt like she was starting an addiction to them. Too bad she didn't have any milk. She leaned back, resting her elbows on the landing above her. Taking a bite of the first one, she laughed at herself. Quite the imagination. All those Nancy Drew books she read as a girl were having an effect on her brain.

"Did I hire you to be an art critic?" His harsh voice rasped.

Annie winced as he slammed the phone down, swearing. Sounds of touch-tones made their way up the stairs as he dialed a number. Out of the area, Annie thought, ten digits. She waited to move till she heard him talking again.

Art critic, huh? So much for the blackmailing theory. And yet, she thought as she cleaned up, there was something unsettling about him. Why else would she be dreaming up these elaborate crime-filled stories, with him as the mastermind? Something about him felt off-kilter. Leaning over the banister, she gauged her ability to sneak down the stairs again unnoticed. She had to go, badly. Every bedroom on the second level had a bath, but Annie didn't feel comfortable using them.

Like it would be an invasion of their inhabitants' privacy.

"I hope to have it to you within the next ten days," she heard him say. Then he started saying "Yes" again, but this time in a brisk, friendly tone.

This conversation sounded more civil. As if he'd been talking to an underling before, and now to his boss. Remembering that he ran his own law firm, Annie tried to imagine who would earn such deference. A client, maybe? That would be a nice thought.

"I know that," he said, his voice a bit petulant, "but there are certain . . . protocols . . . that need to be followed in this situation. The extra precautions are imperative." The grating in his voice became more pronounced as politeness began to wane.

Her foot reached the landing and she moved silently across the expanse to the other set of stairs.

"I will not compromise this venture. Not now, not after . . ."

Too late, Annie realized that he was a man who paced as he talked. Now he was in the den's doorway, a look of fury on his face. She froze, her hand reaching for the downstairs banister as he stood stock still, the phone at his ear. Their eyes locked for a chilled moment and his features darkened. She could see a look of concentration pass over his face, almost as though he was replaying his conversation and determining how much she'd heard.

Nonchalance. That was what she needed now. To feign oblivion.

"Hi," she mouthed, giving a little wave, hoping that the panic in her heart didn't project through her eyes.

He glared at her for what seemed like an eternity, then stepped back into the room and slammed the door.

The door was still closed when Annie made her way back up the stairs. She'd planned on accomplishing a lot more this afternoon, but didn't care for the uncomfortable feeling she was having, here alone in the house with him.

Get a grip, she told herself.

Looking around the pencil-scratched walls, she berated herself for her skittishness. *So I overheard a conversation,* she thought, *let's not make a federal case out of it.* She was here on a professional basis. And she would behave accordingly.

Right.

Picking up her pencil and thumbnail

sketch, Annie took a deep breath and went back to work.

Gina had given Annie several of the boys' favorite books, two of which lay open on the floor next to her. One of the things she'd requested was that the sky not be blue, but black, with stars and planets, since Kevin, the younger one, had recently developed an interest in space. A four-year-old studying astronomy. Seemed a bit far-fetched, but the client would get whatever she wanted.

Gina hadn't provided a book on the solar system, but Annie knew Uncle Lou would have something on the subject. She'd have to remember to ask him about it. And she'd have to give some serious thought to this trade-for-services situation that the DeChristophers had come up with. It might just be better to be paid for her work and go out and find a new attorney on her own.

Annie couldn't remember the last time she'd felt so intimidated by another person. He'd be a powerful advocate, no doubt. But could she deal with it? Pulling her hair back from her face with her left hand, and holding it on top of her head, she blew out a breath. Was nothing easy anymore?

"You've gotten much further into things than I'd expected."

Mr. DeChristopher's soft pronouncement made Annie jump.

He stood, like a pillar in the entire doorway, his hands behind his back. The sun poured in from the floor-to-ceiling mullioned window in the stairway behind him, putting him in silhouette. Annie couldn't make out his facial expression, and his eyes were deep in shadow.

"Oh, hi," she said, trying again for casualness, knowing her words came out a little too high-pitched to fool him. Her hand dropped and she fluffed her hair a bit; it was something to do. She cleared her throat and gestured to the wall, saying, "What do you think?"

He entered with a nod of thanks. As though he needed her invitation to come into the room.

He kept his hands behind his back and Annie noted the gold cufflinks that poked out from the charcoal gray sleeves of his suit jacket. Twin initials, "D" stood out on them, formed by tiny, individually set diamonds. Stepping back to give him a wide berth, she hit the corner, making a small thump. He didn't turn, but continued to move farther down the wall, nodding, saying nothing.

Abruptly he stopped, tipping his head slightly as if he'd only just noticed something. Still with his back to her, he turned his head, offering a profile. His nostrils flared, almost imperceptibly. His question was smooth, direct, "Do you smoke, Ms. Callaghan?"

"No." The word came out short, surprised.

"Hmm. Then I must speak to the maid."

He returned to his musings, and turned to her when he finished walking the length of the wall.

"You have a gift, Ms. Callaghan. You're very fortunate to have found your niche in life. May I call you by your first name? Anne?"

"Of course, but most people call me Annie."

"Annie . . ." he looked upward as though considering it, then back down to her. "No. You are an intelligent woman. I know these things," he tapped at his temple with his index finger. "Annie is a girl's name. A woman of your talents deserves something stronger. I will call you Anne. Unless, of course, you object?" His manner was gentle, inquisitive.

"No, that's . . . uh . . . fine, I guess."

"Good." He turned away to face the wall again. "Anne. What do you know about attorney-client privilege?"

Taken aback, Annie said the only thing she could think of in answer, "I know what it is."

"I was certain you did. An individual who has such cleverness to create something like this would certainly be aware of many of those mundane things that we lawyers have to deal with on a daily basis."

Annie had no idea how to respond to that.

Continuing, still with his back to her, he said, "And you realize that whatever you tell me with regard to your divorce will be kept confidential."

"Yes . . ."

He turned and faced her. His dark eyes met hers and she felt as though she didn't dare look away. "I consider that privilege sacred."

"Of course." Annie flipped her hands in front of herself, trying to lighten the moment.

"Sacred." Tracing his finger along a brachiosaurus' neck, he said, "But I like it to go both ways. I like to feel confident that my clients can keep things to themselves, you understand what I mean?" He wagged his fingers in the air, like a Mafioso don granting dispensation.

"Mmm-hmm," she said.

"What do you usually charge for a project this size?" he asked, and she wondered about the abrupt change in subject.

Having had a chance to think about it, Annie told him.

Mr. DeChristopher shook his head and the rasp in his voice became more evident as he spoke in quiet tones. "You're selling yourself short, Anne. That figure is far too low for what I'm getting from you. Why don't I come up with an amount that's more realistic? And you realize of course, that your legal fees will be taken care of as well."

"But Mr. DeChristopher . . ."

"Please," he said, "call me Richard. After all, I am going to be your lawyer, am I not?"

Annie's mind raced. To be paid for her services *and* to get free legal representation was an offer she couldn't afford to refuse. She nodded.

"As long as we trust each other, Anne, our mutual benefit is assured." He turned with almost military crispness, and walked out the door. "Carry on."

Chapter Nine

Sam started to hand the shake over the tall fountain counter to Annie, then pulled it back with a grin as she reached for it. "Hang on," he said, "almost forgot the best part."

Standing on tiptoes, Annie leaned both elbows on the counter and looked over, watching Sam as he shot whipped cream, sputtering, onto the top of her shake. His eyes glanced up in question.

"A little more," she said. "I'm eating for two, you know."

Shaking the container, Sam piled the cream high, until the white fluff threatened to topple over. He grabbed two maraschino cherries and placed them gently on top. With a wink, he handed the glass back over the counter. "Now that," he said, "is a shake."

Annie took it with both hands, and a smile of thanks. "You going to sit down for a while?" she asked.

He lifted one shoulder. "Sure."

Annie carried it over to their regular booth and stretched her legs as she sat down, unwrapping the straw, and pushing it into the thick confection. She almost enjoyed feeling the aches and pains that followed a period of intense work. Made her feel like she was accomplishing something. Fatigue was another matter entirely, but she'd been able to combat that impediment most days, by napping in the afternoon in anticipation of long nights at the ice cream shop.

All weekend she'd been looking forward to being back here. Itched to get back to her fairy tale wall, to leave thoughts of dinosaurs, planets, and angry men behind her. When she'd pulled up tonight, after ten, the teenagers who worked there were just leaving, spilling noisily out the door. It was a Monday night after an unseasonably cool and misty day and they seemed eager to take advantage of getting out early.

By the time she made it to the front door, however, it had slammed behind them. No matter, she thought, and pulled out her key.

To her surprise, it didn't work.

She tried again, twice, before realization dawned. The key was almost indistinguishable from the one Gina DeChristopher had given her. While Mr. DeChristopher had acquiesced to his wife's one-key request, he'd obviously made up for any safety concerns by providing the house with an industrial strength lock. In her hurry from the car, Annie must have grabbed their key by mistake.

With a murmur of annoyance, Annie returned to the Escort to retrieve the right one. Sitting in the passenger seat, she dug her hand into the glove compartment and fished around through the papers and junk she kept in there till her fingers reached the small piece of metal. Making a mental note to buy a couple of big, hard-to-lose chains to prevent this from becoming bothersome, she pulled it forward and examined both keys in the pale moonlight. Unless she would be able to memorize the peaks and valleys of their cuts, she'd never be able to tell them apart. Their color and brand were identical.

Reaching around to the backseat, she pulled at the small bag of emergency items she kept there in yet another backpack. Somewhere in here were two bottles of nail polish, one clear to handle pantyhose runs, and the other . . . Yes. There it was. Black nail polish, leftover from Halloween several years ago, when she'd been the Wicked Witch of the West. Perfect. She opened the top, wrinkling her nose at the chemical smell, and placed a large dot of polish on the shank of the DeChristophers' key. Waiting, blowing on it to help it dry, she congratulated herself on her improvisation and efficiency.

Still, she'd pick up those keychains as soon as she could.

"Quiet night?" she asked Sam as he came to join her. He leaned forward to slide into the booth's opposite bench.

"Oh yeah," he said, "how's the shake?"

"Great, as always, but how come you're still here? You have to be exhausted."

"I came in late today. I've got Jeff opening for me now, four days a week. It doesn't get really busy here till late afternoon, so I've only been here since five." He shrugged, shook his head. "Gives him some responsibility. And I don't mind staying here late."

"Four days a week?"

Sam nodded, but he didn't look away. Annie noticed wisps of redness creeping up from his collar.

She lowered her head to take a sip of her shake and ask, in as offhand a tone as she could muster, "Really? Which days?"

"Monday through Thursday," he said, a bit too casually.

Annie nodded, then looked up at him. "Well, I'm glad," she said in a quiet voice, "I enjoy the company."

Sam smiled. "Me too."

Something had been different about Sam tonight, Annie thought, as she glanced up and down the street, finally pulling her car up to the curb. The closest she could get to the front of her house was halfway down the block. Life would be so much better if she could use her own garage. This Saturday, she vowed, as she slammed the car door, come hell or high water, she'd load Gary's stuff into the back of her little car and haul it over to that scummy apartment. She didn't care if it took four trips, she was going to get that garage clear again.

But tonight. She sighed. What a gorgeous night. Even though it was technically morning, and the sky at one o'clock was about as dark as it could get, Annie breathed in the damp cool air and listened to the soft rhythmic scratches of her own footsteps. Tonight something had been very different.

The street was deserted. And for the first time in a very long time, the night seemed to hold promise rather than dread. Moved by a sudden burst of ebullience, Annie spread her arms out and flung her head back to face the heavens. "Star Light, Star Bright, First star I see tonight." Whispering, she felt a rising tide of emotion work its way up to her chest. She closed her eyes, letting the cool breeze lift the ends of her hair, taking pleasure as the silken current swept against her skin. "I wish I may, I wish I might, have the wish I wish tonight."

Standing utterly still, listening to the night sounds of crickets and far-off traffic, she made her wish. Opening her eyes, she lowered her arms to stare at the distant star for a long moment.

I wonder, she thought. *Is he wishing on a star right now?*

There was a song about that, an old one. Yeah. Annie started to hum it, then started singing softly as she took light, cheerful steps to her front porch. She didn't remember all the words, but as she reached the top stair, she turned and stared at the sky again, her voice reaching a quiet crescendo, her arms reaching out again, singing, making it up as she went along.

She couldn't come up with the real words, but it didn't matter. With a sigh and a smile, she dropped her arms and turned to open her front door.

To her surprise, the big oak door was being opened for her.

It took a moment for it to register, to pull herself back into the reality that stared at her through the glass of the outer door.

"What the hell are *you* doing here?"

"I heard a car door slam," Gary said. "Figured it was you. Come on in." As though there was nothing unusual about it, he pushed the metal door open and held it with his left arm.

Annie's hands made two fists at her side. They shook with the fury she held, knowing that if she let go, she would lose control completely. She felt her eyes blaze beneath outward calm. Gary pushed the storm door open further and invited her in. Invited her. To her own home. Without budging, almost afraid to move, she repeated herself in tight words. "I asked you what you were doing here."

Gary shrugged. His brown hair was flattened on one side, messed on the other, as though he'd been sleeping. Moths danced around the porch light. One of Gary's bloodshot eyes squinted against its bright beam as he turned his face from it. "Just come on in, okay? The humidity is giving me a headache."

Annie grabbed the silver handle of the screen door and whipped it wide, crossing the threshold past Gary as it swung shut, hitting him with a high-pitched, metallic thwack. God, she wished the glass would have broken on him. Then she could call an ambulance and be rid of the idiot.

He winced and swore. Shuffling backwards, rubbing his head, he closed the big oak front door with quiet deliberation. She heard the solid click of the bolt. He was wearing his old beat-up brown house slippers and the ratty green corduroy robe that he'd had since before they were married. She'd packed both of those things in the boxes that were stored in the garage.

The stuff in the garage!

Just then she noticed the open boxes, all of them, strewn down the hall into the kitchen. He'd emptied every one of them. Still in fists, her hands raised to her head.

"Agh!" she said in frustration.

"Listen, I know it's late . . ." Gary yawned, rubbed his hand down the front of his face in a gesture Annie hadn't seen for a long time. It made her cringe.

"How did you get in?"

"Key." He dug into his pants pocket and produced the item.

Annie silently berated herself for not changing the locks.

He spoke again. "But I didn't know you'd be out till all hours, now, did I? I was worried, Annie."

"Worried?" Her hands shook in rage. "Get out of here. Now." She pointed at the door.

His hands came up in a placating gesture and he swayed a bit, blinking his eyes as though he still wasn't used to the light. "I understand you bein' surprised to see me. Listen, I just wanna make things easier for you."

"What does that mean?" she asked. "That you're hoping I'll 'put out' again? Well, forget it."

He opened his mouth to speak, but stopped himself with a frustrated sigh, causing a waft of his breath to assail Annie's nose.

She pointed at him, then pulled her curled index finger to her lips to hold herself back. "Have you been drinking?"

"We're not starting out so good here, are we?" Attempting a smile, he looked around the room, then gestured for Annie to sit down. Not knowing what else to do, she sat, taking the middle cushion of the couch and she glared at Gary when he looked as though he was going to sit next to her. "Okay," he said, his hands coming up again, as if to ward her off. "I'll sit in the chair if it makes you feel better." His brown eyes strove for sincerity, but there was a cloudiness to them, as if focusing was difficult.

"You *have* been drinking."

"Just a couple of beers. I told you I was worried about you. And, come on, we talked about this. Don't you want to give our baby every chance in the world? I mean, hey, two of us working are gonna be way better than one. You need to take it easy. Working till one o'clock in the morning ain't healthy."

Nearly forgotten, thoughts of Sam popped into her mind. She wildly wished she would have stayed there with him instead of coming home to this. Gary stared at her, blinking occasionally, an insipid grin on his face. He really believed that he was here to do her a favor. She gave a short angry laugh. Gary smiled.

Did he really believe she'd be happy to see him here? He always did what was best for himself, but camouflaged it to make it seem as though he'd been looking out for her. She'd fallen for that before, but no longer. Never again.

"Gary?" she said, in a calm voice, giving a lips-only smile.

"Yeah?" The hope on his face was palpable.

"Get out. Or I'll call the police."

He scratched the top of his head. "Well," he said, "I don't think you wanna do that. If I get taken in, we'll lose all that bail money you put up."

"I don't want you here. I'm asking you now, please." Her teeth were clenched behind tight lips. "Go home."

He had the decency to look abashed. "I . . . can't. I can't go back tonight anyway, not unless you drive me and, hell, you gotta be tired." He shrugged one shoulder. "No car. Can't I just sleep in here on the couch? I won't bother you, I promise."

Annie ran both hands up her face and grabbed at her hair, holding it in a tight grip over the top of her head. She stared at the floor and whispered. "You're such an asshole."

"Did you just call me what I think you called me?"

Sudden exhaustion washed over her like a wave, leaving her feeling battered and bruised. The thought of trying to marshal her strength for some protracted domestic squabble wrenched her stomach.

Annie looked up. "I'm going to bed. Don't," she said, standing, wagging a finger at him, "don't come anywhere near my bedroom or I'll rip your stinking eyes out. Understand?"

"You never called me an asshole before."

She turned. Fatigue was taking its toll. It hurt just to look at him. "Well then maybe you should quit behaving like one."

"Please let it have been a bad dream," she said aloud, as the sun spilled in through her bedroom window coaxing her eyes open. "Please."

She sat up in bed. The smell of fried bacon and fresh coffee wafting from the kitchen put an end to her hopes. A glance at the clock told her it was after ten in the morning. She reached over to her nightstand and grabbed a handful of the saltines she kept there. Better safe than sorry, Karla had told her. "Eat just a few before your feet hit the floor and you'll ward off hours of morning sickness."

So far, it had worked like a charm.

Annie padded out the door, turning to see Gary setting the table. "What?" she said, the exasperation she felt coming out in a whine.

He was grinning. "I forgot how beautiful

you look in the morning."

She glared at him.

"Here," he said, pulling out her chair. "I went shopping after you went to bed. One of those all night places — I couldn't sleep. Hope you don't mind I took your car."

Annie sat. This was surreal.

"And I had to borrow some money too. I found some in your wallet." He backed up a little at the look she gave him. "Just took enough to buy groceries, that's all. I didn't touch your emergency stash. I remember where you keep it though. Bet you don't remember where I always kept my safe stuff?"

He was pouring coffee into her favorite mug and he pulled out a jug of half-and-half. He'd bought that too. She was out of it and she hated using milk instead of cream. Feeling like a fly getting trapped in a spider's web, she shook herself awake.

"Do you?" he asked.

"Do I what?" Annie couldn't keep the snappiness from her voice. Nor did she want to.

"Do you remember where I keep my safe stuff?"

A platter of steaming scrambled eggs and bacon appeared before her with a little clunk. The heat from the plate drifted up, bringing gentle waves of hickory past her nose. It smelled heavenly. As his green corduroy sleeve pulled from her line of vision, she answered, just to shut him up.

"I remember. You keep all your important stuff in that smelly old robe." She gestured toward him with her chin. "You still have those fake pockets you sewed in?"

"Yep," he said, with apparent pride. "And nobody but you knows about them." Gary began to untie the belt and moved to open one side. Annie prayed he had something on underneath.

He did. She breathed a sigh of relief.

"See," he said, holding the left side of the robe open. "Down here, in the low pocket, the big one? Here's where I keep all the stuff that's important. I could keep that bail receipt here, if you want. It'd be safe, and I'd make sure you get your money back when it's all over."

"No thanks, Gary." She took a sip of the coffee.

He shrugged. "Toast coming up."

Annie picked up her fork. Maybe with a little food in her, she'd be better equipped to handle Gary's nonsense. "Don't think you're staying," she said with her mouth full. The eggs were made with just the right amount of butter and salt. And they were hot. Annie took another forkful. This was so much nicer than the two vitamins and the handful of granola she grabbed every morning. Grabbing her coffee mug, she held it in both hands, watching the steam from the eggs curl around the bottom of it and blend with the steam of the coffee above.

Gary sat at the table across from her, his brown eyes wide. "Annie," his voice cracked. "I didn't wanna tell you last night, but I don't have anyplace else to go."

"What?" she joked. "Pete kick you out?"

"Pete's been evicted."

"But I was just there the other day . . ."

"We knew it was coming. We just never thought they'd do it. And now neither of us has a place to stay."

The light began to dawn. "No." Annie said. "No way am I having that little weasel in my house."

Gary stood and moved back over to the stove to grab the frying pan. "It's still my house too, Annie. Don't forget that." He smiled at her, "More eggs?"

Chapter Ten

"He's out right now, Karla," Annie said into the phone, her feet resting on top of one of the empty boxes Gary had left on the floor. She twisted the phone cord on her finger and untwisted it again. "Picking up Pete."

"He's such an asshole."

Annie, who'd been about to continue, started laughing so hard that Karla couldn't understand her.

"Annie? Are you okay?"

"It's just," she held a hand over her mouth, trying to quiet herself, "that I said the exact same thing to him last night. Took him by surprise, too."

"Yeah, well," Karla said, "he sure had all of us fooled."

"Isn't that the truth?"

"So tell me . . ." Karla said, "this Sam fellow. I keep hearing 'Sam said this,' and 'Sam did that.' There something going on you want to tell me about?"

"No. Not at all."

Annie heard the snort over the phone.

"Do you like him? And you know what I mean."

Annie listened to several tiny clicks from the clock on the wall while she tried to decide how to answer. Best just to face it. "Yeah," she said, rubbing the sockets of her eyes and cringing at the little quiver in her voice. "I do."

Karla was silent for a long moment. The ticks almost seemed to grow louder.

"And what about him? Does he feel the same way?"

Shifting herself on the kitchen chair, Annie stood up. "I don't know. Sometimes it feels like he does, but . . ." she looked out the window, at the tree over the garage, and gave a deep sigh. "I don't know."

"He's not married, right?"

"No. He got divorced about five years ago."

"Well, then he's got to be sympathetic to your situation, don't you think?"

"Except that wasn't the end of it. Two weeks after it became final, his wife and son died of carbon monoxide poisoning when their furnace malfunctioned."

"Oh geez."

"They lived in northern Georgia and almost never used the furnace. He blames himself for not being there, figuring had he been, he would have checked it for problems before turning it on."

"Oh Annie, that's terrible."

"It is, isn't it?"

Terrible, Annie thought, and yet, not the entire truth.

Sam had talked in careful, measured words. Nancy and Brian. When he said their names for the first time, his mouth gave a peculiar wrinkle and he looked away. It was the same look Uncle Lou wore as her mother's casket closed. That hold-tight moment that men have where they try to gain control over some internal struggle. Most often they win. Uncle Lou had not.

Though Sam regained control, his look told her this story stayed fresh in his heart.

Talking as if to the picture, glancing up occasionally to meet Annie's eyes, Sam began by explaining that it had all been his fault. That the furnace should never have been turned on.

The divorce had been his idea. Nancy, his high-school sweetheart, had been floored when he'd broached the subject right before their thirteenth wedding anniversary.

"Lucky thirteen, huh?" Sam said to

Annie with a sad smile. "We'd gone to dinner. To a new place, kind of a long drive, so that she wouldn't have bad memories associated with places closer to home. But every time I tried to start, she changed subjects. It was as if she knew. At a minimum, I'd hoped the empty evening would bring home the point I'd been trying to make. Let her see how unimportant we'd become to one another. We had nothing to talk about, nothing in common."

Picture still in hand, he gestured, for emphasis, "And even our mutual indifference wouldn't have been insurmountable." He took a deep breath, then blew it out slowly.

A notion skittered across Annie's mind. Maybe another woman had been the cause of their problems.

As if reading her thoughts, Sam answered, "There wasn't anyone else, you see. Nothing quite so capricious, nor quite so clear cut." He'd cleared his throat before continuing. "I believed Nancy had no passion. No willingness to venture beyond her little social circle and their inbred concerns."

There seemed nothing to do at the moment but listen.

"Once Brian was born, we became more

like brother and sister than husband and wife." His eyes narrowed a bit as he spoke, clearly self-conscious. "In every sense. She made it clear that she no longer needed me . . . physically." His eyes belied the indifference in his voice. "But that my business acumen and income were quite welcome. I began to realize she wanted nothing more than a successful husband, a child to coddle, and a home large enough to make her friends green with envy.

"I wanted more. I wanted adventure. And joy. You know, that *Carpe Diem* sort of stuff. Even if it meant simply walking home instead of driving everywhere, or taking a class that taught me something new. But there was no room for that in Nancy's life. She was content to entertain and visit with a few carefully chosen friends, on specifically assigned days." He looked up at Annie. "I wanted a wife who wanted me."

Above the faint buzz from fluorescent lights, a few gentle bars of ragtime music drifted into the room.

She cleared her throat. "That's your home in the picture?"

"Yeah . . . that's where we lived. Where they died." He passed her the photograph. "Can't seem to make myself sell it."

"But you aren't from the South, are you?"

He chuckled at that, and Annie was relieved to see a bit of the somber mood dissipate. "No, the South I grew up in was here . . . the south side of Chicago. My accent gave me away, eh?"

When Annie handed the picture back to him, he looked at it a long moment before speaking, "I thought she didn't have any passion. That she couldn't move herself to act with her heart if her life depended on it. Guess I was wrong about that."

"You don't think she did it on purpose?"

Sam took a deep breath, his chest rising and falling with the weight of his words. "Inconclusive." His eyes watered up, for the first time since Annie had sat down. "But I know what I believe." His lips pulled together, tightly, and she wanted to reach over, to comfort him, but she held back. "Why?" he asked in a quiet voice, obviously not expecting an answer. "Why did she have to take Brian with her?"

Karla was talking again. Annie shook her head and asked her to repeat what she'd just said.

"I was just thinking that that's an awful lot of baggage for you to handle. I mean, if you were thinking about seeing him."

Annie returned to the kitchen chair, curled up one foot, and sat on it. "But look at the baggage I'm carrying, Karla. I'm no great catch right about now."

"But your sparkling personality makes up for it."

Annie laughed, and it felt good.

"Hey, new subject. How's Uncle Lou?"

"How is Karla?" Uncle Lou asked, his arms full of bundled newspapers. Tied with strong white string, they looked ready to be taken to the curbside. He carried them from the dining room into the kitchen and leaned over one of his chrome and vinyl chairs, letting the pile fall with a plop.

"She's doing great, sends her love. You tossing those out?"

As he righted himself, he reached into his pocket and pulled out a brown plaid handkerchief. Wrinkled and misshapen, he wiped it over his entire face and head, clearing away the sweat. He snorted. "Nah. Organizing. These are the papers from the week of April sixth, last year. Thought I'd try to start arranging them according to date. Then line them up in the basement."

"Do you have anything on the Solar System?"

"Like what?"

Annie opened the refrigerator and grabbed a can of iced tea. "Pictures, something I can use as a guide for this new project at the DeChristophers' house."

"Richard DeChristopher?"

"Yeah," she took a sip of the brisk beverage, "I didn't mention the name before? Have you heard of him?"

"He's a pretty high-powered lawyer. From what I've heard he takes very few clients, but the ones he takes have clout." Uncle Lou rubbed the fingers of his right hand together. "And money."

"Boy, I don't fit that description."

"I got a couple of *National Geographic*s somewhere in the back room from when Pluto was discovered. 'Course those might be a little dated. I got some with those recent Hubble pictures too, hang on." Uncle Lou scratched his bald head as he walked to the bedroom, then stopped and looked at her. "But he's not your lawyer."

"He is now."

"Hmm. I'll have to see if I can find any articles about him around here. I think he's been involved in some questionable dealings, if I remember correctly. You know," he said, pulling on his ear, "I really should think about designing some master catalogue. What do you think?"

Annie didn't want to wait for him to search through the entire back room for the star information. Grabbing her backpack, she started to head out. "You need anything from the store?"

"If you're going, I could use a new pack of yellow highlighters."

"You got it," Annie said, finishing her tea with a gulp and tossing the can in the overfilled recycle bin. "Hey, any word on that missing artwork?" With her back to Uncle Lou, she squeezed her eyes shut. The moment the words left her mouth, she wished she'd bitten her tongue.

"Yeah . . . come here." She followed dutifully back into the dining room where Uncle Lou spent several minutes digging through a pile on the buffet. He came up with whatever it was he was looking for in record time. "You can take this one home. It's a clearer shot of that Durer and it brings the story up to date. They still haven't found it. Don't know where to look. But there's a chance they might have had help from the inside. Read it. Really interesting." Something apparently caught his eye and he pulled another magazine from the middle of the stack. "There's some other interesting art news too. Somewhere in here, I think . . ."

"Thanks," she said folding the article and pocketing it as she inched toward the door. "Oh, by the way, I've got guests. Gary and his slimy friend Pete are staying with me for a while."

That got Uncle Lou's attention. Hands full of clippings, he stopped, mid-search. "You're not getting back together with that loser, are you?"

"No."

Uncle Lou pursed his lips before speaking. "Be careful, okay, honey?"

"Don't worry, it's temporary," she said as she walked out the door. Then muttered under her breath. "It better be."

Annie pawed through her cache of supplies. They had to be here somewhere. She'd picked up a couple of paint tubes at the art store yesterday. Colors she'd specifically needed for this next section of the wall at the DeChristophers'. She'd felt up to putting in some extra hours and Gina hadn't had a problem with that, having returned from taking the kids to their morning soccer practice only moments ago. Lot of good the added effort did her when she didn't even bring the right equipment.

Patting at the piles of supplies on the floor, she lifted to look under some of the drop cloths she'd thrown. Coming across a crinkly plastic bag, and convinced she'd found her paints, she pulled it up in triumph. When she saw it was just the hardware store bag from her morning shopping trip, she gave a little rumble of exasperation.

She remembered putting the bag away last night and couldn't imagine where it could have gone. Unless it fell out in the car. Certain it hadn't, and that she'd simply overlooked, she kept searching.

No luck. Even after going through everything twice.

Well, at least she'd remembered to stop at the hardware store today. Grabbing the bag again, she pulled out two large acrylic keychains. The clear one was shaped like a key, though way oversized, the red one shaped like a heart. Having had the foresight to bring both keys in with her, she dug them out of her pocket and went to work, fussing until they were firmly attached to their respective chains: De-Christophers' on one, Sam's on the other.

Her hand stopped before returning

Sam's key to her backpack. She held it up. The clear red acrylic caught the sun's rays from the window over her shoulder, making the heart twinkle in the light. Like a giddy school-girl suffused with the excitement of a new crush, she'd chosen it in a moment of impulsiveness. What would Sam think if he saw it?

I wonder, she thought, watching the keychain spin slowly in the sun, *if you have any idea.*

With a sigh, she shoved it into the bag, and decided that he probably didn't. And that it might be better that way, at least for now.

The newly purchased paints were still AWOL. "Might as well do what I can," she said aloud, and proceeded to mix Payne's gray with yellow ochre in one of the big glass jars. Slowly she added other pigments, trying to get just the right shade of dinosaur.

"There's a good-looking guy here for you."

Annie, crouched on the floor of the DeChristophers' playroom, stopped stirring the deep gray paint and looked up. Gina stood in the doorway, an interested, yet puzzled look on her face. "Says he's your assistant."

Could it be Sam? The thought brought a smile to Annie's lips as she made her way down the steps to the foyer. And it made her disappointment more acute when she rounded the turn of the staircase.

Gary.

Annie's heart dropped. She steeled herself, wanting to verbally rip him to shreds, but not in front of Gina. He'd gotten a haircut. Probably used her money to do it, too. Clean-shaven, wearing jeans and a fresh T-shirt, he didn't look nearly as grubby as he had only hours ago.

"Did you follow me?"

Gina scooted to stand behind Gary. Pointing to her own ring finger and then to his back, she energetically mouthed the words: "Is this the husband?"

Annie bit the insides of her cheeks to stop the sniping comment that came to mind, and nodded. Gina widened her eyes and appeared to stifle a giggle. She backed out of the room with pantomimed exaggeration, while Gary, oblivious to the antics behind him, held a weighty plastic bag out to Annie, with a grin that she felt like slapping off his face.

"You forgot this when you left this morning."

Gina, who hadn't quite made it out of

the room, turned and raised her eyebrows with a sly smile. "Maybe you ain't gonna need my husband's services after all, huh?"

Gary grinned at the woman, running his eyes up and down her body in an appreciative manner. "Your husband is one lucky guy," he said. Gina preened, clearly pleased.

Once she was out of earshot, Annie grabbed the bag out of his hands. Even before she looked, she knew it was the missing paint.

"How did you get here?"

"Pete dropped me off."

Annie pushed a corner of the front curtain aside to look out. "He's not still here?" she asked, afraid, but half hoping he was so that Gary could leave. Then she furrowed her brow. "I thought he didn't have a car."

"He borrowed one."

Annie put up her hands; she didn't want to know any more.

"I thought maybe I'd help you today. You know, paint."

"Think again."

Gina clattered over, slinging a large black purse over her shoulder. "Gotta run, Annie. But listen, there's enough food for two in the fridge. And, weren't you just saying today how hard it was to paint that ceiling all black? Maybe your 'assistant' can help you with that." Stressing the word, she winked, and pulled the door closed behind her, calling outside for Timothy to bring the car around.

Gary grinned. "I could help. I'm good at painting. You know that. And besides, I don't got a ride home. Unless you drive me."

How did these things keep happening? The harder she tried to manage her own life, the more difficult the people around her made it.

She thought about Sam. He was the exception. The one bright spot in her life right now.

It was true that painting the high parts of the walls had been excruciating. The dark color didn't cover in one coat and she'd painted the narrowest upper wall twice with the black paint before she'd been happy with it. She hadn't even begun the ceiling, knowing that, owing to her short stature, she'd be required to stand near the top of the ladder and have to reach over her head for hours on end. She wasn't looking forward to that part of it. The constant standing was already straining her back, and she hated being so high up on the ladder, feeling every moment as if she was going to lose her balance. She'd found herself pressing into her lower back with her left hand as she painted with her right, reminded, with a shudder, of the waddling woman from the doctors' waiting room.

"All right," she said, warning him with her voice. "You can help me for now. You owe me that, at least. But you do what I tell you, understand?"

Encouraged, he smiled. And in that brief flash of white, Annie caught a glimpse of the man she'd fallen in love with all those years ago. It hit her like a blow to the stomach. Her breath caught in her throat. For just that second, his eyes had held a fleeting look of hope and promise, taking her by surprise. She couldn't ever believe in him again, whether or not he assumed she did. Shaking her head, she returned the smile, wincing at his eager-eyed response. Those days were better left in memory.

She gestured with her head. "Come on up, I've already started."

As they climbed the stairs, he spoke in a muted voice, "Wow. How'd you ever land a gig like this?"

He gave a low whistle as they passed through the hallway, rubbing his fingers over a large, multicolored vase.

Just as they reached the playroom, a thought occurred to her and she turned. Gary stood one step below her and she pointed her finger in his face. "You touch anything in this house, *anything* that doesn't belong to you or me, and you're going to be out on your rear end before you can say 'bail money.' Do we understand each other?"

Realization dawned, "I'm not going to take anything. What do you think of me?"

She looked at him for a moment without speaking, then said, "You don't want to know."

Annie, wearing a navy blue Chicago Bears baseball cap to keep paint splatters from lodging in her hair, looked up with a measure of satisfaction. Expansive enough to handle a dark ceiling without overwhelming it, the part of the room Gary had completed looked almost space-like already and Annie nodded her head. While it would certainly need some work, the painted night sky was just the thing little boys would get a kick out of. She would add glow-in-the-dark paint for stars and planets later. In the past couple hours Gary had made it almost halfway through. He'd started working immediately after she'd explained how she wanted the job done.

"Not bad," she said, as he climbed down from the ladder.

Since she hadn't brought a second hat, Gary's face and hair had gotten flecked with black. Like dark freckles, they stood out from his cheeks, pink from the exertion of keeping his arm over his head for such an extended period of time.

"This is a lot of work," he said in surprised voice, swiping his right arm across his forehead, making little black smears.

"You made pretty good time, so far."

Gary looked up too. "It's coming along." Moving to the far corner of the room, he knelt and clanked the metal stir-stick around inside his empty paint can. "We're gonna need more paint."

Stretching her arms to work out the kinks, Annie thought about that. She didn't feel like heading out to the paint store just now. The dinosaurs were taking shape and it just didn't feel like a good time to stop. She liked the way it looked, the unfinished shapes of the drawings standing out from the darkness of the background paint. Not only had Gary gotten a good portion of the ceiling done, he'd also finished the side walls above her horizon and around the roughed-in dino-saurs' heads. Unpainted, several of the long-necked reptiles and their prehistoric counterparts stood out as white silhouettes in the black background, giving the room an eerie ambiance.

"What's that one called?"

"Apatosaurus."

"Never heard of it."

"I put in a lot of different types in the picture, not just the typical T-Rex and all, because I'm hoping that the boys get interested and maybe learn something about them."

"That's my Annie, always thinking."

She shrugged.

Gary sidled closer to her, making a move to put his arm around her waist, but then pulled himself back. "You're going to make a great mother."

Annie rolled her eyes. "Let's go get some paint then, shall we?"

In a tentative movement, Gary reached out and touched her arm. "I'll go for the paint. That is, if you don't mind me driving your car?"

His hand dropped as she stepped just out of reach, shaking her head, but he interrupted. "Listen, you could use a break. Let me go, and you can just sit for a while, okay? Don't be pushing yourself so much.

This project'll get done."

The idea of resting, if only for a half hour, was tempting. Searching his eyes for some sign of deceit, she tilted her head and cautioned him, "No funny business."

He gave her a withering look, then asked, "How do I pay for this?"

Digging through her backpack, she came up with a small business card. "This is where I get my paint, and this . . ." she turned it over to show him the digits written on the back, "is my account number. Just tell them that you want it put on my bill."

She wrote down quantities, colors, and finishes as Gary ran a comb through his hair. "Okay," he said, grimacing as it snagged on dried paint flecks. "I'll be right back."

Annie had grabbed a clean drop cloth, ready to bunch it up and use it for a cushion to sit on, when she remembered.

"Wait a minute."

He turned in the brightness of the open doorway, silhouetted just as Mr. DeChristopher had been the other day. She noted, almost absent-mindedly, that Gary was much shorter, and didn't hold himself with the same precise carriage that the other man did. And what would *he* say if he knew

the soon-to-be-ex-husband was here helping her paint his house? Annie would have
to remember to tell Gina not to mention
that small fact to him. Even though it
shouldn't be any big deal, she sensed that
he would express strong disapproval.

She dug into her backpack again, pulling
out the large clear acrylic keychain. "When
you come back . . ." she started to hand it
to him, then thought better of it and
yanked it back.

He flipped his outstretched hand in a
motion that asked, "What?"

Gripping it in her hand, she said,
"Nothing."

"What now?"

"Nothing. Listen, just ring the bell when
you get back."

Gary gave her a curious look before he
started for the door, but said nothing.

"Let me walk you down. I have to reset
the alarm anyway."

Sometimes, Annie thought as she headed
back up the stairs, *I'm such a twit. I was
about to give my client's house key to a burglar.* She rolled her eyes before getting
back to work, correcting herself, *Oh yeah,*
alleged *burglar.*

Gary wiped the perspiration from his

face with the back of his hand as he drove. Even with all the windows down the car was hot. How did Annie stand it? Especially being pregnant. He'd heard how hard it was for women to carry in the summer, and the poor girl didn't even have a cool car.

It was his fault, no doubt about it. He'd racked up the credit card bills and she'd bailed him out time and again. Finally, she'd taken steps to protect herself and kicked him out of the house. He didn't blame her.

It felt good to be driving again, despite the sweat pouring into his eyes. When he'd taken the car for his short jaunt to the grocery store and back, it had been cool and he'd been on a mission to surprise Annie with breakfast. This drive was longer, more scenic, through the upper-class homes of the far southwest suburbs. What did people do to afford homes like these?

The car coughed, sending a plume of dark smoke out behind him. Playing with the gas pedal, he managed to keep the engine from dying.

He'd make enough money to fix things. To improve her standard of living. His own too, of course. But mostly to make her proud.

They were having a baby. A baby. He'd have to buckle down now, there was no way around it. And, despite Annie's pro-testations, he knew that they would be to-gether. This pregnancy guaranteed it; it couldn't have come at a better time.

Tapping on the steering wheel to the music while he waited for the light to change, he grinned, listening to the radio, some rocker singing about teaching his woman to listen. He bobbed his head with the beat and sang along.

He pulled into the paint store parking lot and got out, happy to stretch in the sun. Despite the powerful rays hitting him from above and reflecting up from the asphalt ground, it was much cooler than sitting in the hotbox he'd been driving.

Fifteen minutes later, paint cans loaded in the trunk, he headed back. Who were these people Annie worked for anyway? DeChristopher?

Annie had admonished him to park on the street, and as he did so, he saw Mrs. DeChristopher alighting from a large gold-colored Lincoln. She'd seemed so nice this morning, almost as though she wanted him and Annie to get back together. He liked her. Two little boys scampered into the backyard, which by the look of it, was out-fitted with a large colorful playground and separately fenced in-ground pool.

Gary was about to get out of the car when he noticed the driver getting out of the Lincoln. Mrs. DeChristopher had called out to him this morning. Timothy. Didn't Annie say the husband's name was Richard? Must be the gofer. And what a pansy name.

But this guy was big. A gorilla in a white shirt and dress pants, he looked hot and uncomfortable. His biceps appeared ready to burst through the taut white fabric of his sleeves at any moment. His left arm encircled a flat, brown, rectangular package. Gary thought it might have been one of those oversized coffee table books, but he could tell by the way the big man carried it that it didn't have much weight. His firm grip on the package and the way he held it close to his side led Gary to believe that it was something of great importance.

This guy was a goon, no doubt about it. Even though he'd never met this Timothy, Gary had seen his type before. He looked more like a secret service agent than a member of the family. On a hunch, Gary waited.

Several minutes later Timothy emerged, empty-handed, got back in the car and drove off.

Gary wondered about that package.

Chapter Eleven

"Crowded today," Gary said.

Annie pulled up to the DeChristopher home, surprised at the number of cars parked up and down the street. Balloons attached to a nearby mailbox and one of those blow-up jumping trampolines set up in a backyard told Annie that some rich little kid was celebrating a birthday today. She found a spot far down the block, squeezing her small car between two luxury SUVs.

"Gina said she'd be out when we got here. She's getting her hair and nails done for some fancy black-tie dinner tonight," Annie said, reaching across the small car's interior to grab the house key from her glove compartment, wondering what sculptured nail design Gina would choose today, "but I always ring the bell a few times first, just in case."

Gary moved his knees out of the way and nodded.

"And when you're done with the ceiling, you can quit tagging along, okay?"

"Is that the thanks I get for all my help?"

She sighed, staring straight ahead. It was cooler today, thank goodness, and Annie rolled up her window, wincing at the high-pitched scraping sound it made as it jerked upward. She motioned for Gary to do the same on his side. "I'm taking your help as a down payment on the room and board you and Pete owe me."

"You could afford to be a little nicer to him. He's been on his best behavior since he moved in."

She rolled her eyes. "That man is a pig," she said, reaching for the door handle.

"You know Annie, you've been up on your high and mighty horse ever since you started this business of your own. Like you don't need no one. And yet, here I am, helping you out, and all I'm asking for is a temporary place to stay for me and a friend of mine." Staring out, his gaze seemed focused far beyond the windshield as he shook his head. "You don't have to make us feel so . . . small, you know."

With both hands on the steering wheel, Annie looked out over the hood of the car. Was she doing that? It was possible. Maybe she was being too hard on Gary. Maybe he . . .

"Wait a minute," she said in an angry voice.

"What?" Gary looked confused.

"Don't even go there, buster. I'm not going to start feeling guilty. Not when I've been tired and pregnant and working to try to make my place in this world, only to have you butt into my life, screwing it up, literally mind you, bringing that scum of a friend with you. Don't even try to make me feel guilty, because I don't. And I won't." Her voice had risen, loud to her own ears, in the small car. The pressure that had been building over the past few days was near its boiling point and she could feel heat rising from her chest, reddening her face.

"Annie, hang on —"

"I will not hang on. Every time I turn around, you're there making my life difficult. And I've had it, do you understand?" She crossed her arms over the steering wheel and rested her head against them.

"I'm sorry, Annie."

Without lifting her head, she said, "I just want to make it on my own, Gary. And you guys," her throaty laugh sounded as heavy as it felt, "you guys were not part of the deal. I'm forging my way here, too, and if I'm hurting your feelings, I apologize." She sat back to look at him. "It's simple, really. Just move out."

The bright sun on the dark car was bringing up the interior's temperature again.

"We're working on it."

"Pete isn't," she said, her voice sounding snappish again. "All he does is sit in that damn vibrating chair all day and complain about how his giant TV doesn't fit in my house and so he's stuck watching my little set." She closed her eyes for a moment and took a breath. Trying to fix a bland expression on her face, she said, "You mentioned something about having a job lined up?"

Gary's quick nod and cautious look let her know that she probably shouldn't have blown off his big news earlier. He'd started to tell her something about it this morning, but she knew the man was facing burglary charges from his last place of business. No one in his right mind would want to hire him. Sighing, she realized that this was not the time, nor the place, to bring that up. Better to keep the subject neutral. With an attempt at softening the indifference in her eyes, she asked, "How's that looking?"

"Great," he said. "Really great. I told you I knew a guy who could help me as long as I got off that charge, right?" Gary wiggled in the passenger seat, his words tumbling over each other in his hurry to get them out. "My court date is a week from Wednesday. The lawyer says he thinks he can get me off on a Motion to Suppress."

"What does that mean?" Annie wiped the perspiration from her brow with the fingers of her left hand and considered rolling the squeaky window back down. She was about to open the door to get some air when Gary answered her.

"It means, he says, that some evidence they conjured up won't be able to be admitted in the trial. And without that evidence, they got nothing." His smile widened.

"Conjured up."

"Yeah. Not guilty, remember?"

"So you said in court. But is that the truth?" The car's stuffiness was starting to get to her. Not expecting an answer, Annie grabbed the door handle and opened it. The cooler air rushed in.

"Annie," he said, and when she turned she was surprised by the earnestness on his face, "I made a mistake. I admit that. But I swear, if I get off on this, I'm not gonna ever get caught making that kind of mistake again."

She pursed her lips, processing his words. Then bit her tongue to keep from replying. "Let's go."

They rang the doorbell four times before letting themselves in with the key. Annie motioned Gary in quickly, then shut the front door. Moving to the access panel, she opened it and inputted the code to disarm, then reactivate, the burglar alarm now that the door was closed again. The little green light blinked on to tell her she'd been successful.

Turning to go up the steps, she eyed Gary. "You weren't watching me, were you?"

"Watching what?"

"The access code."

Gary shook his head. "Nah."

As they rounded the top of the first flight of steps, Gary walked over to one of the open bedrooms. "Whoa," he said, his head shaking with disbelief. "Look at the stuff in these rooms."

"Stay out of them."

"I'm not going past the doorways, see?" He gestured down to the tips of his blue gym shoes, still safely outside the bedroom. "It's just that," his shoulders dropped as his voice took on a wistful tone, "Annie, you deserve a place like this."

"Puh-lease," she said, tugging at his arm, "let's not go *there*. Come on, I've got lots to get done today."

"Hang on." The door to Mr. DeChristopher's study was ajar, and Gary nudged it wider with his left hand. It opened without a sound. "Who is this guy anyway?"

"Why?" Annie moved closer to see what had captured his attention.

"Look at this room. It's like a museum or somethin'."

Annie's curiosity got the better of her. She peered around the corner, even while chastising Gary. "You shouldn't be prying into other people's lives, you know." Then, "Wow."

As opposed to the cool unfussy elegance of the rest of the house, this room was jammed to the teeth with an assortment of artwork, sculpture, and antiques. So profuse was the collection that it startled Annie when she stepped in. At first glance, she thought it might be a storage room for all the knick-knacks that didn't have a place elsewhere, but within moments recognized some semblance of order. Other than the enormous antique desk, which stood out in stark uncluttered beauty near the back window of the room, every surface was covered, whether it was the walls with paintings, or the shelves with works of art. Crowded, yes, but each and every item had a place.

"I recognize this," Annie said, as she moved into the room, forgetting her initial reticence. A still-life bore the brass-plated title, *Goldenrod*. Resisting the urge to touch the frame, she pointed instead. "This is either an original Fred Holly, or it's one heck of a reproduction."

"Hey," Gary said, moving behind the desk to the table under the window, "that guy Timothy, what is he anyway? A bodyguard or something?"

"He's their driver," Annie answered without looking at him, moving farther down the wall to examine the next painting. "Must be nice, huh?"

"Yeah, well I saw him carrying some kinda package like this yesterday. Looked to me like he was pretty protective of it."

Annie looked up to see Gary lifting a crinkling sheet of brown mailing paper sporting long creases, suggesting it had been used to wrap something a little bigger than a shirt box. "Don't touch anything."

"Don't matter. Whatever was in here is gone now." Gary dropped the paper with a frown, looking around the room.

A rumbling mechanical sound beneath

their feet let them know that the home's garage door was opening. "Let's go," Annie said.

They worked without talking the entire time Richard DeChristopher was home. Annie, thinking about the creaky floors in her own house, realized how fortunate she was that the DeChristopher residence was so new. It would be disastrous for him to find Gary working here, in his home, with his client. With a minimum of stealth, she and Gary were able to move about in relative silence. Annie tried to focus on some of the new sections she hadn't drawn in yet, but her heart wasn't in the job today.

Kneading her eraser again, she lifted it to the wall and gently rubbed away the beginnings of a pterodactyl beak she'd just drawn. Since it was Friday, she wouldn't be working at Millie's tonight. Taking a step back, she looked at the wall again. The birdlike reptile's head seemed misshapen all of a sudden. She erased that too.

Too much on her mind today.

With a deep breath, she began again. The pterodactyl would have to cooperate.

Wiping pencil smudges off her hands, she stood back again, thinking about her situation. She had difficulty referring to

Mr. DeChristopher as Richard, even though he'd specifically requested she do so. Moving back to paint in the eyeball of the very brachiosaurus he'd stopped to admire the other day, she wondered how he'd react if he discovered them up here.

He stayed less than fifteen minutes, talking on the phone in the upstairs study. For such a big home, Annie would have thought it harder to hear conversations from one level to the next, but perhaps due to the utter silence of the house, she was able to make out most of what he said. The sounds drifted up the staircases, and Richard DeChristopher didn't seem to be working overly hard to keep his voice down.

"Yes," she heard him say, "it's here. Arrived yesterday . . . In perfect condition."

Deferential tone. Must be the boss/client person he was talking to the other day. A combination of frustration and tension made her grip her pencil so tight that her finger knuckles were white. Annie tried to ignore the one-sided conversation, but her mind was putting a scenario together, yet again.

Gary sidled close and whispered in her ear, "Arrived yesterday? I bet he's talking about that package I saw the driver . . ."

The downstairs voice continued.

"No. It's quite safe. No need for concern." They heard a few indistinct sounds. Then, "I've pulled it out from the wall safe. I'm looking at it right now. And let me assure you that, even in my humble estimation, this piece is magnificent. It will make a stunning addition to your collection."

She looked at Gary, "Get back to work."

They both stopped at his next words.

"Yes, I've heard the ten-million-dollar figure myself. But, I'll be willing to part with it for half that."

Annie moved, as if to speak again.

Gary held a finger up, silencing her. Then mouthed the words: "Ten million dollars?"

She heard Mr. DeChristopher's resigned tone, "I understand that, of course."

Gary, attentive to the conversation, had stopped painting and leaned out the open doorway, holding the paint roller aloft. Annie caught his eye and gestured toward the ceiling in silent exclamation. She didn't like the way her hand shook while she pointed.

The rest of his exchange consisted of a series of monosyllabic responses. Moments later, he said, "I don't want to chance taking it out again. Too great a risk." He paused for a few moments. "Not tonight at any rate. I'm attending the annual Citizenship Award dinner at the Bar Association." Chuckling, he added, "No, as Guest of Honor." A few seconds passed before he spoke again. "Would you be able to? Then yes, of course. It will be no problem. I'll have them set places for another guest. Do you have the address?"

Silence hung in the air after the receiver hit the phone with a solid click. Annie, hearing the blood pounding in her ears, abruptly stopped moving, as though he'd be able to hear her breathe. She took a cautious glance over to Gary, who had stopped moving as well. They looked at each other and Annie saw Gary's eyes widen in a look that said, "I can't believe I'm behaving like this."

All of a sudden she wanted to laugh. Kind of like she sometimes felt at a wake when something humorous happened. While a situation might be funny, in the context of the somber situation, it took on hilarious proportions. She could feel a little giggle working its way up her chest and knew that if she didn't fight it, she'd lose it right there. Without putting words to it, she understood that her having overheard one of Mr. DeChristopher's conversations could be excused, but that if he caught her up here right now, after this second eavesdropping incident, she'd be kicked out on her ear in a heartbeat.

Mr. DeChristopher whistled as he headed back to the garage. Moments later the garage door rumbled again, and Annie chanced a look out the front window to see him pulling away in his silver Jaguar. When his car turned the far corner, she let out her breath and turned her attention back to the room.

The black painted ceiling was nearly done. With any luck, Gary could have it finished today.

Annie stretched, pushing her arms out to her sides. "Well. Wasn't that fun?"

"Wonder what he was talking about."

"Who knows?" she said, then looked at her watch. "We're probably better off *not* knowing. Next time he comes in when we're here, I say we make lots of noise and say hello right away. I don't think I can take that kind of pressure again."

"Yeah," Gary said, but he sounded as if he hadn't heard her.

"I'm going to run downstairs and grab a bottle of water before he decides to come back. You want anything?"

"No, thanks." Gary moved to reload his roller as Annie headed to the door. "Hey wait."

She turned.

"Let me go get it, okay? You shouldn't be taking so many trips up and down the stairs. And five minutes after you drink the water, you're going to need to run downstairs again anyway. Save you a trip."

Annie turned back to the foliage she'd drawn on the west wall and tried to crack her back in another stretch. "Sounds good to me."

As her hand moved in bold lines over the wall, adding details, she shook her head. This was exactly what she didn't want to have happen. To have an amicable divorce was one thing. This kind of togetherness, and Gary's living with her was another. Pete along as part of the bargain was beyond tolerable.

Glancing up, she hedged. The ceiling, nearly complete, looked great. It *was* a big help to have that part of the project finished. Adding the stars and extras later wouldn't be so bad now that the background was in. And Gary had done a nice job.

But still.

After her fourth erasure of the diplodocus' small head, Annie mumbled a gripe and stamped her foot. Nothing she did felt good today. DeChristopher skulking around downstairs had distracted her for a few minutes, but she couldn't shake a feeling of disquiet. She'd left Sam's last night in a funk. A far cry from the evening she'd come home singing.

Yesterday, she'd mentioned Gary's involvement on the DeChristophers' project. She'd expected Sam to react by cautioning her against letting Gary back into her life. But he hadn't. He hadn't said a word. Later that evening, when she was ready to leave, she'd stopped in his office to talk, as was their habit of late. He looked up at her and smiled, but something was missing. His eyes weren't in on it.

"What's wrong?" she'd asked.

"Nothing."

Every other time they'd talked, he'd been engaged in the conversation. They'd been in sync, even when they'd discussed things that were hard to talk about, and heaven knew they had plenty of that between them. But tonight the Sam she thought she knew wasn't there.

Annie had gravitated toward one of the chairs in a half-move, her fingers grazing its back, anticipating an invitation to sit.

It didn't come.

Forearms resting on the desktop, he maintained a cool, pleasant look on his face. Sliding a pen from hand to hand, he was otherwise still, his eyes unreadable. Fighting the instinct to reach out and touch him, to grasp his hand and ask him to talk, she instead gathered up her supplies as quickly as she could, waving as she left. He'd raised his chin in reply and bent back to work.

Annie knew that last night's interactions kept her from being creative today. Sam's behavior weighed on her. Like a stone in her stomach, she couldn't ignore it, yet couldn't make it go away until she saw him again. Maybe not even then.

Every creative bone in her body had dried up. It hurt. Sitting down, resting her back against the wall, she tapped her pencil on the side of her hand, trying to decide what to do.

Visit Sam.

She sat up.

It came to her so suddenly that she couldn't believe she hadn't thought of it sooner. Just because she wasn't scheduled to work there tonight didn't mean she couldn't go there for a hot fudge sundae. Tucking her hair behind her ears, she considered the idea. If she showed up there unannounced, just to visit, then he'd have to know that she liked him, right? Leaning back again, she looked up and rubbed her eyes. It was like being a teenager all over again. This was ludicrous. Why didn't she just walk up to Sam and tell him how she felt?

Because she was married, that's why.

Annie sighed. The sooner Gary was out of her life, the better, as far as she was concerned. But today while they'd been working, she'd mentioned the divorce again. He'd changed the subject. A second time he'd walked away, her calling after him, "We're going to have to talk about this sooner or later."

Where was he? She looked at her watch, but couldn't remember how long it had been since he went downstairs. It felt like a long time.

Standing at the doorway, she called, "Gary?"

No answer.

She tried again.

With a sigh of frustration, she put down her pencil and called down to him as she went down both sets of stairs to the kitchen. "Gary?"

He wasn't anywhere. Puzzled, she looked at the burglar alarm. It was still reset, so he couldn't have left. "Where are you?"

Her hand on the banister, she moved halfway up the first set of stairs, looking from side to side, up and down. Berating herself for letting him wander alone, she hissed her anger, then called his name, louder this time.

When he stuck his head out of the upstairs den, she jumped, irritated. "What were you doing in there?"

His face strove for innocence. "I went to the bathroom, that's what took so long. And on the way back up, I just thought I'd take a quick look in here again."

She glared at him. "My God. You didn't touch anything, did you?"

"No, no. I swear," he said. Rather than indignation, his face registered shock at the question and somehow she knew he was telling the truth.

"You know what, Gary? I think we're about done for the day."

"Hang on just a minute, Annie," he said, gesturing with his fingers. "C'mere, I want to show you something and ask you a question about it."

Clenching her teeth, Annie felt the tension build as it worked through to every extremity. Bright lights of anger exploded in her head and she had to wait till they passed to answer him. "Get out of there, now."

Gary looked as though he wanted to say something, then thought better of it.

Annie continued. "It was bad enough we looked in there earlier, but I'm not about to go snooping around in my client's home. And you know what?" she asked, her voice rising. "Neither are you. I told you. Get out. Now."

Gary started to move out the door, but cast a longing glance backward. "Listen, Annie, there's something in here I think you might want to see."

Standing with her arms folded at the bottom of the stairs, she tapped her foot on the cool marble, trying to keep the angry trembles from taking over. Gary shook his head as he started toward the stairs.

"Grab my backpack before you come down," she said, trying to inject some power into her voice. She could feel a shiver working its way through her body, and pulled her arms in tighter. Gary wandering around the DeChristophers' home made her shudder. If he'd stolen or broken something, or if he'd even just moved an item from its proper place, they would know someone had been snooping in their home.

It was her reputation on the line. This was her livelihood and she'd been close to squandering it. And for what? To give Gary something to do? To take it easy on herself by having the ceiling done for her? What had she been thinking?

He came down the stairs, looking less sheepish than she'd have hoped, carrying her backpack in one hand and the DeChristopher house key in the other. "I closed up your paints for you," he said, handing her the key, "and I figured you'd need this."

She whipped the key from his outstretched hand, moving back to the access panel to set up the burglar alarm for their exit. As she was about to enter the code, she turned, "Turn around."

Gary rolled his eyes. "You inputted the code before, sweetheart. How do you know I didn't see it then?"

"Just . . . just shut up," she said, tapping the numbers, then shutting the panel door. "Okay, it's clear. Let's go."

At the car, Annie dug through her backpack for her car keys, surprised when Gary's hand covered hers. "Let me drive," he said.

"Why?"

"You're tired. And I screwed up. I know

I did. Let me do this small thing for you."

She slammed her car keys on the roof. "Fine."

Inside the car, Annie tossed the DeChristophers' key back into the glove compartment and sat back. Watching as they passed the big, beautiful houses, she wondered if she'd ever get out from this mess she'd married herself into. Financially, she was still okay, at least for a little while. And if her business took off, she'd have enough money to keep herself afloat and take care of the baby, too. The baby. Seems like something she'd forgotten over the course of the last few days. But it was easy to do, what with not having the requisite morning sickness. Bathroom visits and fatigue were her two biggest hurdles, but she'd learned to cope with them, so far.

She lifted an arm to lean it out the open window, and winced. Her breasts were sore, too. That was something she hadn't expected, but Karla said not to worry. Just meant that they were getting a little bigger. Not too much bigger, she hoped.

It dawned on her that Gary had asked a question.

"What?"

"I said," Gary seemed to draw out the words, "that a guy I know paid me some money he owed me, so I can help out a little at home."

At home. Annie bit her tongue.

"And there's even enough to maybe take you out for lunch today. Whaddya say?"

Rolling her head his direction, she mouthed, "No way."

"Come on," he said, cajoling. "You want to talk about the divorce, right?"

"It's not like I *want* to do anything with you."

"Okay, we *need* to talk about the divorce," he stretched out the word and rolled his eyes. "And we can do it at home, if you want. No problem. But don't forget, Pete's there."

Chapter Twelve

"Pete, it's me," Gary said, his hand cupping the mouthpiece of the cell phone. Standing just inside the door of the men's room at Donagan's, head down, he leaned his butt against the speckled beige Formica counter-top, righting himself quickly as spilled hand-washing water soaked through the back of his jeans. Moving across the dank room, he leaned instead against the brown tile walls and scowled at the plastic device over his head dispensing bursts of air freshener at regular intervals.

Leftover paint from the DeChristophers' black ceiling marred one of his gym shoes and he used the bottom of his clean gym shoe to try to wear the stain away.

"Pete?" Gary's eyes shot to the floor, verifying yet again that no one occupied any of the stalls. No matter how low he kept his voice, the sound bouncing against the ceramic tiles made it feel like he was shouting. He stage-whispered, talking quickly, hoping no one would come in.

The restaurant was nearly empty on this early afternoon, but Gary knew that any minute some old coot might decide he needed the facilities and wander in to overhear the conversation. And unless the geezer was deaf, he'd hear Pete's side of it too because the fool talked so loud.

Gary grimaced, holding the phone away from his ear while Pete finished yawning. "Oh yeah? Hi, Gare. Didn't expect to be hearing from you till late tonight." Sounds sputtered through the phone; stretching noises. "How's it goin'?"

"Pete, listen. Listen close," Gary kept one eye on the door as he spoke. He knew that Annie wouldn't venture near the men's room, but still. The sooner he could put his plan in motion the better. He spoke quickly into the phone, trying hard not to let his voice carry. Trying not to let his excitement show.

If this worked the way he hoped, he and Annie would be set for life. She wouldn't approve of course, but it was her own fault, really. He hadn't hatched this plan till after she shagged him out of the DeChristopher house. If she'd come up to the den when he'd called her, it would have been an entirely different story.

"Gary, Gary. Slow down. I can't make

out a word you're saying. Where are you anyway?"

"Don't matter. I can't talk long." He jumped when the washroom door shuddered a moment, but it was just the air current. "You remember all those newspaper clippings that Annie has that she keeps on the coffee table in the living room?"

Pete yawned again, making a little grunting noise and Gary heard him smack his lips. "Yeah . . . I think so."

Pacing now, Gary tried to make himself clear through Pete's fog of sleepiness. "Do me a favor, okay? Take 'em. All of 'em, and go make copies over at the gas station down the block."

"Make copies of the newspaper articles?"

Gary squeezed his eyes shut. "Yes."

"Whaddya want copies of those for? Why dontcha just read the ones that are here?"

"Because I don't want Annie to know that I have them." Anger shot out from his voice. "Pete," he said in a calmer tone. "Let's just keep that between us, okay?"

"You mean you and me?"

"Yes. You and me. Make the copies, then put the originals back on the table, okay? And then, meet me . . ." he glanced at his watch, "in about an hour at that bar we went to last Friday, okay?"

"Should I bring the copies with me?"

Gary grimaced as the bathroom door creaked, then wiggled ajar. An elderly man pushed it open, with difficulty. Shuffling two steps for every repositioning of his cane, he smiled as Gary pulled the door open for him, and thanked him in a wheezy voice. Gary nodded an acknowledgment, then said into the phone, before slapping it shut, "Yes, bring them."

Annie watched Gary make his way back to their table. Even the way he walked annoyed her now. Smiling at the people at a handful of other tables. Like he knew them or something.

Sliding into his seat, Gary handed Annie's cell phone back to her.

"What was that all about?" she asked.

"If I don't check in with my attorney from time to time, he forgets me." Gary smiled, lifted his linen napkin, and snapped it out before dropping it on his lap. Leaning forward, he laughed in a contrived way. "You see, my case is such small potatoes, that he isn't even worried about it."

She shoved the phone back into her

pack. "You were gone a long time."

"Yeah, well, he's hard to track down. Good attorneys are like that."

Annie decided not to pursue the matter. "I ordered you a Coke."

Elena returned to the table, delivering their beverages with practiced ease. When they'd first arrived, she'd given an interested murmur when Annie had refused a glass of wine and ordered iced tea instead. Now, holding the empty tray against her hip, Elena sighed, "Ahh," with more than a little dramatic flair, "eet is so wonderful to see you both here again, together." She pressed a red-chapped hand against her ample bosom. "I knew it when I saw you here last time, that it would not be the last. I am so happy."

Whether an affectation or sincere, Annie didn't know, but Elena touched the corner of her eye with a daintiness that belied her size, as though to wipe a tear. If she only knew that they were here to discuss a divorce. The situation was almost laughable. As the woman took their orders and made yet another comment about what a nice couple they made, Annie's chest heaved with an unvoiced scream. She wanted to stand up and tell the whole restaurant crowd, of which there were probably eight people, that she was getting divorced, god-dammit.

Instead, she picked up her iced tea and smiled.

Gary grinned at Elena's departing figure. "I'm glad you suggested we come here instead of that other place we went. You just can't beat stuff like that."

"You wanna bet?"

"Annie," Gary said, reaching for her hand.

"Don't."

He pulled his arm back across the table and mustered up enough petulance in his voice to tease up her anger again. "I'm just trying to find a little common ground here."

She weighed her words. "We aren't going to find common ground anymore, Gary."

"What are you, joking? Except for the business right before we left, we were doing great. Working together. Having fun." Looking at her, he added, "At least I was having fun. I liked being able to help you."

Annie pulled her lips together in a tight line and stared at the fat red candleholder in the center of the table. Today had gotten out of hand. She'd let her guard down. Again. Every time she did, she found herself in a deeper mess. "I thought we were here to discuss the divorce. If you have something else in mind, tell me now, because then I'm outta here." She held her hands out in an inquiring gesture and made ready to stand.

"No, of course," Gary said, in a hurry. "That's what we're here for. Definitely. We need to talk about the divorce. So sit tight, okay?"

"You understand that I'm not changing my mind?"

Gary looked at his watch. "Yeah, I understand that."

"And you understand that you and Pete have to find other living arrangements."

"Well . . ." Gary hedged, "that may be tough, at least for a little while."

"You've got two weeks." Annie surprised herself with her forcefulness.

"That's not much time," he said.

"Two weeks."

Gary stretched his arms on the table and looked down at his watch again. "Didn't you say you needed a new lawyer? It'll take you at least that long to find one. Let's wait till the thing is in motion again. Until then, I can help you out by painting and you can help me out with a roof over my head. Whaddya say?"

"I've *got* a new lawyer. Mr. DeChristopher is handling the divorce. We've already discussed it."

Gary's mouth dropped open. "You're kiddin' me."

Annie felt a measure of satisfaction. "Nope."

Gary ran his hands through his hair in frustration, scrubbing his fingers on the back of his head before speaking again. "Okay, fine. We need to think about the baby."

"What about the baby?"

"I've got it all figured out, Annie. Just give me a couple of months and I swear I'll be set. I promise everything will work out. I just need some time."

"We're getting divorced. Or did you miss the first half of this conversation?" Angry now, her sarcasm shot across the table.

"I didn't miss a thing," he whispered. All of a sudden his eyes lit up, and he continued, not attempting to quiet his voice, "You are pregnant with my baby, aren't you?"

Annie's eyes widened. "Gary!"

"I mean, if that's not something we have in common, I don't know what is."

"Forget the baby." Annie surprised herself with her sharp tone. "What I'm trying to say," she threw down the straw wrapper she'd been fiddling with, "is that I don't . . ." her voice caught for a moment, less in sadness, than in knowing she was about to hurt him. No matter that their relationship was over, it was difficult for her to deliberately hurt anyone. She looked at him, knowing by the flicker of a reaction in his eyes, that he sensed her strength. In a low voice, speaking slowly, she continued, "I don't want to have anything to do with you. Nothing."

"Nothing to do with me," he repeated, looking away.

"No." Her quiet answer felt loud, like a gong.

His face reddened. "And when this baby's born, what then?" His hands flew outward and his voice grew louder in indignation.

Annie lowered her head, but maintained eye contact. Although she whispered, she knew he heard every word. "When the time comes we'll work something out, like visits and stuff. But I plan to raise this child alone."

The quieter she grew, the louder he got. A bumpy blue vein stood out in his neck as he leaned forward, almost shouting, "I have rights too, you know."

"Keep your voice down," she said, her brow furrowing as she stole a glance around the room. A couple of people across the room looked over at them. She glared at him, speaking in a heated undertone. "I don't care what rights you think you have. As far as I'm concerned, you have nothing to do with this baby."

His face flushed with the immediate red of intense anger. Shouting an expletive, Gary slapped the table with both hands. "Oh really? I had nothing to do with you getting yourself pregnant?"

Now every eye in the restaurant shot their direction.

Beads of perspiration popped out all over Annie's face and she took a deep breath, refusing to make eye contact with the other patrons. She put a hand up, but Gary wasn't finished.

"Maybe I misunderstood your little confession the other day, sweetheart. When you told me you were pregnant I just *assumed* the baby was mine." His face screwed up in a scowl and his voice grew louder with each syllable.

Gary looked around the restaurant with outstretched arms, playing to the dining audience. "I find out my *wife* is pregnant," pointing at Annie, scraping his chair against the floor as he pushed backward to stand. "And, fool that I am, I'm happy about it. I'm thinkin' hey, sure we have our problems, everybody does, but now we're a *family*." He shot a look at Annie so angry it burned. One of the elderly women sat frozen, her mashed-potato filled fork poised midway between the plate and her open mouth. Only her eyes moved, from Gary's dramatic pose, to Annie's infuriated and embarrassed face.

Without stopping for a breath, Gary continued, his voice booming throughout the room, bouncing off the large windows nearby, "Now I'm thinking, 'What am I — stupid?' Maybe this baby isn't mine after all."

Annie jumped up, causing her chair to fall backwards. "Stop," she reached across the table to grab his arm. He yanked away from her, feigning pain.

"What's the name of the guy you've been spending your nights with? Sam?"

"Gary!" The shock of hearing Sam's name coupled with the suggestion of an accusation startled Annie for a moment. A half-second later, her wits returned; she wondered how he knew Sam's name. How dare he bring him into this? How dare he make such a spectacle of her? She grabbed at him, reaching across the table again, but he sidestepped her. "Stop it. Now." Her own voice had risen several octaves, but as though distanced from her own actions, she couldn't control herself.

Their voices mingled in a jangled contest of volume. Annie could feel the heat in her face, saw the blinding lights in her head again as her eyes scanned the area for something, anything to put an end to this madness. Blindly she searched for some way to shut him up. Her hands fell on her iced tea glass on the table before her. Acting on instinct, without stopping to think, her entire being consumed with the sole thought of shutting Gary up, she wrapped both hands around the heavy tumbler, and threw it at him. The glass itself barely grazed his shoulder but the liquid hit its mark, dousing his head, stopping him mid-sentence, covering his hair and shoulders in tea.

Horrified at her own actions, Annie pulled herself back. As though the moment had frozen and only Annie could move, she took in the sights in slow motion. Gary, across from her, dripping, looking hurt and angry all at once. The other diners sat wide-eyed, not bothering to feign indifference. Blue eyes, brown ones, green ones, all pointed in her direction, all shooting identical looks of entertained shock. Aware of everyone, the diners, Elena, even the cooks, who'd come forward to watch, Annie grabbed her backpack, and fled to the ladies' room.

Banging the hollow door open with the heel of her hand, Annie held her breath till the door squeaked closed behind her. One red vinyl chair sat in the corner of the small, poorly-lit space and she sat in it, happy to find the room unoccupied. Breathing hard, she used every ounce of fortitude to keep herself from crying. One of those automatic hand dryers sat perched at eye level next to her and she rested her forehead against the cool metallic box, re-playing the last few moments in her mind.

"God damn you, Gary," she whispered. "If you only knew how much I wish this was Sam's baby. Anyone's baby but yours."

She sat up as the door creaked open. The older woman who'd been eating mashed potatoes peered around the corner. Her eyes, nearly as pale blue as her hair, registered satisfaction as she spied Annie.

"I have five children," she said, moving forward. Nodding, smiling, approaching her like one would move toward a sleeping tiger, eager to touch, afraid it would bite. Was she waiting for a response?

Annie felt strength seeping away from her. All she wanted was to be left alone, to go home and go to sleep. She rested the side of her head against the hand dryer again and watched the woman, who moved closer yet again and blinked repeatedly before she continued to talk.

Wearing a shiny purple jogging suit with a big white "v" running down the center, straddling the zipper of the jacket, the woman looked to be around seventy. "Five of them," she continued, nodding her head toward Annie's abdomen. "Is this your first?"

Annie nodded, too tired to do otherwise.

"It's a boy," she said. "Carrying boys always made me crabby, too." She took Annie's hand and patted it. "Don't feel bad, honey. Start thinking of boy names, now. And don't mind how things went. Once they put that little bundle of joy in your arms, you both'll forget today ever happened." The woman's face wrinkled into a wide smile, "Well, I just wanted to check on you, honey." Her large-knuckled crooked finger wagged, "But, mark my words."

The older woman turned to leave, pulling the door open again. Annie rested her elbows on her backpack and put her face in her hands. So now the entire restaurant thought of her as a hormonally challenged pregnant female who couldn't hold her temper in public. If they only knew. Annie rubbed her eyes, pinching her eye sockets near her tear ducts. She would not cry. It didn't matter what these people thought. Didn't matter that Gary had been able to get a rise out of her. No. Nothing mattered anymore except her own well-being. Hers and the baby's.

Taking a deep breath, Annie checked her reflection in the mirror, and satisfied that she looked like a calm human being once more, she realized she'd have to face the restaurant again, sooner or later, so better to get it over with.

Turning to the door, she was surprised to see it open again. The jogging suit woman peered back into the room, her face expressing distress. "Honey, I hate to tell you this, but I think your husband left you here."

"What?"

"Just now, out the front door, I saw him get into a car and pull away."

"A little dark blue car?"

"Yeah, honey, I'm so sorry. Do you need a ride home?"

She'd let her guard down again when she let him drive. He had her car keys. Annie threw her backpack onto the red chair and swore. Running her hands through her hair, she mumbled a few choice words about Gary, then turned to the woman, who waited. "No, actually I live nearby. I can walk."

"You're sure?"

Annie nodded. The woman moved forward as if to comfort her, but then appeared to think better of it and left the bathroom.

Annie waited a while before leaving. No rush now. She steadied herself, tried to calm her racing mind. Slinging her backpack over her shoulder, she headed to the cashier. Elena tried to smile, but her eyes were sad.

"Did he pay before he left?"

"No, Ahnnie, he didn't." Elena made brief eye contact, then began to stack and straighten the green and white receipts from scattered piles next to the cash register.

"Fine," Annie said, pulling out a credit card. "I'll take care of it."

"I'm so sorry," Elena said, whisking the plastic card through the reader. "You want

I should call you a cab?"

"No, I'll be fine."

Annie followed an older man to the front doors. Dressed in shiny brown too-short pants, a striped shirt, and gym shoes, he made his way slowly ahead of her. He leaned heavily on his cane and took small, careful steps, stopping as he encountered the heavy glass doors of the vestibule. His skinny spotted arm grasped at the handle, then stopped, as if to marshal his strength before attempting to open it. Annie scooted from behind him and pushed the door open, allowing him to pass. He shuffled through, thanking her, while she moved forward to open the next ones. As she waited for him to clear the second set of doors she scanned the parking lot beyond him, remembering where they'd parked the car. The woman had been right, Gary was gone.

Once the man was safely outside, she let go of the handle. Shaking her head, she muttered, "I'm gonna kill him. I'm just gonna kill him."

The woman from the bathroom pulled up in a light blue Cadillac. Jumping out, she ran around the car. She took the older man's arm to guide him into the passenger seat. Over her shoulder, she winked, "Good luck, honey."

Chapter Thirteen

The walk home wasn't so bad, though Annie wished she had her sunglasses. Just the act of putting one foot in front of the other tempered some of the anger that still seethed. Not too fast, not too slow, her steps were rhythmic enough to settle her nerves. She kicked a small rock out of her path, watched it skitter across the sidewalk, hit a crack, and bounce into the grass nearby.

Her eyes watered from the sun's reflection on the cement. She hated being without her sunglasses and felt a disproportionate anger about missing them. Gary had really taken the cake this time. Not only had he stranded her like some fallen woman, he'd killed her chance to go see Sam tonight.

She'd go to Uncle Lou's house and have to hope he'd be home because she didn't have his key with her either.

Just ahead, on the south side of the street, her park beckoned. She'd always considered it her own because she and Karla had spent so many hours there on the swings, on the slides, and climbing the trees. But mostly on the swings.

The grass near the street, freshly cut, smelled of summer and green. The sun glinted off the metal slide, nearly blinding in its brightness. One of those old-fashioned slides, it hadn't yet been replaced with the colorful plastic kind that dotted the newer neighborhoods and the suburbs. A tall, scary slide, with two matching drops, it had no safety features other than a rusted metal railing near the top. Kids could fall off, but never did. Annie remembered the fast rides down if you picked your feet up and searing hot burns on the backs of your legs if you didn't.

Annie had taken a stray kitten down that slide once, when she was seven, thinking the animal would enjoy the ride. Confused, the poor thing had tried to escape, using the only means available, clawing up her arms, chest, and face. Panicked that the cat might fall to the ground, she held tighter, but the cat only scratched harder. It took a couple weeks before she healed completely. But the cat was okay. And Annie never tried that again.

Her eyes shifted over the playground area.

The swings were open.

She rested her arms atop the silver cyclone fence that surrounded Dolorosa Park. The afternoon had gotten hot, the cool promise of the morning forgotten as the sun shimmered bright above clear skies. She ran a hand around the back of her neck, grimaced at the wetness, then wiped the perspiration on her jeans. Toward the back of the large park, beyond the playground area, the sprinklers provided a cool respite for about a dozen kids.

The colorful children, some in bathing suits, some fully clothed in shorts and shoes, blurred as they danced and jumped, shouting through the sparkling sprays. Annie wished she had a camera to capture them, their skins, pink, brown, black, glimmering wet in the afternoon sun. It would make a beautiful watercolor.

Her eyes shifted back to the swings. These were the good kind, the ones that were hooked onto sturdy metal piping set solidly into the ground. Strong enough, high enough, for an adult to swing. Annie walked around the fence into the park, her hand straying a moment to touch the welcome sign. Just for a minute, she thought.

Dropping her backpack on the gravel near the corner post, Annie took the first swing and settled herself into the u-shaped seat. Just lifting her feet a little caused her to sway. She grasped the metal chains with both hands and kicked her feet back, causing a bit of a breeze on her face as she swung forward.

The children's squeals and laughter were suddenly muffled by the sound of machinery. Two men on matching yellow industrial-sized lawn mowers kicked their engines into gear, moving to the center of the ball fields to cut the grass. The steady roar from her right, and the hum of traffic along the main street to Annie's left as she sat there, rocking on the swing, provided comforting background noise.

"I want to see Sam," she said aloud.

There, she admitted it.

Kicking her feet forward, she gave herself a little boost. Her plan to visit Sam tonight, to stop in there casually for some ice cream, for a visit, was shot. Gary had her car and Annie knew that he was gone with it. For how long, she had no idea. She knew that with no means of getting there, she could kiss good-bye the idea of "just happening by" Millie's Ice Cream Parlour tonight.

Swaying, allowing her thoughts to roam, she wondered exactly how Gary had known Sam's name. She'd taken great care never to mention it to him. But he knew.

She put her feet down for a moment, stopping herself. He must have followed her. There wasn't another explanation that made sense. Annie closed her eyes, trying to purge frustration from her body. The sooner he was out of her life, the better her life would be. She lifted her feet to start swaying again. But now what?

Going home held no appeal with Pete there. Asleep, most likely, on that wretched vibrating chair. One of the things she hadn't noticed about the chair at first, was that the leather back had a removable outer casing. She'd found that out late last night when she caught Pete hiding girlie magazines in the zippered backside. She'd pretended not to notice, but as she exited the room she noticed him reaching to pull them out again. To be home alone with that creep was too much for her to bear.

Maybe she could stay the night with Uncle Lou. He'd be more than willing to put her up, but where? There wasn't a horizontal surface in his home that wasn't covered with books or papers or collections of magazines. He'd have to clean up for her. Though he'd be willing to do it, she wasn't willing to put him through it.

She could go to a hotel. For a few nights at least. The cost would hurt, but Annie didn't see too many other options. Getting there, though, would be a problem.

Straightening out her legs, then pulling them back as she crested forward, Annie got a good rhythm going on the swing. She leaned back, stretching her whole body as her feet pointed skyward again. It had been years since she'd been on these. Her hands perspired around the solid chains as she pulled back, closing her eyes against the brightness of the sun, enjoying the wind in her face.

It used to frighten her to lean all the way back, to hang her head far behind her and see the world upside down as she swung. But she always did it anyway, enjoying the little thrill of fear that tickled her stomach. She dropped her head back now, wondering how close her hair was to touching the ground below her. The world flew by, tilted and weird, moving up and down in a gentle rocking motion. It was still a little scary, but she was braver now.

Or was she?

Sitting up, Annie dragged her feet along the bouncy white pebbles below her and skidded to a stop. What she wanted more than anything was to see Sam. To make things right with him again. And what was she doing? Sitting alone, feeling sorry for herself, and lamenting the fact that she didn't have a car.

Reaching for her backpack, Annie pulled out her cell phone. Behind her, the two men on lawn tractors had cut their motors and gotten off their perches to examine something in the middle of the field. Perfect timing. Maybe it was an omen. Or not. Maybe there was nothing between her and Sam other than a comfortable working relationship.

There was only one way to find out, she thought, as she dialed Millie's number.

He answered the phone himself.

"Hi, Sam?" Annie said, hoping to quell the tiny tremor in her voice. "Got a minute?"

"Annie?" Her stomach did a little flip-flop when she heard the warmth in his voice. "I've got as long as you need."

She let out the breath she'd been holding and tried not to sound as relieved as she felt. The sky looked bluer all of a sudden, and she closed her eyes a moment before speaking. *Now or never,* she thought to herself. "I have a favor to ask . . ."

"Jeff?" Car keys in hand, Sam called into

the kitchen area, getting the teenager's attention. "I've gotta run out for a few minutes. Can you handle the place?"

"Sure. Everything okay?"

"Yeah, I have to go pick up Annie. She had . . . ah . . . car trouble."

"She doesn't usually come in on Fridays, does she?"

Sam scratched his neck, "No. She's not working tonight. Hey, if I needed you to close for me, could you do it?"

"Sure, Mr. Morgan. No problem."

With his index finger in the round key ring, Sam played with his keys, flipping the bunch into his palm, over and over. Pushing the flat brass plate of the front door, he stepped outside, wincing as he hit the outside heat. Annie was waiting in this miserable humidity. Waiting for him. He wanted to get to her as quickly as possible, knowing how low a pregnant woman's tolerance for high temperatures could be.

Sliding into the driver's seat, about to put the key in the ignition, he stopped. Sam the rescuer sat back and took a moment to assess the situation. She'd called him. She'd needed a friend and she'd called him. He smiled at that.

He lifted his key toward the ignition again. Stopped again.

Why was he so anxious to get to her? The beating from his heart seemed a bit louder than normal. Quicker too, but he had just jaunted across the parking lot. Clammy hands, but what else could he expect coming from the nice air-conditioning into this inferno?

Sam started the car, eased it into traffic, and made his way toward Annie. He'd been surprised and relieved when her voice came over the phone line. Yesterday she'd poured out her heart about the husband, Gary, and his friend. He'd listened and then . . . done nothing. No words of encouragement. No support. Annie's pained reaction, and her hurried departure, had made him feel enormous guilt all day.

He had to admit that the idea of Gary living back at the house with her bugged him. Realistically, he knew that she wasn't living with him in the marital sense — but still.

Twenty minutes later, Sam pulled up to a red light just a half-block short of where they were to meet. He could see Annie sitting on a park bench, her ankles crossed and pulled far back under the seat, her back straight. Her reddish brown hair glinted in the sun as her head moved, scanning the passing cars.

As the light changed to green, she stood up, spotting him. She gave a little wave. Sam pulled up to the curb and Annie got in, bringing with her a blast of hot air, her skin glistening with a sheen of perspiration. Her eyes seemed even brighter than usual against the pink of her cheeks. Her breathless "Hi" and her apologetic smile gave Sam the impression that she was nervous.

"Back to Millie's?"

"That'd be great, Sam. And maybe I can work on the mural a bit."

As the car's air-conditioning kicked in, Sam watched the cool air reach Annie's face, pick up the ends of her hair and play with them, making the tips wiggle and dance around her eyes. She brushed the stray hairs out of her way and smiled at him.

"Tell you what. How about you come back to the shop with me for a while, but not to paint? I'm all caught up with the bills and payroll, and I wouldn't mind a little company. You can tell me more about everything that's been going on, and if you need a ride home later, I'll take you. How does that sound?"

"That," she said, with more relief in her voice than Sam had expected, "sounds wonderful."

On the drive back, Annie tried to make the episode sound humorous, describing the woman with the mashed potatoes and the diners who looked like they were watching a soap opera. She downplayed her humiliation, instead focusing on how much tea she'd managed to hit Gary with. When she looked over at Sam, she could see that he wasn't buying her lightheartedness.

They were about halfway back to the ice cream shop, when she got to the part about the woman coming into the bathroom a second time. Sam pulled the car over to the side of the road and looked at her.

"And then he left you there?"

Annie nodded. Sam shook his head, facing outward, his gaze fixed on his small crystal pentagram hood ornament. She knew he was feeling sorry for her. "But it's not like I haven't walked home from Donagan's before. It's not that far, really."

"Annie," Sam turned to her, without smiling, "don't try to justify his actions. The man's an idiot."

"I know." Annie wrinkled her nose, replaying the scene in her mind. "But I guess *anybody* who just got doused with iced tea is going to be pretty upset. Anybody would be mad enough to leave."

Sam took a moment before speaking, and when he did, his mouth curled up in a sad way. "I never would have left you there. No matter what."

Looking into his intense blue eyes Annie felt a little tickle in her stomach. His left arm was propped against the steering wheel in a way that turned his whole body to face her. The top button of his dress shirt was undone. The bow tie, vest and garters from his sleeves were gone and it made him look more casual than usual. She could see his tension from the set of his jaw and the whiteness of his knuckles as his hands made fists.

Annie touched his hand, "I know that, Sam. But you're not just anybody."

Something shifted in his eyes. His fists loosened, and his face broke into a smile. God, she loved that smile. He returned both hands to the steering wheel and looked out again, deep in thought.

"You're not going back there tonight, are you?"

"No," Annie heard the hesitance in her voice. The more she'd thought about a motel, the less she liked the idea.

"Will you stay with your uncle?"

"He doesn't have the room for me. I figured I'd stay at that new hotel they just built off of Harlem."

"And your clothes, your stuff?"

Annie gave an embarrassed smile. "Well, it's not like I've had a chance to give it a lot of thought. But it seems like my best option."

Swiveling his head her direction, he asked, "You trust me, don't you?"

"Completely."

"I have an idea. Before you say no, hear me out, okay?"

Annie nodded.

"Let's drive back to your house . . ." Sam held up his hands at her reaction, "just to pick some things up. And then I'll take you back to my house." His words rushed out. "You can stay with me . . . until you can get these two losers to move out. To be safe, okay?"

Dumbfounded, Annie said nothing.

"I have spare rooms; you can pick the one you want. It may be weeks before they get their asses in gear, and it just seems wrong for you to be living like that, uncomfortable in your own home. If we go back now, it'll be better, in case they're there, for you to have someone with you, anyway."

"Sam . . ."

"We're friends, right?"

"Yes, of course."

"Then let me do this for you, okay?"

Annie rarely cried at sad movies. The ones that always got her were the happy ones, the ones where the most unexpected wonderful thing happened to the worthy hero. Looking at this unexpected wonderful man who'd become such an important part of her life, she had to fight the hot lump twisting in her throat before speaking.

"Thanks, Sam."

Her car was nowhere to be seen when they got back to her house. Still, Annie called out as she walked in.

"Gary?" she said, trying to make her voice sound sharp.

No answer.

"Pete, are you here?" There was no mistaking her tone with him. She walked from room to room in the small house, with Sam behind. But they were gone.

Returning to the foyer, Sam examined the leaded crystal oval of the front door. "This is beautiful," he said, running his finger along the wood grain frame. He swung it back and forth a few times, causing rainbows of light to dance on the walls and ceiling behind it. "Where did you get this great door?"

Annie stood in the center of the living room, tapping her lip with her index finger, concentrating on what she would need to take. "Hmmm? Oh. The Kane County Flea Market."

"I haven't been there in years," he said. "We should go sometime."

Annie looked up and locked eyes with Sam, who wore an expression of surprise, as though he'd spoken before thinking. "I'd like that," she said, and felt her heart skip a little when he smiled at her answer.

Necessities in hand from the bathroom, Annie moved to the bedroom, where she pulled out some jeans, a few tops, and one casual dress, just in case. She didn't know how long she'd be at Sam's, and while his offer was generous, she wondered how uncomfortable she'd feel staying there. Although, truth be told, she felt more comfortable around him now than she thought wise. She'd have to contemplate that, but right now packing needed her undivided attention.

So far all her clothes still fit, but Karla told her that first pregnancies take a while to show. She should be safe for at least another month, and her stint at Sam's certainly wouldn't be that long. Recently Annie felt as though some of her jeans were getting snug, but that might be from all the milkshakes.

Poking her head out the doorway, she checked on Sam. He was leafing through a stack of her watercolors, slowly. Taking his time with each one, before moving it forward to see the next.

Back at her task, she opened her underwear drawer and grabbed the multi-colored stack of dainties. Shutting the drawer with her hip, she stopped for a moment and bit her lip. Bending, she opened a second drawer, rooting around before she pulled out her lacy bras and silken underwear, holding them for a thoughtful moment. She could hear Sam walking around in the living room. It was a comforting sound.

What had he said? That they were friends. That she should trust him.

With a sigh of regret, she shoved the fancy underthings back in their drawer and slammed it shut.

"All set?" he asked as she emerged.

"Ready as I'll ever be." Annie looked around the room, trying to decide what she might be forgetting. She glanced down at the coffee table. "Wait a minute, my newspaper clippings are gone."

"The ones your uncle gave you?"

"Yeah," Annie said, drawing out the word in puzzlement. "I was sure I left them right here. I thought I'd take them along. He still wants me to do some research on that Durer drawing."

"What for?"

"I'm not entirely sure, but once a reporter, always a reporter, and I'm his resident Art Expert, whether I deserve the title or not." Annie laughed, looking under some of the books on the side tables. "I could have sworn . . ." she said. "No matter, I'll call him and see if he can't get me new copies."

Sam reached to take the oversized gym bag from her shoulders and gestured with his chin to the stack of paintings he'd been looking through. "Take those, too."

"My watercolors? Why?"

"They're wonderful. Just breathtaking. And if this Gary character comes back and sees you gone, he's going to be mad. He's going to want to hurt you somehow. What better way to do that than destroy the things most important to you?"

With new eyes Annie looked around her house, realizing for the first time the precariousness of her situation. Gary could do so much damage if he knew she'd left with Sam. And she was afraid he would. She blew out a breath of frustration as she gathered the paintings and dug around the back of the table for one of her portfolios to transport them in.

"This the chair?" Sam asked.

"Isn't it hideous?"

"It's . . . big."

"Takes up half the room, doesn't it? This Pete character sits there all day, no shirt, no shoes, watching *my* television and complaining about how small the screen is. I wish you could see this guy." Annie shook her head. "No, on second thought, be glad you don't have to."

"If I did, I'd make him sorry he met me."

Annie smiled and laid her hand on his arm.

Sam's face reddened, but he beamed. "You ready to go?"

He did indeed have extra rooms.

"I bought this place years ago," he explained as they walked through the attached garage and small hallway to the kitchen. "Thinking that maybe we'd live up here for the summer and take our winters back in Georgia. But, Nancy wouldn't hear of it."

"It's beautiful," Annie said. Though not opulent like the DeChristopher home, this house also had room to spare. But while their home boasted knick-knacks galore, Sam's could be considered utilitarian. A flowery sofa took up the back wall of the family room, a matching loveseat sat at an angle, opposite. The sofa was flanked by two pink wing chairs and the three seats faced a television and VCR on a shaky-looking stand.

"I didn't pick the fabric," Sam said, indicating the sofa. "Nancy got tired of it in our Georgia house, so we had it shipped here. Said she was sick of all the bright colors."

Annie's gaze swept over the kitchen as Sam moved toward the sink. "I'm sorry," he said. "I haven't done dishes in a few days . . ."

From the look of it, he hadn't done dishes in longer than just a few days. Filled with coffee mugs, drinking glasses, and crusted plates, the sink overflowed with proof that no maid had been hired for this house. The surrounding counter, as it rounded into a peninsula toward the eating area, was covered with stacks of old mail, some opened, some not. Sam's ever-present white dress shirts draped the backs of all four wooden kitchen chairs. Two or three shirts each.

"Sam . . ."

"And I've been meaning to get to the cleaners," he said, grabbing at the shirts and bunching them into his arms. "Let me clear this up for you to sit. I'm so sorry. This place is a wreck."

"Sam."

He stopped, his arms full, his face pink with embarrassment. "Yeah?"

"You live here, right?"

He shrugged the affirmative.

"So, stop worrying. Homes are supposed to be comfortable. And this is . . ." Annie gave a contented sigh, taking in the mess, the lovely imperfection of it all, "very comfortable."

Chapter Fourteen

Gary sat on a tall stool, his elbows propped on the shiny bar top, massaging his eyes. *Where the hell was Pete?* The old coot to his left, Emil, made no attempt to stifle a deep belch, causing rancid alcohol-laden air to waft up between them. No matter what time Gary came into the bar, this guy was here, in the same spot, in the same position, his elbows propped on the bar, a cigarette smoldering between his age-spotted fingers. He hardly spoke, but when he did, it was so slurred and nonsensical that Gary usually ignored him. Right now he was making some sort of low humming sound, like a motor left idling, as he stared, unseeing, across the bar toward the mirrored back wall.

The bartender and another customer stood watching an overhead television at the far end of the counter. They shouted the same expletive in unison as the Cubs blew a double play in the tenth inning. Gary toyed with his empty beer glass, rolling the base of it in circles, making patterns of wet on the countertop. He glanced to his right, seeing the easy camaraderie between the two men as they leaned inward from opposite sides of the bar. The guy couldn't be older than thirty, wearing suit pants and a tie, and the comfortable air of a successful businessman taking an afternoon off. Al the bartender was a grizzled older fellow. At the commercial he shifted from leaning on one massive arm to folding both on the bar in front of him to talk baseball.

"Hey," Gary said, getting his attention by lifting his beer glass, "how about you set me up again, wouldja?"

Pushing himself from the bar with reluctance, Al sauntered over, a bright red dishtowel slung over one shoulder. "You ain't paid for the first one."

"Yeah. Hang on." Gary dug into his back pocket, slapped a five on the bar. "Okay?"

The bartender nodded, grabbing the money and making change before taking Gary's glass to the tap. "Don't forget the other transaction we been talking about, either."

"Yeah, I remember," Gary said, looking toward the bathrooms where the public phones hung. Sliding off the stool, he began making his way to them when the door opened. Turning, he squinted as the bright light shot through the open door.

"Hey, Gare," Pete's voice clanged, disturbing the lonely quiet of the room, "Wow, sure is dark in here."

"Where have you been?"

"Well . . ." Pete said, drawing out the word as he waved hello to Al. He licked his lips. "We got time for a brewski?"

"Yeah, but we gotta make it quick," Gary said, gesturing toward the booths along the far wall.

Pete ambled over and sat down. "What happened to you?"

"Don't ask," Gary said. He ran a hand through his tea-sticky hair and pushed a tall glass of beer across the table as he settled himself. "We don't have a ton of time, and I got a plan we need to work out."

"You got a plan?" Pete leaned back against the dark wooden booth and laughed out loud. His teeth were straight and fake-looking and although Gary'd asked him repeatedly, he swore they weren't dentures. But the pulled-in and drawn look of his jaw made Gary suspect otherwise. "Is it anything like the last one, Gary? Where you were gonna make us both rich because nobody at your company ever counted inventory? And you figured nobody was gonna miss a couple of pallets of laptops?" He laughed with his mouth open and his tongue hanging out, making little sucky noises as he breathed. "I'm just glad it was you got caught and not me. Don't think I'd get away without doin' some time this time."

Gary's foot fidgeted against the center table leg. He kept his eyes on the beer quivering in his glass until Pete stopped laughing. "Listen," he said, raising his eyes, suddenly still, "you want in, or not?"

Pete rolled his head from side to side, bunching up his face, as though uncomfortable answering. "Well . . ." he said. He scratched his face and sighed. "I dunno, what is it?"

Gary wished he could handle this on his own. Not involve Pete at all. The guy was stupid, no question. Fortunately the role he would play was small. "Where are the copies?"

"Oh. Yeah."

"You didn't forget to make them, did you?"

Pete pushed his dark-framed glasses up his nose with the point of his index finger. "No," he said, stretching out the word and leaving his mouth hanging open, effecting an air of indignation. "Got 'em right here."

When Pete pulled the original clippings

from his back pocket and smoothed them out on the table, Gary rubbed his forehead in frustration. "I told you to make copies," he said in a tight voice.

"I did." He looked down. "Oh." Digging into another pocket, Pete pulled out the duplicates. Each of the four white sheets held an off-center article and the unmistakable picture of Pete's thumb holding the corner. From being held in Pete's pockets the pages, folded in quarters, were slightly damp from a combination of sweat and humidity. Gary glared across the table as he smoothed them out.

"You were supposed to put the originals back on the coffee table. And now that they're all folded up, she's gonna know someone was looking at them."

"Hey, sorry, okay? I had some problems, y'know. The machine at the gas station wasn't working, so I had to hoof it all the way down to the library, but then, the one there . . ."

"I don't care." Gary's foot started fidgeting again as he tapped the papers. "Okay, here's what we'll do. Before we get going, we'll take the originals back to the house, maybe Annie won't notice they're missing. We'll take these . . ." Gary pulled a pen from his back pocket and started making notes on the copies, "and hide them somewhere safe, once we get all the details down. We don't want to have these on us, just in case." He looked up into Pete's slack, uncomprehending face. "Got it?"

Pete shrugged and nodded.

Gary took a deep breath then looked around. He leaned forward, and in a hushed whisper, began to explain.

"I'm hot," Pete said for the fourth time. He ran a finger along the white collar of his shirt and loosened his tie.

Gary pulled Annie's Escort up and parked it half a block away from the DeChristopher home. He looked up at the darkening sky as he got out of the car, reaching back in for a stack of small papers he'd left in there. "Fix your tie," he said, in a sharp whisper to Pete.

"Awww," Pete got out of the car shaking his head, but he complied. "You're not going to make me wear the suit coat too, are you?"

Gary lifted his own suit coat from the back of the driver's seat and thrust his arms in with an angry look across the top of the car. "Did you ever see any of those Jehovah Witnesses walking around *without* a suit coat?"

"No, but . . ." Pete lifted his chin up as though his collar was too tight.

"But nothing, you idiot. How else are we supposed to walk around in a neighborhood like this without looking suspicious?" Gary reached into the back seat to pull out a portfolio he'd borrowed from Annie's supply. It looked enough like a thin briefcase to go with their cover story. "Grab those Bibles, okay? And take a stack of these papers. Make it look like something you'd be passing out."

"But these are coupons for pizza. Shouldn't they say something . . . holy?"

"You're stupid, you know that? We're not passing anything out. We're just looking like we will. And believe me, no one's going to ask for one. If anybody comes near us, they'll be relieved when we don't talk to them."

"Seems kinda dumb."

Gary ignored him, shut the door, and walked around to Pete's side. Reaching in, he shuffled through the glove compartment till he came up with the DeChristophers' key. "And this, Petey, is our ticket to fortune. Here." He tossed the car keys over to Pete. "When we go, we *go*. I'll take the drawing, you drive."

"Wish the car had air-conditioning."

"When we're done with this, buddy, we're gonna be able to buy all three of us new cars. And they'll all have air-conditioning."

Stars were beginning to peek out in the deep blue purple of the sky. Gary tried several different ways to hold the Bible and the portfolio as they walked, none of which felt right. He settled on carrying it down by his side, the portfolio on the other. Pete held his up near his chest as he took springy steps. Gary reached over and turned Pete's Bible right side up, telling him to slow down, to stroll. "And if anyone here asks us anything, just open up the book and make it look like you're gonna start reading aloud. That'll chase them off."

Pete shrugged.

Gary glanced at him but said nothing. He didn't believe they'd encounter anyone. This neighborhood was quiet during the day, quiet at night. A couple of homes had lights on out front, and one car went by as they made their way to the home. Otherwise the street was silent.

"How are you gonna sell this thing, Gare? Ain't it gonna be hard to get rid of?"

"Nope," Gary said. "I got a contact.

Somebody who deals with stuff this big all the time. I figure the hardest part is tonight — getting it."

"You got the key, and you got the alarm code?"

"Yep."

"That don't sound so hard."

Gary shrugged, keeping his eyes open for movement nearby. Nothing. They were just about there. The house took his breath away, again. Whoever these DeChristophers were, they deserved to get robbed. Wasn't fair for all the money to be spread around so few people. For some people to have houses like this while other folks got evicted.

The best part about the plan, though, was that he was stealing from a thief. That meant no cops, no reports. Once the drawing was in his hands, the money would follow.

Walking up the steps, Gary pulled out the house key. "I'm thinking maybe the best idea is to take the drawing, then call these guys and get them to pay us to get it back. Maybe we don't make ten million, maybe we make two or three. But," he grinned, "that'd be enough for me."

Getting inside had been as easy as Gary had made it sound. What a spread these people had. And such idiots, to leave so many expensive things lying around, unguarded. Pete's mouth hung open as he watched Gary input the code for the alarm. They'd entered noiselessly, the front door swinging open without a sound.

Gary indicated with his eyes that Pete shouldn't move, and so he stood in the foyer, and thought about how some people pronounce it *foy-ay* and how this is one of the places that could get away with fancy sounding words like that. Even in the dark he could see that the tables in the living room were covered with neat little doohickeys. Pete knew he could sell any one of them on the street for more than just a couple of bucks. He began to edge toward them when Gary's whisper stopped him cold.

"Hey," he said, "upstairs."

"Why we whispering if nobody's home?"

"I just feel better being quiet, okay?"

"Didnya say they were gonna be out all night at some fancy shmancy dinner?"

"Just shut up."

They crept up the stairs, holding the handrail and keeping both eyes and ears open for the sound of the family coming home. Other than house noises, a gentle hum from the kitchen refrigerator, the

267

solid ticking of the grandfather clock in the hall, the house was silent. And dark. Once their eyes had become accustomed to the dimness, they moved a bit faster. Moonlight shone in from the windows that faced the front of the house and the blue light was enough for them to navigate.

Pete followed Gary reluctantly, wanting to stop and look around. Pick up a few things, if truth be told. But Gary seemed focused, more than Pete had ever seen him before. Slowing in front of the master bedroom, Pete looked in, open-mouthed. Beyond the king-size bed was a tall chest that no doubt held the wife's jewelry. Probably a lot. Probably real stuff, too. From this distance, the chest didn't look to be locked. Too bad, it would have been a fun one to pop.

Pete felt the fire in Gary's eyes, urging him forward.

All thoughts of lifting trinkets from the bedrooms rushed out of Pete's mind when he saw the stash inside the den. Not only were there several cases with antique-y, expensive-looking jewelry, but also small, easily transportable works of art that appeared to be made out of solid gold. On the table next to him was an array of jewel-encrusted egg-shaped goodies. He slipped one into his pocket when Gary wasn't looking, then reached back for more. He grinned. It was almost too easy. With the sharp edges of the gems poking through the light fabric of his pockets every time he shifted, Pete moved with ginger eagerness. As long as he kept his suit coat on, Gary probably wouldn't notice the bulges. He sidled up to his friend, trying to look innocent.

"It's over here," Gary said, moving further into the room.

Pete watched as Gary felt his way, his hesitating fingertips touching the furniture only where necessary. They should have picked up latex gloves on the way, but Gary had refused to take the time, saying he was determined to get this job finished fast, and just told Pete to be careful not to touch anything.

Gary stopped at an easel set on an angle in the corner. On the shelves above it were about a dozen old gold coins in frames. Pete glanced at the picture and squinted his eyes. It didn't look like much, but the room was dark. He bent at the waist to bring his face closer and saw that it was the same drawing of a bunch of naked women washing themselves that they'd seen in those newspaper clippings.

Gary's bright white teeth shone in the moonlight as he grinned. "This is it, buddy! We are home free!"

Pete pointed to the woman depicted on the far left of the drawing. "That one looks like she's scratching her ass!" He let out a bark of laughter, then tried to suck it in, but snorted instead.

Gary's eyes widened in alarm. He put down his Bible and picked up the drawing, muttering about Pete's idiocy, stooping to unzip Annie's portfolio. Pete saw that his friend's hands were shaking and he felt kind of bad. "C'mon Gare. Nobody's here . . ."

But Gary looked old all of a sudden. Kneeling on the floor, taking care to place the drawing safely in the side pocket, he looked up at Pete. His face had lines Pete hadn't seen on his friend before. "You ain't worried, are you, Gare?"

"What do you think? Of course I'm worried. There's still something else I need to do. This is where you come in. Over there, see that filing cabinet?"

Pete nodded.

"This art collector jerk is representing Annie in the divorce. I have no idea what kind of dirt they have on me, but I want to make things difficult for them. I want what's in there. How bad does that lock look to you?"

Pete licked his lips, tossing his Bible on the desk. "Piece a cake."

"Then go, boy. Get that sucker open."

Pulling a few key tools from his back pocket, Pete walked over to the filing cabinet and assessed the lock again. Now he understood why Gary wanted him to come along.

"You sure you want me spend time on this, Gare? It's gonna take a few minutes."

Gary stared at him. The moonlight spilled in, coloring half his face blue with cool light, leaving the other half in shadow, but caught the glitter of anger in his eyes. "I could have done this myself if all I wanted was the picture. The only reason you're in on this is for that lock, so quit talking and get moving."

Pete set to work without arguing again. Breaking and entering carried hefty prison time for guys like himself with convictions on their records, but Gary had said he'd make this heist worthwhile. The sharp edges scratching against his upper thighs reminded him that he'd already made this night profitable. He just hoped the rest of this worked out like they thought. Gary might be good at coming up with plans, but he stunk at the really important stuff, details like remembering to bring gloves, or how to find a buyer for some ugly but priceless drawing. The guy mighta been book smart in school, but he had no street smarts. And he couldn't pick a lock to save his skin.

It would have gone a lot faster if Pete didn't have to keep worrying about leaving prints. He wished for the latex gloves again as he wiped the side of the cabinet with his sleeve. Gary hissed in the background, telling him not to worry, reminding him that these guys wouldn't be able to report a burglary on an item they themselves had stolen. Pete swore under his breath. He figured that folks who lived in places like this were probably real well-connected. If he left even one print, they'd be screwed. He knew it.

Actors made it look so easy in the movies, Pete thought. He wiped his forehead with the sleeve of his right arm, his left hand holding the two metallic picks steady. Licking his lips, he shut his eyes and turned his left ear toward the lock. A combination of sound and feel usually let him know when he was close. He whispered, "Don't they got air-conditioning in this place?"

Gary stood at the room's window, shifting from side to side, alternating views up and down the street. "It's not that hot in here. It's just your nerves. Shut up and keep working."

Easy for him to say, standing there with his arms wrapped around the black case like a lover. His part was over. Sweat dripped into Pete's eyes, the saltiness stung. He shook his head like a wet dog, causing the tools to slip from his hands.

"Shit!"

"What's taking you so long? I thought you said it'd be a piece of cake."

"Yeah well, I was wrong, okay? So sue me. This guy got himself some heavy duty lock here. I need a coupla more minutes."

Gary rubbed his eyes, took a deep breath and returned to staring out the window.

Pete repositioned his tools, moving closer in, feeling his way more than seeing it. A little pressure, a couple of clicks. His breathing came faster as he sensed being almost there. He pressed his hip against the side of the cabinet and twisted his left hand ever so slightly.

With a metallic twang, the lock popped.

"Ta da!" Pete said, stepping back, with an expansive lift of his arms.

Gary rushed over, pulling at the top drawer.

"Watch it, you're gonna leave prints."

"Screw that," he said. "This is paper, they're not gonna get much off of this."

Pete stepped back, shaking his head. This guy didn't know anything. Paper was like one of the best surfaces to get a print from.

"Do you think it's under her maiden name, or under Randall?" Gary asked, talking to himself.

"I dunno," Pete said, moving back toward the wall of shelves, looking for a trinket, small, expensive, to pick up.

"Ho! Would you look at this?"

Pete turned.

"He's got a whole file on the crazy drawing here. Look," Gary flipped open a manila file folder and scanned the pages. "Man! Are we in business or what?"

"Hurry up, Gare, I'm startin' to get nervous."

"Yeah," he said, stuffing the file into the portfolio before digging back through the drawer. When he slammed it shut, Pete headed for the door. "Not so fast," he said. "Haven't found what I'm looking for, yet." Gary pulled out the second drawer, tilting his head to the side to read the file folder titles. "These are all according to date, like from the past coupla years." He pulled one out. "Nothing recent."

"Gare, he probably keeps that stuff at his office at work, dontcha think? I'm thinkin' that this is just his like, hobby or something."

Gary's shoulders slumped. He swore. "I didn't think about that. I just thought . . ." He made a noise of frustration. Slamming the second drawer shut, he reached for the third.

"Gary. We got the picture, right? Let's get outta here."

"Two more drawers. I'll make it quick."

"It ain't here. You know it."

"Watch the window. I'll be done in a minute."

Pete moved to the window but didn't look out. He watched Gary flip through the files, examining each one quickly, but thoroughly, throwing a couple into the portfolio as something caught his interest. This didn't feel good. They'd had it easy so far and Pete just knew they were pushing their luck. Gary didn't have good instincts for these kind of jobs.

Gary stood up, kicked the last drawer shut. He scowled at Pete. "Let's go."

With a sigh of relief, Pete left his window

post and they walked down the stairs, less quietly than they'd come up, their shoes making solid pounds on the carpeted steps as they ran down, eager to leave.

"Hang on to this a minute," Gary said, handing the portfolio to Pete. He moved to the alarm panel and began to input the code when they heard the hum of the garage door, opening.

"Gare!"

"Hold on," Gary said, gritting his teeth, moving his fingers to hit the proper code. "Shit."

"I ain't waitin'." Pete reached for the door handle.

"Don't touch it." Gary hissed. Pete's fingers made contact with the ornate metallic knob. Gary hit "clear," then began again. The garage door noise had stopped. They heard the faint slam of a car door.

Gary blinked a couple of times, touched his forehead, then moved to input the code. As if in slow motion, he hit one pad, paused, then bit his lip, his hands shaking. In that instant Pete knew that Gary had forgotten the sequence.

The garage door motor sounded again. Closing. A door opened nearby. Very nearby.

Pete heard a monosyllabic grunt, followed by "Hey!"

The enormous shadow moved like lightning, but even as Pete took in the man's massiveness, frozen with fear being caught here, realization dawned. In the darkness, with only a sliver of light shooting through the nearby window, the big guy couldn't see him. But he obviously saw Gary.

Pete shrunk further back toward the wall, keeping as close to the door as possible. The nearby window illuminated Gary, standing stone-like, caught with his fingers poised over the keypad, staring at the approaching giant.

The big guy raced forward. In a split-second, Pete knew he would be seen. He'd have to move quick. Even as he thought this, he saw the guy reach to his right side and pull out a gun, moving to block Gary's path. But it gave Pete his chance.

He wrapped his fingers around the door-knob and pulled.

"No!"

Gary's whispered scream almost stopped him, but he tore out of the house at a flat run.

A second later he heard the shot. But he didn't stop running.

Chapter Fifteen

Richard DeChristopher leaned back, reaching to place his arm around the curved wooden frame of his wife's banquet chair. He watched as tuxedoed waiters cleared the table, taking the half-finished desserts away, refilling coffee cups, never making eye contact with the diners. When they pulled out the small metallic wands and scraped away crumbs from the white linen tablecloth, Richard smiled. Their round table, placed front and center near the stage, the deference of the wait staff, and even that of his fellow diners, pleased him.

Gina chatted with the woman to her left, Kamila Stewart, the wife of the master of ceremonies. Though his own wife's clothes were expensive, and Richard knew just how expensive they were, she never managed to look put together like so many of the other women did. It had to be the extra weight she carried. Since having the boys, Gina's figure went from lissome to paunchy. The gold dress she wore today, made of some kind of sparkly stretchy fabric, would have looked much better on a woman three sizes smaller.

That painter, Anne Callaghan, now she had a nice little shape. Curvy but slim, petite all around. Richard's eyes roved Gina's body as he pictured Anne next to him instead. The dress color was wrong. Anne would look better in blue. Royal blue, backless. Gina caught him looking, smiled up at him, and winked. He squeezed her shoulder in return. Unfortunately, Anne was a client and Richard made it a point never to get involved with his clients. Still, she was a sweet thing. And even better, the girl had class.

He wished Gina had a bit more class. When he'd suggested she take some college courses, thinking that expanding her horizons, she'd evolve somehow, she'd laughed in his face, reminding him that she'd barely made it through high school. There were times he cringed, knowing that his wife would accompany him to dinners and occasions such as this. Served him right for marrying so young. But she'd been a tempting little thing back then, with strict parents. And he'd been foolish enough to pop the question before he'd had a chance to test the merchandise.

Not that it mattered anymore. For reasons that baffled him, Gina always managed to hold her own at these doings. People gravitated to her; they liked her earthy, friendly personality. He remained grateful for that. Gina kept him entertained when he stayed home, and he couldn't complain about her performance in the bedroom. Always willing to try things he suggested, she never once asked where the ideas came from. Good girl.

Tonight turned out as perfectly as he'd planned. Immediately following his acceptance speech for the Bar Association Citizenship Award, the ceremonies would be complete and the attendees free to mill about. After pressing the flesh with all the saps who'd nominated him for this award, he'd be able to make his way over to see the real reason he was in such a good mood.

It hadn't been difficult to wrangle an invitation, even on such short notice, for Charles Bernard. Wealthy, handsome, famous, he'd made the cover of *Newsweek* once, *People*, twice. Not only a self-made man, his personality loomed bigger than his bank account. The type of fellow who whisked supermodels and entertainers to his yacht, his chalet, his penthouse, he found ways to talk about it without being obvious. His name opened doors, inspired hushed conversations. When Richard called to see if table space could be made available, the folks in charge bent over backward to assure him that everything would be perfect.

Richard magnanimously suggested seating Bernard at a different table than his own. That too, was perfect. Had they been placed together, they'd be limited to chat about unimportant drivel at the dinner table, conscious of eager ears. And when the time came to visit, to mingle, they'd be expected to move about the room, to interact with those who'd paid for the opportunity to hobnob with the upper class. Noblesse oblige.

Now, after dinner, after the required speeches, it would be only natural for Richard and Charles to seek each other out, to be seen talking, privately, even for an extended period of time. Then the deal could be finalized.

Charles Bernard came in shortly before dinner began, moving into the ballroom, shaking hands, smiling. Rugged and handsome, the man in his late fifties commanded attention. Richard watched him work his magic. A middle-aged woman gazed up in awe as Charles bent forward to listen to whatever it was she said. His eyes never left her face as she spoke, and even from this distance Richard could see the red blush creeping up from her neck. A dark curl from his full head of hair spilled forward, just as he smiled at her, laughing in a self-deprecating way at a flattering remark, no doubt. The blend of rakishness and sincerity he exuded, coupled with his warmth — he took the woman's hands in both of his and leaned forward to kiss her on the cheek, still smiling — gave credit to every juicy word written about the man.

Richard caught his eye and he nodded, taking his attention away, ever so briefly from another woman, waiting her turn to share a moment in his presence.

All through dinner, Richard replayed their earlier phone conversation in his mind. Charles appeared agreeable to the five-million-dollar price. For one drawing. Setting his coffee cup down with a clink, he grinned. Once the particulars were arranged, all he'd have to do was collect. Maybe even tonight. Richard could just about taste it. How sweet. How wonderfully ironic. Not a soul in this place suspected, even for a moment, that he, Richard DeChristopher, model citizen, champion of justice, had masterminded the scheme that had been front page news for the past two weeks.

Gina said something.

"What, dear?" Richard leaned forward, his face impassive.

"I asked if you were nervous. They're gonna be introducing you soon."

He patted his wife's shoulder, leaning back as Wayne Stewart, the master of ceremonies, left their table to take the podium. "No," he smiled at her, then at the rest of the table, listening in. Their eyes were on him, the rapt attention giving him a feeling of power. The men's faces wore a mixture of respect and envy while their women glanced between him and Gina as if to gauge their relationship by their interplay. He broadened his grin. "Should I be?"

Gina flipped her hands up in mock exasperation, looking around at the table, too. "He's not nervous. Can ya believe it? I'd be shakin' in my boots if I hadta make a speech in fronna all these people."

Polite chuckles, then all eyes turned to Wayne, who'd cleared his throat into the microphone, causing a ripple of silence to drift over the ballroom. Richard tilted his head and stretched his chin in an effort to loosen the bow tie's grasp around his neck.

His many philanthropic efforts were being listed, and he nodded acknowledgment as those around him leaned forward to touch his arm or whisper congratulations. Across the room, Charles looked over, with what could have been a smirk on his face.

Wayne Stewart drew out his words as he neared the end of his introduction. "And so without any further delay, let us extend a welcome to our Guest of Honor tonight, Our Bar Association Citizen of the Year . . . Richard DeChristopher."

Having perfected over the years a self-effacing air, Richard moved toward the podium affecting a shy smile. Every person stood, applauding as he grasped either side of the podium with his large hands. The guests, a sea of colored gowns and black tuxedos, sent him high-voltage smiles as they clapped so enthusiastically that he could see the water in a nearby glass tremble. He blinked and nodded slowly, to his left, then his right, then center, waiting for the din to die down.

"Thank you," he began, lowering his head to the microphone's height. Straightening, he adjusted it upward, to his level. "Thank you," he said again, "for that warm welcome."

He waited as the guests slowly took their

seats, almost in a wave, starting from the very front and dropping backward. This moment epitomized the life he'd created. As the group quieted, his heart beat faster. Honored, respected, revered. And still able to create lucrative business arrangements that kept his family comfortable and his passion for collecting alive. Keeping his eyes on the crowd, his fingers reached into his inner pocket, pulling prepared note-cards out in a fluid movement. Tapping the stack to straighten the edges, he laid them down, centered, against the tiny ledge, and gripped the edges of the stand again. The warmth of the lights above didn't make him feel uncomfortable; rather they reminded him that he stood center stage, that every awe-struck or envious eye was upon him. An almost out-of-body feeling came over him. He could see him-self poised, assured, ready to accept this honor with grace. He took a deep breath when the crowd quieted.

"When I was informed of my nomina-tion for this prestigious . . ."

Beep. Beep. Beep.

The pager's chirp echoed through the room, its high-pitched alarm deafening in the silence.

His right hand flew to his side, silencing

the device as he stopped mid-sentence. In that split second all possible scenarios ran through his mind as he cursed himself for forgetting to switch it to vibrate instead of chime. The kids were at his mother-in-law's. She had Gina's pager number, not his. Everyone from his place of business was here. Charles Bernard was here. No one else should be calling him, unless . . . Momentarily rattled, he smiled at the audience and said, "Excuse me," while his fingers made deft motions at his side to bring up the number on the screen. Turning as though to shut it off, he took the opportunity to glance down at the number. Timothy's cell phone.

The interruption lasted barely two seconds, yet felt like an eternity under the steady gaze of the spectators. Returning to his speech, he held out his hands in a helpless gesture. "Technology today," he said with a chuckle, "can't get away from it, can we?"

He waited for the murmurs of understanding to quiet before reaching to caress the tall crystal prism-shaped award next to him.

"And yet technology has been a boon, hasn't it? Helping us in so many ways to do good for our fellow man." Giving the trophy an affectionate tap, he continued, "In my experience . . ."

They were on their feet again, clapping, cheering.

His speech finished, Richard forced himself to smile, his left hand already gripped around the cell phone in his jacket pocket. Timothy knew better than to page him for something frivolous. It took all his willpower to stand on the dais, to receive the accolades rather than rush into the vestibule and make the call.

Wayne Stewart wore a puzzled look as he applauded. They'd discussed Richard's acceptance speech at length. Worked together to prepare the notecards for a fifteen-minute speech. Richard had spoken less than ten.

"What happened?" Wayne asked in a low voice, the first to move forward, clasping both Richard's hands in his.

Richard noted that the man's smile never wavered. He returned it, leaning in to whisper in Wayne's ear. "Nerves."

The master of ceremonies cocked an eyebrow, then moved backward into the group, allowing others to step forward.

Richard shook hands, surreptitiously making his way to the far doors. Charles

Bernard stood at the fringe of the crowd, waiting. With a small hand gesture, Richard let him know that he'd be right back.

God damn hangers-on, Richard thought, attempting a graceful exit. "Thank you," he said to an older fellow with cold wrinkled hands who'd just spoken to him. "I have been quite impressed with the soup kitchen project."

"Soup kitchen? I said, 'Stadium renovation.' "

Inching sideways, Richard grimaced at his mistake, "Beg your pardon, but I need to see someone. . . ."

Furrowing his brow, the older man stepped aside and muttered to himself. Richard spied his assistant, Patty. He gestured her over, telling her to take down the old guy's phone number so he could get back to him about the stadium. You never knew how much power some of these elderly folks could wield.

Pushing open the double doors with both hands, Richard felt better as the fresher, cooler air from the less-crowded hall met him, causing a breeze on his face. The press of the hot bodies, their eager warm breaths mingling as they all tried to come over to make his acquaintance caused droplets of perspiration to form on his face, under his arms, and around his waist. Richard prided himself on maintaining his composure, but the short hair framing his forehead began to curl from the sweat, a sure sign of his uneasiness.

Stragglers in the entryway, nursing their watered-down cocktails, looked up at his entrance, some moving forward, then returning to muted conversations as Richard strode through to the outside doors and the parking lot beyond.

Slamming the glass door open with his right hand, his left pulled the phone up and flipped it open in a swift, angry gesture. He looked around to ensure he was alone as he hit the speed dial command.

Timothy answered before the ring registered on Richard's phone.

"Got a problem," he said.

"Yeah. So I gathered. What is it?"

"You had a coupla visitors," Timothy drew out the last word in emphasis. "One of 'em is still here. The other one left early. Took off with the ladies."

Richard, about to lean his back end against a nearby pillar, stopped and straightened as he processed the information. Timothy stayed silent. Richard cleared his throat. "Who?"

"Don't know, boss. Never seen this guy before. And the other one, I didn't get a good look at."

Pacing, rubbing his fingers against his left temple, Richard fought the urge to slam the phone to the ground. "How?"

Gina pushed open the glass door and stood with her hand on her left hip. "There you are," she said, the shrill of her voice loud in the quiet night. "What was that in there anyway?"

"Gina, not now."

"Whaddya mean not now? You come off the stage and don't even give your wife the time of day? What's up with that?"

Richard's index finger flipped up. "Gina," he said, not bothering to mask the anger in his voice, "I said, 'not now.' Now get your fat ass back in there and stall for me. Do you understand?"

Gina's chin came up in defiance, but her hand dropped to her side. "Fine," she said, shrugging one shoulder, staring at him, "but you need to start remembering what's important." She turned with a flounce.

Richard massaged his eyes; he knew very well what was important. His head pounded with questions, with rage. In the distance he heard fire sirens racing to some other emergency, their eerie noises compounding the pain in his brain. "The visitor you've still got there," he said, resuming his conversation with Timothy, his voice tight, "see if he'll tell us who he's working for." Could he have been set up? Only Charles Bernard knew he had the drawing. Knew it as of this afternoon, and knew he'd be here tonight.

The sirens' wails obscured Timothy's answer.

Bernard came out the front doors just then. "Problem?"

"Take care of things. I'll be there when I can," Richard said, as he snapped the phone shut. He looked at Bernard, taking him in from head to toe. "No, not at all," he said, pasting a smile on his face. "Why ever would you think so?"

Chapter Sixteen

She'd taken forever to fall asleep last night. Annie thought about that as she walked softly down the stairs in the morning, determined not to wake him. Being in the same house with Sam, knowing he was there, had been . . . difficult. While there was a certain pleasant tension knowing that he was in his bed not thirty steps away, that pleasant tension was exactly what kept sleep at bay. She'd had the foresight to pack an alarm clock and she'd watched the green numbers glow, changing ever so slowly as the night stretched into morning.

A tiny part of her brain wondered, as she watched the digits change, if Sam would make some overture. She tossed and turned, knowing in her heart that he would not. She was vulnerable right now; they both knew it. There was no way Sam would take advantage of that. He was too wonderful of a guy. Too decent.

And yet, part of her felt a twinge of disappointment. She'd played so many different scenarios in her mind, trying to decide how they would get together, but she knew that when he'd used the word "friends" he might have meant just that. Only that.

"How did you sleep?"

Surprised to see Sam up so early, Annie gave a start. Wearing a black university T-shirt and blue jeans, he sat at the kitchen table, reading the newspaper, holding a mug of coffee in his right hand. She could see the steam twisting upward and caught the smell of the brew as she moved farther into the kitchen. With his left ankle supported by his right knee, and a slow smile spreading across his face, he came across as the picture of relaxation. "It's still dark out," she said. "What are you doing up at this hour?"

"Same thing you are. Trying to be the first one up."

She noticed that his combed-back hair was wet. "I didn't hear your shower."

"I heard yours. You want some coffee?"

She gave a self-conscious smile. "I got it," she said, moving to the center of the kitchen's work area. The dishwasher hummed. All the dirty dishes from the night before were gone. The counter sparkled. Guessing, she opened the cabinet above the coffee maker and found several mugs. Choosing one, she poured herself a cup and opened the refrigerator.

"You have cream," she said, pulling out a container of half and half.

"Uh huh, you want milk instead?"

"No, not at all," Annie said, "it's just that no one else usually keeps cream at home except me."

"Got used to it at the restaurant," he said with a shrug. "So I make sure I keep some at home now too."

As Annie turned, she glanced out the window over the sink. It was early, very early, not even six o'clock. The skies were dark, but the promise of sunlight in the eastern clouds made her smile. The warm overhead lights of the room and the darkness outside gave the home a coziness she hadn't anticipated. Sam had his back to her, and she took a moment to watch him.

What was it about him that she found so attractive? He was handsome, sure, but not in the classic sense. He probably wouldn't ever be asked to be a male model, nor the next James Bond, but something about him, his wonderful smile, his gorgeous eyes, something did it for her. When they were together she couldn't keep from trying to memorize his face. He had tiny wrinkles near his eyes and around his mouth that deepened when he looked at her, little lines that let her know this was a face that liked to smile.

Sam, sitting at the head of the table, folded his newspaper and turned to see Annie watching him.

Startled, she moved toward the coffee pot, "Want me to warm you up?" then nearly bit her tongue, worried at how her words sounded.

"Sure," he said, draining his mug before she refilled it. If he noticed her slipup, he was too much of a gentleman to react. "Thanks."

Annie took a seat, holding her mug in both hands. Sam took a drink from his. They looked at each other.

"Well," Annie said, not knowing what to say. For half a moment she imagined what it would be like to be with Sam, to share his life. In this quiet morning atmosphere, she could almost pretend it was real. She smiled, trying to banish the thoughts, worried that they'd somehow broadcast themselves on her face. He was a treasure. One that she wanted to keep forever.

Sam sat back. "The mural's really shaping up."

"You think so?"

"I had four people ask for your card this week alone."

"Really?" Annie's voice rose in excitement. She'd heard from two potential clients since the mural had begun, but so far no definite jobs.

"Four. And a lot more people admiring it, asking who the artist is." Sam got up and walked into the little alcove that jutted outward from the dining area of the kitchen. Two windows flanked the back door. He twisted the mini-blinds open and stood there, staring outward for a moment. He pointed downward, "Hey, looks like my bunny's back."

Annie stood up and craned her neck to see a small brown rabbit with a white puff on his backside sitting on Sam's patio, facing away from the sunrise. She moved for a closer look, standing right in front of Sam, near enough to feel warmth emanating from his body. Sleeping next to him would probably be like sleeping next to a furnace.

Annie shook her head. She shouldn't be thinking things like that.

"What?" he asked.

She turned. He was right there. Inches away. Though caught a bit off guard by how close their faces were, she couldn't help but think how easy it would be to reach up and kiss him right now. She shook her head again. "Nothing." But she had a peculiar feeling that he'd read her mind.

Sam nodded, turning away from the window, but his hand grazed the small of her back, just for a second, sending a shiver up her spine. "I've got to meet with some produce vendors this morning before I go in. Will you be okay here by yourself?"

Annie nodded, wishing he'd stay. She cleared her throat. "I just want to thank you again, Sam."

He brushed her thanks off with a gesture, "My pleasure." Rinsing his coffee cup, he headed to the door. "Make yourself at home. I'll call later to check in, okay?"

She waited in the front window till his car pulled away, trying not to let him see that she was watching. The house was completely, utterly silent. It was as if its spirit had gone when Sam left.

Annie headed back into the kitchen. The dishwasher had finished its cycle, so she opened it to dry the glassware and put it away. When she'd finished, it was still before seven. She glanced over at the phone. She didn't want to call Uncle Lou too early. She'd planned to call him last night, but had forgotten and wanted to let him know where she was, in case he'd tried to reach her.

Make yourself at home, Sam had said. Annie walked upstairs to the bedroom farthest from Sam's. Though there were beds in each of the four bedrooms, he'd carried her things up to this room last night. She'd made the bed, wanting to be a tidy guest, although truth be told, she didn't always do that at home. Thinking it presumptuous to use the drawers, she'd instead folded her clothes and laid them out on top of the dresser, having taken a moment to brush the heavy dust away.

Wandering back out into the hall, she thought about this man, "her Sam" as she liked to think of him. She moved toward his room and looked in. Actually entering the room seemed to her like an invasion of privacy, so she simply stood in the doorway, wanting to know more about him, looking for clues. His bed was unmade, which made Annie smile. So, she wasn't the only one. A picture of his son stood on the dresser next to one pile of books. Another pile sat on the nightstand next to a clock radio. He must sleep on the left side of the bed. The right hand nightstand was bare. She wished she could make out some of the titles, she'd like to know what he read, but the distance from the door to the bed made it difficult.

Annie leaned in the doorjamb and thought about what it might be like to be with him. She laughed then, rubbing her hand over her abdomen. She was a pregnant woman. Pregnant with Gary's child. What would ever make her believe that Sam would find her attractive? And yet, she knew she felt something when he looked at her.

Wishful thinking, perhaps.

The phone rang four times before he answered.

"Annie!" Uncle Lou's voice came over the phone, a mixture of relief and alarm. "Thank God!"

"What's wrong?"

"I think you better come home."

Annie looked at the clock. Eight-thirty. "Why? What happened?" And how did he know she wasn't home?

The small sounds that came through the receiver led Annie to believe that Uncle Lou was rubbing his hands over his face. His raspy breathing came through with a sonorous rhythm as she imagined him gathering the courage to tell her something terrible. She felt an irrational fear, as if her house had burned down. He said, "Ah . . ." with a reluctant pull to the word. "It might be best if you just come on home. Where are you, anyway?"

"I'm at . . ." She stopped. How would it sound to tell him that she'd spent the night at Sam's house without having the chance to explain it? "I'm . . ." She needed to know why her uncle sounded so upset. "Uncle Lou. Tell me what's happened."

She heard him blow a breath out, and she sat down, knowing without knowing how she knew, that she'd need to be sitting to hear this.

"I don't know how to tell you this, honey," Uncle Lou said, his voice cracking, "Gary's dead."

Chapter Seventeen

"Here you go Mrs. Randall," the officer said.

Annie didn't really want the water, but extended her free hand to take the Styrofoam cup from the young man with a murmur of thanks. Her other arm hung tight around her backpack, and her finger traced up and down its side, rubbing over a bump in the fabric over and over. They'd called her Mrs. Randall since she'd walked in the door, despite the fact that she'd introduced herself as Annie Callaghan.

Gary was dead.

But he couldn't be. She'd just seen him. They were together yesterday and he'd been alive. How could it be? Annie couldn't make herself believe it, and yet when Uncle Lou had come to get her at Sam's house, his face wore the pained, shocked look of terrible news.

Annie's molded plastic chair wobbled when she moved. She found herself trying to sit very still, to keep the metallic legs from tapping on the tile floor of this long narrow hallway. Bricked on both sides and illuminated at either end by tall windows, she felt the warmth of the early afternoon sun as its rays sliced through the skylights above, hitting her square in the face. Other than the chair next to her, occupied by the silent young Officer Schlosser, the hall was vacant.

She held the backpack protectively to her chest, and stared into the cup of water, wondering why she was here. Soft voices from the rooms she'd been escorted through, reflected against the triangular-shaped windows, only to be absorbed by the brick, distorting their sound, rendering them incomprehensible. Too quiet. Her hand readjusted around the small white cup and she took a sip, wanting to have something to do.

When they said he'd been killed, she'd immediately assumed a car accident. But Uncle Lou had brought her home, and she'd found her car parked in front of her house, the keys dropped on her kitchen table, no note. Gary had obviously been back since she and Sam left. That put him at her house sometime after three o'clock yesterday. But there was no sign of Pete.

Uncle Lou could tell her nothing because he knew nothing. Despite connections in the world of news reporting, he'd come up empty.

But then came the visit to the morgue. Annie had never been there before, and on the drive, Uncle Lou at the wheel, she'd stared out the passenger window, barely registering the outside world as he navigated through the city to Harrison Street. Part of her, a quiet detached fraction of her mind, saw the boarded-up homes and the dirt where grass should be in front lawns and knew that under other circumstances, she'd be fearful right now. This crime-ridden area was one she took pains to avoid. And here they were, hurtling through it, just over the speed limit, without a second thought.

Once there, they were met by a man in uniform, who took her information, had Annie fill out forms and show her driver's license, and who then directed them into a waiting room, its cinder block walls painted two bland shades of beige. They sat on the plastic covered orange couch in the corner for a few minutes before a second door, near the back of the room, opened.

"Mrs. Randall?" A short, bleached-blond woman in a green jumpsuit held open the far door with her back end, motioning them in.

"Yes," Annie said, not bothering to mention that she used her maiden name. It didn't seem to matter one way or another at the moment. She and Uncle Lou got up together, the couch making a squeak as their weight lifted from the hard cushions.

She didn't want to walk through that door. Her gut knew what her mind still rebelled against. Like a reluctant child being led to the doctor's for a shot, she knew that nothing good waited down that corridor. Walking toward the technician in green, she searched for some sign of compassion. There was none. The tech, in paper booties, skooched backward, pushing the door farther into the looming corridor, one hand holding a clipboard, the other gesturing them forward.

"This way," she said, glancing up to Annie's face, not reacting at all to whatever she saw there. She seemed to be making a mental note of them, but without any interest whatsoever. Annie could feel her stomach clench. Her feet still propelled her forward, one in front of the other, but for the life of her, she couldn't figure out how she wasn't collapsing. It was unreal.

The walls down the short corridor, as well as those in the small room ahead, were painted a shade of green that matched the tech's outfit. Putrid green, Annie thought. Some mishmash of shades that would never be used for painting nature, it had a fake, unpleasant look to it, as though the color were engineered for this purpose alone.

The tech whose name, Belinda, hung from a tag on a long woven strap around her neck, stopped them at the point where the corridor widened and the room began. She gestured above her head as she looked down at the clipboard in her hand. "That's the closed-circuit television. We can send the picture by camera, so you don't have to see him in person, if you want?" She ended her statement as a question.

Annie shook her head, confused.

The tech continued, this time looking directly at them, "What we try to do here, is we try to take it easy on you folks having to see your loved one dead and all. So, like, if it's on a TV, it's kinda like easier to take." She shrugged, her explanation complete. "Do you want me to tell the guys to set up the video?"

Annie glanced at Uncle Lou, then up at the monitor attached to the ceiling and wall. "I . . . don't think I want to use the television. I think I need to see him in person."

"Suit yourself," Belinda said, moving into the room beyond them. "But it isn't really in person. It's still behind some glass. That's the best we can do, okay?"

Annie nodded. She wanted to be anywhere else but here.

As they arranged themselves in front of the center of three large Plexiglas windows that lined one wall, the tech spoke into a walkie-talkie. Moments later, a gurney rolled into view, pushed by a young Oriental guy who maintained a lively conversation over his shoulder with someone out of view. As though in pantomime behind the thick glass, his silent laughter and animated body language were, absurdly, normal. The ugly walls, the musty smell, and the zoo-like feeling of watching from behind safety bars were what seemed strange. Annie wanted to be part of a life that could share the joke, to feel the lightheartedness, instead of the fear and ache that pinched in her gut.

With a shake of his shiny dark head, the tech returned his attention to the black bag in front of him, and arranged his face into solemn neutrality. The gurney stood between him and the Plexiglas wall, and, keeping his eyes on his task, he moved to unzip the bag from right to left. Midway through, he glanced sideways and Annie watched his studious look lighten for a second, before regaining control. She noticed that he bit the insides of his cheeks and didn't look up again, as his face pinked up.

She could imagine his friend, off to the side, making some comment or movement, trying to get him to laugh. As the young man moved the plastic bag away, Annie shut her eyes for just a moment. One moment before it all became true.

For a second, maybe two, she didn't know it was him. All she saw was the brown-encrusted blood. It seemed to cover most of his forehead, and the entire right side of his head. But it was Gary. His eyes and mouth were open in a still, frozen reaction to the shot that had killed him.

Annie leaned her forehead against the glass, staring ahead, believing, not believing. Hot tears of frustration worked their way up, and she let them fall, quietly. Not like this. No one should die like this.

Her breath made tiny puffs of condensation against the window. Still, she stared, wondering everything and nothing at once.

"Is this your husband, ma'am?" Annie caught Belinda's movement in periphery. The woman had pulled a pen from her pocket and held it poised over her clipboard. Annie wondered why the rush. It wasn't as though a line of people stood outside, holding numbers for their turn.

Annie said, "Yes," but it came out quiet, almost breathless. She cleared her throat. "Yes. This is my husband."

"Can you state his name for the record, please?"

"Gary Benjamin Randall."

Her job done, she clicked the pen closed and began to leave the room. Turning at the door, she said, "You can stay as long as you like. Just wave to Hiroshi to let him know when you're done. 'Kay?"

Uncle Lou, silent till now, moved forward and stood next to Annie. "I'm sorry honey," he said. "I just don't have any words . . ."

Turning to her right, she saw the tears well up in her uncle's eyes as he pulled out his crinkled handkerchief to wipe his nose. She reached over to put her arm around him and they stood there a long moment.

With a sigh, Annie signaled to Hiroshi.

"Mrs. Randall?"

Startled, Annie sat up fast in her wobbly chair, causing a few drops of water to splash over the side of her cup. Reliving the morning at the morgue, she'd lost track of the fact that she was sitting in the middle of a police station, waiting for them to tell her what to do next.

Standing over her, the man who'd spoken didn't look like a policeman at all. He was gray. Thin, with an unhealthy pallor, wearing lightly patterned gray suit pants, a dress shirt, and loosened tie, he motioned for her to follow him. The movement of his arm caused a waft of air that made it clear he'd just finished a cigarette. She followed him down the hall, cup in one hand, backpack swinging against her hip. His wrinkled shirt, with its white sleeves rolled up mid-forearm, was threadbare at the elbows. Late fifties, with military-short dark gray-flecked hair and a hint of beard stubble, even at mid-day, he moved almost silently as he shut the door behind them. Annie looked around, noting the faint smell of stale smoke and the pattern of smudges and fingerprints on the shiny painted walls, most of them at about waist level.

Annie sat in the chair he pulled out for her, laying her backpack on the table beside her.

"Mrs. Randall, I'm Detective George Lulinski."

Annie, resigned, closed her eyes. Mrs. Randall.

Dropping into the chair across from her, he stopped when he saw her face. "Is there a problem?"

Annie shook her head, "No."

Detective Lulinski picked up a manila file folder from the table and leafed through a few papers. "Hmmm. You were in the process of a divorce?"

"Yes. That's right." Annie didn't know why every word that came out of her mouth sounded stilted, but it did.

"Says here you use the name Callaghan. That your maiden name?"

"Yes," she said, nodding, trying to feel casual. Failing. "Callaghan. I've been using it again now for about a year, I guess." Her eyes wandered about the room. Small, it had two doors, the one they entered through from the hall to her right, and one behind Detective Lulinski that remained closed. Next to it was a large window with mirrored glass. Annie thought it odd-looking and then saw a flash from behind it. As though someone had lit a cigarette . . . A cigarette? It was no mirror; it was one-way glass. And there were people on the other side watching her. Suddenly, she found it hard not to feel like a criminal.

"You identified your husband at the morgue this morning, is that right?"

Annie tried to block thoughts of the visit from her head. She nodded, looking away for a moment.

Scratches in the wood tabletop beneath her folded hands made her wonder about other people who'd sat here before. Behind her, a low bench ran along the back wall. Metal rings were attached to either end. She imagined handcuffed prisoners attached to them.

"I'm very sorry for your loss, Mrs. Rand— Ms. Callaghan." The detective's eyebrows furrowed over his dark eyes. "Sorry. Which do you prefer?"

Annie's hands fluttered in front of her. "No matter. I'll answer to either one, I guess." She tried to give a smile, but knew it fell flat. She dropped her hands to the table, one on top of the other. The detective spent a few more moments reading over the papers in front of him and she uncrossed her hands, recrossing them the opposite way. She felt like a disobedient fourth grader, waiting for chastisement.

Her hands were cold, from nervousness perhaps, and she felt her fingertips begin to tingle.

"So, Ms. Callaghan," Detective Lulinski

pulled out a blank sheet of paper before closing the file. He pulled a pen from his shirt pocket and clicked it twice, poised to write. He looked completely at ease. "When did you last see your husband?"

A long question mark–shaped stretch of inkstain decorated the area over the detective's pocket and Annie's eyes were drawn to it as she spoke. "Well," she said, tucking her hair behind her ears and using the moment to relocate her hands to her lap. "It was yesterday. We went to a restaurant, called Donagan's, for lunch."

Slow nodding on the detective's part made Annie feel as though she should keep talking. "We, um, were there to talk about the divorce."

"How did that go?"

"Not too good." Annie cringed at having to bring it up.

"Where were you last night, around seven o'clock?"

Annie's mind raced. She fidgeted in her seat, aware of the man's intense scrutiny. Except for a fan that hummed in the ceiling above her, its motor making a metallic click every so often, the room was utterly silent. It felt wrong to tell him that she'd stayed the night at Sam's. There was no way to explain that and have it come out right. And yet she couldn't lie.

She cleared her throat.

Just then, Officer Schlosser poked his head in, requesting a moment of the detective's time, out of the room. She couldn't make out the low conversation beyond the open door. From the cadence of the voices, however, she gathered that whatever Officer Schlosser was saying was of some interest to the detective.

Annie pulled her shoulder blades together in a small stretch. How could she tell them that she'd spent the night at Sam's house? It sounded so meretricious.

Detective Lulinski eased back into the room with a paper in his hand, speaking a few more moments out the door before closing it and resuming his seat, the chair emitting a plastic squawk of protest as he settled himself.

"Sorry for the interruption, Ms. Callaghan. I have another question for you." He shifted papers around on the table, not looking at her. Took his time shuffling. Then looked up at her with a smile that didn't reach his eyes. "Where was your husband living?"

Annie's hand came up from her lap to tuck her hair behind her right ear again, even though it didn't need tucking. "He moved back in with me. Last week." She waited for him to write, but he watched her instead. Unsettled, her words rushed out. "He and another guy, whose name is Pete — they both moved in. I didn't want them to, but Gary said that he could get in trouble with the court because of his burglary charge if he didn't have somewhere to live." The detective nodding again made Annie want to scream.

"Weren't you concerned when he didn't come home last night?"

"No." Annie bit her lip to stop herself from explaining further.

"Why not?"

"I didn't know he hadn't come home."

"Because he wasn't living with you. He had an apartment." The detective asked, but it came out as a statement.

"No. He was living with me. Since . . . since . . ." Annie was so flushed with heat that it felt like her face was pounding as she tried to remember what day it had been that Gary met her at the door. Tiny beads of sweat popped out on her forehead, and over her lip. She still had her cup of water and she took a sip, to give herself a moment to gather her thoughts. Before she could speak, he continued.

"This is the address we have in our computers." He passed a printout across the table. "He didn't have a driver's license on his person, so we looked it up." His chin lifted her direction. "That correct?"

Annie pulled the paper closer and scanned it. "That's where he was living, yes. But they got evicted. Last week."

He pointed to the information, causing the paper to crinkle. "This apartment got broken into last night. We haven't had a chance to talk with the owners of the building yet, just the neighbors. Nobody mentioned an eviction. Estimated time of your husband's death is between seven and nine p.m. yesterday. Police were called to a disturbance at this apartment just after midnight."

Annie shook her head, not understanding.

"While it's possible that the two incidents are not related, it's also likely that they are," he said, continuing. "The place was ransacked. Tossed. And yet all the high-priced items were left untouched. We find that curious."

"But," Annie said, shaking her head again, looking down at the table and trying to make sense of his words, "they were evicted." She could hear the desperation in her voice, as though saying it could somehow make it true. But tiny pieces of a puzzle niggled in her brain. Annie remembered warning Gary not to even try to bring the big-screen television into the house and he'd grinned at her, telling her that they were renting the TV and a few other things to another friend, for cash. Could they have sublet the apartment, and then lied to her about it? Her shoulders slumped. She'd been conned.

"Do you have any proof that your husband was living with you?"

"His stuff is at my house." Annie could hear the high pitch in her voice as she ended the statement like a question; she knew that could hardly be considered proof of anything.

The detective wrinkled up half his face in a "that ain't gonna cut it" look. He clicked his pen, then clicked it again. "Now, Ms. Callaghan, why don't we start from the beginning. Where were you at approximately seven o'clock last night?"

Annie tried to quell a shudder as she brought her hands back up to the tabletop again. All she wanted to do was go home now, and sleep. Maybe she'd wake up to find this had all been a dream. "I . . ." she said, clearing her throat again, "I spent the night at a friend's house."

His face remained impassive, even as his hand moved across the paper, writing. "Go on," he said.

Chapter Eighteen

Annie's eyes flicked over to the front seat. Sam drove slowly, following the long black hearse, one hand draped over the steering wheel, his left elbow propped against the driver's side door. She'd preferred the back seat, and had insisted on it, despite Uncle Lou's suggestion that he take the back and she sit up front with Sam. Really, she just wanted to be alone, to sort out everything that had happened over the past few days.

A one-car funeral. People made jokes about them, but Annie wasn't surprised. She'd been afraid to face having a wake and funeral with dozens of mourners, all wanting to know how it happened, where it happened, and what was she feeling? Both to her relief, and yet to her sorrow for Gary's sake, few people had turned out.

Sam glanced back at her, checking on her, probably, and he gave a small smile. She couldn't have asked for a better friend. At the police station the other day, she'd suddenly realized that Sam would have no idea where she'd gone. She'd written the number for Millie's on a scrap of paper, pressed it into Uncle Lou's hand, and asked him to call there. Still, it had surprised her to see Sam when she'd come out of interrogation.

Fatigued from the incessant questions, the closeness of the closet-sized area, and the constant repetition, she'd left the room feeling hot and dingy. The cool of the hallway air had been like heaven, and when she looked down the hall, she'd seen Sam. Waiting for her.

Sitting there, his large frame looking uncomfortable on the same small wobbly chair that Annie had sat in earlier, he'd been leaning forward, his elbows propped up by his knees. She could tell even in profile that he was tense, with his folded hands pressed hard together and his jaw set. He stared across the small corridor at nothing but the brown brick wall. But he was there.

All the emotion that she'd kept down in order to get through the initial shock and then the ordeal of being questioned, bubbled up when she saw him, and her voice cracked. "Sam?"

As he stood, the look on his face told her even more than his being there did. A combination of concern, relief, and something else — she couldn't tell what — commingled on his features, sending a warm rush of release through Annie's weary body. Tears burnt a path to her eyes and she moved forward to be enveloped by Sam's strong arms, as if it were the most natural thing in the world.

As Annie regained control, she stepped back a bit, putting some space between them, self-conscious as Detective Lulinski appeared to her right. "And would this be the friend whose house you stayed at last night?" he asked.

"Sam Morgan," Sam said, stepping forward, allowing his arm to drop from around Annie's waist. "And you are?"

The two men shook hands, though Annie felt a tremor of animosity between them. "The detective working this homicide. George Lulinski."

To Annie, Sam asked, "Are you okay to go?"

Annie wiped at her eyes, wanting nothing more than to leave immediately. She turned to the detective, "Am I done?"

He leaned up against the brick wall, scrutinizing them. Dropping one hand into his pants pocket, he came up with a small metallic container. He flipped it open and pulled out a business card. "Yeah," he said, making slow, deliberate movements, "but here's my card. If there's anything else you think of, Mrs. Randall," he said her name with emphasis, "be sure to call." He crinkled up half his face in a way that could have been a wink, had it been friendly. Leaving them, he walked back down the hall to his office, stopping about halfway there, to turn. "And, of course, if there's anything you want to talk about . . . you know . . . get off your chest, you can call me. Anytime."

The low rumble in Sam's throat would have been inaudible if Annie hadn't been standing so close. "Let's get you home," he said.

Once there, Sam had settled Annie onto her sofa. "Can I get you something?"

"No," she smiled, "I'm fine. Really."

Sam sat next to her. "Why don't you tell me what happened."

As she'd talked, Annie had felt some of the tension leave her body. She'd watched Sam's face as she described her trip to the morgue and the subsequent visit to the police station. More than once he said, "You should have called me," and Annie realized that he meant it. She had wanted to call him. Wanted his strength when she went to the morgue. She'd wanted to be with him just because she knew everything was better when he was near. But she'd stopped herself from calling, afraid to burden him. It hit her with a suddenness that nearly took her breath away; he wanted to be part of her life and was hurt that she hadn't called. It was as if she hadn't trusted him enough.

Mid-sentence, she'd yawned for the third time. Sam had gotten up and pulled a quilt over from the loveseat to cover her, before moving into the kitchen.

She'd stared at the ceiling for a few minutes, hearing him open and close cabinets and drawers. Part of her wanted to get up and help him find whatever he was searching for, but she didn't have the energy. As the noises quieted and she heard him turn on the stove, her eyes became heavy and she dozed.

When Sam came into the living room, he sat on the coffee table and placed a cup of blackberry tea on it next to him. "I thought that maybe this would help you sleep, but it looks like you might be able to relax a little after all."

Annie boosted herself up on one elbow and tried to find the words to thank him for being part of her life. None came.

"It's okay," he said, as if reading her mind. "And I've been thinking. Your uncle gave me his number when I saw him at the station. I'm going to have him come over and sit with you for a little bit while I take care of a couple of things."

"What kind of things?"

"Well, for one, we need to change your locks."

Annie reached for the tea, boosting herself up a little more. "Why?"

"You talked about that Pete fellow, and how he gives you the creeps. Well, he might very well have Gary's keys right now and I don't think you want him popping in here to surprise you."

Annie's eyes strayed to the corner of the room, at the big white leather vibrating chair. "I hadn't thought of that. But my door takes a special kind of lock. That's why I never replaced it; it was too expensive."

"I have a friend who can work his way around any lock. Did all mine at Millie's. They're tough, heavy-duty, the kind that would take a professional all day to pick. The only way to get past them is to virtually break down the door itself. I'll get him out here and have him change them tonight."

He'd mentioned a couple of other stops he planned to make, then got up to call Uncle Lou. Within minutes, the older man had arrived and the two of them talked in low murmurs in the other room. Still reeling from the ordeal at the police station, Annie had closed her eyes, wanting nothing more than to escape reality and to let the two wonderful men in her life take care of her.

She remembered that feeling now in the middle of this quiet cemetery, as the wind whipped around them, its brisk fingers snatching away the priest's words, even as he raised his voice to compete with Mother Nature. Annie didn't care, really. She didn't need to hear the blessings. Blustery sounds of the air shot through the branches overhead, making the leaves reach and twist in the breeze, providing enough background noise to allow her thoughts to take flight. She knew Karla was thinking about her right now. She'd wanted to come, but she was due to deliver any minute, and Annie had refused to let her take the risk.

Beneath the overcast sky, the small group stood in a semi-circle along one side of the casket, the spray of red roses resting atop, their unmistakable scent hitting her with a vengeance, only to vanish as quickly when the wind changed direction. Annie felt her hair dancing in the sharp breeze, making movements above her head like that of a wild campfire. Uncle Lou kept his head bowed, the breeze unable to do much more than lift the back flaps of his suit coat. Sam stood silent as well. He'd been with her yesterday as she made the arrangements, to lend moral support and, she suspected, to make sure she held up.

With a sprinkling of holy water that missed its mark, flying instead against Annie's cheek, the priest closed his small black prayer book, and stepped backwards. She accepted the holy man's condolences before he walked away to his car.

It was over.

Uncle Lou and Sam moved toward her, both of them wearing the same look of fearful anticipation.

"I'm fine," she said.

Annie stared straight ahead as they made their way back to the car, turning only briefly when she heard bumping metallic noises behind her. Two men dressed in gray stood at either end of the casket as it lowered into the ground.

Sam drove home, the three of them silent, Annie deep within her own thoughts. She was supposed to feel something, wasn't she? They'd been married for five years and even produced the child she carried. But that fateful night had been an accident, an anomaly. Gary's death had rattled her, to be sure, but what she felt was guilt rather than sorrow. Guilt at knowing, deep in her heart, that she wouldn't miss him. For all the time they'd been separated, she'd never once hoped to stay married. Even that fateful night that they had gotten together had been more about her needs than about Gary. She leaned on the armrest built into the car's rear door and she watched out the window, seeing nothing. Feeling empty. She'd been married to the man for five years and was surprised she felt so little.

Detective Lulinski didn't seem overly interested in the fact that Annie's elderly neighbor had seen a man trying to get into her house through a side window. Upon examination of the front door, it appeared as though he'd attempted to jimmy the lock first. Mrs. Trumbull, the neighbor, had been out sweeping her front steps when she'd seen a man balanced on a trash can, trying to reach the side kitchen window.

Mrs. Trumbull had been more than happy to talk to Detective Lulinski, assuring him that while her eyesight wasn't great, and admittedly, she hadn't been wearing her glasses, she knew what she had seen. A tiny woman with pale white hair, she spoke whirlwind fashion, having to wipe at the corners of her mouth every so often at the spit that gathered there. "I shouted at him," she said, the pride evident in her voice. "And he took off like a bat outta hell. Just like that." She snapped her bony fingers with a solid crack.

Her exclamation as she crossed the street had surprised the man and he fled before she'd been able to get a good look at his face. From what she could tell, however, he was of average height and build, and she thought he might have dark hair. Probably somewhere between twenty and fifty years old.

Annie, absolutely certain it was Pete, found herself discouraged by the detective's reaction. Average height and build didn't give him much to go on, he'd said. "Half the population fits that description."

He'd walked around the house, taken a look at the garbage can that had been dragged from the alley, and made a few quick notes.

"Don't you think it's suspicious that Gary's apartment was broken into and now an attempt has been made on my house?" Annie asked.

The detective had smiled at her, in a way that made her feel small, like a child. "Only if someone knew he'd left his old apartment to move in here. And this Pete fellow — you don't happen to have remembered his last name, do you? If this Pete guy was his roommate, then I don't see him breaking in at either place. He'd know where Gary was living, and he probably had keys to both places."

"Sam changed my locks. Just a couple of days ago."

"Well now," the detective said, in a slow, patronizing voice, "that was probably a real good idea."

Annie blew out a breath of frustration. "What I mean is, even if Pete had the key, he wouldn't have been able to get in. Maybe that's why he tried the window."

The detective had stood up and closed his notebook. "I appreciate you calling me to let me know this latest development, but truthfully, I don't see that it holds much bearing on your husband's homicide. But, we'll look into it. Let me know if anything else happens though, okay?"

Just as his hand reached the knob, Lulinski turned around. "That day you and your husband went to lunch. At . . ." he consulted his notes. "Donagan's?"

Annie nodded.

"Bunch of elderly folks were there too, right? Having lunch?"

"Mm-hmm."

"Turns out they go there kinda regular. So I stopped and talked with a couple of them. You know, just to see what their observations were." Lulinski's eyes were steady beneath his gray brows. "Nothing official, mind you."

Annie didn't know where this was going.

He squinted. "You talk with any of them?"

"One of the older ladies came in to talk to me," she said, adding, "in the bathroom."

"What about her husband?"

Annie tried to remember. "No. I don't think I said a word to him."

Flipping to the next page of his notebook, he read for a moment, then looked back up at her. "That's funny," he said. "The old guy distinctly recalls you saying, 'I'm going to kill him.'"

Lulinski tapped his fingers to his forehead in a mock salute, and left.

Sam shut Annie's front door behind the detective's departing figure.

"Well," she said.

Sam shrugged. "Let it go, Annie. We know you didn't do it. Let's just be patient here. We can get through this."

Annie noticed that Sam used the word "we." Something about that made her feel good. Hopeful. Despite Lulinski's attitude. She walked back into the kitchen and started to clean up. They'd offered the detective coffee, but he'd declined. "Want some?" she asked, holding up the pot. She took her time pouring both mugs of coffee and pulling out the cream from the fridge. Sam stood, leaning against the countertop with his arms crossed in front of him, looking exactly how she felt, confused.

"What now?" she asked as she sat down.

Sam pulled out a chair across from Annie. "Not much, I suppose. But I have to tell you, whatever the detective says, I think this *is* somehow related to whoever killed Gary. And I think Lulinski thinks so too. He just doesn't want to tip his hand."

"Why not?"

"Annie, we're suspects, both of us. Whether we want to believe it or not, he thinks that we might have done Gary in because we're having some torrid love affair." Sam made it sound matter-of-fact, but she heard the anger in his voice.

Annie sipped her coffee. "Okay, let's say that the two burglaries are related. What do you think they're looking for? I don't have anything of value. I don't think that Gary did either."

Sam shook his head. "I know that I'm not comfortable with you staying here alone. Makes me nervous."

Annie reached across the table to touch his hand, causing him to look up. "Thanks, Sam. It means a lot to know you care."

Sam's face reddened slightly before he changed subjects. "I ought to get going. Lots of stuff I've let slip through the cracks."

"I'm sorry," Annie said as she stood to walk him to the door, "I've taken up so much of your time."

"Don't worry about it. I'm just glad I was able to help out in some small way. Your uncle told me he'd stay here with you the next couple of nights, just to make sure everything is okay. But you feel free to call me anytime, all right?"

Annie nodded. Bright sunlight shone in through the crystal panels of the front door and made tiny rainbows on the side of Sam's face. He seemed reluctant to leave.

"By the way, have you told the DeChristophers what happened?"

"I called Gina on Monday, but didn't say a lot. I told her I wouldn't be over for a few days due to a death in the family. Didn't mention it was Gary, though. Maybe because she met him, maybe because I'm embarrassed to say that my husband was killed gangland style and that I'm a suspect in his murder." She felt her voice rising as she spoke, but quelled herself. "I'll eventually have to tell them, of course." Annie stopped for a moment, thinking. "You know, I wished so hard that I didn't have to deal with Gary or with the divorce or with Mr. DeChristopher as my lawyer." She made a noise that attempted to be a laugh but came out a sob, instead. "Teaches you to be careful what you wish for, huh?"

When Sam opened his arms, Annie felt as though she'd come home. She wrapped her arms around his waist and held her head against his chest. The room was so silent she could hear his heart beat. He was warm and solid, and when his hands gently rested against her back, pulling her in ever so slightly, she felt her body mold itself to his.

She didn't want to let go, but she didn't

want to hold him back from his responsibilities either. With a sigh, she pulled back, but he didn't.

She looked up into Sam's face. His blue eyes stared at her, holding a look of such intensity it caused her heart to lurch.

With the tiniest of movements, Sam's head bent as Annie reached up. Their lips met in a soft, moist kiss, and as they drew away, their eyes searched each other's and in a moment they came together again. They held each other gently at first. Annie could feel a pull in her heart, as though there were nowhere else she'd ever want to be again. Her right hand caressed his cheek, then slid around the back of his neck, drawing him closer as she parted her lips. He gave a groan of pleasure as his arms pulled her in, hard, till every inch of their bodies touched one another's.

"Oh," she said as they parted.

Sam pulled back, blowing out a ragged breath. He looked away. "I'm sorry."

Annie cleared her throat. "Don't be."

"It's too soon, Annie."

Even though her mind knew he was right, her body rebelled. It felt as though a delicious hot fluid was coursing through her veins, reaching every extremity, making her tingle. She reached up with both hands to touch his face, and stared into those beautiful eyes. Her voice cracked as she spoke, "I want to be with you, Sam."

He held her with one hand, and brought up the other to push a stray hair out of her face. "Someday, Annie, we're going to look back on the first time we were together. And we'll want to remember the beauty of it, the newness of it. We won't want to have that memory overshadowed by all that's happened recently." He smiled a little. "We'll wait. Till the time is right."

He kissed her again, this time chastely on the cheek. "I'll call you later," he said.

She stood in the doorway and watched him leave, wondering how life could be so cruel and yet so beautiful at the same time.

Chapter Nineteen

Gina met her at the door.

"I'm so sorry, honey," Gina said. "How did it happen? He was so young."

Annie stepped around two burly men hoisting a roll of new carpeting into the living room and foyer area. The floor had been stripped clear of the old carpet and wallpaper had been torn from adjacent walls.

"What happened here?" Annie asked, as Gina led her to the kitchen.

"That Timothy," Gina said, rolling her eyes. "He's such a good guy, but doesn't have a lot of brainpower, you know? He was here, watching the house the other night and my mother called him to bring little Drew's teddy over to her house. So he goes upstairs to get it, right? With a friggin' Bloody Mary in his hands. And on the way back, you guessed it, he spills it everywhere."

Annie thought it was amazing that one spill could warrant new carpeting and wallpaper, but she kept quiet. Maybe if she had their kind of money, she'd spend it freely, too.

Gina continued as they sat at the table. "And I thought Dickie would go through the roof, but he handled it like it was no big deal. Men," she said, derisively. "Can't live with 'em, can't live without 'em." She looked up at Annie. "Oh, honey. I'm so sorry. That was kinda thoughtless of me. Tell me about your husband now. What happened?"

Annie struggled to find the words. "He was shot, then dumped in an industrial yard, not far from his apartment. I have a hard time talking about it. I hope you don't mind."

"Not at all, sweetie. And I thought the two of you made a cute couple, you know?" Gina poured Annie a glass of water and herself a diet pop before sitting back down at the kitchen table. Noise in the background grew steadily louder till Gina stood up and walked over to the basement door. She opened it and screamed for the boys to be quiet, before turning around and smiling at Annie again.

Annie had been going stir crazy at home. Between Uncle Lou and Karla calling every few hours to make sure she was all right, and the after-funeral paperwork and bills that needed to be done, Annie knew that the best thing she could do to keep her mind off her troubles was to get back to work. In some ways she was sorry, though. By the end of the week, the dinosaur project would be complete and she'd have to start cultivating more jobs.

Gina wrinkled her nose. "So it looks like you won't be needing a divorce attorney after all, huh?"

Taken aback by her forthrightness, Annie lifted her water, taking a sip. She nodded. "I'd appreciate it if you'd let your husband know."

"Let me know what?"

Richard DeChristopher strode into the kitchen, having made his way noiselessly from the adjacent hallway.

Gina reached for her husband's hand, pulling him to stand by her chair. "Oh, terrible news, Dickie. Annie's husband died. That's why she hasn't been here for a few days." She stage-whispered, even though Annie was right there. "He was shot."

DeChristopher's face underwent a change. "Shot? When did this happen? How did he get shot?"

"Dickie," Gina said, chastising, "she doesn't want to talk about that. It's been hard on the poor girl. She's been through enough. And she's pregnant, besides."

Annie thought DeChristopher's next movements looked orchestrated, as though he were striving for nonchalance when really he came across wound tight as a drum. She wondered briefly what could be causing the strain that telegraphed from his eyes. Wrinkles bracketed his lips, more so than normal, and his mouth drew tight. "I'm so sorry for your loss, Anne. Excuse my ignorance. Must be the attorney in me, always trying to find the answers."

Annie murmured something incomprehensible, even to herself.

"If there's anything we can do . . ." he continued. "Please feel free to call on us."

"Yeah, honey, you do that."

"Thank you."

Richard DeChristopher sat down at the head of the table. "So, was it an attempted robbery? A carjacking?"

"Dickie? What's up with that? Why are you asking her so many things?"

Richard's head swiveled his wife's direction and though his words were gentle, his eyes blazed. Annie didn't understand. Had they had a fight earlier? Anything Gina said this morning seemed to set him off. "Sometimes it helps, dear, to share things about our loss. Helps us cope with the difficult grieving process."

"What is with you today?"

DeChristopher ignored her. "Since you and I never had our meeting about your divorce, I never had the opportunity to meet Mr. Callaghan."

Annie shook her head. "Not Callaghan. That's my maiden name. I took it back when we separated. His name was Gary. Gary Randall."

Mr. DeChristopher stared at her a minute, then nodded. "As I said, I'm very sorry for your loss."

"Yeah," Gina sighed, "and I met him. He brought Annie some paints last week. Nice-looking guy, too. You know, I really thought you guys were gonna get back together, honey. I really did." Gina leaned forward and patted Annie's hand. "Weren't you two tryin' to get back together?"

"No," Annie said, shaking her head.

"But didn't he say you 'forgot something at home' that one day he came here?"

DeChristopher asked, "He was here? Inside?"

The conversation was taking a turn Annie didn't want to go down. She stretched a bit, in an effort to look like she was ready to start work. "Yes," she said, reluctance in her voice, "he'd been staying at my place temporarily. It wasn't my idea."

Richard stood up, walked over to the desk in the working part of the kitchen, and rummaged through it for a few seconds before he looked back up at them. "I'm sorry. I just remembered a commitment for this morning." He looked at his watch and pulled a cell phone out of his pocket as he began to leave the room. Turning back, he looked at Annie. His lips curled into a smile, but his eyes were cold and distant. "You'll be working here all day, I presume?"

"Yep. Just about done. A couple more days and I'll be through."

"Splendid."

Through the dings, whirs, and digitized sounds of three busy video poker games and the heavy layer of smoke settled above the heads of those playing, Pete watched the rest of the patrons at the bar.

He sat in the same booth he'd shared with Gary last time they'd come here. A little busier today, a majority of the stools were occupied, the backs of the mostly overweight men lined up one after another, with elbows leaning on the bar, their faces turned toward the baseball game on television in uniform rapt attention. Today was the Crosstown Classic, the unique annual contest between Chicago's White Sox and their northside nemesis, the Cubs. The southsiders had beaten them handily for the past few years, and it looked as though there was no danger of ruining the streak.

The men cheered together, their shoulders rising upward to express non-verbal delight at a play on the screen above them. Pete missed it, but the replay would be shown again, at least three times from three different angles. What he saw was one of the young players, a kid practically, jogging and high-fiving his teammates, a grin on his face.

It wasn't fair. These kids nowadays had everything handed to them on a silver platter, getting private lessons in batting and pitching when they were six years old. No wonder they got these multi-million-dollar contracts. It was the poor fools that had to work for a living that paid for it. So you had to grab for the brass ring whenever you saw it and hope to hell you got a good hold, and you had to do whatever it took to make your own breaks. For guys like him, anyway. And when a shortcut came his way, Pete knew he'd take it. It's just that things got so screwed up sometimes.

He lifted his empty beer glass to his lips.

He had only about forty bucks to his name till next week when his unemployment check came in. Still, he needed time to think and to plan. Gary had blown this one big time, the poor son of a bitch.

And so had he.

It should have been clear sailing when Annie had headed out for Gary's funeral, but some idiot had put in new locks on her doors. Good ones, expensive ones that he couldn't pick fast enough. And then that damn old broad had seen him trying the window.

Pushing himself upward from the table, he meandered over to the bar, where the men talked amongst themselves, joking and calling to Al the bartender for refills while the commercials were on.

"Hey, Al," Pete said.

The burly man looked up. He lifted his chin toward Pete in acknowledgement. "What can I getcha?"

" 'Nother one." Pete lifted his glass, tilting it slightly in the air.

Picking up a red terrycloth towel along the way, Al slung it over his shoulder. "Hey, you remember when you were here the other day?"

"What of it?"

"Well . . ." Al said, drawing as he tipped

the mug under the tap. The golden liquid caught the scant light as it rippled into the glass. "I ain't seen Gary around since then. You know where he is?"

"Why?"

"He owes me a C-note from a little wager. Hasn't paid up yet." He flipped up the tapper and handed the glass to Pete.

Pete snorted. "Good luck collecting, bud."

"Why? He leave town or something?" He moved forward and began to wipe down the bar with the towel.

"Something like that. The guy's dead."

Al stopped mid-motion. "No way." He shook his big head, his mouth set in a line, then started wiping again as he looked up. "I just saw the guy. But you know, he wasn't lookin' too good lately. Guess he was having some marital problems too. What was it? He didn't do himself, did he?"

"Nah, it was sort of an accident," Pete said, drawing out his wallet to pay. "Real sudden."

"Good friend of yours?"

Pete looked up, sensing an opportunity. "My best friend."

Al waved the proffered money away. "This one's on the house, man. Sorry to hear."

Back at the table, Pete took a long drink of his brew, licking the foam from his lips as he considered his next steps. So far as he could tell, those DeChristophers didn't know he existed. He was safe there, at least. But they probably knew the connection between Gary and Annie. Probably had her place staked out, even now. He'd have to be real careful getting back into Annie's house. But the chick was home every night nowadays. And the daylight break-in hadn't panned out.

He'd have to go in at night, to pick up that crazy drawing. Not that he had any idea how to fence it. Not yet. In his panic, he'd stuffed it away at her house, but had forgotten to hide the jeweled eggs he'd pocketed until he'd gotten back to his room at the YMCA.

Still, it was the picture that held the promise of big bucks. He had to figure out a way to get in and out of there, hopefully without her knowing. He didn't want to have to hurt her, but he would if it came down to that. Two million dollars. That Gary had been one crazy son of a bitch. No way he'd get that kind of cash for an old picture of naked women, but he'd done some homework on this drawing and maybe, if he played his cards right and if he could find some high-end fence, he could clear a few hundred grand. That'd be enough to go down to Mexico and retire among the pretty senoritas. He could live like a king on that for a good long time.

Cheers from the bar area brought him out of his reverie. The southsiders had done it again. Slowly, the men left their barstools and made their way to the washroom, then out the door. With each opening, the bright sunlight spilled in, brightening up a sliver of the dark bar, illuminating the dinginess that stayed hidden as long as the door stayed closed.

Pete's beer glass was empty again. He played with it, weighing the pleasure of another cold brew against the lack of money in his wallet. Slouched in the booth, he played with the glass, the noise as its base made circles on the table soothing him, letting him think and plan.

Al came by with a fresh beer in a new glass. "Here ya go, bud," he said. "Lost a friend of mine 'bout a year ago. I know just how ya feel."

Pete sat up a little, pulling his feet from the opposite seat where they'd been resting. "Yeah?"

Al still had the red towel draped over his

shoulder. He scratched at the stubble on his chin and glanced over to the bar. "You okay there, Emil?" he called out in a loud voice.

The old guy turned in slow motion, looking afraid that any large movement might cause him to fall off his stool. "Al? Yeah. I'm okay."

Rolling his eyes, Al lowered himself into the booth opposite Pete.

"Now, I know this ain't none of my business, but I gotta tell you, I see a lotta guys in a place like this. And I get to the point where I can tell who's got real problems and who's just passing time here, ya know?"

Pete nodded, taking a mouthful of beer. He wondered where in that estimation he fell.

Al continued, his manner friendly, inquisitive, almost like he wanted to get to know Pete. "You got the look of a guy who's kinda lost. And I know that your buddy's death has a lot to do with it, but there's something else about you. Like maybe you had some business with him, and now that he's gone, that's gone too." His beefy arms rested on the tabletop. "That about right?"

"Maybe."

"You say he was your best buddy. And buddies that close share stuff, don't they?"

Pete couldn't figure where this was going. "We shared some stuff, yeah."

"Like for instance, he mentioned that he got you guys a place to stay for free." Movement near the bar caused Al to look up, but it was just one of the guys heading to the bathroom. "Told me a little bit about that setup. I'm guessing that you might be having some issues with income now that Gary ain't around no more."

Sitting back in the booth, Pete realized that the contacts Gary had mentioned might not have disappeared after all. "Yeah," he drawled, settling in to tell the sad tale that might just make him look needy enough to keep this guy's guard down, "I got screwed. Big time."

Al looked at Pete's half empty beer. "Hang on." He lumbered back behind the bar, talked for a couple of seconds with the guys leaning, smoking, and staring into the mirror opposite the stools, then made his way back with a shot of whiskey and a pitcher of beer. "Here ya go. Times like these call for something stronger than a brewski, don't they?"

Pete grinned. This guy was a real soft touch.

Al took a deep breath and looked around again before speaking. "Truth is, Gary and I didn't have no wager. And it wasn't for no hundred bucks neither. He told me he was coming into some big money. That jibe with what you had going with him?"

Downing the shot, Pete made a noise of great satisfaction and smacked his lips. "Maybe."

"Listen, bud, I'm thinking we can work together on this one."

"What else did he tell you?"

"Not a lot," Al's eyes were watchful, "but he promised me a grand for a couple of things I did for him." With a half-shrug, as if the information were of no consequence, Al continued, "I set him up with a friend of mine. A guy I know who deals with merchandise. High-quality merchandise, you know? Gary made off like he had something kinda pricey to move. And my friend is a real go-to guy. Would trust him with my life. Believe me."

"Promised you a grand?"

"Yeah. And I set everything up. They were supposed to meet on Tuesday, but Gary never showed." He made a helpless gesture with his hand in the air. "Now I know why."

"Let me guess. You'd be willing to do the same for me?"

Al licked his lips. "Seein' as how you're a friend of Gary's, I suppose something can be worked out, yeah."

George Lulinski exchanged a look of frustration with his partner, then knocked on the apartment door again. Ringing the bell twice brought no response, but after his first knock someone peered out from the sliding door curtains to his right. George had flashed his badge at the young man whose baleful eyes stared out at him, the kid leaning back in a chair, not exerting more effort than necessary to see who was at the door. At the sight of the two policemen, the curly-headed fellow's mouth had dropped open, the curtains fell shut, and the scuffling began. Muffled voices raised while the two men stood outside the door, losing patience.

Several moments after the second knock, the door opened. The same dull-eyed kid who'd checked them out leaned against the jamb, pulling the door close to his other side. "Yeah?"

Detective Lulinski introduced himself and his partner, Bill Schumann, before adding, "We'd like to ask you a few questions." He didn't wait for the fellow to acquiesce, but put his left hand spread-fingered on the door, and pushed. "Can we come in?"

"Hey, you ain't got no right to barge in here. You ain't got no search warrant or nothing." His eyes bounced back and forth between the two men, his pupils wide. "Do you?"

George didn't enter the apartment, but he noted that there were two other males present, both of whom panted as though they'd just run a marathon. They sat in positions of relaxation, but their attention focused on the conversation at the door rather than on the large-screen television in front of them. One sat on an old sheet-covered couch, the other on the floor next to him, his hands behind his back. None of the three could be older than twenty-five, and while the fellow at the door had dark curly hair and brown eyes, the other two were blond and fair, looking as though they could be brothers. Thin, haggard, and going prematurely bald up front, they sported duplicate extra-high foreheads.

A coffee table, its wooden surface scratched and dented, but nonetheless shiny, stood out from the clutter of the room by being the only surface completely clean. Knowing in his gut that only moments before they'd knocked, this one had been covered with drug paraphernalia, George looked over to Bill, who chomped on a wad of gum and smirked. They'd be sure to mention this apartment to some of the guys back at the station, but right now illicit drug use wasn't high on their list of priorities.

"What's your name?"

The curly-haired guy's eyes jumped from Bill to George and back again. He squinted at the sunlight, even though it wasn't all that bright right now, then wiped at his nose. George knew that Bill would follow his lead. They didn't want to antagonize these guys any more than they had to. Two cops trying to come across to some doper as unthreatening made the task more difficult. "Listen, buddy, I don't really care what you've got going in there. I'm looking into a homicide and I need some answers. Now, *you* can make this easy or *we* can make it hard."

Bill narrowed the space between them, bringing himself up to his full six-and-a-half feet. When he wanted to, Bill could look tough. The tall, hefty guy was twenty years younger than George's fifty-six, and had the kind of build that people backed away from. He'd been promoted to the detective division just six months before, and George thought he showed promise. If only he'd give up the gum-chewing.

George was bluffing. He had no probable cause to be able to enter this apartment, nor did the kids have any reason to cooperate with him, but he counted on their fogged brains not to put that together. A long minute passed as decision worked its way across the muddled fellow's face. The two guys inside the apartment sat open-mouthed, watching him.

"My name's Ethan," he said at last. "Homicide, huh? That means somebody's dead?"

"Yeah," Bill said, cracking chewing gum as he spoke, "somebody's dead all right. And somebody else killed him."

"Hey, it wasn't me!" Ethan said, his eyes growing wide.

"Yeah, we figured as much," George said, "but you want to make us go away, you gotta answer a few questions. How does that sound?"

Ethan half-turned to the two guys in the room who looked at each other and shrugged. Turning back, his face registered a change, as if he'd just remembered something. "Hang on," he said, then pushed the door nearly closed so that only a sliver remained open. They heard him stage-whisper, "Kyle!"

A moment later, he reopened the door. Gone was the guy who'd been sitting on the floor, but they heard noises from the adjacent bedroom. George scowled at the combination smells of body odor and something sweet, like perfume. He looked around the dark room shaking his head, though he'd experienced worse. The older of the brothers still sat on the couch, but he shifted to one side, as though to make room for the two detectives to sit.

Bill declined for both of them.

Kyle came back, rubbing his hands on the sides of his jeans. Except for different sayings on their dirty white T-shirts, the three were dressed almost identically in faded baggy jeans with rips in the knees. George took down their names for the record. He addressed all three with his questions. Ethan, Kyle, and (he'd been right) Kyle's older brother Ryan settled themselves on the couch, all three looking up at the two policemen with the appearance of mischievous schoolboys, their elbows resting on their knees, hands folded.

"You guys know a Gary Randall?"

They shifted, moving legs and arms and

eyes all at once. Ethan spoke, "He usedta live here. We got the apartment when he moved out."

"You rented it from him?"

"Yeah. Him and his buddy."

"You met them? Both?"

"Yeah."

Bill moved to lean against the wall, chewing his gum slowly, making loud popping noises, showing perfectly even teeth. "What's the other guy's name?" George started to rethink his gum aversion. Even the cracking sounded menacing.

More shifting. They looked at each other as though someone had just asked them to divulge state secrets. Ethan shrugged, "Pete."

"Last name?"

"Don't know it."

George knew Ethan was lying. He looked over to Bill, who watched the trio through squinted eyes.

"Where do you think we can find this Pete?" Bill asked.

Kyle and Ryan were content to let Ethan handle the interview. They flanked him with rapt expressions on their faces. "Don't know," Ethan said, looking away.

"This apartment got broken into just a couple of days ago, right?" Bill straightened himself and stretched a bit, as if by changing the subject, he was lowering his guard.

The three nodded. "We didn't call, though. I swear we weren't here. Some neighbors called."

"Anything taken?"

They looked at each other and shook their heads amongst themselves before Ethan looked up at George and said, "Nothin'."

"They just messed everything up," Kyle said. "Like, totally."

As if this were safe conversational ground, Ryan chimed in, "What kind of an idiot breaks in and don't take nothin'?"

George was tempted to make them arrange their hands around their faces so they'd be the "see no evil, hear no evil, speak no evil" monkeys, and he felt a small grin try to make its way to his face.

Bill shifted his weight from one foot to the other, bringing him slightly closer to the scrawny boys. He affected a tone of pure friendliness, "Nobody even touched your coke?"

Ryan shook his head, his eyes full of wonder, "Yeah, can you believe it?"

Kyle and Ethan's eyes widened at Ryan's mistake, but the older brother was scratching his head and grinning, like they'd gotten away with something.

Bill rolled his eyes at George. His look said, "Idiot kids."

George moved in a little closer too, feeling their discomfort, ready to take advantage. "How about I ask you again about this Pete guy . . ."

Fifteen minutes later George and Bill stood outside the apartment and listened as Kyle and Ethan's voices rang out, belittling Ryan for his big mouth. Not that it mattered. These guys weren't their target, but knowing their propensity for drugs could make them useful in the future. George grinned at Bill as they made it to the car. "Let's go for a cup of coffee and sort all this out. My treat."

Just as Bill moved to get in the passenger seat, George dropped his arm across the top of the car's roof with a thump. "And hey," he said with a grin, "lose the gum."

Chapter Twenty

Annie had just picked up Gary's old bathrobe when the doorbell rang. She looked at her watch, wondering who'd be coming over at eight o'clock in the morning. Piles of Gary's clothes, along with incidental items he and Pete had brought into the house, waited to be folded and boxed and disposed of. She'd been at it since six, working under the power of her allotted one cup of coffee per day and some Oreo cookies. She'd planned to have a healthier breakfast once she'd finished, but sorting between Gary's and Pete's things had become difficult. She'd arranged several piles: one for Gary, another for Pete, and one for the items for which she couldn't decide ownership. She'd donate Gary's stuff, and offer the rest to Pete, if he ever showed up. And when he did, she'd get his last name.

Stepping over a pile of things she considered garbage, she threw Gary's ratty green bathrobe over the back of a kitchen chair and complained aloud when the doorbell rang again, but then quelled her annoyance when she found Uncle Lou standing there, covered plate in hand.

"You're up early," she said, opening the door wider to let him in.

"Yeah, couldn't sleep. Too much going on around here lately." He walked directly into the kitchen, still talking. "How are you doing?"

"I'm okay," she said, following him. She pointed to the extra bedroom as he sat down. "Just sorting through some of Gary's stuff."

Annie sat across from him, removing the bathrobe from the back of her chair and tossing it next to her while Uncle Lou, with obvious pride, unwrapped the dish he'd brought. "Made it this morning. Thought you might like some."

"What is it?" Annie asked, leaning forward.

"Banana bread. Got a knife?"

As Uncle Lou removed the shiny crinkled tinfoil, the scent of the freshly baked bread wafted up, its sweet, warm smell making Annie's stomach growl. She touched the top of the browned loaf and smiled. He must have brought it straight from the oven. "Yeah," she said, and returned with plates and two mugs.

"Milk?" Uncle Lou asked, peering into

Annie's cup as she started a pot of coffee.

"Yep. Had my ration of java for the day already. Got to start thinking healthy." She sliced them both a hunk of the bread before she sat down.

Uncle Lou took an enormous bite, then sat back to chew, watching Annie.

She felt a question in his look. Smiling self-consciously, she shook her head. "What?"

He finished chewing and eyed the remaining portion on his plate as he leaned forward resting his arms on the table. "This guy, Sam . . ." he began, "he's the guy who owns the ice cream parlor where you're painting that mural, right?"

"Yep, that's him."

"How's that project coming along?"

"Well," she said with a wry look, "it's been put on hold a bit lately, but it was shaping up. I think I might have another week or so, and it'll be done."

"One wall, right?"

"One wall."

"The DeChristopher house is a whole room, right?"

"Yeah. That one's almost done, too. Maybe one more day. Maybe more."

He took another big bite and glanced over to the coffee pot. Getting up, he put the drip mechanism on hold and poured some of the hot brew into his mug as Annie took a drink of her milk. "Seems like the dinosaur room should have taken a lot longer than one wall."

Annie shrugged. "I don't get as much time at Sam's as I could use sometimes. And it is a more intricate project."

Uncle Lou nodded and finished up his bread, stretching forward, his stout arms reaching out from the narrow short sleeves of his shirt to slice another piece. "And maybe you don't want to see the castle project end?" Annie started to shake her head, but he held up a piece of the banana bread to stave her off. "I like this Sam fellow."

She sat back, confused.

Uncle Lou continued, unabashed. "Like him a lot. Didn't ever get the kind of feeling from Gary, God rest his soul, that I do from this guy."

Dumbfounded, Annie listened. Uncle Lou was a fact-based person, always had been. For him to be offering an opinion on Sam's character was odd, to say the least.

"Don't know if you've got something going with this Sam," he said and she felt her face redden as he scrutinized her, "but I think this one's a good guy. Just my opinion, of course."

Annie opened her mouth to respond, although she didn't know what she was going to say, but he changed subjects abruptly, "So, what's the scoop on Gary's case, have you heard anything?"

"No, not a thing. I was hoping that detective would keep me informed about what's going on, but he hasn't. I guess since I'm one of the suspects, he really can't, but still." She lifted a shoulder as if to say it didn't really matter, but it did. Gesturing toward the bedroom behind her, she said, "I've been searching through his stuff, what little he had here. Think I might find a clue?"

"Worth a look," he said. His face wrinkled in thought. "You remember anything he might have said or done that could give you an idea of what he was up to?"

"Nothing. That Pete friend of his hasn't been around either, which makes me wonder about him. And all the stuff I've been going through," she gestured again, "is just old clothes and junk like that. Can't imagine I'll find anything of interest in stuff like this." Her left hand reached over to the other chair and she picked up the bathrobe. Holding it, she stopped, then looked across the table to her uncle. "Except . . ." she said. She could feel her heart pound in her chest, hear it in her ears. Her right hand raised up to her mouth as ideas raced through her mind.

"What is it?"

"It's just . . ." she stood up, staring at the garment in her hands. Bunching the worn green fabric around the sleeves, she moved her hands down, slowly, feeling her way in tentative movements. Gary had sewn in the pocket himself, years ago. She'd found a gift once early in their marriage, by accident, as she grabbed the item to throw it into the wash. The robe had rattled. Curious, she'd shaken it again until she'd found the source of the noise. Inside sat a small gray velvet jewelry store box. She'd opened it to find earrings. Ruby earrings. Which Annie found curious. Her birthstone was topaz and she'd often commented on how much she liked the pale golden color. She wore a marquis shaped ring on her right hand, a gift from her parents, with a nice-sized tawny stone set in silver. Nestled in this tiny presentation case were dark red gems surrounded by heavy gold halos. Gary knew she didn't like rubies and these certainly had to cost a great deal.

Just as she'd begun stuffing them back into their hiding space, considering how to react when he gave them to her, realization dawned. At that very moment Gary walked in, catching her with the clamshell box in hand. His reaction — the wide-eyed flash of panic and subsequent cover-up, the careful nonchalance in his eyes — told her volumes.

"Oh, you found it," Gary had said, his voice neutral.

Rattled, she held up the bathrobe. "I wasn't looking for anything."

He took both the robe and the box from her hands and showed her the hiding spot, smooth as can be. Without a moment's hesitation, he lapsed into a story about how he always hid items of value in the back of this robe and how he hadn't expected her to find it.

While he'd talked, Annie gathered some courage. "These weren't meant for me, were they?"

A flicker of something crossed Gary's face. While he was often able to dance around subjects and to worm his way out of difficult situations by turning on the charm or by dissembling, she knew when caught he crumbled. "No," he said. "But it isn't what you think. I've had these for a very long time. They were meant for someone else, a long time ago. I just haven't had the chance to figure out a way to sell them or trade them for something different. Something special for you."

She'd wanted to believe him.

Now she held the bathrobe, the memory of his explanation in her head. He'd hidden other things in it since then, but had always mentioned it to her in the way a person who's about to go into surgery tells his family where all the insurance policies are hidden. "If something happens to me . . ." he'd say, "you know where to look." Dismissing his warnings as paranoid, she'd given the robe little thought over the years. But that was before his burglary arrest.

Now that something *had* happened to him, she didn't know what she'd find. It took every ounce of Annie's courage to upend the garment and root around to find the big pocket. Her hand moved from the belt downward, grabbing bunches of fabric, hearing nothing, feeling nothing out of the ordinary.

But then, her hand crept down again. She squeezed and heard a crinkling noise. Felt resistance, felt something bend and it wasn't fabric. Uncle Lou sat across from her, his eyes alert. She understood that he was confused, but she didn't want to stop to explain. It wasn't as though she knew what she was looking for anyway. She had no idea what could be in this pocket. It could be old pictures, or his birth certificate. But she hoped for a clue. For something that could give her information about his killing. For something that could serve to exonerate her in Detective Lulinski's eyes.

Her left hand held the robe by the belted center, and she lifted it high, reaching down with her right to dig into the fabric pocket. She pulled out an assortment of papers. With varying shapes and sizes, the pile looked like a bundle of garbage, but she laid them on the table, feeling at once triumphant and alarmed, almost afraid to unearth any secrets they might contain.

Reaching back in, she searched again, coming up with a few more smaller pieces of paper and a wad of money. Twenties, tens, fives, and singles. Counted out they added up to just over a thousand dollars. She and Uncle Lou exchanged perplexed looks as she sat down.

"Well," she said with a grimace, "looks like I hit the jackpot."

Uncle Lou nodded, tugging at a corner of one of the papers, bringing it over to his side of the table. Holding the paper an arm's length away, he tilted his head back and narrowed his eyes before making a sound of frustration and reaching for his glasses. The black-rimmed, half-moon shaped spectacles resisted his attempts to open them, but he managed, using his mouth and one hand, keeping his attention on the paper he held aloft in the other.

Annie recognized the writing on a large white paper and picked it up in a flash of anger. The receipt for Gary's bail money. He'd taken it from her. That meant he'd been in her room when she hadn't been home. He'd gone through her things, pawed through her drawers. She'd hidden this one deep, under socks and pantyhose, along with her emergency money. Standing, she squelched a noise of pure fury and headed to her room, knowing before she got there, that her emergency money was gone.

Uncle Lou raised his eyes as she returned, spouting her anger. "Well, I know where some of that came from," she said in clipped tones, indicating the roll of cash on the table. "My secret stash." She sat down in the chair with a whump, leaning her elbows on the kitchen table and massaging her eyes. After a moment she glanced up and said, "How can I still be so angry at a person, even after he's dead?"

Uncle Lou wasn't paying attention. He'd pulled a few more papers from the stack and was going over them word by word. "Why would Gary have been interested in that missing Durer artwork?"

Annie reached over and pulled at one of the sheets her uncle had discarded. "I don't know." Picking it up she wrinkled her nose in thought. "These are copies of the articles you gave me. The ones that I thought were missing the other day. Sam and I looked all over for them, but they weren't on the table where I'd left them."

Getting up, Annie walked into the living room and returned with the original articles in hand. She held them up as if to fan the air with them. "But here they are." So much had happened between the time she'd left for Sam's house and when she'd returned, that the articles hadn't crossed her mind at all. Now, she'd found them under a book on the coffee table, and knew she hadn't put them there. "This is strange," she said.

Uncle Lou dug through the papers again, making little grunting noises as he read. Shuffling through them over and over, he picked up, put down, then picked up again, as Annie stared off into space, trying to piece wildly disparate information together so that it made sense. "You don't think Gary had something to do with the theft of the artwork from the museum, do you?"

Her uncle shook his head, his eyes never leaving the papers in front of him. "Definitely not. From the information I've gathered, this was a surgical strike. Took the efforts of more than one person, by far. Whoever pulled that caper off had access to state-of-the-art technology, professional contacts, and a lot of money. If Gary pilfered cash from you," his eyes flicked back to the bills lying on the table, "there's no way he could have been in on this. This job took sophistication. And that's one thing Gary didn't have."

"You can say that again," Annie said. She experienced a small measure of relief. At least he wasn't a big-time crook. Stopping to think, she realized that made him a small-time one. For a wry, amused instant, she wondered which would be considered worse.

Doorbell chimes interrupted her thoughts. She and Uncle Lou exchanged worried glances, as though sorting through Gary's things had conjured up whatever evil had led to his murder and now waited for them at the door. Annie shook herself and smiled, more to bolster her own self-confidence than anything, and went to answer it.

Though his silhouette was blurred and disjointed by the prisms of glass of the front door's oval window, Annie recognized Sam's form immediately, throwing open the door in a mix of happiness and excitement.

He stood there, leaning against the doorjamb, too casually, in a way that made Annie believe he was nervous, his left hand gripped around the leash of a large black and gray German Shepherd. "Hi," he said with a cautious smile.

Annie looked from Sam's hopeful, apologetic face to what appeared to be an identical look on the dog's upturned gaze. Staring at her with bright brown eyes, the animal sat, shifting its front paws a little, giving her the sense that it wanted to come inside, but was too polite to do so without an invitation. The pooch's long pink tongue hung out the side of his mouth.

Annie held the door open wider. "A new friend?"

Sam's face hinted at a grin as the duo came inside. "Well," he began, scratching the side of his head. "I was thinking about how you're all alone here at night and how someone tried to break in that one time. And, well . . ." he left the thought unfinished, and shrugged, as red crept from the collar of his T-shirt, making its way up to his cheeks. The pinkening of his face and the shy way he half-shrugged as his eyes met hers gave Annie a tiny shiver. Even now, with his face passive, uncertain, she loved looking at him. But him standing in her front hall, with a dog, was a surprise she hadn't expected. Unsure how to react, unsure how exactly she felt, she stood there, trying to decide what to say.

"What a great idea," Uncle Lou's voice boomed as he offered his hand to the dog to sniff. "Male or female?"

"Male," Sam said, looking relieved to have something to say to break the silence. "His name's Max. That's what they told me at the shelter, but he can probably be taught a new name," he turned to Annie, "if you don't like it."

Annie looked from Uncle Lou to the dog to Sam. Three sets of eyes stared at her, hazel, brown, and blue, waiting for a reaction. The only sound in the room was the dog panting and the occasional drip of saliva from his mouth onto the floor. "He — he's for me?" she finally managed.

"I know. I probably should have asked

you about this first, but I just don't like the idea of you being here alone at night. But . . ." Sam faltered as he spoke, "I figured that if you really didn't like him, I could keep him. He seems like a really nice pet and they said at the shelter that he's a great watchdog."

Something in Sam's voice let Annie know that this was really important to him. Taking a breath to get over the surprise, she nodded and reached over to greet Max. "Hey, boy," she said in a soft voice as he nuzzled her hand. She reached over and scratched him behind his pointed ears, noticing that his eyes were alert, flicking between the three of them, watching every move. "He's got to be nervous," she said to Sam.

"Do you like him?"

Annie grinned down at the dog who'd started to lean against her leg as she stroked his fur. "Yeah," she said. Glancing up, she caught a look in Sam's eyes. With a force that nearly took her breath away, it hit her. *He loves me.* She turned her head back down quickly, afraid that he'd read her thoughts from her face. *Oh my God, he really loves me.* Annie's knees felt ready to wobble and her hand shook a little as she pulled Max closer, for support.

Sam cleared his throat. "I picked up some supplies and stuff at the pet store on the way here. How about I go get them?"

Uncle Lou grinned at Annie while Sam headed to the car. "I'm going to take off myself. It's not the company, it's the hour." He glanced at his watch then at Annie with a rueful smile. It couldn't be later than nine in the morning. "Got up too early. Let me know what you find in those papers, okay? And if there's anything I can do . . ." He leaned down and took the dog's head in his hands. "You take care of Annie, you hear?" The dog blinked, as if he comprehended. Uncle Lou took off his glasses and headed toward the door, looking pointedly toward Sam out front. He grinned at Annie. "But I have a feeling you aren't going to be alone here much at all."

Chapter Twenty-One

Max lapped up his water with noisy eagerness, the action of his long pink tongue flinging droplets around the side of the bowl. Annie thought he seemed happier than he had at first, maybe because now he knew that he had a home. She smiled to herself. As if a dog could reason that way. Still, when he finished drinking and plopped himself down in the corner, she thought he gave a whuff of contentment. With his head resting across one large paw, his eyes followed Annie as she moved away from the sink toward Sam, who stood at the kitchen table, all of Gary's notes and paperwork spread out before him.

She watched Sam in profile, knowing that at any second he'd feel her gaze, look up, and she'd lose these precious moments to study him. His brow furrowed in concentration and the fingers of his left hand came up, massaging his temple, which she knew meant he was deep in thought. From the slight curl of his light brown hair to the way he studied the information before him, she found herself attracted to every inch of this man. Contented, she took a deep breath, trying to memorize every curve, every line of his face.

He must have heard her sigh because he looked up. Caught her staring. But when he did, it was almost as though she'd been waiting for him to do so. She managed a small smile without breaking eye contact, asking him a silent question, half-afraid of getting the answer she wanted. Sam stood up straight, but didn't avert his gaze as a grin played at his lips. "What were you looking at?" he asked, his voice light.

Annie answered simply. "You."

She watched as his eyes smiled then, too. Could he be feeling that same invisible tug, that welling up of emotion she felt every time she looked at him? Feeling a red blush creep up into her face, she bit her lip. The need to touch him overwhelmed her, but she didn't move.

Tapping the pile of papers on the table, Sam said, "We should go through these." His voice wavered a little. "Maybe there's something important here."

Annie nodded because it seemed like the right response, but she wasn't really listening. Something about the papers. Something. But it didn't seem all that important at the moment. The sun coming in from the window to her right caused a brightness in the room, but one that paled in comparison to the light in Sam's eyes. They'd picked up the blue from the T-shirt he wore, but behind their sparkle she sensed a seriousness she hadn't seen before. And when he gave a shy half-smile, she finally understood the term "took her breath away."

Pointing behind herself with a vague motion, Annie started to speak, her words coming out in nervous spurts, "There's something I need. Um. In my room."

Turning, she headed to her bedroom. She stood at the side of her bed in the small room with her back to the open door. Closing her eyes, she listened to her heart pound as she whispered, "Please. Follow me."

For a long moment she heard nothing. Then the floor creaked behind her, and he was there. She let out the breath she'd been holding.

"Annie?" he asked, touching her shoulders. His fingers traced a slow shivering path around the back of her neck.

She turned, opening her eyes. Any doubts she had about his desire for her tumbled away in a rush. Sam cupped her cheek in one hand while his other arm encircled her waist. He brought her face up to his and their lips met, sending a torch of fire through Annie's body, lighting up every crevice, every secret place. Her breath uneven, Annie reached forward and upward for more, feeling Sam's lips encompass her own, pressing her mouth to deepen the kiss. As they pulled apart, they stood motionless, catching their breaths, their bodies carrying on the conversation that their words could not.

Annie reached up to trail a finger along the side of Sam's face. "Do you know how much I love looking at you?"

Surprised, as if he'd expected her to say something else, he leaned back a bit, but spoke in a soft voice, "Me? What's there to look at?"

She let her fingers trace his jaw line, then move further down, playing under the neckline of his shirt. "You're beautiful," she said with a sigh. "You're perfect."

Sam laughed, and Annie felt his warm body shake as he pulled her closer. "Nobody's perfect until you fall in love with them." His eyes became serious as he looked down at her. The weight of the unasked question hung in the air, sending weakness to Annie's knees. She felt as though she'd loved him forever. And would love him forever.

So close now that she felt her body mold to his, Annie could sense Sam's readiness. She felt a sweet wash of warmth course through her own body, as it wept with joy at the thought of being with this man. Their lips met again, touching, releasing, tasting, like a dragonfly's dance on the water at the lake.

"Annie, it's . . ." Sam began. He took a deep breath, "It's been a long time."

"For me, too," Annie said. She looked away, then back at him as she amended with a wry smile, "Since it meant something. Since it felt — right."

A shyness crept up between them. Annie shuddered with anticipation as they stood there, waiting to take the next step. Her heart welled up with a burst of affection. She trusted him, loved him in a way she'd never experienced before. She wanted to be with this man. More than anything. With trembling fingers Annie reached for Sam's belt buckle and moved to loosen it, not wanting him to see that she was biting her lip. It came undone easily, more easily than she would have expected, and she looked up at him, hoping for guidance.

His hands, which had remained chastely

around her hips, moved up, pulling her in with a swiftness that surprised her. She felt them move across her, roving at first, then become more insistent as they tightened around her back. Their mouths touched, parted, then came together, moving as though with one thought. Annie felt as though they were meant to fit together, as their mouths opened, wanting more of each other, inching impossibly closer. Sam's hands moved from her back, reaching around her sides, till they brushed against her breasts, sending shivers of delight down her spine. She pulled her T-shirt up over her head, then reached back to unfasten her bra. The look in Sam's eyes and the rumble of pleasure in his chest made Annie's heart quicken till she thought it couldn't beat any faster.

A tickle of fear caused her to give a tiny shudder. Sam reached for her, at once both gentle and strong, caressing her flesh with pleasurable pressure. His warm hands moved in tender slowness, but she sensed unleashed power just beneath the surface of his calm.

Annie raised both her arms to wrap around his neck, pressing herself forward, feeling as though she couldn't get close enough. He slid his fingers down her sides, causing her skin to explode in gooseflesh. She moved her hands downward, instinct taking precedence over rational thought, and tucked her hands inside his waistband, coaxing his jeans downward, and their lips met, not softly this time, but with heat and intensity as he crushed her body to his.

They pulled apart for a moment and Annie heard her own shallow breaths, felt the pounding of her heart in her ears. She reached a nervous hand out to help Sam remove the rest of his clothing.

"You're beautiful," she said as she ran her hands up his bare chest, leaning forward to brush him with her lips.

Wrapping his arms around Annie, Sam lowered her to the bed. She felt the heat and gentle pressure of his warm body over hers. They kissed, deeply, their bodies, their hands, their mouths exploring with an eagerness Annie had never felt before. "I'm in love with you," Sam said, never taking his eyes from her face. "And I want to be with you, Annie, but if you think we should wait . . ." his voice was ragged, his eyes, ever bright, concerned.

Annie reached up, silencing him with a touch to his lips. She kissed him in a long slow display of her own readiness, then reached to hold his face in her hands, feeling as though she knew love for the first time in her life.

Annie took a deep breath and blinked away the heat gathering in her eyes. "I love you, too. So very much. I don't want to go another day without having you know that. Please," she said, her voice a hoarse whisper, "don't stop now."

Later, as she lay on her side with Sam's strong arm wrapped around her, she sighed, contented. His breathing, which had almost reached the level of evenness that indicated sleep, now sounded a bit more shallow. She felt his arousal against her back and she smiled, feeling more comfortable and satisfied than she had in a long time. His hand shifted now, his fingers tracing an imaginary line along her naked hip, not stopping, but moving upward until he reached around to cup her breast. Turning toward him, they kissed, deeply, lazily. With a low moan, Sam pulled Annie over himself, settling her on top with his hands on her hips. She smiled as they began to move together, taking it slow, knowing that they had all the time in the world now, to learn to love each other.

Chapter Twenty-Two

"You're telling me you got that picture everybody's been talking about?" The big man smirked as he sat back in the booth and folded his arms across his chest.

Pete didn't like the guy's tone. As if the bastard didn't believe he could have gotten his hands on something this big. "Yeah, that's what I'm tellin' you." Pete affected a look of boredom as his eyes swept the room to the left. Al was leaning forward behind the bar, talking with one of the regulars, though his eyes flicked up now and then, as if to gauge how Pete's meeting was progressing. Al licked his lips as he nodded to the fellow talking and gesturing on the barstool in front of him, but Pete bet his mind was on the finder's fee he expected once this deal was done.

Al had brought the guy over to the booth, introducing him with a casual, "Hey, this here's my buddy Don Romas. You and him have some friends in common, I think." And then he'd left.

As Al walked away, Romas remained

standing next to the booth, just staring down at him for a few moments. Pete didn't like looking up to anybody; it made him feel like he wasn't the one in control. The guy was huge, everywhere. Paunchy, flaccid cheeks dropped down to become wiggly jowls. His full head of hair looked like it might be glued in place, its dark brown color contrasting with the long gray hairs sprouting from bushy eyebrows, and curling out and around his ears. More long, wiry strands made an appearance from within the v-shaped neckline of his pale green golf shirt. His gut could rival that of a ripe pregnant woman's and when he moved down closer, pressing his finger-tips onto the tabletop, Pete caught a glimpse of the man's nails. Manicured. Not the sort of guy he was used to dealing with.

He hadn't offered his hand to shake, not that Pete minded. Instead, he pulled his head low and looked straight at Pete. His eyes were a peculiar shade of brown with sort of yellowish flecks that Pete couldn't help but notice with the guy's face so close. Romas spoke with the voice of a heavy smoker, "You mind switching sides?" he asked, with a nod of his head to the empty seat of the booth.

Pete's hands were around his beer mug. He'd curled in his chewed fingernails, and held them against the glass. Lifting his chin to this guy, he narrowed one eye, "Come again?"

Romas tapped the table in front of Pete. "I prefer to sit on this side," he said, his manicured nails making a tiny clicking sound as he did so. "Facing the door. Makes me feel more secure, you understand?"

Despite the fact that it was a small request, Pete felt his position of strength slipping away. He sighed theatrically and moved to the other side, carrying the weighty plastic bag he'd brought along. He reached to drag his beer across the table, glad to hear it make a rumbling sound as it skittered across the uneven wood. Romas smiled, showing capped, tobacco-stained teeth, lowering himself into the seat Pete vacated. For a moment he wondered how the guy would fit, with a gut that big. Without missing a beat, Romas grabbed the table with both hands and edged it forward, repositioning it so that it accommodated his bulk, but pinned Pete in further, pressing lightly, but noticeably against his chest.

"Do you have this *alleged* masterpiece with you?"

"What are you crazy? You think I'd bring it here?"

Romas shook his head, then lowered his face and spoke in a quiet, terse voice. "You don't have shit, do you?" His face, wide with an undisguised smirk, loomed close. Mocking.

Pete sat with his arms on the table, crossed in front of him, feeling like a kid in an oversized desk. This wasn't going the way he'd anticipated. He snuck a look over to Al, but the bartender was busy adjusting some control on the television.

And now this Romas guy was laughing at him. Or looking like he was about to start. But beneath it, a cold-steel anger flashed in his eyes as he spoke. "I don't have time to waste with pissant guys who think they've made a score," he said, pursing his lips. "I deal with the real things. I deal with fine merchandise. I can look at you and know you've never seen anything of real value in your life. You're stuck in a rut, lifting cheap crap, trying to fence it for a couple of bucks. Barely making it. Am I right, or am I right?"

Pete felt a tremor of anger work up through his body. But Romas wasn't finished.

"And I don't have time to educate a nobody like you on what is valuable and what isn't. Because you're not ever going to find yourself in possession of something that I'd be interested in." He smiled then. Pete wanted to shove his beer mug down the guy's throat. "What did you do, buy some old drawing at a garage sale? Think you found a masterpiece?" He was really laughing, now.

Pete bit the inside of his cheek to keep himself from making a retort. He reached down to his side and snaked his hand into the plastic grocery bag next to him. He'd been so nervous about someone seeing what was in the bag, or the bag ripping, that he'd wrapped his treasure in newspaper, then overlapped it with four grocery bags to conceal its shape.

Right now, he cursed himself for his caution, as his fingers fought the plastic and fumbled around, looking for an inlet into each bag. The bags crinkled, the noise amplified by the small confines of the booth. He grabbed a handle from the outermost bag and pulled it up onto his lap, allowing himself a quick glance at Romas across from him. The man was ready to bolt, his half-lidded eyes expressing both disdain and impatience.

Romas placed his two plump hands on

the table, fingers spread, and began to boost himself up. It pushed the table further toward Pete's chest and he looked up to see the big man watching him grope through the bag. Romas shook his head with a smile that didn't reach his eyes. Then the sucker winked. "Pleasure doing business," he said with a snort.

Pete stopped digging long enough to shove the table back. It caught the other man by surprise and he stumbled a bit, sitting back down hard. The expression on his face was one of pure fury. He wagged one fleshy finger Pete's direction, "Don't you ever — " he began.

Pete brought the bag up to the table with a whump. "You," he said to the other man, "will wait till you see what I've got. Then you decide whether you want to stay or go. Got it?" Pete needed this guy to wait. He didn't have any other connections that could fence the kind of merchandise he and Gary had gotten their hands on. It was time he stopped taking this guy's shit and started acting like someone who knew what the hell he was doing.

His hands shook as he reached into the grocery bag, finally feeling the crumpled newspaper wrapping. He took out the lumpy parcel and laid it on the table between them. "Now," he said, attempting to come across more confident than he felt, "I'm gonna give you a look at this. Just a look. I don't want all the bozos over there to see what I'm carrying, you understand?"

Romas held his gaze for a moment. "Yeah, you show me what you got here, little man. I have a couple of minutes and I could use a laugh."

Pete's mind flew all directions at once. Both he and Gary had assumed that everything in that study was genuine and valuable. The truth was, neither of them knew a priceless piece of artwork from a scribble. If it wasn't for that newspaper article, they wouldn't have had a clue about the drawing. Maybe that DeChristopher fellow dealt with reproductions, and this wasn't the real thing. His gut told him the stuff was real though. Besides, it was too late to turn back now and there was only one way to find out.

Pete took a breath and moved aside one corner of the newspaper. But it was enough. Despite the low lighting, the diamond-encrusted egg shot a rainbow of color across Romas' face and his eyes grew large. He looked up at Pete, then back down at the egg. Pete watched him. He licked his lips and shot a nervous glance over to the bar, but no one paid them any attention whatsoever.

Romas used the newspaper as a shield, so that a passer-by wouldn't see the egg, but he caressed one smooth side of it, and nodded to himself. Bringing his other arm up, he cupped the egg in both of his ample hands, bringing it in for closer inspection, turning it gently one way, then another. After several moments of silence, interspersed with small sounds of appraisal, Romas looked up. "Where did you get it?"

Pete, emboldened, sat back, his arms across his chest. There was no mistaking the venal glint in this guy's eye. The egg was real, he thought with satisfaction, and though Romas was careful to keep his face passive now, he'd obviously been surprised to see something this valuable fall in his lap from a guy like Pete. Now, he'd pay top dollar for this little trinket to make up for his rudeness. Pete tried to decide what the egg was worth. More than he'd bargained for, that's for sure. "Same place I got some other stuff," he said with a shrug. He was careful not to look too anxious.

Romas nodded, pulling his lips into his mouth, then pursing them. He appeared to be deep in thought. Finally his eyes flicked up to meet Pete's and Pete was struck again by the odd color in them. "How much other stuff?"

Mentally kicking himself for not lifting a few more items while he was in that room with Gary, Pete squirmed in his seat. He was here to unload the drawing, and didn't want to lose focus. "The picture," he said, "the one I told you about? That's just as real as that egg you got there."

Romas nodded again, seeming neither impressed nor disappointed. Pete felt like one of the big guys all of a sudden, dealing in the big leagues and being asked to join the team. These trinkets might turn out to be his "nest eggs" after all. He smiled to himself at the play on words.

Pete held his hand out for the return of the egg. As he rewrapped it in the newspaper and shoved it back into the plastic bags, he thought he noticed Romas cringe. "What?"

"Nothing," the big man said, but he held up his hand in a signal to Al.

Two drinks arrived as Pete tucked the bag next to him in the booth, snug against his leg. Al stood there, the ever-present towel on his shoulder, holding a tray. A tray. Like he was serving some sort of royalty or something. Filled just short of brimming, the on-the-rocks glass sparkled, its amber brew catching the light as it was set before Romas. Al placed a shot and a beer in front of Pete, but asked, "Something you'd like better?"

Pete shook his head, and downed the shot, following it up with a gulp of beer and a smile. He could get used to this kind of life. He saw Al scanning the table, apparently looking for some clue of what they were discussing and, finding none, his face registered a shade of disappointment. "Anything else you gentlemen need right now?"

Romas raised his hand in a gesture of dismissal. "I'll let you know," he said.

As Al walked back toward the bar, Pete could feel his chest bubble up with the desire to laugh. What a rush. These guys wanted to do business with him. With him. He could write his own ticket now. Laying his right hand on the package next to him, he looked down for a moment at the tabletop and fought the mirth that kept creeping up. The score of a lifetime. And he had Gary to thank for it.

He managed to keep himself to a smile, but in his mind he thanked his dead friend for including him on the heist. And, even better than that, thanked him for getting himself shot so that he didn't have to share the take with anyone.

Chapter Twenty-Three

Sam looked up as Annie came into the kitchen. "Have a nice nap?" he asked.

Annie, who'd thrown on her T-shirt and shorts in a hasty attempt to get dressed, didn't think she'd ever seen anything more wonderful than Sam as he sat there, completely at ease, in her kitchen. She walked behind him and wrapped her arms around his neck, kissing the top of his head. "Thank you," she said.

"For what?" Although the question was asked innocently enough, Sam's eyes twinkled as he turned to her.

"For making me feel . . ." Annie came around and sat down. Her eyes began to feel hot again and she wrinkled her nose to keep from getting emotional. "For making me feel. Again."

"When I said I wanted to be with you, I didn't mean, only . . . that." Sam reached for her hand. "I meant I always want to be around you, Annie. When I'm not with you, I'm thinking about you."

Annie smiled as she reached up to caress

his hand in return. "I thought it was just me who couldn't get enough of you." At Sam's grin, a touch of shyness returned, so she shifted in her seat. "So, what have you been up to while I was sleeping?"

Sam nodded his head toward the table. "I've separated these into three piles," he said, pointing. "Newspaper articles, official forms, and," Sam turned his palm upward in a gesture of uncertainty, "notes. Most of which don't seem to make much sense."

"It's all stuff he considered important, I guess." She lifted a paper from the first pile, giving it a cursory glance. "But why he'd be collecting information about the missing Durer drawing is beyond me. And the rest of this stuff, I just don't get. Look." She picked up an index card from the third pile, reading aloud. "Portfolio. Suit. Bibles? What do you think that means?"

Sam shook his head. "I have no clue." He held up a beat-up cocktail napkin. Across the decorative gold-monogrammed "Q" surrounded by a wreath of leaves, a name had been scrawled in blue ballpoint pen. Annie recognized Gary's handwriting at once. Despite the fact that the ink had skipped as he wrote, the name was clear.

"Do you have any idea who this is?"

"Donald Romas," Annie read, trying to concentrate. "No. None." She picked up a note from Sam's third pile and started reading again, confusion in her voice. "This one's another list. Car, copies, Pete, file, Al." Puzzled, she glanced up to see Sam leaning forward, focusing on the back of the card she held.

"Any idea what 433831 stands for?" he asked. "It isn't a phone number."

"Huh?" Annie flipped the card over to look at the scribbles penned across the back of it. Her mouth dropped open as she recognized them.

Sam looked up. "What is it?"

Blinking, Annie put the information together in her mind. Her voice was soft as she spoke, trying to sort it all out. "Those numbers are the code to the De-Christophers' burglar alarm. Gary must have watched me when I input them. Oh my God. And . . ." she bit her lip, as it occurred to her, "my key." She jumped from the table and headed out the front door. Max leapt to attention, accompanying them as Sam followed, looking perplexed.

At the car, she rummaged through the glove compartment but came up with only one keyring — Sam's key to Millie's on the heart-shaped chain. The other one was gone. Sam started to come down the front stairs, but she waved him back and scratched Max absent-mindedly behind the ears as she came inside and headed toward the kitchen.

"I knew there was something wrong," she said, worry and excitement making her voice rise and her words speed up. "Something was missing when they showed me Gary's things at the police station. I just wasn't thinking. Wasn't concentrating." Sitting down, she blew out a breath of frustration and looked at Sam. "It was there. The DeChristophers' keyring. I'd bet my life on that. But the key wasn't on it."

"Annie?"

She got up again and started pacing from the back door to the sink. "He took my key from the glove compartment. And he had the code."

Sam, his head slightly canted, watched her. "You think he went back to the DeChristopher house? You think he was planning to break in?"

Annie stopped mid-pace. Rubbed her eyes. "Let me think. Let me think." Staring at the ceiling, she began to recreate that last day aloud. "I got mad at him. He'd gone wandering through the house and called me over to see something. Something in Richard DeChristopher's study."

"What was it?"

Annie stomped her foot in exasperation. "I didn't look." She shook her head and threw her hands up in an angry gesture. "The fact that he was going through the house without anyone watching him made me so furious that I made him leave, immediately. Maybe if I would have gone over there, maybe . . . I don't know." She pinched the bridge of her nose, took a deep breath. "That's when we headed to the restaurant and had the big argument."

"And he left you there, taking your car."

"With the key in the glove compartment."

"Do you think he set you up? You know, orchestrated an argument so that he could have access to your car and then the key?"

"You mean like he'd been planning a break-in ahead of time?"

"Yeah."

"I don't know," Annie answered slowly, piecing it together. "Going out to lunch *was* his idea. Right after we overheard that the DeChristophers were going out to some fancy dinner that night. So he knew they wouldn't be home. But still . . ."

"He might have hatched the plan that morning, when he saw things start to fall into place for a hit."

Annie sat down. "I hadn't thought of that. But the argument did seem to come out of nowhere. It was so sudden, and so strong." She let her hands drop onto the table, with a thump of frustration. "I wouldn't put it past him. Not for a second." She looked up at Sam, who leaned against the counter. "So what do you think happened? Do you think he ripped off the DeChristophers and then Pete killed him for whatever it was they got?"

Sam sat across from her. "Mrs. DeChristopher didn't mention a burglary, did she?"

"No."

"Maybe Gary never got the chance to break in. Pete, or whoever killed Gary, might not have tried to get in there, yet. Maybe now that they have the key and the code, they're just waiting for an opportunity."

Annie's eyes widened as she started to get up. "Then I'll have to warn them." She pressed her hand against her forehead as she berated herself for not thinking. "Gina was so trusting. She didn't want her husband to know that I had a key. Now it's all going to come out and she's going to get into trouble."

Sam reached for Annie. "Hang on a minute. We're just guessing here. There's no evidence. No *real* evidence. And you don't want to get them all worked up for nothing." Sam pulled out the copies of the newspaper articles. "This, for instance. What do you think this missing artwork has to do with anything?"

Annie shook her head again. "Have no idea. But Richard is quite an art buff. Maybe Gary thought that he saw something there that reminded him of this drawing."

Sam sat back. "You don't like Richard DeChristopher, do you?"

"No. I know it's silly, but the guy scares me."

"And he's got some sort of bodyguard who hangs around?"

"Timothy, yeah. He's not so bad, kind of stays in the background. But he looks like a tough guy."

"Do you think that Richard DeChristopher is capable of perpetrating a crime?"

"Perpetrating a crime? My, aren't we sounding professional here." Annie felt herself smile despite the fact that she didn't know what was going on, didn't know what to do. Call Gina? Call Detective Lulinski? Or chalk up all her thoughts to her wild imagination? Sam sitting across from her had a look of deep concern. His brows furrowed together as he sat back, his arms folded across his chest, reaching out now and then to sort through the papers, trying to help make sense of it all. She was glad to have him with her. They were facing this together and knowing he was by her side made her feel stronger.

"What if . . ." Sam sat forward, leaning his elbows on the table, "What if Gary *did* see the missing Durer artwork at the house?"

Annie's voice was dismissive, "That would mean . . ." she stopped, then spoke more slowly, ending her thought with a question, "that Mr. DeChristopher had to be the person who stole it in the first place?"

"What do you think?"

It felt like a cog had clicked into place. "Oh my God," she said. Then, "No. It can't be. He was just honored for being some kind of citizen of the year. And I don't think he'd keep something worth . . ." Annie pulled the paper closer to read a couple of lines, "ten million dollars in his house. Do you?"

"He might, if he had a working burglar alarm and a bodyguard."

Annie shot Sam a look that was half warning, half fear.

He held his hands out as he spoke again. "Where would you hide a missing piece of artwork? One that the entire city knows about. Heck, that the entire world knows about? You can't just walk into a safe deposit vault with it under your arm, you know."

Annie nodded. "Plus, these things require special humidity and temperature to preserve them. You don't want to keep something that valuable in less than ideal conditions. At least, not for an extended period of time."

"If Gary was thinking of stealing this from DeChristopher, he was in over his head. And he probably wasn't about to attempt this alone. I think we have to find this Pete guy."

"I wish that detective would take me seriously with that. He didn't even seem interested. Completely dismissed the idea that Pete could have been in on Gary's murder." Annie's mouth wrinkled in a frown. "Especially since he was found not far from that apartment where they used to live. I would have thought for sure he'd want to follow that up."

Sam reached for Annie's hand. He held it in a soft grip, absent-mindedly rubbing his thumb across the tops of her fingers. Annie felt her body respond, but forced herself to keep her mind on matters at hand. "And you know what?" he said with a smile. "We might be blowing this totally out of proportion. What are we working with? A few newspaper clippings and conjecture. Let's stop worrying about it for a while. If Gary and Pete were working together, then it's all over now because Gary's dead. The only thing that worries me is your job over at the DeChristophers'. I don't really like the idea of you going back there. Just in case we're right about parts of this."

"I've only got a little bit more painting to do till the project's done."

"Can't you figure out some way to avoid going back? At least till we can clear this up?"

Annie sat up straighter as a thought occurred to her. "Hey, I know. Listen," she leaned forward, placing her free hand over their entwined ones. "I told Gina I'd be there tomorrow afternoon. What if I go back there, one more time? Just to put the finishing touches on the mural. Anyway, it would look fishy if I don't complete the project." She wiggled forward in her seat as she continued. "And while I'm there, I'll try to get a look in DeChristopher's study and see if that drawing is there. Then we'll know for sure if our suspicions are right."

Sam shook his head, a look of incredulity on his face. "And what if we are right? Do you have any idea how much danger you could be in?"

"Why? Why would I be in any danger at all? How are they going to know that Gary was plotting to rob them? I'm perfectly safe."

"If the guy is capable of stealing from a place as tight as the Art Institute, and if he's holding onto some artwork worth ten million bucks, then he's capable of a lot of things you're best off avoiding." Sam's voice rose as Annie shook her head, her mouth set in a line of determination. "Come on, Annie, think about it. You're not Nancy Drew, you know."

"Of course I'm not," she snapped, knowing he was right but not wanting to admit it. "Nancy Drew wouldn't be pregnant."

Sam's eyes held hers for a long moment

before a small grin appeared on his face. "Well, not that we know about, anyway."

Annie felt a smile creep up. "All right," she said. "I'll come up with some excuse to not go back right away. But we should probably tell that detective about this stuff." She started to gather the papers together, arranging them into as neat a pile as she could. "I guess Gary's pocket is as good a place as any to keep these."

Sam put his hand out. "Tell you what. Give them to me. When I have some downtime today, I'll go over all of this again. You never know."

Max leapt to his feet.

Sam and Annie looked at him, standing alert at the back door. Sam stood up. "Think he needs to go out?"

Just as he said that, Max moved forward. Pressing his snout up against the crack between the door and the jamb, he growled. Annie saw the fur on his back stand up on edge. "Here, boy," she said. But he didn't move.

Growling deeper, Max leaned further forward and then stopped and sat back. Without taking his eyes from the door, he began to bark. The low-timbred sound coming from this animal made her realize how glad she was that Sam had brought him. He'd scare anyone away with that bark.

Sam headed to the back window and looked out. "Nobody out there," he said. "Maybe he sensed a rabbit or squirrel or something running by."

Annie opened the back door and Max raced out and sped to the back gate next to the garage, where he stopped and barked till Annie felt almost hoarse herself from listening to him.

Once back inside, Max panted and paced back and forth, wearing a path from the front door to the back door again and again, stopping only occasionally for a drink of water from his new purple bowl. Eventually he sat down, then lay down, but his eyes flicked back and forth, the long gray hairs above his eyes shifting with each movement.

"Guess he needs to get used to being here," she said, amused by the dog's antics.

Sam pulled Annie close. She loved his smell and the feel of his strong arms around her. It was as if nothing could touch her when they were together. She felt safe. He kissed her forehead, keeping his lips there as he spoke, "That's something I wouldn't mind getting used to myself."

Chapter Twenty-Four

Richard DeChristopher leaned forward, listening to the one-sided conversation as his wife spoke on the phone. She had her back to him as she cradled the cordless handset against her cheek, chattering so much that he wondered how much information she could possibly glean without listening. And he wanted her to find out as much as she could. From what he could tell, it was Anne Callaghan on the other line and he leaned over to whisper to Timothy when Gina moved farther into the kitchen.

"It sounds like our little painter friend isn't going to make it here today."

Timothy's face was impassive. "How do you want me to handle it?"

Richard's eyes were on Gina's back. He didn't answer. He knew that the longer Gina spoke to Anne, the better their chances of finding out what they needed. In all probability, Anne was unaware of her husband's involvement in the theft of the Durer, but she was still their best link for getting it back. Whoever that other guy was who'd made off with it, Anne was likely to know how to find him. The only difficulty was getting the information from her. She was a smart one, that girl.

Gina opened the refrigerator, standing in front of the door, with a hand on her hip. The cool air rolled out from the lighted compartment in graceful waves. It was too hot in their house. He kept telling her that. But the woman was always cold. You'd think with the extra layer of insulation she carried, she'd always be warm. Her eyes scanned each shelf, as though her mind could process all the different combinations and options, even as her face contorted into a sad, empathetic frown.

"Oh, no, honey, not really?"

Richard and Timothy exchanged glances. They needed patience at this point, but Richard was finding it ever more difficult to maintain a calm exterior. Charles Bernard's wire transfer into Richard's offshore account for half the agreed-upon price had arrived safely two days ago and the playboy's anxiety was mounting. He'd been calling several times a day since Monday afternoon to check on the whereabouts of the drawing.

Gina lifted the tinfoil cover of a platter, pulling out a wide slice of ham. She folded it in two and took a bite, lifting the microphone part of the receiver high so she could listen, but evidently so that Anne couldn't hear her chew. Just as she was about to take another large bite, she stood up a little straighter and brought the phone back near her mouth. "Hang on a second, honey, okay? I got a beep."

Pressing a button, Gina said, "Hello?" They watched her roll her eyes, say "okay," and then press the same button again, connecting back to Anne. "Listen, sweetie, my husband has a call. The guy's on his cell phone, and says it's about some legal thing that's real important. Sounds very wound up, if you ask me. Like paying for a few extra minutes is gonna break him or somethin'. I'm going to give you a call back again one of these days though, okay? Talk with you later. Buh-bye."

Gina handed the phone to Richard and plunked the platter of ham down on the table between herself and Timothy. "You want anything to eat?"

Richard stood up when he heard the voice on the other end of the connection. "Hello, Charles," he said easily, walking toward the back of the kitchen to look out the triple set of doors. The overcast sky felt as dark as Richard's mood, the rumbles in the distance ominous and loud.

"I haven't made this many calls in a row to one person since I was a horny teenager looking to get laid for the first time," Charles said. His voice attempted humor, but Richard could hear the strain beneath the levity. "But back then when I finally got screwed, it was a good thing."

Richard made noises to approximate a hearty chuckle, but his mind was working, gauging the other man's mood and the best way to approach this situation.

"Well, old friend," Richard said. He drew his words out, attempting to give the other man the impression that there was nothing to be worried about. "I hope you aren't suggesting that I intend to take advantage of your trusting nature." He chuckled again, his fingers tight around the handset of the phone. "I'm certainly not out to screw you. I mean, what would Gina have to say about that?"

No laughter came through the phone line. Richard winced as he stared out the doors. This was going to be a tough sell.

Fat raindrops had begun to fall, making a polka-dot pattern on the redwood deck outside. A bright streak of lightning traversed the dark sky, purpling up the clouds. If he hadn't been so wound up about this drawing, he might have found it beautiful.

For a long moment the phone was silent. "Maybe I'm not being clear," Charles finally said, as a hard edge crept into his voice. "I sent you two and a half, with the understanding that upon receipt, a certain package would be brought to me. And at that point I'd planned to give you the other two and a half."

"I know that."

"Do you? Then I don't understand the holdup. You've had my funds for two days. And I'm still here, sitting in this lame Chicago hotel, waiting for my picture. I have things to do, Richard. And I don't like waiting."

"I understand, and I assure you —"

"Do you realize those are the exact words you used yesterday? I'm not a patient man, never have been." His voice came over the line, tight and vicious. "And I have the means to make things happen. You do get my meaning?" Richard heard the man take a deep breath before he continued in a more reasonable voice. "I'd be more than happy to send a messenger over there to pick it up. A fellow I trust. Someone who will do exactly as he's told and not *modify* the plan."

"Look," Richard said with a sigh. "I don't have it here. I should have let you know that sooner. That's why the holdup."

He could almost hear the gears working in the other man's head. "Didn't you tell me that you had it right there in your study? The night of that dinner. It was there."

"Of course it was here. And it will be back here shortly. What I'm trying to tell you is that I decided to find a safer place to hold it until our transaction took place." The fingers of Richard's left hand beat against the side of his leg. "Didn't want to take any chances with something that valuable. You can see the wisdom in that, can't you?"

The silence hung for a long moment as Richard pressed the phone to his ear, his mouth tight in a line, as he waited. Charles heaved a theatrical sigh. "When will you get it back?" And then he continued, just as Richard opened his mouth to answer, "You know what? I don't care when it's good for you. Don't tell me. I have a reception to attend tomorrow night. You can bring it by afterward. Call me," he said, and hung up the phone.

George Lulinski and Bill Schumann stepped out from the glass doors of the police station into the grayness of the bleak day. George meandered down the seven steps to the asphalt parking lot, turning to see Bill, still just outside the back doors, stretching.

"Looks like more rain," Bill said before following George down the steps.

George nodded as the sky rumbled above. Despite the puddles on the ground and the promise of more precipitation to come, the day was heating up. It was only ten o'clock in the morning and already George could feel trickles of perspiration making their way down from under his arms, soaking his shirt.

As they reached the unmarked squad car, George removed his suit coat, draping it over the seat behind him. Bill did the same, but then dug through its inner pocket before settling into the passenger seat. He came up with a pack of gum and started to open it. Glancing up, he caught George's look and shot him a grin. "How about I try to chew quietly?"

"How about you forget the gum while we're in the car," George countered, serious. "You go ahead and masticate to your heart's content while we're interviewing this guy, but just keep it out of the squad, okay?"

Bill shoved the pack into the breast pocket of his shirt. "You got it, boss," he said.

Minutes later they pulled up in front of Quint's After Five. The corner tavern, obviously built in the 1950s, had somehow survived the neighborhood's renovations. A two-story structure, with living quarters upstairs, it was both business and home to its owner, Al Quint.

"It ain't gonna be open at this hour," Bill said as they spun their suit jackets back on. "You want to try the owner's place first?" He indicated a white side entrance, displaying the same address as the bar.

George was already moving to the door set into the corner of the structure, beneath a plastic sign that gave the bar's name in small letters, the logo of a major beer brand in bright shades of red and blue. He propped open the lightweight screen door and pushed at the heavy inner one, shrugging at Bill with a look that said, "How do you like that?" when it opened.

Stepping into the dark, stale room, George stopped a moment to adjust and assess the place. There were three booths along the wall to the right, four tables to his left. The bar itself, set against the north and west walls, was small, but despite the aroma of old beer and cigarettes, the place appeared well-kept. The bartender looked up as they moved into the room, squinting his eyes their direction. He was a big fellow, nearly bald, leaning over the counter, in conversation with a gray-haired guy, his only patron.

That guy, sitting on a red-topped bar-stool, looked like he might have frequented this place since it'd opened decades ago. He held a cigarette in his right hand, the smoke wafting upward in lazy curls, as he focused his attention on the two men by the door. George met the two pairs of eyes and nodded a greeting.

"We ain't open yet," the bartender said, grabbing a towel from his shoulder and rubbing his hands in it.

George moved up to the bar, taking the stool next to the old guy. Bill went around to the other side, flanking him. The two detectives presented their identification briefly, George noting that the old guy reacted with dulled curiosity, and the bartender had no reaction at all. No reaction to a visit by the police meant only one thing to George. This guy wasn't surprised. It meant they'd been expected and the reaction was practiced. Maybe there was more here than he'd figured. Over the old guy's shoulder, George watched Bill pull out his pack of gum and shove two sticks in his mouth. Shaking his head, George started the interview.

"I'm looking for Al Quint," he said, addressing the bartender. "That you?"

The guy flipped the towel back up to its shoulder perch. "I'm Al. What's up, officers?"

"We're looking for someone. A guy named Pete. Pete Munro. You know him?"

Al appeared to think for a minute. He dragged the towel back to his hands and wiped them, looking down. "No," he said slowly, "don't know him."

The old guy at the bar watched the interchange from beneath shaggy eyebrows, his red-veined cheeks letting George know that sitting here with a drink at ten in the morning wasn't a fluke. Bony, wrinkled arms leaned forward on the bar, the age-spotted hands meeting in the air near his face, the cigarette not three inches from his mouth. He appeared to be trying to follow the conversation, turning his head toward whomever was speaking, but he was several beats behind each time.

George narrowed his eyes at Al. Bartenders were usually pretty easy to work with. They met so many guys on a first name basis, that it was rare to find one who could say "no" right off the bat. The usual response was a shrug and a request for a description.

"I got a picture here," George said, reaching into the file folder he carried. He pulled out the first one. They'd obtained it from drivers' license records after interviewing the three druggie boys in Pete's old apartment. Fearful of an arrest, they'd given the detectives everything they knew, including Pete's last name and frequent haunts. While they didn't know where he was staying now, they did know that he'd been talking about some big score coming up.

If the license didn't work, George had some mug shots too, from Pete's prior arrests. The most recent one had provided the two detectives with a bona fide reason to pick the little guy up. An outstanding warrant. Perfect. Now if they could get him into custody, they could squeeze him on the homicide.

Al reached a beefy hand out and took the picture. He made a show of taking it back near the bottle racks where the light was better, and he held it at arm's length, as though scrutinizing carefully. Walking back with his arm outstretched, he said,

"Nope. Never saw him. Sorry."

Instead of putting the photo away, George placed it on the bar, while digging out the mug shots. As the old guy's eyes slid over to check it out, George moved it closer to him on the pretense of needing room on the bar to place his folder.

Al tilted his head toward the folder. "What'd this guy do, anyway?"

Bill leaned in on the bar, his mouth working the wad of gum in his mouth. "We just want to question him, is all. About a homicide."

George placed four mug shots of Pete on the bar, facing Al. He noticed out of the corner of his eye, the old guy had snuck a finger over and pulled the first picture close.

"Homicide, huh?" Al said, the towel back in his hands. He didn't look at the shots spread out before him. "Who'd he kill?"

"Well," Bill drawled, "we're not saying he killed Gary Randall." Al's eyes shot up at the mention of the name. "We just want to ask him a couple of questions."

"You knew Gary Randall," George said. He didn't phrase it as a question.

Al scratched his forehead, frowning. He started to say, "I — yeah . . ." when the old guy cut in.

"Hey Al, you do know this guy. Dontcha remember?" The old guy's words slurred and George's eyes met Bill's over the slicked-back hair of his gray head. "He was just in here yesterday."

"Yesterday?" Bill asked.

"Emil don't know what he's talking about, detectives. He's seeing things." Al bent, came close to the old guy's face, but he seemed unaware. "I think you had too many this morning. Maybe you ought to head on home."

George turned the other mug shots so they faced the old guy. He moved the empty glass to one side, to accommodate them. Coming aware, it seemed, that all eyes were on him, the old guy gave a grin. "What'd you say this guy did?"

"Just want to ask him some questions, old-timer. About a homicide."

The guy grunted. "This guy ain't no killer," he said, pushing the picture back to George. "Is he, Al?"

"I wouldn't know, Emil," Al said, his towel back in his hands.

"Sure you would. You better tell these guys that too, you know." His shoulders lifted for a moment, stifling a belch. "Otherwise when they get wind of that deal . . ." his gaze lost focus and he reached for his glass again, upturning it till the last drops fell onto his tongue. "Can one of you fellas . . . ?" He lifted the glass in question.

George nodded to Al who protested. "Listen guys, this guy's talking out his ass. The last thing he needs is another drink."

"Fair enough," George said, "but if you won't let me buy him a drink, then I guess I'm gonna have to give both of you guys a free ride to the station instead. How's that?"

Al pulled out a bottle from beneath the bar and poured. Leaving the bottle up top, he held onto the edge of the bar with clenched hands.

"What were you saying about a deal?" Bill asked.

The old guy moved his head in slow-motion, and it took several seconds before he answered. "Listen. Now this is important," the words came out choppy as he enunciated each syllable. "Al here, is my friend." He reached across the bar to grasp the bartender's hand and he held it, tears forming in his eyes. "He's been letting me come here since my Johnny died. Twenty-eight years ago." Pulling his hand back, he used the back of his other arm to wipe at his nose. "And I'm not gonna let him get caught up in some kinda murder problem. I know him too good for that."

"Emil —" Al said.

"Let him talk," George warned.

"You pick up this guy, you'll find out. My friend here don't deal with no murderers."

George sensed they were losing him. "This guy," he asked, pointing, "he was here yesterday?"

"He was sittin' back there," he gestured with his thumb behind himself, "in the booth with your other friend . . . that big guy, what's his name? Don Romas."

"I don't know who you're talking about, Emil," Al said, his words staccato behind clenched teeth.

"Back up, back up, a minute," George said. "Did you say Don Romas?"

"Yeah, he's Al's buddy, he does lots of good deals for him, don't he Al?"

George and Bill exchanged a look. "*The* Don Romas?" Bill asked.

Al shook his head. "Don't know what he's talking about. He never makes sense. Probably read something in the paper and thinks it's real, you know? I don't know the guy."

The old man waved his hand out toward Al, nearly losing his balance on the bar stool as he did so. "Sure you do. Some big business deal you were cooking, remember?" He turned toward George again. "But don't think nothin' of that. Al's always got business deals going. But they're on the up and up." He pointed toward Al. "That's my best buddy. The best guy in the whole world."

"Emil doesn't remember things so well, anymore," Al said, interrupting.

What anger could come from glazed eyes, shot across the bar as Emil sat up a bit straighter. "I can remember everything like it was crystal clear." He settled down again, his back stooping like an old woman's, as he muttered to himself. "Young guys nowadays. They keep tellin' us old guys that *we* forget, like we all have Alzheimer's or somethin'. But they forget more'n we do."

George turned to Al, whose mouth was set in a thin line, his eyes angry. But Emil wasn't finished. "Hell, I can tell you what I had for breakfast this mornin'," he held up the amber-filled glass, "an' I can tell you what I had for breakfast the mornin' I heard my son got killed." Tears welled up in his eyes as his voice cracked. "Twenty-eight years ago." His gray head bowed over the bar and he fell silent.

George stroked his chin, lifting an eyebrow toward Al. "Tell me about Pete."

"Okay, maybe he was here. You know, I see a lotta guys. I can't remember them all."

Bill tapped on the bar as he spoke. "Yesterday, though, huh?"

Al threw a hand out in a gesture of defeat. "It coulda been yesterday."

"And Don Romas?" George let the question hang, as he glanced around the room. Way down on Romas' food chain. To get the big man down here himself, this bartender had to have something impressive to offer him.

"He stops by for a brew once in a while. Just like any other guy who comes in here now and then."

Bill tapped again, attracting Al's attention. "Look. We need to talk to this Pete guy. We're not interested in your business dealings, but if you don't want to cooperate with us in our homicide investigation here . . ." He let the sentence hang.

Al slapped the towel down against the bar with a thwack. He shook his head at Emil, but the old guy was muttering and drooling over the bar, his hands wrapped around his drink, the cigarette nearly burnt down to the filter.

"Okay, fine. He was here. I don't know nothin' about him bein' involved in a homicide. He told me Gary died, but he said it was an accident."

As George listened, he felt a piece of the puzzle push to the forefront, stopping just shy of dropping into place. Maybe Pete Munro didn't kill Gary Randall, but it was a good bet he knew who did. Now it was just a matter of finding the little creep.

Back outside, George started up the car, opening the windows for fresh air, even as the rain began pattering down again.

"Where to now?" Bill asked.

George put the car in gear and drove down the block, parking further down, but still keeping the bar in sight. Bill gave him a quizzical look. "What? You think that the bartender's gonna hurt that old drunk or something?"

George shook his head and tapped a cigarette out of his pack, gesturing for Bill to spit out his gum. "Just a hunch," he said.

DeChristopher slammed the phone into its cradle and turned around to face Gina and Timothy. Charles' manner had broken through Richard's normally calm reserve.

The bodyguard stood up. "Problem?"

Richard's lips were pulled tight against

421

his teeth. Gina stopped chewing, looking at him, a puzzled expression on her face. "What's wrong, Dickie? You don't look so good. Something happen?"

He pushed himself to maintain a neutral air, even managed to force a smile. "No," he said in as soothing a tone as he could muster. "Nothing at all." He walked over to the back doors again, his hands clasped behind his back as he looked out for a moment before asking, "Gina?"

"Yeah?" she answered. From the sound of her voice, her mouth was full again.

"Is that playroom mural about finished?"

"Yeah, about." Gina finished chewing and swallowed before continuing. "As a matter of fact that was Annie on the phone just now. She was supposed to be here, but I guess she can't make it today."

Richard turned toward his wife. "Oh really? Did she give you a reason why?"

Gina lifted an eyebrow, and he knew that his question had surprised her. He rarely concerned himself with projects around the house. Gina wiggled a little, as if to signify getting her back up, and affected an air of sass. "What's it to you, mister?"

Richard recognized the actions of a jealous wife. As if he had something like that on his mind right now. He didn't have time for games. His voice lowered in impatience. "Gina. Why isn't she coming today?"

A little bit of light went out of Gina's eyes, to be replaced by hurt puzzlement. Her mouth opened and she blinked, but didn't answer right away.

"Gina!"

Regaining her composure, Gina's eyes flashed. "She ain't got a car. Hers broke down or something. Or, that's what she said."

Richard lifted his glance to Timothy. "Call her," he said. "And go pick her up. Tell her anything. We're having a party or something. I don't care. Tell her we need the room finished today and don't take no for an answer."

Timothy nodded, moved toward the phone.

"Wait," Richard said. "Gina should call her. It'll be less suspicious if Gina makes the call."

"Suspicious? Dickie? What the hell are you talking about?"

He chewed the inside of his mouth as he tried to placate his wife. "It's a long story, honey, and I wish I had time to explain it to you. Anne might have, um, seen something while she was here. And I need to talk with her about it."

Gina pushed the platter across the table with a huff and watched her husband with narrowed eyes. "You got something going with *her* now?"

"Don't be ridiculous," he said in clipped tones.

Gina stood up and advanced on him. "I ain't as stupid as you think I am, Dickie. Don't think for a minute that I don't know when you got a girl on the side. I know. I always know. I just pretend, so's you have a place to come home to."

He raised his hands in an effort to calm his wife down, but her face was reddening as her voice rose, "I've heard you talk, asshole, and I know you don't 'get involved' with clients. But she ain't a client anymore and now you got the hots for her." Gina pushed at him with angry hands, but couldn't budge him. Instead the movement caused her to momentarily lose her balance. Richard reached for her arm to steady her, gripping hard and not letting go.

"Gina," he said pulling her with a rough tug. Her features contorted with rage and she looked about ready to cry. Richard bit back his anger and cursed the situation, not for the first time. The moment called for desperate measures. Over her head he saw Timothy, waiting for direction. Richard's voice was low. "You will make that phone call, you hear? And you'll be convincing. I don't care what the hell you think is going on between us, and I assure you, madam," his voice took on a condescending tone as his grip tightened, "that your imagination has run away with you once again."

"Call her yourself," she said, wrenching her arm out from his grasp.

Richard felt a rush of fury as Gina stepped back, massaging her arm, just out of his reach. He wanted to slap that woman silly. If she had any idea what a fool she was making of herself. Taking a deep breath, Richard turned to Timothy and spoke in a quiet voice, afraid of losing even a small measure of control. He knew he was capable of doing serious harm. "Take my wife and the boys to her mother's house, will you?"

Timothy nodded and moved toward Mrs. DeChristopher, reaching his hand out, but not touching her. She shot an angry glance at her husband before moving to head out of the kitchen. "Screw you," she said.

"Timothy," Richard added, waiting for the big man to turn. "I better go down to visit Charles. Settle him a little. He needs some reassurance if we're going to do business and I can't let this deal fall through. I should be back in a couple of hours." Gina had moved out of earshot. "After you drop off my wife, go directly to Anne Callaghan's house and pick her up. Have her work on the playroom till I get back. I'll call her and let her know you'll be coming."

Timothy nodded and they were gone.

Alone, Richard reflected on the morning. Anne was his best chance at finding the drawing and he needed her here. The key would be to get information from her without her becoming suspicious of his intentions. He'd need to be friendly, inquisitive. She wouldn't respond as well to intimidation. At least not yet. But time was running out and he needed answers.

With one eye on Anne's business card, posted on the refrigerator with a colorful magnet, Richard dialed the phone. She would be there. He willed it. There were so few options left and he refused to accept the possibility that the drawing had slipped through his grasp forever.

She answered on the third ring.

He tucked his left hand into the back of his suit pants and conjured up his most ingratiating voice, "Good morning, Anne."

Chapter Twenty-Five

"Jeff?" Annie spoke into the phone, dragging a gym shoe onto one foot and hopping on the other one as she spoke. "Is Sam there?"

"No he's not, Annie," the boy answered, then added, "hang on one second." Annie heard him speak to someone in the background. From the sound of it, he was directing a delivery.

"I'm sorry," Jeff said, speaking back into the phone. "Sam said that he'd be in later this morning. He had a meeting with someone, but he didn't tell me where. Do you want me to tell him you called?"

Through the phone line Annie heard the sounds of things being moved in the background as she laced up her sneakers, one foot at a time, propped on a kitchen chair in front of her. "Please. I'll try reaching him on his cell phone, but in case I can't get through, let him know I had to go to the DeChristophers', okay?"

Kitchen sounds surrounding Jeff grew louder. "You had to go where?" he asked, his voice rising, as though Annie would have as much trouble hearing him as he had hearing her.

"To the DeChristophers'," she said. "Make sure you tell him, okay? It's pretty important."

As she hung up the phone, she turned to the corner of the room where she kept her paint supplies and gear. A brief check assured her that she had everything she needed to finish the job. She replayed the earlier phone conversation with Richard DeChristopher as she snapped shut the lid.

When Annie had explained that her car wasn't working, hoping her lie sounded convincing and apologetic enough to get through the conversation quickly, Richard had graciously offered her Timothy's chauffeuring services. Annie had declined three times, before Richard's insistence became too difficult to refuse. He was sorry to hear that her car was out of commission, but they were preparing for some big bash at the house tonight and Richard wanted to surprise Gina by having the playroom done. This way, he said in a voice so warm as to sound forced, she could show it off to their guests when they arrived. He hated to impose, he said again, but stressed how important this would be to Gina.

Something didn't ring true, but she

shook her head. *Imagining things.*

Annie would have much preferred to drive herself, to be able to come and go as she pleased, but she'd literally painted herself into a corner with the fib about her car.

She had a few minutes before Timothy was due. Annie reached for her phone again, this time dialing Sam's cell phone number, relieved to hear it ring. She'd been afraid he might have forgotten to turn it on this morning. After the end of the first chime, however, realization dawned. A shrill sound coming from her bedroom corresponded exactly with the sound from the handset by her ear.

Listening, waiting for him to pick up, she started toward her room, knowing at once what the sound was, but hoping against hope that she was wrong. The small black tip of an antenna stuck out from beneath her flowered bedskirt. She picked up the small cell phone and watched it, feeling her shoulders fall in dismay even as she took her home phone from her ear and hit the "off" button. The ringing in her hand stopped.

She'd counted on getting ahold of Sam before Timothy got here. Just in case. Just on the off chance that some of their suspicions about Richard DeChristopher were right. "Damn," she said.

Annie stood in her bedroom, trying to gather her thoughts. Turning her phone on again, she dialed Uncle Lou's number, letting her eyes drift toward the clock as the other line began to ring. At this time of the morning, he was most likely still sleeping. She let the phone drone on and on, silently cursing the fact that he'd never gotten around to hooking up the answering machine she'd bought him three Christmases ago.

Walking back into the kitchen, she slammed the phone back into its cradle and decided she'd run over to his house, just for a second, before Timothy got here. She wanted someone to know where she was. Uncle Lou's house key hung on a hook near her back door. She grabbed it and headed for the front door, thinking that if he wasn't there, she'd leave him a note. But then remembered that finding a pen and unused paper at his house might be problematic.

Congratulating herself for thinking ahead, she hurried back to the kitchen to scribble a short note explaining where she was. Just as she made it to her living room, Max leapt up and ran past her to the door, with a growl. He started barking at the prismed glass, his paws tapping a frenzied dance on the floor.

It must be Timothy. Annie frowned her disappointment. He was early. She wouldn't get a chance to let Uncle Lou know where she was after all.

"Quiet boy," she said to the dog, as she reached for the shiny doorknob. Then she thought about it. "Good boy," she said in a more appreciative tone.

Opening the door, her jaw dropped. "Pete," she said, surprised. "What are you doing here?"

Max growled, his face lowering to the vicinity of Annie's knee, nose inches away from the screen of the storm door.

Pete's eyes shifted from Max to Annie. His chin lifted, indicating the dog. "When did you get him?"

Annie ignored the question. He was wearing the same suit he'd worn the first time they'd met at the courthouse. Even more wrinkled than it had been then, the shirt was just as rumpled, sporting a shadow of dirt near the wide open collar. No tie. "Where have you been?" she asked, surprised at the instantaneous anger that had jumped into her chest.

Pete put a hand up, as though to explain.

"What's your name?" she asked, not even trying for civility.

"Huh?"

"Your name," she said again, with impatience. "What's your last name? I never got it."

Pete scratched at the side of his face. "I just stopped by to pick up some of my stuff, you know. Don't need to bother you. Just want to get my clothes and some other stuff that belongs to me."

Annie widened her stance a bit, and placed a hand on her hip. Max continued to make low rumbling noises next to her. "Give me your last name, and I'll consider returning your things," she said, with finality.

"Come on, Annie, I need my stuff. It's my property, you know." His voice started out petulant but then his tone altered. "I could report you holding stolen property if you don't give it to me."

Annie laughed at that. Her hand reached out to stroke Max's fur. Having him nearby felt good. "Go ahead. Report me."

She saw Pete bite the insides of his cheeks, as he strove for control. Whatever it was she had here of his, he was adamant about getting it returned. "Listen," he said, wheeling now, craning his neck to see inside the living room. "I just need ten minutes in there. Ten minutes, okay? I'll get what I need and be gone." He raised his eyebrows, encouraging her agreement. "And I swear to you, I'll make good by it. I'll make good on what Gary would have wanted. Just give me the ten minutes, okay?"

"What are you talking about?"

Pete's fists clenched, but just as he was about to speak again, the gold-colored Lincoln pulled up, Timothy at the wheel. Pete glanced behind, then back at Annie, as he started to move. "I gotta go, okay? But don't let anybody touch any of my stuff. You got that? I'll be back tomorrow, and I'll make good on it." He'd edged down the steps and was on the sidewalk, moving down the block. "I swear."

Annie still had the note for Uncle Lou in her hand as Timothy got out of the car and headed up the stairs. Each step creaked as he climbed to the porch, and Annie noticed that the blonde highlights on his spiked hair seemed brighter than they had before. He nodded in the direction Pete went and furrowed his brows. "Who was that?" he asked.

Thinking it peculiar for him to ask that question, she lied. "Lost his dog," she said, one hand on Max. "And the neighbors told him I just got one, so he came by to check."

Timothy's gaze settled on Max, who hadn't moved from his position next to Annie. Max bared his teeth. "Nice pooch," he said. "You ready to go?"

Annie remembered the note in her hand. "I have a phone call I need to make, then I'll be all set."

Timothy shook his head. "You know, I gotta be somewhere. How about you use my cell phone to make any calls you need."

"This'll be real quick," she said.

"Miss Callaghan?" Timothy said, his hand gesturing toward the car. "We really need to get going."

So much for trying Uncle Lou one more time. She left the note on her coffee table and grabbed her paints and tools. At the last second, she spied her backpack. There was nothing in it she needed, but she hoisted it over her shoulder nonetheless. "Bye Max," she said, scooching past the dog to get out the front door. "Take good care of the house while I'm gone, okay?"

"You know, Emil," Pete heard Al say to the drunk old guy in front of him as he heaved himself away from the bar, "this place shouldn't be called 'After Five' anymore. It should be called 'Before Noon.' " To the door he raised his voice, "We ain't open yet, for Crissakes."

Pete let the door swing shut behind him. "Hey, Al," he said.

The bartender ran a hand over his shiny head, "Holy Mother of God," he said. "What the hell are you doing here?"

"I got a problem."

"Yeah, I'll say you do. Two detectives were just in here looking for you."

"What?" Pete's hands splayed on the bar in front of him, and he half-swiveled to face the door as though the cops were expected to return any minute.

Al leaned forward on the bar. "Just a little while ago. They showed me your picture and said they were investigating a homicide. Thought you told me Gary got killed in an accident?"

Emil raised his head, his eyes blinking, not focusing. "That was today?"

Pete headed over to the front window and looked out for a long while before sliding onto one of the swivel-seated barstools. "They were just here?"

Al shook his head. "Settle down. I don't think they're coming back for a while."

Pete felt a cold sweat break out from beneath his arms and across his forehead. He swallowed. "What did you tell them?" he asked, his voice sounding creaky to his own ears.

"Me? Nothin'. But our buddy here . . ." Al's eyes slid over to Emil, who seemed oblivious to the fact that they were talking about him, "made you. Made you good."

Al plunked a shot of whisky in front of him. "Do you think they have the place staked out?" Pete asked, downing the shot with shaking hands.

"Naw. They were just asking questions, but I think you better watch your back, you understand?"

Pete nodded, and pushed the empty glass toward Al for a refill.

Complying with the silent request, Al poured, clinking the bottle back into its place between all the others before he spoke again. "Now listen, I don't mind covering for you, but you better make sure I get my cut on this deal between you and Romas."

"You and me both," Pete said.

"What's that supposed to mean?"

"Ran into some problems today."

"What kind of problems?"

Pete stared at the drink. "I couldn't get the picture."

Al's eyes widened. "What do you mean you couldn't get it?" He gestured to Emil with a nod of his head and moved out from behind the bar, heading for a booth. "Maybe we better take this over here. The friggin' walls have ears."

Pete sat down, and wrinkled his nose as his own body odor shot up in a puff. Most of his clothes were at Annie's too. He'd been able to get by while he stayed at the YMCA, but pretty soon his stash was going to run out and he'd be out on his butt. Again. He thought about all the fine things the money from this heist would buy him, things that shoulda belonged to him anyway. At least the drawing was hidden until this business was through.

"It's at . . ." Pete stopped himself. No sense in telling Al where the thing was. "It's in a safe place. I just can't get to it today."

Al's face turned red. "I took a chance on you. I set you up with Romas. And now with these cops sniffing around, I could get screwed for doing that. You better come through, you understand?"

Pete felt the thrill of playing ball with the big guys slipping through his fingers as he massaged his forehead, muttering to himself.

"When were you supposed to do the exchange?" Al asked. The front corner door of the bar opened again. Al squinted. "Oh shit."

"What do you mean you don't have it? Did we . . ." Romas turned to Al, as though looking for confirmation, "or did we not agree to an exchange of valuables this morning?" They were sitting at a table this time, Romas, Al, and Pete, far enough out of earshot of Emil who looked as though his nose was about to hit the liquid in his shot glass.

Al held his hands out. "I wasn't in on the arrangements. All's I know is that this guy," he gestured pointedly with his thumb, "was supposed to come through, and he didn't. Listen," he said, directing his comments to Pete, "I still get my cut, you understand?"

Pete's foot slipped from its perch against one of the table's feet, causing the top to wobble and the men's drinks to splash. "Sorry," he said.

Romas' eyes were small, with enormous pouchy bags, but their anger shot like an arrow through Pete's exterior calm. "You ain't sorry, pal. Sorry's what you're gonna be if you don't cough up that picture. I put

438

some feelers out yesterday and got some-one biting on it already." He licked his lips, and for a second Pete caught a glimpse of just how big a job this really was. A sheen of perspiration glimmered over the big man's upper lip and he gripped his untouched drink with his right hand, gesturing with the other. "If I find out I risked my reputation on a man who doesn't know how to honor his commit-ments, well . . ." Romas let go of his glass and sat back.

Al cleared his throat, "And my cut?" His beefy arms were crossed over the table, and he picked at the hairs on his right arm, looking nervous. "I held up my end of the bargain, buddy. You owe me."

Pete's hands spread themselves outward of their own volition and he cringed at the weakness the movement implied. "I can't come up with that kind of cash until we make the trade," he said, chancing a look over to Romas. "He's the guy with all the money."

"Yeah. Money you're never gonna see if I don't get what you promised me."

"I didn't say I couldn't get it, I said I couldn't get it today," Pete said, trying to keep the tremor out of his voice. "Just give me a couple days. It's in a safe place and I'll get it, I swear."

Romas stood up, looking at his watch. He pursed, then bit his lips as though thinking, staring as he did so, toward the front door. "Tell you what, little man. I'm gonna give you just one more chance. And you know why? Because I feel sorry for you." He reached over and slapped Pete's cheek twice, in an artificially friendly move. It stung. "I got business that's gonna take me out of town till Thursday. I'll be back here at ten sharp. Ten in the morning, you understand. Thursday."

Pete nodded, relieved. He knew he could get the drawing out of Annie's house by then. He felt his body relax as the big man began to move away and Al stood up to go back behind the bar. Just as Romas reached the door he turned around. "And you will have it by then. Right?"

Pete nodded, his head bobbing up and down like a flocked dog on the dashboard of a car running over potholes. He sent Romas a thumbs-up, feeling more confident watching the two men depart. "Gotcha."

Al had his back to him, and Pete heard the clink and rushing water sounds of glasses being washed. He stared down at the beer in front of him. He'd get that goddamn picture if it was the last thing he did.

Then who would be the big man? Downing the beer in three large gulps, he set it down with a heavy thunk, keeping one hand wrapped around the glass. Al didn't turn around.

All of a sudden the brew didn't feel so good in Pete's gut. "Screw it," he said aloud in frustration, shoving the empty glass across the table. He stared at it a minute, then stood up and headed out. He pulled open the heavy door with a violent gesture, slamming it against the wall before it boomeranged back to close.

Pushing through the flimsy screen door, he stood for a moment in the emerging sunshine, and jammed his glasses up his nose, letting his eyes adjust to the brightness. Putting one hand on his hips, he stretched out his back. It was going to be another hot one and the sudden change from the dismal bar to this outside fresh air made his sinuses ache.

He shook his head looking upward. Time to regroup. Time to plan. He nodded to no one, assuring himself that this was going to be a piece of cake after all. The only thing standing between him and the big score was Annie, and she wasn't worth the hassle. Not with that kind of money at stake.

He needed it by Thursday. Today was Tuesday. Not a problem.

Pete grinned to himself and stepped off the stoop.

"Peter Munro?"

He didn't see them come up. Two guys, "cop" written all over them. Moving now, to stand too close for comfort. He felt his mouth hang open and he closed it quickly, stepping backwards. They stepped forward again, minimizing the space he had to maneuver. They must have been staking him out after all. He slid his eyes between the two, judging his chance at a run.

Still, he attempted a touch of bravado. "Yeah, well, who wants to know?"

The guy closest to Pete introduced himself and his partner as the two pulled out their identification. Pete made a show of reading the IDs, as though he'd never seen one before. The older one a slim guy, took a last draw on his cigarette and flicked it to the sidewalk, grinding it out with his shoe.

"We have a warrant for your arrest, Mr. Munro," he said. "If you'd like to come with us." He gestured, palm outward toward the unmarked car at the curb.

In a split-second, Pete knew what he had to do. He nodded, making it look like he was cooperating. But as the two men fell in behind him, he bolted.

"Shit," he heard one of them say. The big guy, he figured. That was the one who scared him. He looked like he was in good physical shape. But Pete knew his own speed and he thought he could do it.

The sounds of rhythmic pounding behind him fought for dominance with the deafening thud of his own heartbeat in his ears. He scanned the area ahead, trying to decide his best path of escape. Ducking into a gangway between two three-flats, he shot toward the alley and went over the back gate with ease. He could hear the man behind him talking, into his mike, no doubt, but the voice came out breathless. Pete careened down the alleyway, looking for a promising yard.

As he turned into a gateless throughway, he heard his movements reported again by the guy running behind him. He didn't chance a look back, but the voice sounded farther back this time.

Streaking through to a shadowed space between two more homes, he checked right and left, then sprinted to the right. The car had been pointed north. Chances were, if the other guy was trying to head him off, he'd be coming from the left. He ducked into another gangway, doubling back and creeping along the bungalow's brick wall, checking to see if the guy chasing him had waited. He took in the row of neat yards, separated by matching cyclone fences. No one. He headed back to the alley, with stealth.

As he crept around the back of a white-sided garage, he knew he'd chosen the wrong direction.

"Freeze, asshole." It was the big guy, panting. "And put your hands up."

"Can I get you something?" Richard DeChristopher asked. "Diet pop, coffee?"

"No, thank you," Annie said, reaching the landing in front of the door to the play-room after a trip to the washroom. "I'm fine." Since he'd arrived home, he'd kept up a conversation, and now escorted her up both sets of stairs to the third level. He spoke to her differently than he had in the past, too. Eager, almost.

As she approached the room, she took a deep breath. Maybe now she'd be left alone to finish. Stepping inside, she reassessed it. Nearly finished, all it required were touchups. An hour or so for painting and another to rip up all the newspaper, masking tape, and drop cloths that she'd left strewn about the room. Then she'd be done.

Crouching over her tackle box of supplies, she felt a bit uncomfortable, as though her jeans were suddenly too tight for such a position. Rearranging herself, she sat down on the floor and looked around for one of her fine line brushes.

Richard DeChristopher didn't leave. Feeling his eyes on her, Annie turned. The man made an imposing figure as he stood in the doorway. Unhurried, he shifted his gaze from her to the rest of the room, taking it in, wall by wall, nodding. Even though he smiled in a gentle, beneficent way, his body stood rigid and his jaw clenched.

"You've done a magnificent job," he said.

A prickly feeling came over Annie's stomach. While he'd never been anything other than the picture of courtesy, all of a sudden the fact that she was alone in this big house with only Richard DeChristopher and Timothy made her feel uneasy.

"Thank you," she said, wishing he'd leave her alone.

Taking two steps in, Richard reached out to touch the wall, "So real," he said. "It's almost three-dimensional. Like I could reach over and break one of these vines in half," he snapped his fingers, "like that."

As he spoke he watched her. She felt her cheeks warm under his scrutiny and fought a sick feeling gnawing in her gut. Something was not right. She needed to get out of here.

Annie blinked. "You know," she said, her voice wavering, "I could probably use a glass of water, after all." She stood up. This job wasn't worth the fear she felt. Once she got downstairs, she was out of here, even if she had to walk all the way home.

DeChristopher nodded in a feigned subservient way, a little grin playing at his lips. "Of course."

Annie moved to the door, but DeChristopher blocked her way. "I was going to go down to get it," she said, trying not to look intimidated.

"Allow me," he said.

Annie heaved a sigh as he moved toward the landing outside the room's door. Good. Once he was in the kitchen, she'd make her way out. She glanced behind her. She'd leave the paint box and tools here, but she'd grab her backpack on the way out. She'd left it by the front door when she arrived.

"Timothy," he called from the top of the steps, never moving far enough out of the doorway for Annie to get around him, "would you be kind enough to bring Ms. Callaghan a tall glass of ice water?" He turned to her. "You do take ice, don't you?"

Annie, numb, nodded.

Turning back, he clasped his hands together. "Go ahead," he said, gesturing inside the room. "Don't let me stop you. I just thought that while you worked we could have a little chat."

Chapter Twenty-Six

George and the station receptionist stood outside the interrogation room. He held one foot in the doorway, keeping the occupants in sight. Bill sat across the table from Pete. They had been about to launch into their good cop, bad cop routine but Tonya's knock had interrupted the momentum. They'd have to start all over again.

"He says he'll only talk to you, Detective," Tonya said with a shrug of her shoulders. At George's look of impatience, she glanced back down at her note. "A Mr. Sam Morgan."

George eased himself halfway back into the room, nodding to Tonya. "Have him wait," he said. "Pete. Buddy," he said addressing the suspect, "I got a visitor. Somebody here who's got some interesting evidence," he said, embellishing on Tonya's information. "And guess what? It's all about you."

Pete's Adam's apple bobbed.

"So, you got yourself a reprieve for a few minutes. Detective Schumann here will

448

keep you company while I'm gone and anything you want to tell him? You go right ahead. And maybe, if you're real co-operative, things'll go easier for you."

"Mr. Morgan? What can I do for you?"

Sam carried a black leather folder into the office where two rows of steel gray desks crowded opposite walls, leaving a narrow aisle in which to walk. Detective Lulinski's desk was the second on the left. Except for the two of them, the room was unoccupied, which made Sam feel a bit more at ease.

The detective pulled a side chair from one of the unoccupied desks, and settled it next to his, effectively blocking the aisle if anyone needed passage. "Have a seat," he said.

Sam settled the folder on his lap, and tapped the pads of his fingertips together, measuring his words. "I have . . . that is, Annie and I, have found some notes and papers that make it seem as though Gary Randall was planning a theft." He tried to read how the detective was taking the information. "A big one."

"A big one," the detective repeated, showing no reaction whatsoever.

"Gary had a place he kept things, a safe

place. Annie ran across it yesterday morning and I just thought that there might be a clue." Sam spread his hands out. "Or, something."

Detective Lulinski sat back. "And you're hoping that this evidence you have will shift our investigation away from Ms. Callaghan and focus it on someone else."

"Annie had nothing to do with Gary Randall's death. You have to know that."

"In my line of work, Mr. Morgan, I never assume I know anything."

The two men locked eyes for a moment before Sam pulled out Gary's paperwork. "Well then, you'll be open-minded, I guess," he said, trying not to let his sarcasm show. "Here's what we found."

George played out several scenarios in his mind as he stood up, tapping the papers on his desk after he and Sam had finished. "Do you have some time, Mr. Morgan?"

Sam nodded.

"I have someone I need to talk to, right away. If you wouldn't mind waiting here for a while." He gestured vaguely out the door, "There's coffee in the break room. Help yourself."

George called Bill out of the interrogation room with an impatient motion. Pete's eyes were large as he caught the signal and George knew that every delay in his questioning now would only serve to make the suspect sweat a little more. Good.

"What's up?" Bill asked.

George told him.

A few moments later, both detectives resumed their places opposite Pete at the table.

They knew.

Pete licked his lips and switched his gaze from the thin guy to the big one and back again. They knew about the drawing. He could see it in their eyes.

"Mr. Munro," Detective Lulinski said.

"Yes?" Pete's voice cracked as he answered.

"You realize that we were able to bring you in on an outstanding warrant. Let me see," he said. The guy made a pretense of consulting his notes, but Pete knew it was just for show. He knew exactly what he was going to say next because the whole job had been blown wide open. "Yes, here it is. Fraud. Assumed name."

Pete nodded, not trusting his voice again.

Both the detectives shifted positions, as though arranging themselves for a long conversation. The other guy spoke. "But we all know that's not why you're here today, don't we?"

Pete shrugged, his mind working, playing out all his options.

Detective Lulinski affected a sympathetic look. "Mr. Munro. You have quite an extensive record here," he said as he pulled up the bottoms of the anchored sheaf of papers, letting them flip one by one back down. "But nothing of the magnitude of murder. This is a whole new ballgame for you, isn't it?"

"Murder?"

"Gary Randall."

"I didn't kill him."

"Well, we have some new evidence, Mr. Munro . . ." Detective Lulinski let the thought hang.

"Who was out there? Who'd you talk to?"

Bill leaned forward. "You don't need to know."

Pete's fingers worked their way to his mouth and he bit at one fingernail before realizing it. Pushing his hand away, he tried again. "What kind of evidence?"

The detectives looked at one another.

"We've got Gary Randall's notes."

Pete felt his body go limp. He'd begged Gary not to write that shit down. Told him it could be used against them someday. But Gary had insisted. His only concession was not taking the notes with them during the burglary. They'd stopped at Annie's, where Gary assured him he'd hidden them in a place where nobody'd ever look.

After escaping the DeChristopher house, Pete had headed back to Annie's, frantic, looking everywhere for those damn notes. Everywhere he thought Gary might have hidden them — but he came up empty. At that point, he should have made the decision to keep the drawing with him, but hiding it at Annie's had seemed safer for something that valuable. Like not putting all his eggs in one basket. This should have been the take that would change his life. Missteps. So many missteps. This one could have been beautiful.

Visions of his life down in Mexico, living like a king, evaporated before his eyes to be replaced by life imprisonment if he was convicted of murder. Why hadn't he figured that the rich bastard would manage to come out scot-free? He played out the scenarios in his head. The two men across the table watched him as he looked up.

Well, he reasoned, he wasn't going to go down on a murder rap.

"I could use a cigarette," Pete said, leaning forward, his arms in front of him on the table. Detective Lulinski pulled out his pack and slid one over, holding up his lighter.

Taking a deep drag, Pete decided. These weren't the big boys he'd hoped to play with, but at least he still had the ball.

"I might have something to trade," he said.

"Chat?" Annie asked.

Her face must have registered surprise, because he tilted his head and said, "You don't mind."

"No, of course not," she answered automatically.

He reached into the closet to pull out two folding chairs and proceeded to set them up next to each other in front of the open door. Settling himself in one, he smiled. "Wonderful. It's about time we get to know one another better. Now that your project is nearly complete, it behooves me to find some other venue to utilize your talents. I don't want to let you get away."

Timothy appeared at the door with two large glasses filled with ice and a pitcher of cold water. He didn't move until Richard stood up to allow him passage. He set the three things down on Annie's makeshift table and headed back out the door. Richard replaced his chair in front of it and took his seat. "You'll stay nearby, won't you, Timothy?"

"Yes sir."

"Thank you."

Annie eyed the other chair. Did he expect her to sit down? Moving to the far wall, she opened the small window; it was getting stuffy in here. And she wanted as much distance between her and Richard as possible. Near the window was her T-Rex. This was the last section that needed polish.

At the table, Timothy had poured two glasses of water, the iciness causing droplets of condensation to gather on the glasses. Choosing one, she took a long, cool drink, watching Richard watch her.

"Anne."

Richard's voice, mellow and soft, still pierced the silence with intensity. She glanced up at him.

"Have you ever been in my upstairs study?" he asked, his face passive.

Annie heard barely controlled anger under the otherwise genial tone. "Yes," she answered, her throat feeling suddenly tight. "I have."

"And what did you think of it?"

Taken aback, she answered, "It's beautiful. Stunning, actually. You have an impressive collection."

He nodded in acknowledgement. "Thank you. I'm quite proud of it, if I do say so myself." Looking upward toward the ceiling for a moment, he pointed. "Your sky is excellent. I could almost believe I've died and gone to heaven when I sit here and stare upward. Do you ever wonder what death is like? Is it all beauty, like your sky here? Or is it existence in a state for which we mere mortals can't possibly imagine?" He seemed to muse on the question for some time. "In any case, the sky is lovely."

"Thanks." She could barely get the sound out.

"Now," he said, and the word came out slow, yet precise, "I have a most difficult question to ask you, Anne."

She leaned on her fingertips against the top of the table.

"You didn't take anything out of my study, did you?"

Annie's mind raced even as she answered, "No!" with vehemence. So someone *had* broken in. Was it Gary? Or the person who'd killed him? She swallowed, shaking her head, wanting to look innocent but realizing that the thoughts running through her mind made her look anything but. "Something's missing?" she finally asked.

"Yes. Something is . . . missing," he said.

"What . . . ?" she cleared her throat, "What is it? What's missing?"

"Some Faberge eggs. Very unusual, very old Faberge eggs. Each worth more than I make in a year."

Annie let out a breath of relief. She'd let her imagination run away with her. She'd immediately assumed he was talking about the missing artwork from the Art Institute, the Durer drawing. Richard watched her, curiosity on his face, as though he could sense her relief. That really wasn't the reaction she wanted to project. "That's terrible," she said.

"Yes, it is."

Annie shook her head again, her composure returning in welcome waves. "I didn't take them. I wouldn't ever take anything."

"I was sure you wouldn't. You're a woman of high morals. I can sense things like this," he said with a dismissive wave, "and, I would venture to guess, high ideals as well. In any event, although such trinkets are beautiful, you're much too strong of an individual to succumb to trifling temptation."

Annie stood there wondering what would come next. She could hear the seconds tick by in her head. Richard's fingertips, spread out before him, tapped together in a slow rhythm, his face the picture of concentration.

"But the eggs are missing nonetheless. I have interviewed our maid and believe her to be innocent as well. The only other possibility is that we had an intruder the night Gina and I attended the Citizenship dinner. And since you were working here that day, I thought perhaps you could shed some light on what might have happened."

"I'm sure I don't know," she said, fighting the urge to tell him about Gary having access to the front door with the key and knowing the burglar alarm code.

"You didn't see anything unusual? Hear anything?"

"No."

"Odd," he said.

"What?"

"How did you get in?"

"How . . . what?"

"How did you get in that day? As I recall, you weren't here when Gina and I left in the morning. I came back, briefly, but still didn't see you."

"Maybe . . . I *wasn't* here that day."

"Ah, my dear, but you were." He stood up. "A man doesn't get to the level of success I've achieved by losing track of details. As it happens, I'd come up here that morning, just to see the progress. Gina wanted me to." He lifted his hands in a mock gesture of defeat. "I was impressed. Very impressed. And . . ." he wandered over, nearer to Annie, but farther from the door. She eyed the exit, mentally calculating the odds of getting there before him. He stepped up to her, blocking any path of escape. "I looked at this dinosaur." He pointed, moving closer to her. "This very dinosaur. What is it called?"

She blanked out for a second, then remembered. "Brachiosaurus." Each syllable was a labor.

"Thank you. And I thought how odd it looked without its eyeball painted in. Blind, you understand?"

Annie's legs weakened under his glare.

"And this. What do you call this?"

"Pterodactyl."

"You are a clever girl, aren't you? This pterodactyl wasn't here. I specifically remembered thinking about the large blank space over this creature's head." He tapped the wall again, as he looked at her. "The interesting part comes after the break-in. Yes, there was a break-in. We both know that, don't we?" He was calm, frighteningly calm. "After the break-in, I went through the house. Every room. I wanted to be sure I knew precisely what had been taken and how the thieves had gained access."

Annie bit the inside of her lip, tasting the metallic tang of blood.

"And to my great surprise," his voice rose an octave as his hands came up for emphasis, "I had a new pterodactyl. And my brachiosaurus could see." His hands extended upward and his eyes glittered as he widened them, as if amazed. "It was a miracle."

Annie's stomach clenched. "I swear," she began to say, "I didn't take anything."

"Of course you didn't." Richard's face tightened. "But we both know who did, don't we?"

Annie's mind raced. He knew. He knew it had been Gary.

"Where is it?"

"It?" she asked. "You mean the eggs?"

"The drawing." He said it so softly it was

almost as though she felt his answer rather than heard it.

My God, Annie thought. Sam was right. The Durer. That meant Gary had gone through with it. She looked up into DeChristopher's dark eyes and knew at that moment what had happened to Gary. Sounding almost graceful in her head, the pieces fell into place, one after another. Gary dead. Evidence that his body had been moved. The new carpeting in the DeChristophers' foyer. The missing artwork. Pete showing up at her house this morning. Her face must have registered her shock when she realized the implication of Pete's visit.

"What?" DeChristopher asked. "What do you know?"

Annie shook her head, her hand up to cover her mouth. Ten minutes, he'd asked for. Ten minutes to get something. The drawing was in her house. Gasping, she felt light-headed, but fought the dizziness. If this man was capable of killing Gary, he was capable of killing her. She needed to get out. If only she'd listened to Sam.

"Where's Annie now?" Detective Lulinski asked as he strode into the room. Sam looked up, surprised that he'd used

461

her first name. It'd been "Ms. Callaghan" or "Ms. Randall" all along.

"She's home."

"You're sure?" Now at his desk, he reached for the phone.

"Yeah, she was supposed to paint again at the DeChristophers' but called them and said she couldn't make it today."

Lifting the receiver, Detective Lulinski handed the phone to Sam. "Call her."

Sam shifted in his seat, surprised. "So, you believe me?"

The detective didn't answer. His mouth was set in a thin line. "Call her," he said again. "Tell her we're sending a squad car to pick her up."

"Listen," Sam said, getting up. He couldn't read this guy. Something about his manner had changed though, and Sam berated himself for coming down to talk to him at all. Doing that had somehow made Annie's situation worse. "I'm telling you she didn't have anything to do with this."

George's voice lowered. "Mr. Morgan. We've got Pete in custody. There's a lot more going on here than you even suspected. If Annie's home alone, she could be in serious danger. Call her."

Sam didn't need to be told again. He dialed Annie's number at home. It rang several times before her answering machine kicked on. He listened to her message, "Annie? It's Sam. If you're there, pick up, okay?" He waited a couple of seconds. "Annie?"

Sam replaced the phone with both hands, and looked up at Lulinski.

"Not home?"

"She told me she wasn't going to leave today. Let me try my restaurant. She might have gone there," Sam's voice was unconvincing, even to himself. A trickle of worry began to creep into his chest as the phone rang.

"Jeff? Sam. Have you heard from Annie?"

Sam felt the color drain from his face. He turned to Lulinski. "She's at the De-Christophers'."

Chapter Twenty-Seven

"Who was with your husband that night?"

Annie shook her head. She needed to think before she gave up information.

"You know something. I can see it in your face."

Annie tried to keep her thoughts clear. He wanted the drawing. "What if," she asked, her voice in a pitch so low it sounded as though she was ready to break down, "what if I could get you the drawing?"

DeChristopher's eyes lit up. He advanced on her. "Don't try to tell me you were in on this. I know better. I'm looking for the fellow who was with your husband that night. That's it. He hands over the drawing, you go free."

"No, I won't," she said, the bleakness of her predicament making her brave. Her voice strengthened. "You get the drawing, I'm dead. That's how it's going to work, isn't it? You killed Gary, didn't you?"

A corner of DeChristopher's mouth turned upward. "As a matter of fact, I did not. It was handled before I got here."

Handled. Annie fought the tears of anger as she pulled her lips inward, biting them in an effort to stem the rising tide of emotion. She needed her wits about her right now and couldn't afford to let her fears weaken her. She didn't want to be "handled."

"The drawing's at my house."

DeChristopher narrowed his eyes. "I don't believe you."

"The other guy, the one you're looking for — his name's Pete and I swear I don't know his last name." Annie's words tumbled out, her panic rising as her voice attempted calm. "He came to my house this morning. He was looking for something. But he left fast, really fast, when your bodyguard showed up."

Annie watched as DeChristopher's face underwent a change, going from incredulous to skeptical, his eyes searching hers, as though looking for a sign of deceit. "You're telling me that you have the Durer."

Annie's body trembled as though cold, but sweat was pouring down her back, forming into beads near her hairline. She brushed her bangs away with the back of her hand, then rubbed her hands together to get rid of the wetness. "I don't know where exactly, but it's there. It has to be. It's the only thing that makes sense. Let me go home and look for it." Even as she said the words, she knew he wouldn't let her out of his sight. "And I swear I'll get it to you."

Richard lowered his head, lifting his hand to rub his eyes. He chuckled to himself. "Give me your keys," he said, looking up.

"What?"

"The keys. To your house. Once the drawing is back in my possession, we'll discuss your future."

"You're going to my house?" she asked.

He grasped her elbow and pulled her toward the door. "We're going together, but don't worry," Richard said, chucking her under the chin, "You're safe. For now."

"You're not coming with us," George told Sam, as he strapped his bullet-proof vest on.

"The hell I'm not."

"Listen, she's probably fine. If what this guy told us is true, then I want Annie out of there because DeChristopher is a dangerous fellow. But we know she's been working there all along without incident. He may not have made the connection be-

466

tween her and Gary Randall. And if he didn't, she's safe. For now."

"Then you're not expecting a confrontation."

"No. Not at all. We're just going to ask him a few questions."

Sam watched as he and Bill covered their vests with shirts and jackets. Fear for Annie's safety grabbed at his heart, not letting go. Fear of not knowing what would be going on was even worse. "So, this is just a routine visit?"

George nodded.

"Then there's no reason why I can't come along." He watched Bill and George exchange a look. Sensing an opening, he persisted. "Come on, I won't get in the way. I just need to know what's going on. You can understand that."

"Go home, Mr. Morgan. We'll call you when we know anything."

"But . . ." Annie said, trying to wrench her arm out of DeChristopher's hold, to no avail. "You can't just kill me. Too many people know I was coming here."

Richard held tighter as they neared the second level, preventing her from falling as the inertia from her futile movement caused her to stumble. He pulled her close as they reached the landing. Over his shoulder Timothy stood back, watching passively. Holding both her upper arms in a tight grip, Richard's face was inches from her own. "You disappoint me, Anne. And I was convinced you were a creative thinker." His eyes bore down on her and she felt his hot breath as he spoke. He tugged again at her arms, pinching till she nearly cried out. "There are many options available to a person of my position."

Turning behind him, he spoke again, "Timothy, why don't you bring the car around? We're taking a field trip to Annie's house."

With a nod the giant was gone.

Annie thought fleetingly of the baby she carried. Too afraid to cry, the thought of never being able to see her own child galvanized her and she kicked out at DeChristopher, kneeing him in the groin. It wasn't a solid hit, the disparity in their heights making the blow less intense, but his grip loosened and she managed to pull out from his grasp and head for the stairs.

She could hear the sounds of the garage door opening. That meant Timothy wouldn't stand in her way out the front door. DeChristopher lunged for her, missed, although she could feel the tips of his fingers as they grazed the back of her shirt. In the scant four seconds that it took her to reach the bottom of the stairs, she mentally calculated how best to grab the doorknob and unlatch the deadbolt at the same time.

DeChristopher stumbled behind her, but then she tripped over her backpack, still lying at the bottom of the stairs. Half a stutter-step later she reached the door, knowing she'd made it. Her fingers flew to the deadbolt, but in a second she was grabbed from behind. Her arms pinned back, she was lifted bodily into the air. Timothy had her in a steel grip, heading back up the stairs. "We got company, boss," he said.

George rang the doorbell again.

"What do we do if he doesn't answer?" Bill asked.

"Somebody's home. That garage door didn't open by itself."

Bill took a step back, assessing the house. "We don't have probable cause, do we?"

George ran a hand over his face. "No, but I got a real bad feeling about this one," he said as he pressed the doorbell again, holding it till he could almost hear the electricity buzz back into the switch. "Let's see if he'll invite us in for a friendly chat."

The click of a deadbolt grabbed their attention.

Richard DeChristopher opened the door himself. "Yes?"

George and Bill introduced themselves as they displayed their identification. "I'm glad we were able to find you at home, Mr. DeChristopher. When no one answered the doorbell after two rings, I became apprehensive. Especially with your garage door left open like that."

"Well, thank you for your concern, Detective. And I apologize for the delay in answering. I'm just getting ready to leave, myself. I must not have heard the earlier rings."

George nodded. "We have a few questions to ask you."

"Of course," he said, amiably. "Is this in regard to one of my pending cases?"

Bill answered him. "No."

The well-known lawyer appeared bewildered. "Then I don't know if I can make the time for you gentlemen right now. I'd be happy to talk with you later, if you'd be so kind as to call ahead."

As he began to close the door, George stepped forward, catching a glimpse of the foyer and remembering all Pete had told them. "Looks like your wife has been doing some redecorating," he said with feigned interest.

Richard DeChristopher ignored the comment and looked at his watch. "Really, gentlemen, I am pressed for time. If you'll excuse me."

"Can we speak with your wife, then?"

"I'm sorry, she isn't here at the moment."

Bill scratched his nose, then pointed to the garage. "Both your cars are here."

DeChristopher moved to open the door a little wider, emphasizing his terse words with a gesture. "She isn't here, Detectives. I'm home alone."

George caught a glimpse of something behind him as the door cleared his line of vision. A backpack, looking out of place in the otherwise impeccable hall. Patterned with a collection of masterpieces, it looked familiar to him. He knew he'd seen it before. George smiled. "I'm very sorry, Mr. DeChristopher, but this is important."

"So is my meeting with the mayor."

Bill took a half step forward. "Well then, if we can get started, sir, you'll have a better chance of being on time."

Sam watched the two detectives from the corner of a neighbor's garage. There was no way in hell he could stay back, not knowing what was going on. He'd parked far enough down the block to keep them from noticing him and he'd worked his way over on foot to have a look around. Annie had driven Sam past the DeChristopher house once before and she'd pointed out the high window that faced out the right side of the house. She'd used that window as the focal point in order to describe to him what the playroom looked like inside.

Richard DeChristopher was at the door, gesturing. So, this was the man. Sam paid attention to his body language. It didn't appear as though the detectives were having any luck getting inside. He knew Annie was in there. He just knew it.

Sam banked on DeChristopher keeping his attention on the two detectives at his door. He wandered around the side of the house till he could see that upstairs window. Very high up. He'd held half a hope that there would be some way to access the room while DeChristopher was occupied. He walked backward, secreting himself in a small forested berm with a great line of sight, trying to see if there was any movement in the room.

Annie's mouth, secured shut with her

own masking tape, began to bleed from paper cuts from the tape's edges. Timothy had warned her to be quiet, but as though he'd read her mind, when he spied the tape on the table in the playroom, he'd used it to assure her silence. She stood in the corner, her hands bound together in front of her and she felt prickles begin as the tight stricture restricted her blood flow to her fingers. The tape around her head itched against the sides of her cheeks, and the edges cut into her lip, but under his constant gaze, she couldn't even attempt to remove it. Standing in the doorway, his bulky presence eliminated any chance of escape.

She moved her head to try and adjust the tape wrapped around her head. The movement caused the stickiness to pull out strands of her hair and a waft and taste of glue assailed both her nose and her mouth at the same time.

Timothy kept an eye on her, but he leaned out the room's door, obviously straining to hear the conversation going on in the hall downstairs.

Thoughts of Sam, her worry for him, and her fear for her own predicament welled up and a single tear slid down her cheek, lodging under the edge of the tape and spreading downward toward her ear. Leaning her back against the wall, she stared out the window at the blue sky, wondering where Sam was, hoping to send him her thoughts and trying to figure a way out.

A movement caught her eye below. Her body reacted, standing straighter, and she stifled a small gasp. Sam. Looking up at this window. She willed her body to slacken itself, so as not to arouse Timothy's suspicions, but she stood directly in the window, watching as Sam held a hand over his eyes, shielding them from the sun. Staring up.

Timothy hadn't noticed her movement, remaining intent on the conversation downstairs. She heard her breathing come faster and her heart jumped at the chance of rescue. If Sam was outside, he had to know she was here. He had to. But he didn't move. He continued to stare upward, his hand at his eyes. It dawned on her then. He couldn't see her because of the brightness of the sun.

If there were only some way to let him know . . .

Voices from downstairs rose, grabbing Timothy's attention and he turned his body more toward the stairs, giving Annie a moment to move. She looked around for something to signal Sam with, her panic and fear that he'd walk away soon driving her to distraction. Annie sidled over to her open tackle box of art supplies, her mind repeating a thought, like a prayer, as she hatched what little plan she'd devised. *Don't leave, Sam. Don't walk away. Not yet.*

Her hands shook and she waited till Timothy turned, facing down the stairs as if to hear better. She wiggled her hands into the bottom section and pulled out one of her small glass jars of paint. Great. Green. It would blend in with the grass. She palmed it and grabbed in again, hoping to beat the return of Timothy's gaze. Quick, she reached, in and out, coming up with another glass jar, this one gray. She moved back to look for Sam as quickly as she dared.

Timothy straightened up, a perplexed look on his face. He started toward her, whispering, "What are you . . . ?"

Stepping away from the window, she shook her head. Timothy came up, grabbing her arm to keep her from running and he looked out the window, muttering to himself when he saw Sam. He reached into his back pocket, pulling out a cell phone. He dialed with one hand.

Timothy held her so close Annie could hear DeChristopher's tight voice answer, "Yes."

"We got a problem, boss. We got some guy snooping around outside in back."

She heard a hiss of anger come through the phone and DeChristopher's words, clear. "Well, take care of it. I'm with some police officers now."

Timothy hit the "end" button, terminating the call. He pushed Annie into the corner nearest him and kept her there with a look of pure malice in his eyes. He reached around his back, pulling out a pistol and a silencer, which he attached without needing to look. "Don't move from there," he said, giving her a hard stare. He turned back toward the window. "Unless you wanna watch. One hit from this and he's history. And nobody's gonna find him in there for hours."

With a deft movement, he propped his hand against the bottom of the window frame and aimed the long pistol out the window. Annie reacted by throwing herself against him, clawing at his face. Half afraid of being hit by a bullet herself, she kicked and fought, lifting her bound hands high, pounding the two glass jars against Timothy's head, until one broke with a solid

476

crush, cascading green paint all over the big man's face. He took a couple of seconds to react and Annie jumped up, looking for Sam, but he wasn't there any longer. Still, she heaved the other jar of paint out the window.

Timothy muttered under his breath, wiping at his eyes. Shards of broken glass in his skin sent rivers of red down from his temple to drip from his cheek. He backhanded her hard, and she felt herself reeling as he shoved her into the closet. Black spots swarmed in front of her eyes. "Stay in there and keep quiet." His harsh whisper seethed with rage. She tried to bang on the doors, and attempted to yell, hoping to make her voice heard over the tape, but caused herself to gag in the process. Timothy's voice warned her. "Listen. I got my gun here. I got a silencer. You keep quiet or I'm gonna use it. You understand?"

Annie leaned her back against the wall of the small area and let herself sink to the floor. *Please Sam,* she thought, *please go tell the police.*

"And I'm telling you that I don't have time for this!" Richard DeChristopher's voice rose in indignation.

George knew he was on shaky ground. DeChristopher didn't need to let them in, wasn't required by law to answer any of their questions. Being a high-powered lawyer, he knew that as well as they did. The man's cordiality had disappeared and he was close to slamming the door in their faces when George, pen in hand, pointed to the floor behind him. "Whose backpack is that?"

As DeChristopher looked back, they heard a series of scuffles from above. George and Bill looked at one another and Bill asked, "What was that?"

Something flashed in DeChristopher's eyes before he regained his outward calm. He pulled himself up to his full height and stepped backward as though to shut the door. "I have two sons, detectives. They're rarely quiet."

"I thought you were home alone?"

Richard blinked. "Forgive me. I was referring to adults at home. In that sense I'm home alone," he said, clarifying. As he was about to continue, the phone in his suit pocket rang for a second time. He hit the "talk" button with one hand as he closed the door with the other. "Call my secretary to set up an appointment, detective. Have a good day."

★ ★ ★

Into the phone he said, "What the hell was that?"

Timothy was on the line. "We got a problem. She might have thrown something out the window."

"To the guy out there?"

"Yeah, but he was gone by then."

"Okay, listen. Forget about that. I need time to sort all this out. Those two cops are going to follow me, I can feel it. Let me head over to my office. They'll think they have me covered. You take her to the house and find the goddamn picture. Call me when you have it and I'll meet you back here. Got it?"

"Got it."

Richard hurried to his Jaguar, making a show of looking at his watch several times for the benefit of the two men, now settled into their own vehicle. He pulled away fast, screeching his tires as he spun out onto the street.

Sam raced from around the side of the home, holding a broken glass that dripped with dark gray paint. He'd turned the corner just in time to see the detectives' car pull away.

He stood in the shadow of the big house,

paint staining his fingers. Annie was up there. He needed to get to her.

Richard chuckled to himself. These cops were so predictable. So lame. They would follow him all the way downtown and then what? Wait outside his office for him to make an appearance and try to question him again. By then Timothy would have gotten the drawing, and taken care of the Anne problem. Charles would be satisfied and another two-and-a-half million dollars would make its happy little way into Richard's offshore account. Of course he was going to have to come up with some alibi when Anne turned up missing. He shook his head. He was a lawyer, used to manipulating the facts to suit his purposes. This wouldn't be a problem.

He looked into his rear-view mirror and saw the dark sedan drop back. So, they were going to try and be unobtrusive. He could play this game.

"What are we doing?" Bill asked as George let a fifth car slip between the unmarked and DeChristopher's.

As the Jaguar left their field of vision, George tossed his half-smoked cigarette out the window and pulled a hard right to double-back the way they came. "Just a hunch," he said.

Timothy tossed away the towel he'd used to try cleaning himself. He hadn't been successful. The streaks of paint, mixed with the seeping blood, made his face a mask of crimson and green. He reached down and pulled Annie up by her elbow. His grip pinched into the softness of her arm and Annie tried not to cry out as her body banged against the closet doors. He held her arm with his beefy left hand, and kept the silencer-laden gun down by his leg, in his right. "Come on," he said. "We're gonna go find that picture."

Sam dropped the paint, rubbing his splattered hands against his jeans. She was in there and he needed to get inside. DeChristopher had pulled away in a flash, too fast to have been able to get Annie out of the attic room to join him. Quickly checking the backyard and the other side of the house for easier access, Sam ignored his nagging fears and headed back to his original position. "Annie?" he called up, in a stage-whisper to the open window. She couldn't hear him, he was certain of that. There was nothing else to do but go to the front door and confront whoever answered.

He'd just turned the corner to the front of the house when a hand clapped over his mouth.

"Be quiet," George warned in Sam's ear. "I thought I told you to stay home."

"She's in there," Sam whispered. "She threw some stuff down to me."

George nodded, taking the lead position, gesturing Sam to stay behind. Within minutes he saw the DeChristophers' garage door rise again, the Lincoln inside already backing out. He ran forward toward the car, shouting into his radio, then at the car backing up down the driveway.

"Freeze!" he yelled. "Police!"

The car responded by speeding its descent, but Bill had already pulled up, blocking its path off the driveway. The Lincoln, still in reverse, careened onto the lawn, in an attempt to get around the unmarked sedan. George sighted the tires and shot, blowing one out.

A buzzing bullet, shot through a silencer, went high and wide over George's head as the driver returned fire through the open passenger-side window, his accuracy blown when the car hit a red and yellow Big

Wheel that'd been left on the grass. George watched the guy adjust his weapon, grateful that this guy had the silencer attached, since that meant he had to manually rack the slide on the automatic back each time to chamber another round. George aimed, and shot again, taking out another tire. He waved Sam over, indicating for him to stay low to the ground and he shielded Sam as the two ran for cover on the far side of the police car, to join Bill. Knowing he had only seconds to decide his next move, George tried to predict what this guy, the bodyguard, would do next. He tried to get into the big lug's mind. A loyal employee was still only an employee. No matter what went down here, DeChristopher's cover had been blown and he wouldn't be able to explain his way out of it. This bodyguard couldn't do anything to change that. His best bet now was to get out, alive.

As if on cue, he jumped out of the driver's-side door, and using the car as a shield, fired again, poised to run. His face was a grotesque mixture of red and green, glistening as bright drops of sweat dripped from his head. His expression was pained and murderous.

Another bullet dinged the car right by the

detectives' heads. The guy's aim was good, and George knew that unless they got a clear shot of him alone, it was just a matter of time before one of his shots got lucky. Knowing that the backups were on their way gave George added comfort and he decided to wait, to let this bodyguard make the first move.

Silence between the two cars lasted less than ten seconds when the reassuring sound of sirens in the distance played like music in George's ears. He peered over the top of his hood, seeing that the bodyguard had heard them too. The guy looked both ways, apparently judging his best route for a run. The big man looked both ways again, then sprinted to his right. He'd taken two steps when George aimed and squeezed the trigger. Slowly, knees buckling as he attempted another step, Timothy's body crumpled and he fell to the ground.

Sam raced over to the open Lincoln and helped pull Annie out from the back seat. She'd managed to work the tape away with her fingers while she listened to the gunfight. Weak in the knees, she reached out to Sam, who held her as she fought to stop the tremors that shook her body.

"Annie," he said.

Unable to speak, she just held tight, as they waited for the paramedics to arrive.

Chapter Twenty-Eight

Richard DeChristopher snapped his cell phone shut again and glanced at his watch. Surely Timothy had found the Durer by now. Why the hell wasn't he answering? Scenarios ran through his mind as he stood up and walked over to the window to stare out over Chicago's Loop, his hands behind his back. That Anne Callaghan was a wily little thing. He swore to himself and tried Timothy's number again.

Surprised by the sound of raised voices outside his office, he turned just as the door opened and a group entered. His young, blond secretary stood beyond the doorway, biting a fingernail, shaking her head, eyes wide with undisguised curiosity. "I thought I asked you gentlemen to call first," DeChristopher said, with weary condescension. "Really, I don't have enough time in the day already. You'll have to schedule an appointment."

"Well, as a matter of fact, we did," George said, smiling and holding up his handcuffs. "The guys from Financial

Crimes and the State's Attorney's office are doing that now. They're getting a warrant for your house, your business, and your cars, as we speak. But right now you're coming with us."

"For what?"

He shrugged, "Oh, let's see . . . concealing a homicide, unlawful restraint, possession of stolen property. Conspiracy."

DeChristopher's face reddened. "This is ludicrous. There's been a mistake." He turned to the door, addressing his secretary. "Patty, call Larry. Get him in here right away." When she didn't move, DeChristopher shouted, "Patty, you stupid bitch, get Larry. Now!"

George meandered over to the polished credenza along the wall, trailing his fingers along the top of a bright crystal prism. He lifted the trophy, letting the sun play havoc with the facets inside, sending colors around the room. "Nice trinket," he said, then feigned surprise as he read the inscription. " 'The Bar Association's Award for Citizen of the Year.' " He lifted his eyebrows. "Well let's hope next year's recipient gets to keep this a little longer, hmm?"

"Turn around, Mr. DeChristopher," Bill said, grabbing the man's arm and ratcheting the first cuff in place. He cracked his gum, and grinned. "You have the right to remain silent . . ."

"You understand the strings we had to pull to get you into Witness Protection, don't you?" Detective Lulinski's voice was a growl as he and Detective Schumann escorted Pete to Annie's house. "You don't cooperate, you don't get in. Plus you still got to help us get the goods on this Don Romas guy. Using those two eggs you lifted. And you better be straight about that picture being here."

"Yeah, yeah," Pete said. Geez, if he had a quarter for every time somebody said "you better get that picture" in the past couple of days, he'd be rich already.

Annie and Sam opened the door for them as they approached. It was almost like a reunion the way the detectives and the two of them acted like they were old friends.

As if they'd be anywhere without my help, Pete thought. He grimaced, watching them, annoyed at the way they kept congratulating each other on how things worked out and how they kept explaining parts back and forth. Didn't they get sick of their own voices? He was sick of them. They were all so happy. Even the damn dog wagged his tail at the cops, but then backed up and growled when Pete looked at him.

He sighed. It would have been great to be a real millionaire, but somehow he'd always known that sort of thing was out of his league. After the group chatted for a while, the older detective finally turned to him. "Okay, buddy, where's it at?"

Heading over to the vibrating chair, he heard Annie's gasp of surprise. Maybe this could be fun after all. Reaching around the back to unzip the extra cover, he pulled out three girlie magazines and took particular enjoyment out of Annie rolling her eyes at that. Pete pushed his glasses back up his nose with a grin. Feeling like a magician onstage, he reached in again and pulled out the drawing, covered for protection by a brown grocery bag.

"Ta-daaa!" he said, pulling it out with a flamboyant gesture.

The dog growled again.

"Okay, Mr. Jokester," Detective Lulinski said. "Hand it over, and let's go."

On the trip from Annie's house to the YMCA, Pete had started to call them George and Bill, even though they told him they didn't like it. The Witness Protection people had given him three choices: Arizona, Wyoming, and Louisiana. Pete thought that Arizona sounded good, closest to the Mexican border.

George and Bill escorted him into his tiny accommodations, giving him no privacy. George didn't stop pacing the small room, even though he couldn't take more than five steps before he was forced to turn and pace back again. Bill sat on the bed as Pete scrounged his meager belongings together. The metal drawers of the lone brown dresser gave a shrill squeak with every pull.

"How long's this going to take?" George asked, for the third time. "Chrissakes, it isn't like you got all that much to pack here, you know."

"I'm working on it," Pete said, more to calm his own frazzled nerves than anything.

He'd already packed his clothes into the brand new suitcase they'd provided, and now he rooted around in the drawers to make sure he hadn't missed anything. Even though his room had a lock, he'd never felt as if it was truly secure. So, he'd taken pains to hide things. A leather shaving kit came as a bonus with the new case. He grabbed that and headed into the bathroom.

"You done?" Bill started to stand up.

"I gotta go." Pete gestured with his head toward the adjacent facilities. "And I gotta pack my shower stuff, too. Okay?"

Bill rolled his eyes. "Sure. Go ahead. But be quick about it. We want to get rid of you — pronto."

Locking the door behind him, Pete scrambled to the floor, reaching behind the toilet's inlet pipe. Keeping his face tilted upward, and using only touch to guide him, he pulled at the tiles he'd loosened the first day he'd gotten here. The uneven grout along the edges scraped at his fingers and he grunted, once, but moments later the two big tiles came down in his hands.

"Ah," he said.

Reaching into the space between wall studs — his own personal safe — Pete pulled out a newspaper-wrapped package, gingerly cradling it in his lap as he sat back on the chilly floor.

Stifling a giggle, Pete unfolded the newspaper, letting the rainbow lights of the sparkling gems escape and play against the drab walls of the tiny bathroom.

"You ready yet?" George yelled.

Pete leaned over and flushed the toilet. "Yeah," he answered, raising his voice to be heard. "I'm ready."

He stretched a finger out to caress the golden shell of the third egg, the one nobody else knew about, giving himself a final look before he rewrapped it and stuffed it into the shaving kit. He sighed. Living like a millionaire in Mexico might not be so out of reach after all.

Even a few days later, Annie's hands still shook when she thought about it all.

She slipped her arm into Sam's, as they walked beneath a canopy of tall trees. Max strained on his leash, trying to get Sam to move faster. They'd brought him to this meadow several times for exercise and he evidently couldn't wait to chase the Frisbee in the sunny prairie grass.

The majestic trees' upper branches rippled and whispered in the warm breeze and Annie took a deep breath of pleasure, remembering the first few times they met and how different things were now. How much better. *Things happen for a reason,* she thought.

Sam glanced down at her, and for a moment she wondered if he'd been reading her mind. "Everything okay?"

"Very okay," she said.

He touched her hand, his fingertips playing along the tops of her knuckles.

"What else did the doctor say?"

Annie shook her head. "Believe it or not, everything's fine. All the test results are in now. I'm healthy, the baby's healthy." She glanced downward with a smile, "Even after everything we've been through."

At the mouth of the meadow, Sam reached down to unclasp the dog's leash. Max bounded away, prancing over the high grass, barking. He came back a moment later, tongue lolling out of his mouth, an expectant brightness in his chocolate brown eyes.

"You brought his toy, didn't you?" Annie asked.

Sam dropped his backpack to the ground and rummaged through till he found the bright blue plastic Frisbee. "Go get it, boy!" he shouted, flinging it out across the field.

They watched the dog take off. Annie thought for a moment that if she ever heard joyous barking this was it.

Sam turned to her. "What did your Uncle Lou have to say about all this?"

"He's in his glory." Annie laughed. "The newspaper asked him to come out of retirement just for one more feature, seeing as how his niece was responsible for the recovery of the Durer drawing to the Art Institute. I have no idea how they got all that information, but he's down there right now, working to get it polished for the morning edition."

"He's quite a guy."

Annie felt contentment settle over her; she was a lucky girl. Changing the subject, she made a face. "Do you realize that this all started because DeChristopher's kids messed up our wall?"

Sam laughed, shaking his head. "I hadn't thought about that."

"It's just about done, you know."

"I know."

"I'll miss working on it," Annie said, wistfully. "And I'm even going to miss working on the dinosaurs, believe it or not. But a couple of other people have called me, so there might be new ones to start soon."

Max dropped the Frisbee at Sam's feet, panting. After waiting a moment, he pushed it closer with his nose.

"Okay, boy," Sam flung it out into the field again. "Go, get it."

They were silent for a long moment.

Annie canted her head, listening to the rush of the wind through the weeds, and Max's distant barking. "But how can you be sure he won't run off?"

Sam raised an eyebrow. "Sometimes," he said, "you just gotta have faith."

Warmed, Annie smiled. "Faith. I like that."

"So do I."

"No, I mean for a name."

Sam gave her a quizzical look.

She ran a hand over her abdomen. "The doctors think it's a girl, you know."

Max bounded back again, the Frisbee flapping in his mouth like a wide blue tongue.

Sam grinned. "Faith Morgan." He put his arm around Annie's shoulders and pulled her close, placing a kiss on the top of her head. "You know what? I like that, too."

About the Author

Julie A. Hyzy dreamed of being a writer from the time she was old enough to put a string of words together. Life often gets in the way of dreams, however, and only recently has she been able to make writing a priority in her life. She graduated from Loyola University of Chicago with a bachelor's degree in business administration, but has always remained an English major at heart. Julie is also a graduate of the intensive Oregon Coast Professional Fiction Writer's Workshop. She lives in Chicago's Southwest Suburbs where she reviews movies for a metropolitan newspaper and writes fiction. Julie's short stories have appeared in numerous magazines and anthologies including *Star Trek Strange New Worlds*, Volumes V and VI. Dedicated to her craft, she makes time to write at least two pages every single day. *Artistic License* is her first novel.